Duel With Darkness

(Huntsman's Fate: Book 2)

Liam Reese

© 2018

Disclaimer

This is a work of fiction. Names, places, characters and events are all fictitious for the reader's pleasure. Any similarities to real people, places, events, living or dead are all coincidental.

This book contains sexually explicit content that is intended for ADULTS ONLY (+18).

Prologue

Porantillia floated in a sea of miserable despair, her seething anger an incandescent flame glittering in the sea of hate she had swam in for millennia. Trapped in a prison even her formidable powers could not help her to escape, the Goddess plotted ways in which she would have her revenge when she finally got out.

I will devastate thy creations and make thee watch! I will end thee in the slowest manner I can find! Thee will not share the fate of thy father and burn forever but suffer the eternal nothing of death at my hand!

Her prison, a construct of the Gods themselves, drained Porantillia's will, thought, and life force until she could barely function but her hatred burned endlessly, supporting and nurturing her as she manipulated the lesser creatures beyond the borders of her prison.

Eventually, many thousands of centuries after her incarceration, Porantillia had sensed an evil force in the world of humans. Tiernon had proved to be a useful tool in her plan. He had access to numerous lives he could feed to Porantillia and thrilled in sending those lives to her. Ruthless and needlessly cruel, Tiernon had taken direction from the creatures she had sent to twist his mind. Porantillia's rage had increased when he had been slain.

The Goddess had watched Besmir's son born, biding her time until he was old enough, a blink in the time she had existed.

Now Besmir, as you have chosen to relieve me of my slave, it is thee who can serve me, thee who will free me from my eternal cage and thee who will suffer Hell to do so.

Chapter One

Crown Prince Joranas squatted in the middle of a *curass* bush, the light pink blossoms exuding enough perfume to hide his musky scent. His keen, brown eyes peered out from between the dark green leaves, searching for Ranyeen as she hunted for him. His heart beat faster when he saw her shock of blonde hair pulled back into twin braids by her mother. Ranyeen's head swung from side to side as she read the little signs his passing had left in the bone dry soil. A bent stem here, the ghost of a footprint there, all would be building a picture in her head revealing his hiding place easily, as they had both been taught.

Joranas watched, a smile spreading across his face as Ranyeen's head came up and she sniffed the air, pulling his smell from the bush's perfume like a bloodhound on a scent. Her dark blue eyes shot to his hiding place as she put all the clues together and a little smile crossed her lips as he watched.

"Found you!" Ranyeen cried as she walked straight at the bush he hid in.

Joranas stood up, disturbing a pair of bees collecting nectar, and waded from the middle of the bush towards her. Ranyeen cocked her head to one side and rested one hand on her hip as she watched him struggle free.

"Took you long enough," Joranas said, swatting leaves and insects from his clothes.

"Your mother's going to have a fit when she sees the state of your clothes," Ranyeen said, pointing to the rips and stains.

Joranas shrugged, looking down at the damage. It did not matter how careful he went, how gently he treated the garments she made or bought for him, they always seemed to tear or stain as if some malevolent spirit watched him, waiting for the moment it could destroy his new clothes.

"Not much I can do now," he said. "Come on, let's see what trouble we can get into," he said with a grin.

The pair wandered toward the marketplace at the heart of Morantine's commercial district. Ignored by most of the adults, who contented themselves by bellowing that their wares were the best available at the lowest price, the prince and his best friend went unaccosted. Joranas gave her a little money to buy a pair of fruit pies from one of the stalls. The stall owner glanced at Ranyeen then searched the crowd for Joranas, nodding a little bow when he spotted the prince. He handed the pies to Ranyeen, refusing the money, and smiling at the prince.

Joranas sighed, knowing the trader had given him the food as he wanted him to tell his father how great it was. Unfortunately the trader did not understand how little his father thought of Joranas' ten year old opinion. His father did not care what he thought of anything, it seemed, no matter what he did to get his approval.

Joranas took a bite of the pastry, relishing the flavor and sweetness, the apple and strawberry pie had been lightly spiced and he gobbled it fast, wanting to go back for another. His eyes rolled across to his friend who had only taken a couple of delicate bites of her pie.

"No," she said without even having to look at him.

"What do you mean, no?"

"No you can't have my pie," she said bluntly.

"I'm the prince," Joranas said, straightening. "You should give it to me," Joranas flared his nostrils and stared at her.

Ranyeen looked at her friend, trying to maintain a straight face as she took another bite of her pie, chewing it as she stared into his eyes. She laughed as a grin broke out over his face.

"It was worth a try," he said, nudging her. "Come on."

Joranas led her past his house, the building his father had chosen years before as an alternative to the main palace. Joranas looked up at the immense complex of disused buildings, the forbidden ruins as irresistible as a narcotic. Every stone seemed to call to him, every door a portal to endless adventures he was banned from having.

"Well, well, if it's not the little prince and his wench," a voice cried.

It belonged to a stocky lad of around twelve. He was surrounded by younger children who looked up to him as if he was some kind of messiah. Crallan had taken an instant dislike to Joranas as soon as the young prince had started venturing out of his house and Joranas had no real idea why.

"Come on, let's go," Ranyeen said, tugging the sleeve of his stained, white shirt.

"Yes, little prince, listen to your wife and leave," Crallan said in a mocking tone.

Joranas looked around, searching for any of the guards or other of his father's staff. Seeing none he grinned, stepping across to Crallan.

"Got your group of little children as usual," he observed. "I suppose you're at a similar age in here, after all," Joranas tapped the side of his head.

Crallan's face darkened and his own eyes scanned the area behind the prince for any adults that might intervene.

"We're all on our own," Crallan spat. "No one to come and help you," he grinned at the older boy.

Pain exploded in his face as Crallan smashed his fist into Joranas' nose. He doubled over as tears blurred his eyes. A ringing sound, like someone rubbing their finger around the rim of a glass, came to his ears and nausea flooded his mouth with saliva.

"Leave him alone!" Ranyeen screamed, throwing herself in between the two.

Crallan brought his hand up as if to strike Ranyeen, too, but her piercing glare stopped him in his tracks and he allowed his arm to fall.

"You should be careful," Ranyeen warned Crallan. "He might decide to use his magic on you."

Crallan's eyes widened at the threat and he paled as a pair of the younger children slid behind his larger frame. The stocky boy took a step back when Joranas straightened, blood beginning to crust on his lip and his teeth bared in a snarl.

"Y-You wouldn't do that," the bigger boy said. "The King would..."

"What?" Joranas demanded in a pain filled voice. "What would my father do?"

Crallan swallowed as Joranas approached him, a menacing expression in his wild eyes.

"What *could* he do if I burned you to a pile of ash?"

Crallan's face looked more like tallow than skin. Beads of waxy sweat broke out on his forehead and he looked more scared than anyone Joranas had ever seen. A savage joy rose up in Joranas' chest at the sight and he grinned. In an attempt to save face Crallan swore at Joranas, spitting as many unkind, graphic, ugly words at him as he could think of.

Joranas laughed, sneering at the other boy until he turned his attention to Ranyeen.

"I do not understand why you associate with *that*," Crallan said, pointing at the girl. "Yellow haired freak..."

Joranas bellowed a wordless shout of rage, launching himself at the bigger boy, fists flying. Crallan stepped back in shock as this suddenly savage animal hammered into him, punching relentlessly as he screamed.

Joranas' rage gave his arms the fuel needed to sustain a few good punches to Crallan but his madness meant they landed in soft areas and did little damage. By the time he had exhausted himself and stepped back, panting, Crallan had only one painful area on his right cheek. He barely felt anything from the other punches, the pain already fading. It had been the pure, animal savagery that gave the older boy pause. That almost insane violence combined with the thought the young prince might actually burn him alive was enough to make Crallan back off.

Joranas watched him retreat but felt no sense of victory. Rather, he felt robbed of the opportunity to have beaten Crallan to a pulp. With the adrenaline draining from his system Joranas turned to Ranyeen with his head down.

"You all right?" he asked sullenly.

"I'm always alright when I'm with you," Ranyeen said, a little smile playing about her lips.

"Why did you tell him I was going to use magic on him?" Joranas asked as they plodded through the cobbled streets of Morantine. "You know I can't do that kind of thing."

"But Crallan doesn't," Ranyeen said quietly. "Did you see his face?" she giggled.

"I see it again," Joranas said pointing at the backside of an ox that was straining to relieve itself in the street.

His heart leapt when she laughed, the musical sound washing his dark feelings away.

"We'll always be friends, won't we?" Joranas asked in a quiet voice.

Ranyeen took his hand as they made their way back through the gathered people, squeezing his fingers gently.

"Always," she said.

***

King Besmir Fringor regarded the Corbondrasi ambassador with amusement he did not allow to show. Like all Corbondrasi, Ru Tarn was covered in brightly colored plumage, her feathers clinging to her feminine figure like a cloak. Were she human, Besmir thought she might be attractive, with wide hips, slim waist and large breasts. Her pink and peach feathers, however, muted all this in his eyes, turning the Corbondrasi into a creature from one of the books he read in the orphanage of his youth. Coral eyebrows framed lavender eyes that radiated both mirth and intelligence, however, and Besmir knew his every word would be committed to her memory.

Despite her alien form and odd manner of speech, the king found he liked Ru Tarn's company, her insights and quick wit matched his own, even if she did say very few words.

Arlonius Motcall was a completely different story. Hailing from Waraval, an ancient nation bordering to the east, he was as obscenely superior as the rest of his race, a fact both Besmir and Ru Tarn played on endlessly. At six feet in height, Motcall was one of the largest men in the room, his stocky, muscular frame just beginning to run to fat in his later years. His dark brown hair and neatly trimmed beard were now shot through with gray hairs lending him an almost distinguished air that gelled perfectly with his obscene manner.

"As I was saying, your Majesty," Motcall said in his deep voice. "My King's most gracious offer can only stand for so many hours awaiting your signature. If you truly value the future of Gazluth, you should reach for your quill immediately in order to allow the denizens of Waraval to enlighten your little country."

Besmir glanced at Ru Tarn. The Corbondrasi widened her lavender eyes a little, offering a sarcastic glance at Motcall.

"Well, I really am grateful for the offer, Arlonius," Besmir said, "and please relay my apologies to King Penolan but, as this agreement pretty much gives your country exclusive access to my eastern border and offers nothing in return, I don't think it's the best deal for us."

Besmir held out the parchment to Motcall who took it with a grunt. His displeasure showing.

"I have been king here for ten years, you know?" Besmir added. "You're the first ambassador from Waraval and you've only just arrived. What makes you think I'm going to grant any kind of exclusivity to a kingdom that happily ignored its neighbor for almost a decade?"

"My King did not wish to interfere in the internal politics of Gazluth," Motcall said evasively.

"Ah, I see," Besmir said sarcastically. "So the internal politics, which were basically my people starving, couldn't be interfered in, but now we're beginning to make some headway into bringing this country back from the precipice of death," Besmir leaned forward in his chair. "Now Waraval can interfere?"

Motcall reddened but in anger rather than embarrassment, he adjusted the heavy green and gold robes he wore with a hand garnished with gold rings.

"My generous King simply wishes the best for his simple neighbor and is prepared to help in any way he can to enlighten the people here to the sophisticated ways we enjoy in Waraval."

Besmir sighed.

"I'm getting sick of this," he spat. "A decade ago, when we needed aid, you were nowhere to be seen. The Corbondrasi sent help as did the Ninse, both neighboring countries and both without any expectation of repayment or boon." Besmir looked at the ambassadors from both countries, nodding to them in gratitude.

Ru Tarn bowed, spreading her arms in a mocking display she muted with a massive grin while the squat ambassador from Ninse raised his goblet in salute. Motcall watched the display with barely concealed malice, his pale yellow eyes narrowing as he stared at Besmir.

"Any kingdom unwilling to adopt the enlightened example Waraval sets must surely suffer as a result," he said.

"Well that's just a risk we're going to have to take," Besmir said dismissively.

He managed to keep the smile from his face as the Waravalian ambassador gathered his robes and made his exit, leaving a ghost of perfumed air to mark his leaving.

"Seems a bit put out," Xosux Duntur, the Ninsian ambassador, observed dryly.

At just five feet tall, the Ninsian sat on a chair he had provided as those already in the conference hall had been uncomfortably large for him. His goblet had been filled several times already despite the early hour, although he seemed none the worse for wear. Besmir had wondered if what he sipped almost constantly at was not alcoholic at all until Duntur had offered him some, the little man guffawing when Besmir had spluttered, coughing from the heat.

"How will I ever get to sleep?" Besmir asked sarcastically as he wafted the heavy perfume from his nose. "Why he feels the need to wear so much of that..." he flapped his hands. "Stuff...is beyond me," he added.

"He not wash," Ru Tarn said, her high voice sounding almost as bird like as her plumage made her look.

Besmir grinned at her comment. The Corbondrasi ambassador said little, mainly due to the difficulties most Corbondrasi had speaking Gazluthian. Besmir had toyed with the possibility of learning Corbondrasi but had horribly insulted several members of Ru Tarn's family in the process and they had both decided it was a bad idea.

"Although it is not my place to say anything," Duntur said in a speculative voice, "it might just be worth having him watched," the small man gestured to the door through which Motcall had stomped.

"We are," Besmir said casually. "Checking his missives and eavesdropping on all his private conversations," he smirked. "Like we do to all the visiting dignitaries."

Duntur looked shocked for a second before an expression of wry amusement crossed his own face.

"Ah, Besmir, it is so refreshing to meet a leader with a sense of humor," Duntur said. "Makes it so much easier to sneak things past you."

Duntur sipped from his goblet with a little smile on his face.

"It's not me you have to worry about," Besmir said casually. "Some of my people are almost..." he tapped his chin in thought. "Overzealous? Is that the right word? In carrying out their tasks." He chuckled as Duntur's face fell. "After all, who knows what is happening in your houses at this very minute?"

Duntur looked about to speak and even Ru Tarn appeared a little upset.

"By the Gods!" Besmir cried. "Look at the pair of you!" He huffed a laugh. "You're perfectly safe. All your little secrets are still secret. I don't have you watched," he said. "Much."

Besmir laughed when both ambassadors stared at him.

"To business," Besmir said.

Before the three had gotten anything done the doors to the conference hall opened admitting Queen Arteera. Besmir and the two ambassadors rose as she seemed to glide through the room towards her husband. Besmir watched every move, noting the play of a smile as it crossed her lips. Duntur sighed beside him as Arteera approached and his own smile widened. He had no need of spies, when it came to Duntur, he would spill his guts to Arteera if she merely asked him.

The queen wore a long, flowing dress in a simple design and fabric. Cream and light brown, it hugged her figure perfectly, falling to the floor where it appeared to float just off the ground, suspended by some magical force.

"Sorry to interrupt," she said once greetings had been exchanged. "However, there is a pressing matter that needs your attention, my love."

"Can it wait?" Besmir asked.

"Unfortunately not, my lord," Arteera said clasping her hands in front of her. "It involves the young Prince Joranas," she added with a subtle tightening of her lips.

Besmir noted the set of her mouth and the formality of her speech, indicating she needed his attention now. Whatever royal business the two ambassadors had, it would have to be put off for another time.

"Ru Tarn, Xosux, if you would excuse me, I have a family matter to attend to," Besmir said.

"Of course, Majesty," Duntur said, his eyes fixed on the queen.

Ru Tarn bowed as she left wordlessly with a hiss of her feathers moving against each other.

"What's happened this time?" Besmir asked his wife as soon as they were alone.

"Oh Besmir," Arteera sobbed, collapsing into his arms. "Someone hit him! Both his eyes are bruised and his little nose..." she trailed off.

"Come on, let's go see him."

***

Joranas sat on a simple bed, pain from his throbbing nose and top lip distracted him from paying much attention to his surroundings. The room in which he had been unceremoniously deposited was stark, bare, and made of gray stone for the most part. A simple cot sat in the corner with a hearth in the opposite wall. No fire burned there at present, however, as the room was quite warm. A set of shelves occupied another wall on which sat jars and pots filled with all manner of healing potions, unguents, ingredients, medicines, bandages, and straps. Joranas' eyes roved over the array of enticing items as his young brain tried to decide what each one of them might do.

The door opened admitting a middle aged woman with ruddy cheeks. She wore a white bonnet, tied so tightly beneath her chin the ribbons disappeared into her flesh, and a dark brown dress almost like a monk's robe. Her kind, gray eyes inspected Joranas as soon as she closed the door behind her, assessing his injuries immediately.

"Nasty that," she said, reaching for two of the jars on the shelves.

"It hurts," Joranas said in a sullen voice.

"I expect it does," she said rubbing some of the contents from both jars onto a piece of clean rag. "Never been punched in the face myself, so I could not tell how much, but I bet it is painful."

"Jessa?" Joranas said.

"Yes, your Highness?" Jessa replied as she applied the cloth to his nose and eyes with a gentle hand.

"Is there any need to involve my parents here?" Joranas asked, wincing with the slightest of touches.

"That is nothing to do with me, young Prince," Jessa said. "The guards what found you sent for the queen as soon as they seen the state of your face."

She carried on dabbing at his eyes and nose gently, dulling the pain and easing his suffering.

"Oh," he said sadly.

"You know you're lucky, right?" Jessa asked.

"To have been punched in the face?" Joranas asked in shock. "That's not what I call luck."

"No, no," Jessa said in a dark tone. "You is lucky to have a ma and pa who loves you very much."

Joranas looked into the older woman's kind eyes, seeing the sincerity in them but not understanding her point.

"Ma maybe," he said, "but my father hates me."

"Piffle!" Jessa barked making him jump. "Said like the little kiddie you are. I know you is just ten but there be other children of ten who has to work all day just to be scraping by," Joranas looked shocked at her angry tone, "and lots of them only be having one parent left."

Jessa clamped her mouth down into a tight line as the door opened behind her.

"Majesties," she said, trying to curtsy as Besmir and Arteera filled the small room.

"Jessa," Arteera squeaked as soon as she saw the purple rings around Joranas' eyes. "Is he going to be all right?"

"He will live, Majesty," Jessa said with a straight face before leaving the room.

Joranas felt himself surrounded by soft warmth as his mother wrapped him in her arms and for a few seconds everything felt fine.

"What happened, son?" Besmir asked.

There it is. He thinks it was all my fault.

"Some of the local children were picking on Ranyeen," Joranas said. "I stopped them."

"Good man," his father said. "I can't imagine what Keluse would do if she lost her daughter as well as her husband."

"Besmir!" his mother cried. "Just look at our son's face!" she turned accusatory eyes towards him. "What are you going to do about this?"

"It looks to me as if Joranas has already done all he needs to. Right, boy?"

Joranas nodded while Arteera gaped.

Besmir continued, "Look, if I make a big show of trying to punish whoever did this or have a pair of guards follow him everywhere, it's going to look like he can't stand up to a few bullies. We both said the boy needed to be seen among the people, unguarded and alone, to show that we believe he can look out for himself."

"Well, I've changed my mind," Arteera said stubbornly. "I want him inside, with me, where he'll be safe and cared for," she held up one hand when Besmir went to speak. "No. I'm his mother, I get to choose what happens to him and I refuse to let our only child get beaten up so you can look good to your people!"

Arteera stood and shoved Besmir aside, opening the door to leave in tears. Besmir sighed and looked at his son, head hanging in defeat.

"What was Jessa saying when we came in?" Besmir asked.

"She was telling me I should be thankful I've got two parents who love me," Joranas said.

"Ah," Besmir said, sitting beside his son. "She watched too many children lose their parents when Tiernon went on one of his rampages."

Joranas paled and made a protective sign in front of him. Besmir laughed.

"You said his name!" Joranas said with a little awe in his voice.

"Ah son, I faced him just before you were born. Speaking his name is nothing."

"If you say his name three times he comes to get you in your sleep!" Joranas said.

"Really? Who told you that?"

"Just some boys..." Joranas said evasively.

"Well, I'm no expert, but I doubt Tiernon will ever be coming back."

Joranas looked up into his father's face, wishing desperately he could put an expression of pride or happiness on it.

"Why's that, father?" he asked.

Besmir returned his son's look with one of his own, but turned away with a frown as if debating whether to speak or not. When he did eventually speak again his tone was subdued.

"Because I burned him and shocked him with lightning," Besmir said in a sad voice, "then I stabbed him through the chest and watched him die," he added.

Cold fright and awe dribbled through Joranas as he looked at his father. He had heard the stories, of course, but they had never seemed real. Did this mean his father really killed Tiernon?

"Why haven't you told me any of this before?" Joranas asked accusingly. "Why, father?"

"Your mother forbade it," Besmir said. "Didn't want your young head filled with tales of death and war," he glanced down at Joranas. "But maybe it's time you heard about what happened. Maybe you should hear what the power that runs through your veins can actually do."

Joranas swallowed.

Chapter Two

Agony seared through his veins as he was *exuded* from nothing. He landed on the diamond sharp, gritty earth with a wet splat, the impact sending rills of further agony through his malformed body. A searing wind, filled with acid mist and grit, rasped over his newborn flesh and he writhed on the sharp ground as his body began to take shape.

After what felt like an eternity he found himself able to stand. Pain stabbed up through his feet and he looked down, frowning. Something appeared over the sole of his foot, a protective barrier that stopped the pain. Stretching his arms out he thought again, clothing himself in a simple layer of imagination. The wind could no longer touch him and he felt something on his face. He reached up to examine his features, feeling his lips stretched and the hard things in his mouth exposed.

Smile

The word drifted into his mind.

"Smile," he said.

His voice sounded smooth and deep even in the hollow atmosphere surrounding him. He lifted his foot, leaning forward and smashed into the gritty floor again. Frowning he dragged himself to his feet again and tried a second time. It was complex and hard but with faltering, staggering steps he managed to start walking.

After what might have been seven lifetimes he came to a different place. Something had been built here, a...

House.

"House," he said.

Other names came to him as he looked around. Trees surrounded a pond that was fed by a stream that began in mid air. He put his fingers in the stream, feeling the water that was there. A primitive life form...

Fish.

That lived in the water. He tried to catch it but it dove to the bottom of the pool and hid from his questing fingers. He turned to the house, seeing how it was two shades of gray, alternating to make stripes.

Wood.

Its name leapt into his infant brain as all the others had, knowledge came to him as he needed it, he did not question where it came from. The sound of his footsteps changed as he entered the house, hollow thumps echoing up from the contact. He stamped his foot a few times, watching it hit the wood and hearing the thud at the same time.

Inside he encountered more new items, the names springing into his mind as needed. Couches faced each other with a low table in between. Shelves lined the walls, each holding different things; books, small statues, plates and cutlery, a small box. He examined each item in detail, returning it to its original place after doing so.

"Who are you?"

He turned finding the owner of the voice and the house, standing behind him.

Enemy. Evil. Danger.

He watched as the spirit of Besmir's father walked in. His exile in the Hell dimension had warped his appearance until he was covered in shimmering, oiled scales that rubbed silently against each other and with a head that sprouted horns. The thing was obscene to look at and he felt something harden inside him.

Hate.

"Can you understand me?" it asked him. "I am called Joranas. Who are you?"

"Joranas," he said thoughtfully. "Enemy."

The horned beast's eyes narrowed.

"Do you even have a name?" Besmir's father asked.

"Name," the newborn said tilting his head.

"What do you want?" Joranas asked.

"Portal," the other creature said without hesitation.

***

Joranas thrust his hands out, flame exploding over the stranger, burning and searing. He kept his assault up until he began to weaken, the edges of his vision starting to darken. When the heat dissipated he could see the newcomer stood there completely untouched. Lightning exploded from his fingers, engulfing the outsider in its electric embrace. Joranas spent himself, his power fading as he bent double, panting. Still the newcomer stood untouched.

Joranas attacked him physically then, tearing at him with his clawed, taloned hands, his immensely strong form a match for anything else in this place. His blows were as effective as blowing on a house fire to extinguish the flames, the strange being simply watched him attack.

Eventually Joranas halted, realizing his efforts were in vain and stepped back. The newcomer struck out, his hand a blur, grabbing Joranas around the neck. His grip felt like an iron band around Joranas' neck and he hammered his claws against the creature in a desperate attempt to escape his grip.

"Portal," the infant said in a conversational tone as he squeezed Joranas' throat closed.

Joranas felt himself lifted, his doll-like body flopping, to smash against his own ceiling before being slammed into the floor. Pain exploded through his back, debilitating and severe, and the first edges of panic crept into his chest. Abruptly, Joranas felt himself flung out through one wall into the air. He managed to control his flight, turning to glide back towards his house. Crafted through pure force of his will from the very substance of this world, Joranas watched as his home was systematically torn apart from within by this new being. Created by the creature imprisoned in the absence, it looked perfectly human and Joranas knew it would be able to wreak havoc in his son's world if it managed to get through the portal.

Chunks and sections of his house exploded outwards as the thing raged madly, returning to the dusty ash of the planet he had crafted it from. Joranas floated nearer, anxious and frightened by the power this thing seemed to have. As one of the most powerful beings in this plane, Joranas himself was ineffective against the thing and at a loss as to how to stop it.

With his house smashed back into dust, the portal to his son's world lay bare and unprotected before the creature. Without hesitation the infant stepped into the gray mass and disappeared.

"Cathantor!" Joranas bellowed the name of the God of afterlife. "Help!"

***

"Where are we going?" the young Joranas asked as Besmir led him towards the imposing and forbidden palace complex.

"You'll see," Besmir said with a smirk as he approached the tall gate that broke the curtain wall.

Besmir leaned his palms and forehead against the aging wood bringing a deep click from somewhere within. Slowly the gate swung inward on silent hinges, admitting the pair.

Joranas peered through the door to the place he had been forbidden to enter, to see the overgrown grounds within. He set foot inside, following his father who shoved his way past shrubs threatening to engulf him after securing the gate. Joranas trotted after him, trying to keep up and not wanting to be alone in this alien place.

The paths had been lifted in places by roots, fouling his feet as he tried to keep up with his father. Topiary that had once been kept neatly trimmed into convoluted shapes and sculptures had sprouted grotesque branches and morphed into horrible parodies of their former selves. Shrubs that had once been horses had large growths jutting from their necks, making it appear to Joranas' young eyes as if they had been attacked, weapons jutting from their throats. Other shapes had twisted under the weight of their new growth, leaning towards the path they passed along as if trying to catch him.

Joranas ducked beneath the massive form of a leaning cube that tried to halt his progress and tripped, falling against his father who had stopped at the edge of what had once been a lawn. More a hay field now, it was piled with matted, yellowing stems and weeds poked up offering yellow meadow flowers to the sky. Joranas ignored the flora, however, his attention dragged away by the palace buildings.

Holes gaped in the walls where windows had once sat, the glass or shutters long since gone. All summer scents fell from his nose as a waft of stale air like corpse breath washed over his young face. Joranas traced the lines of the buildings, some of which had begun to collapse without any form of upkeep, and felt a cold hand rummage round inside his guts.

Tiernon's palace. I'm really here.

In his short life, Joranas had felt an almost unbearable need to come here, to see what lay within the tall curtain walls that surrounded the complex. Now that he was here, he had an almost unbearable need to run back to his mother and jump into the protection of her warmest hug. He glanced nervously at Besmir who smiled down at him but offered no comfort or protection.

"Ready?" Besmir asked.

Joranas nodded despite the fact he was anything but.

Banshee screams came from one hinge as Besmir shoved the door open far enough to let them in. Stale air and dust blew across Joranas' face and he covered his eyes, blinking hard to get rid of the gritty feeling in them. He sneezed, the sound like thunder in the tomb like building and he flinched from the distorted echo that came back.

Besmir led him into the dim interior, the door hanging open on its rusted hinge, and through to a large room with marble supports holding the ceiling aloft. The permanent layer of dust that coated every surface lay unbroken until his father strode directly through the middle of the room. Joranas watched as ghostly wraiths curled around his father's ankles, floating off to either side in his wake. Joranas was torn between the need to follow and his fear of the dust that had grown, in his mind, into a malevolent force.

They didn't get father but he's strong. They'll drag me down, I know it.

"The throne room," Besmir said.

Joranas jerked sideways, his chest feeling cold, at his father's words. Even though he had spoken in a normal voice it had sounded far too loud to Joranas' ears and he had jumped. His eyes picked out a number of vertical lines, slightly darker than the gloom of the throne room and he wondered at them.

"Tiernon kept people in there," his father said. "Women he wanted to use...for any number of things."

"Like what, father?" Joranas asked, his eyes wide with suspenseful wonder.

"I...ah...Maybe you need to be a little older," he said. "He starved and mistreated them all. Your aunt Thoran was one such."

"Aunt Thoran!" Joranas squealed, peering at the cage as if he could see her image inside.

"Hmmm..." Besmir hummed. "Come, the throne is this way."

Joranas trotted behind his father his eyes darting all over the place and seeing demons in the shadows. He turned just before running into his father's back and found himself before a platform set above the main floor. On it sat a single chair, large and golden with a pile of dusty cloth behind it.

Tiernon's throne.

"Want to try it?" his father asked.

Joranas' lower belly felt hot, then cold and he abruptly needed to urinate. He stared back at the expectant face of his father with his mouth open. Nothing, no words came from him but his thoughts tumbled like rolling rocks down a mountain.

No! Tiernon will come back and possess me. I have to. Father expects it.

Besmir smiled and squatted beside his son, resting his hands on his small shoulders.

"There is nothing to fear," he said gently. "Just an old building and some horrible memories. I would never let anything hurt you, son. Never."

Joranas took a deep breath and stepped up to the throne. He turned, the throne room filling his vision in its darkness, and sat slowly down.

The gilded wood was cold and hard beneath him. The throne was far too large and he felt suddenly stupid, his childish fears pointless and foolish. He smiled at his father who smiled back, nodding his approval.

Something stirred in the shadows at the far end of the room. Joranas' eyes snapped to it, his young brain trying to make out what it might be at the same time as panic gripped his heart, squeezing hard. A pitiful squeak issued from his throat and his father frowned, spinning to see what had scared him so badly. Joranas leaped from the throne and dashed across to lean against his father's leg.

"I s-saw something move," he stammered, "in the shadows."

Joranas pointed a trembling hand at the point he had seen move, thrilled and frightened when he felt his father start towards it.

Besmir sent his mind flashing through the space, searching for who or whatever had scared the boy. He knew nothing should be in here with them but he also knew there were *other* things. Inexplicable things that came from different worlds and had different values. His consciousness flew round the throne room revealing the few life forces in the room; a few spiders had populated corners, hoping for an easy airborne meal. Those airborne meals flicked around, trapped by the building they had found their way into and a family of mice had made their home just inside the main door to the palace itself. Apart from those few things, they were alone.

Joranas stuck to his father as he crossed the room, hoping whatever he had seen was his imagination but not able to believe it was. The gloom parted as they approached, shadows peeling back to reveal the bare stonework of the wall.

Joranas let out a breath he had not realized he had been holding, the relief in his chest a thing of beauty.

Besmir laughed when he heard the relief in his son's breath, realizing he had felt some anxiety himself.

"Old buildings full of shadows, eh son?" he said as he led Joranas from the room and back towards the other rooms.

Joranas nearly screamed when he saw the figure.

"The Hall of Kings," his father said. "Our family going back generations."

Joranas saw there were a number of statues here, lining the walls, each in a different pose and each dressed in their royal robes. He approached the first, looking into the stone eyes of someone who had died centuries before. The clothing smelled damp and musty, as if water had gotten to it and the boy recoiled from the smell, wrinkling his nose.

"Looks like the roof is leaking now," his father said, walking slowly along the corridor.

Joranas stared at the charred hole where one of the statues had been obliterated by some immense force. He swallowed when he saw his name carved in the stone, the click audible in the hallway.

"Your grandfather," Besmir said. "We named you after him, you know?"

Joranas nodded, the information vaguely familiar to him. The sight of his own name here in this mausoleum had shaken his young mind and he wanted nothing more than to leave, immediately.

His father led him past a door that had been sealed. Heavy iron and oak bars had been attached to the outside and spikes driven into the stonework at either side. He looked at it as they passed, a curious sense of belonging pulling him towards the door.

"What's in there, father?" he asked, stopping.

"The purest evil you can imagine," his father said in a dark voice. "Tiernon's private chambers hold something so malevolently evil I can't remove it, or even destroy it. I don't know how he built it, even *if* he built it, but this is the best solution we could come up with at the time."

Joranas turned to see his father rubbing the beard he had just decided to grow and staring off into nothing, remembering events that had taken place before he was even born.

"Come on, I've got something much better to show you," Besmir said as he turned away from the door.

The subtle tug pulled at Joranas' mind as he dragged himself farther down the corridor after his father, now it had been awoken in him, however, it was something he could not ignore.

Through yet another door, this one carved with intricate details of flowers, plants, and animals, some of which Joranas was unfamiliar with. Tiny, winged people flew between the flowers, dipping an occasional hand into the nectar filled throats as they went. Joranas examined the door in fascination, his mind drawn into the scene as he imagined himself among the flowers.

His young mind fought to comprehend what his eyes told him was inside the room. Stacked from floor to ceiling on shelves that had been built into the walls were hundreds–thousands–of books and scrolls. This room had a musty atmosphere also, but one that was filled with the enticing aroma of parchment, wax, tallow smoke, and polish. Gone was the thick layer of dust that coated the other areas he had seen, kept at bay by unseen hands. Giant, ornate candelabras stood attached to the pillars holding the ceiling aloft, filled with lit candles while oil-filled lamps burned in wall sconces adding to the natural light that flooded through the windows.

The center of the room was dominated by a table, but a table the likes of which Joranas had never seen. His young eyes roved over the image of Gazluth represented there with reverence. Whoever had built it had been a master of his craft as every detail looked perfect. Joranas found Morantine immediately, the city's spires and palace built and painted to be an exact miniature replica. The mountains looked to have real snow, the vast grasslands appeared lush enough for herds to feed on and Gazluth's few forests were comprised of individual trees, each crafted separately before being added to the model.

"Amazing," Joranas breathed. "Is it magical?"

"No," his father shook his head. "Whoever crafted it was a genius, however."

Joranas nodded, running his fingers over the impressive sculpture, caressing cities and towns before stroking meadow lands.

"What brings you two here?" a deep voice asked.

"Uncle Zaynorth!" Joranas cheered running over to hug the old man.

"By the Gods!" Zaynorth cried when he saw Joranas' bruised face. "What happened?"

"Bullies," the king said shortly.

Besmir watched as the old illusion mage tickled his son until he was squealing with laughter, a small smile tugging at his mouth.

"So what are you doing in here?" Zaynorth asked as Joranas resumed his study of the map table.

"It's time he saw for himself what power lies in his blood," Besmir said, casting a glance at his son, "and at what cost."

Zaynorth pulled at his beard, now more gray than black, as his eyes searched his king's face. Besmir grinned.

"Don't look at me like that, old friend," he said. "If he's fighting, I just want to make sure he doesn't incinerate someone's child by accident."

Zaynorth nodded, looking at the boy he had come to love as a grandchild and hoping he would not hate him once he had shown him what he knew he must.

"Joranas," the prince turned, a bright smile on his face, "come here, lad. I have something to show you."

Chapter Three

"Good night mother," Joranas said in a low voice almost as soon as he and Besmir returned. "Aunt Thoran, Sharova," he added solemnly.

Arteera looked from son to father and back before holding her arms out to Joranas.

"A little early for you to be seeking your bed, Joranas," she said. "And it is very unlike you to refuse food. What's the matter?"

Joranas glanced almost guiltily at his father before looking back at the queen.

"Nothing, mother, I'm just tired from today," he said.

Queen Arteera looked at her son as if she could see inside him, see what the problem was, but nothing in his face gave her a clue as to why he looked as if his world had ended so she released him.

"Good night then, my little prince," she said, kissing him on the forehead.

Joranas looked up at her for a few seconds, uncertainty and fear in his eyes. It looked to Arteera as if the boy aged before her very eyes, maturing faster than she liked and a horrible suspicion crept into her heart. She stared coldly at her husband as Joranas made his way, slump-shouldered, from their dining room.

"What did you do?" she asked as soon as the door closed behind her.

Sharova turned to Thoran, his expression strained.

"Maybe we ought to leave for now, love," he said, cutting his eyes to the monarchs.

"I got Zaynorth to show him what it means to have Fringor blood in his veins," Besmir replied calmly as he poured himself a goblet of wine.

Thoran laid her hand on her husband's arm for support as she got awkwardly up from her seat. Her distended belly looked huge beneath the blue dress she wore, making her ungainly and overbalanced. Sharova stood, supporting his young wife until she gained her feet.

"Yes, love," she said. "I do feel a little light headed. Maybe we should leave for now."

"There's no need," Besmir said darkly. "Stay, enjoy your meal. I have work to catch up on."

Without another word, the king turned and left, taking his goblet with him and leaving three shocked people behind.

Besmir stalked through his home, away from the accusing eyes of his wife, the puzzled eyes of his sister in law and the permanently haunted eyes of Sharova. He set the goblet on a table as he passed through one of the hallways and climbed the stairs to the upper level. Pausing outside the door to Joranas' room, he almost sent his mind through to see if the boy was all right.

No, I vowed I wouldn't do that to my friends or family.

His hand hovered before the wood as if he was about to knock but something stopped him. He had shown Joranas what had happened a decade ago. Shown him what the use of his magic, his *birthright*, could do if misused and seen something, some light, fade from the lad.

He hated himself for it.

The Hunter-King of Gazluth trudged along the corridor and slid through the door to his bedchamber.

***

Joranas tossed and turned in his soft bed. Sleep eluded him and he could not rid himself of the images Zaynorth had planted in his mind. He had seen his father burn Tiernon, a wasted husk of a man, burn him, then heal him to burn him again.

Zaynorth's gift as an illusion mage put Joranas right there, as if he had sent him back in time. He could hear Tiernon's screams of agony and the insane laughter that followed, smell the singed hair and flesh as it cooked on the man while he still lived. He felt the heat singe his own skin as his father sent wave after wave of flame at the crouching, broken thing that cowered in the corner of the empty room.

"Not my proudest moment," his father had said when Zaynorth had taken the images from his mind.

Tears had blurred them both as Joranas looked from Zaynorth to his father and back again.

"Why?" he squeaked, his throat tight.

"You had to see that," his father said. "You had to see what magic did to him...and started to do to me."

His father had hugged him then, pulled him into his strong arms and held him as he cried, sobbing tears of fright and repulsion onto his father's shoulder.

"It was me who ended Tiernon's life," his father had said.

Joranas recalled the horrible sound the sword had made as it entered his great-uncle's body, the sickening splash of hot blood as his father had wrenched the blade clear and the coppery stench of blood that mixed with the aroma of cooking meat in the air.

"Yet he was doomed long before I got anywhere near him with that blade," his father explained. "Remember how Tiernon looked before I started burning him? Remember that wasted, ancient thing squatting in the corner?"

Joranas had nodded against his father.

"That was all that was left of him," he had said. "Magic had drained his life force, his soul, to the point there was nothing left. Worst of all," his father had said in a tone of warning, "he sacrificed people to extend his life, give him even more power, and still it ate at him like some disease."

Joranas swung his legs from the bed, feeling the cool floor beneath his feet. He dressed silently in the same clothes he had worn earlier and slipped out of his room. He could hear the low tones of his father and the higher voice of his mother as they spoke in their bedchamber but he turned away from those sounds and trotted down the stairs, skipping the third step from the bottom as it always squeaked.

His father's guards would be stationed at the main doors but Joranas had long ago discovered another exit from the house. He entered the kitchen, the cook fire banked low in the hearth and grabbed an apple from a bowl as he opened the door leading down to the cold cellar.

Darkness engulfed him like a blanket but he had always been able to see with virtually no light and made his way down the creaky stairs into the chilly, subterranean chamber. His breath fogged before him as he passed the massive slabs of ice his father had brought at immense cost to keep the food down here cold. The scents of meat and fruit came to him as he passed various areas of the store on his way through the cellar to the far wall where an iron grate had been set in the floor.

Loosened by years of draining water, Joranas levered up the grate with ease, dropping into the dark sewer that led from the house. He had been repulsed by the stench the first time he had been down here but his sense of adventure had spurred him on. Who else would know of a secret entrance to the home of the royal family?

Roughly half his height and filled with sludge a few inches thick, the passageway led the young prince out from beneath his house and down towards a sluggish river, the water chuckling over rocks. Once free of the sewer he could stand once more and took a deep breath full of the scent of river water and summer flowers.

A sea-foam curl of stars gave more than enough light to see by and Joranas made his way upstream, wandering aimlessly along the riverbank, kicking stones into the water as he went. Something moved in the darkness ahead and he froze, almost laughing at himself as he saw it was just a man who had had too much to drink and had come to relieve himself in the river. Joranas waited until he had staggered back up to wherever he had come from, singing a low tune, before continuing.

He considered his father's words as he walked.

"I'm telling you all this, showing you these horrors, as a warning, son," his father had said. "You have immense power running through you, but using it comes at a cost. Not an immediate cost, oh no," his father had looked at Zaynorth then, almost as if accusing him of something, "but eventually. Simply put Joranas, when you use magic, you use up some of your life force," he had explained. "That's it, gone, used, never to return. There is nothing you can do to get it back. Tiernon tried," he said, "he murdered hundreds of people trying to get back the life he had spent using magic and still he looked like he did at the end."

Joranas shuddered at the thought of ever ending up like Tiernon.

"Why are you telling me all this, father?" Joranas had asked. "It's not like I can do magic any way."

"You can, if I teach you," his father had said. "I can show you how to use your powers to create and destroy, but I had to show you the risks first. You needed to see what using too much magic can do to you."

Joranas looked around, realizing where he was without knowing he would come here. The curtain wall surrounding the palace looked smaller than it had earlier. He crossed to the main gate, leaning his head and both hands against it as his father had done. Something within the wood sensed his being, his identity, and it opened with ease. He stepped inside, the overgrown gardens, only gardens to him now. Even in the strange light cast by the stars and nearly impenetrable gloom he could see the trees and shrubs that had scared him so much were harmless.

He reached the main building in a few minutes, shoving his way past overhanging branches and kicking through piles of dead grass. He paused to look up at the sightless windows and saw they held no fear for him now. There was absolutely nothing in this dead, empty palace to be afraid of. It was himself he should fear, what he might be capable of and the awful power that coursed through his veins.

Oddly the screaming hinge was silent this time as he leaned on the door.

Maybe the rust cleared earlier.

He followed his own footsteps through the palace, turning in a different direction once through the throne room. Down a short flight of steps he found several suites of rooms that had probably been for important visitors. Large, dusty rooms filled with old drapes and furniture that had seen better days. The almost completely dark palace appeared brightly lit to his eyes and he wandered through the rooms and corridors surefooted and at will.

The young prince came to an area that had been opened up for some reason. A hole in the main wall allowed a gentle breeze in, blowing the dusty air away from his nose and his eyes picked out the signs of many pairs of boots that had tracked mud in from outside. He followed the footprints through a wooden door that had been wedged open, and down a corridor with rooms to either side, each one with a pair of bunks.

A guard barracks? Why would Tiernon have needed guards?

His mind cast back to the Hall of Kings and the numerous statues there. Of course *Tiernon* had no need of guards but his predecessors would have had them. The giant Norvasil had been part of his grandfather's guard and he vaguely recalled Herofic telling him he had been a guard at some point too.

Joranas wandered through the deserted, empty hall until he reached the end. His eyes picked out a hole in the wall, the stone blocks looked almost melted and he tentatively approached it to see a rough tunnel leading down into the earth. Tiny pinpoints of light shone from the stone walls and floor and he looked closer at one.

"Thoranite," he breathed, frowning.

So this was the source of the rare crystal his father had mined years ago. This was what had saved the Gazluthian economy after Tiernon had all but ruined the country. According to the stories he had been told, his aunt Thoran had discovered the diamond like crystals after escaping Tiernon's cage and while searching for Sharova…

Joranas swallowed.

If this is where the thoranite came from, this is where Sharova was sealed in!

The young prince had no desire to see where his uncle had almost died and ran back through the guard barracks to the main palace. Heedless of his direction Joranas eventually found himself face to face with the statues in the Hall of Kings, studying the faces of his ancestors.

None of them looked anything like his father or himself, he thought, until he reached the farthest end, just before the plinth that bore his name. There was a passing resemblance, he realized, between the likeness of his grandfather and his father, something about the eyes, the set of his mouth that reminded him of his father. Joranas turned, looking at the hole where Tiernon had blasted the likeness of his own brother through the wall, pounding it to dust, before moving on up the corridor.

He was almost upon the door when he realized something was wrong. The barred, sealed chamber his father said held something evil, stood open. Joranas froze, his abdomen clenching in cold fear.

Something's in here with me!

Yet the subtle pull of whatever lay in that room was more powerful than his fear, and Joranas took a step towards the door, leaning on the wall for support. He took three deep breaths, held the fourth and peered round the door.

To see an empty room.

Feeling silly he stepped inside, looking at yet another cage Tiernon had kept people in and wondering if his aunt had been captive here too. Something glowed to his left, a sickly blue light that formed mesmeric patterns in the surface of a table.

Joranas felt a wash of calm come over him. There was nothing to fear from this, how could his father call it evil? Joranas watched his hand reach out towards the silvery light, just to feel the patterns there.

A locked off portion of his mind screamed relentlessly and pointlessly to stop. To just run, run as fast as he could and never come anywhere near this thing again. Helplessly Joranas watched as his own hand betrayed him, touching the ice-cold pattern.

As soon as the contact was made, Prince Joranas Fringor vanished.

***

Besmir floated above the surface of Hell. Gray and bleak, the virtually featureless landscape stretched off infinitely in all directions. Besmir flowed across the surface of Hell, pulled by an unseen hand that guided him.

He recognized the pulverized remains of his father's house when it came into view. The stream, pond and trees remained untouched but the house his father had built to hide and shield the portal to his world had been ripped apart. A few sections of wall were all that remained and Besmir clearly saw the portal floating harmlessly above the surface of the planet.

"Father!" he cried out, his words coming as a whisper. "Where are you?"

Besmir fought to stay where he was but found himself dragged away from his father's house. He struggled and fought, to no avail, as the image of the ruined house and portal to his home world faded from view.

He felt the presence of the absence before he saw it. A pervasive, hollow sensation that grabbed at his insides even though he was not physically there. He approached the blackness, the absence drawing him in until he thought he would be pulled into it, lost forever inside the awful, crushing nothing.

His flight ended, however, inches from the entrance to whatever abysmal place it led to. His father had once told him the world beyond was so unimaginably awful it would rip his mind just to enter it. Now his nose hovered just beyond that border and fear clamped its familiar cold fingers around his chest.

"I have thy son," a voice echoed from inside the absence.

It sounded like a billion tortured souls screaming for simultaneous release and Besmir felt his mind slipping at the horror of it.

Wait. Hold on. My son?

"What do you mean you've got my son?" he managed to ask.

"Exactly that," the tortured voice screamed at him, "your son now resides in my care. If it is thy intention to see him released unharmed, thy path is clear. Present yourself in this location, stand before me in thy physical body and I may grant you audience."

"Who are you?" Besmir asked as he felt himself thrust away from the absence.

"Porantillia," the scream came as a whisper as he flew from Hell.

***

"Joranas!" Besmir screamed as he jerked awake.

"What?" Arteera asked as she woke, wide-eyed and scared.

Besmir ignored her, dashing from their room, naked to bound down the hall, past startled servants who averted their gaze. He virtually threw himself at the door leading into Joranas' room and halted as if kicked in the stomach by a horse when he saw it empty.

"Where is he?" Besmir demanded of anyone within earshot. "Where's my son?"

The queen floated down the hallway, her diaphanous gown trailing like a ghost behind her.

"What is going on?" she asked looking into the room.

"He's gone," Besmir said in a tone of defeat. "Joranas has been taken by something."

Arteera's face fell and she shoved past her husband, searching her son's room frantically.

"What? What do you mean he's been taken by something?" she asked as she tossed Joranas' bedclothes and opened his wardrobe. "Besmir?" she turned, her face pale and stretched in shock. "Where is he? Where is Joranas?"

Besmir stepped across to take her in his arms but she slapped his hands away, shouting at him.

"Where is he, Besmir? In the city? Guards! Guards!"

Arteera ran from the room, leaving Besmir to stand, naked, in his son's room, his head down as his fists clenched, opened and clenched again.

Chapter Four

"I have every man and woman out searching, your Majesty," Norvasil said solemnly, bowing to Besmir. "Heralds have been charged with crying the news to the people so they can look too." The massive warrior trailed off as he looked at the despair ravaged face of his king.

Zaynorth arrived with Keluse and her daughter, Ranyeen, who looked more frightened than Besmir felt. The king all but jumped at Ranyeen who tried to hide behind her mother as he knelt before her.

"Ranyeen," Besmir said, laying a hand on her shoulder, "has Joranas been saying anything about running away?" his eyes bored into the girl who was paralyzed with fright.

Besmir shook her gently.

"Think, love," he implored. "Did he tell you where he was going?"

"Ranyeen?" Keluse asked. "If you know anything you've got to tell us."

Ranyeen flicked her wide eyes from the king to her mother and back again before shaking her head slowly.

"You're hurting me," she said in a tiny voice.

Besmir snatched his hand away from her little shoulder and hung his head, a posture he was rapidly becoming used to.

"I'm sorry," he said, "so sorry...I didn't mean to...it's just..."

The king took in a deep shuddering breath and looked up into the open, honest eyes of Keluse's daughter. The little girl jumped at Besmir, wrapping her arms around his neck and sobbing. Surprised, he returned the hug, lifting her tiny body and allowing her to wrap her legs around him. A single tear rolled down Keluse's cheek as she watched them.

"How's Arteera?" Keluse asked in a thick voice.

Besmir put her daughter back down and watched as the child leaned against her mother. He sighed again, rubbing at his eyes before staggering backwards into a chair.

"Not good," he said sadly. "You know how she is with him, and since we discovered we couldn't have any more...he's precious to her, you know?"

Keluse nodded, the lump in her throat a gritty ball she could not shift.

After all we've been through!

"I got the healer to give her something to help her sleep," Besmir said to no one in particular. "I...uh...I don't know what to do." Besmir looked at his friends for help.

None of them would return his hurt stare for long and the silence stretched out until Zaynorth spoke up, his voice gruff and tinged with an edge of anger.

"Tell us about this dream again," he said without ceremony.

Besmir dragged in another shaking breath and described his dream in as much detail as he could recall.

"Porantillia," Zaynorth grumbled. "I'm unfamiliar with that name, but I'll consult the palace archives and send word to Mistress Cornay at the university," the old mage hesitated. "If this was a message, rather than just a dream, how does this Porantillia expect you to present yourself physically?"

"I don't know, Zaynorth," Besmir said, shaking his head. "I really don't know."

***

Days passed as Besmir watched his people virtually turn the city of Morantine upside down looking for his son. His love for them grew at the same time as the despair in his heart swelled.

"I don't know if I can bear it," he said to Keluse as the pair walked along the river that flowed through the city. "Half of me wants to kill and burn and destroy but the other half just wants to..." he trailed off.

"Curl up into a ball and shut the world out?" Keluse said.

Besmir stared at her in shock and she smiled bitterly.

"I lost my husband on my wedding night, remember?" she said. "I know what grief and loss feels like."

The same, familiar guilt cut Besmir as she spoke, carving lines of fire on the inside of his ribs. While he had not sent Ranyor to his death he had let the man volunteer for the mission that ended his life at the hands of Tiernon.

"Have you spoken to your wife about how you feel?" Keluse asked.

"She's got her own troubles," he said. "I can't bring this to her as well."

"Typical man," Keluse snorted derisively. "All she needs now is you," she said. "Not medication, not sleep, not to be left alone. She needs *you*." Keluse turned and poked Besmir in the shoulder, hard. "Trust me on this, I know what I'm talking about."

"She doesn't want anything to do with me," Besmir said, "and blames me for his loss."

Keluse grabbed her oldest friend and one time mentor in a tight hug, wishing she could take his pain away.

"She doesn't, Besmir," Keluse said patiently. "She just hasn't got anyone else to lash out at."

Besmir pulled back, staring into the blue eyes of his one time apprentice and smirked.

"When did I become your apprentice?" he asked.

A clattering of weapons on armor and hammering of feet dragged his attention from Keluse and he turned to see two of his house guards pounding towards them.

"Majesty," one panted, her chest heaving. "A discovery...footprints....Joranas."

"Show me," Besmir commanded. "Now."

Besmir followed the guards he had interrogated earlier, trying to get them to recall seeing his son leave their house, as they led him upstream to an outflow that disgorged a thin stream of brown water out into the river. Stagnation and sewage filled Besmir's nose as he breathed and the guards pointed out the single, small footprint that had been almost perfectly preserved in the mud.

Both he and Keluse squatted to examine the footprint, noting the size, direction, depth and the fact whoever had left it walked with toes pointed inward like a duck. Besmir smiled recalling Joranas' first steps and how he had looked so awkward with his toes pointed at each other. He and Arteera had tried so many different things to get him to turn his toes out but the lad had never been able to manage it fully. Besmir laid his fingers on the mud as if it would connect him with his son.

"Where does this go?" Keluse asked, pointing to the drain.

"We...do not know, ma'am," the guard replied, embarrassed. "No one has been inside as yet."

Besmir freed his mind from his body, flicking up the stone pipe at the speed of thought until he came to a grate in the roof. Through that, he discovered himself in some kind of storage area, staring at a face he knew. His cook, Nashal, was busy filling a basket with meats and fruit that had been stored down here. He watched as she moved around the room, apparently in a world of her own until she came to the corner where the grate lay. Besmir watched her look at the ironwork, dismissing the partially open grate as she turned back to her list. A second later his anger dissipated as her eyes widened and she dropped her basket, screaming for guards as she pelted for the stairs.

"The cellar," Besmir said as soon as he had entered his body once more. "It comes from the cellar under my own house!"

Keluse turned back from where she had been scouting along the riverbank, the skirts of her dress wet with mud and worse.

"More footprints here," she said, "going upriver."

"With me!" Besmir commanded the guards, both of whom snapped to attention.

The king trotted up the stony bank searching for any sign of his son. His mind was drawn to the fact Joranas' footprints were the only ones he saw. His son had been alone, rather than taken by someone.

Why Joranas? Where were you going?

They followed the flowing river upstream, past warehouses and businesses that dumped all manner of rubbish into the flow, adding to the stench. Disgust cut at Besmir when he smelled the overpowering stench of decay from the rotting carcass of a sheep that must have washed down from the grasslands above the city.

It was Keluse who spotted the first signs Joranas had turned from the river, a patch of grass he had gone through had almost straightened back up but her keen eye picked it out.

"This way!" she cried, scrambling up the bank.

Besmir followed her, his heart sinking with every step towards the destination he feared the most.

The old palace sat like a brooding hen, the curtain wall broken only by the main gate he had sealed with magic only he or Zaynorth could penetrate. They had come up with the idea to protect people from entering and potentially ending up as victims to Tiernon's altar.

Besmir felt a sick sense of certainty punch him in the stomach as soon as he saw the gate hung open. He dashed through it, running heedlessly through the snatching, grabbing plants that tried to snag his clothing, keeping him from his son. Without a thought Besmir summoned his power, sending a gout of flame exploding from his hand to cut a path through the once elegant topiary.

Burning, scorched wood filled his nostrils and the hiss of steam boiling from leaves filled his ears with the pop and crackle of burning shrubs. Fueled by rage and desperation his flame was lava-hot and it cut an almost instant path through the gardens, revealing the palace door hung as open as the main gate.

The two young guards looked at Besmir in shocked awe having never witnessed his use of magic.

Besmir sprinted for the door, not bothering to track his son any longer as he was almost certain where the boy would be.

That cursed altar!

He pelted through the throne room and into the Hall of Kings where he skidded to a halt, his legs collapsing, forcing him to grab onto a statue for support. Keluse and the pair of guards arrived a few seconds later to see their king hugging the likeness of his grandfather for support.

"What...?" Keluse asked staring at the splinters and burst masonry. "Did Joranas do this?"

Besmir shook his head, staring at the doorway with fear in his heart.

"L-Look," Besmir stammered. "It's been burst *outwards*..."

"That means..." Keluse muttered. "Something opened it from *inside*..." she finished, putting her hands up to her mouth.

Besmir nodded, finally managing to take a few steps towards the door. His guards bustled past him, knocking him sideways in their haste to enter the room first.

"Let us, Majesty," the woman said.

Besmir reached for her as she turned from him to the room.

"Noralynn wait!" he said, missing her by inches.

The king made a second desperate grab for his guard as she walked into the room. Missing her again he stumbled in behind her as her male counterpart shouldered his own way into the room.

It was much as Besmir had left it so many years ago. The disgusting altar still dominated the middle of the room, radiating tendrils of hate and evil. The cages that lined the walls still contained a wooden bucket, the rope handle long since rotted away. The outlined shape of a man was still part of the wall, left by Sharova's body as the stones appeared to absorb him before Besmir freed the man.

The main difference Besmir noticed was the dust. More dust than he had seen anywhere else in the abandoned palace and he looked down to see the tiny footprints as they entered the room, approached the altar and vanished.

"Don't touch it!" he warned all three as they surrounded the altar. "Whatever you do, keep away from it."

"What is it, Majesty?" Noralynn asked as she caressed the table with her gaze.

"Some foul thing Tiernon had," Besmir said. "He used it to drain people's life force, sustaining his own but..." Besmir paused. "It's almost as if it's alive," he added. "Conscious and aware," he looked at Keluse, "and hungry. So very hungry."

Keluse shivered and looked at the floor beneath the shadow where Sharova had once hung. Sadness welled in her eyes as she recalled being brought here to see Ranyor, his corpse cast aside like a used rag once Tiernon had finished with him. A sob escaped her and Besmir appeared at her side, wrapping an arm about her shoulders.

"My King," Lucian said, drawing Besmir's attention.

The king bent down to look at whatever the young man had found. Keluse looked too and both she and Besmir saw what he had found. Beneath the altar, jammed under its wooden base was a single small shoe.

Lucian reached for it but Besmir grabbed his arm, yanking it back hard.

"Don't!" he said. "It's Joranas'. I'm sure he was here."

The trio stood straight once more, turning almost as one to see Noralynn reaching towards the silvery symbols laid into the top of the altar.

"Noralynn!" Besmir barked, throwing his hand out towards her.

His warning came too late, however, and the young woman touched the altar, throwing her head back as soon as contact had been made.

Besmir grabbed Lucian to stop him from approaching his partner, wrapping his arms around the guard who roared as Noralynn's entire body stiffened. Besmir could see the muscles in her arms and neck were rigid with tension, her whole body shaking with whatever horrific power flowed into or out of her form.

"Besmir," Noralynn said in the same voice of multitudes he had heard in his dream. "I have thy son. Present thyself to me and secure his release, or deny me thy presence and I shall torment him in Hell." Noralynn's body shook violently now, her hair flying in all directions.

"Who are you?" Besmir asked as he struggled to stop Lucian.

"I? I am Porantillia, Bane of Gods, destroyer of worlds and devourer of souls."

Besmir saw Keluse clap her hands over her ears to try and block out the horrific voice that came from a thousand throats, her eyes wide with terror and madness.

"Come to me, Hunter King, or lose thy son's soul for eternity."

"Oh, I'm coming," Besmir said, hurling his guard aside. "I'm coming. And when I arrive, you and I will have a reckoning, whoever you are!"

Besmir had dragged the sword from Lucian's scabbard at the same time as he shoved him at the door leading to the Hall of Kings. Brandishing it more like a bludgeon than a sword he swung it wildly at Noralynn as Porantillia laughed at him with the young woman's body. Just before he could hit the guard, however, she hammered against the surface of the altar, her face slamming into the silver inlaid wood with a sickening crunch.

Besmir watched as the color drained from Noralynn's body, looking as if it flowed into the wood, pulling the skin of her face with it until her features were so distorted Besmir could no longer recognize her. Her body jerked a few times, spasms ripping through it as her life was ripped from her by the vile thing. After half a minute Noralynn's limp, lifeless corpse dropped to the floor and lay still.

Besmir, Keluse and Lucian looked at each other, seeing their own horror on the other's faces. Dust flew, filling the air with the stench of powdered bones. Lucian crawled over to

Noralynn's body, shaking her in a futile attempt to wake her lifeless husk. He turned his tear stained face to Besmir, pleading with his king.

"Help her, Majesty," he begged in a pitiful voice. "Please."

"She's gone, Luc," Besmir said as gently as he could. "I'm sorry, but there's nothing I can do."

"She is like a sister to me," Lucian said. "What will I tell her family?"

"Don't worry about all that now," Besmir said, gently. "We must leave."

He trotted back down the Hall of Kings and into the throne room where he gathered an armful of the drapes that had once hung behind the chair. Returning, he helped Lucian to wrap Noralynn in order that they could carry her more easily.

Chapter Five

Ru Tarn pushed her way through the crowds that filled the street. Morantine was awash with the mixture of cultures it had become famous for. Gazluthians mixed with Corbondrasi, Waravalians, Ninsians and others. She even saw a pair of Pitcriss tails as they made their way through the throngs of people she pushed past.

Ordinarily Ru Tarn enjoyed the short walk from her ambassadorial residence, formerly Fleet Admiral Sharova's house. Today, however, her feet could not carry her fast enough and the press of people around her was nothing but a hindrance. The two guards assigned to her fought to keep up as she shoved her way through the crowds earning more than one annoyed glance from people as she pushed past them.

One short Ninsian took more offense than the others and turned from the merchant he had been shoved into.

"Feathered Corbondrasi *powhalli*!" he cried as she continued.

His comment earned him a few nasty looks from other Corbondrasi who had come to the central marketplace just to do business and he turned back to examine the jewelry the Gazluthian merchant had been showing him when he realized he was surrounded by the feathered people.

Ru Tarn approached the mansion Besmir had taken as the royal residence years ago. The guards at the door recognized her and opened the portals, saluting as she bustled past them. The Corbondrasi almost knocked into an old servant who was in the process of carrying a decanter and several glasses balanced on a tray he held in one hand.

"May I assist you, madam ambassador?" he asked in a self-important voice once he had regained control of the decanter and glasses.

"Must see king," she said shortly.

"Unfortunately King Besmir is indisposed and cannot be disturbed at present. May I give him a message?"

Ru Tarn drew in a deep breath, puffing out the plumage on her ample chest in a sign that would, in her homeland of Boranash, be seen as a challenge. She fixed the pompous old man with a stern look in her dark lavender eyes and let out a piercing scream that sounded more like a shrill whistle to all those in earshot.

Drilling like a nail into the ears of all around, the note drew out forcing people to cover their ears. The old servant threw his tray, smashing the decanter and glasses, spilling the contents along the wall and across the floor, so he could slap his hands over his ears.

People appeared from doors and rooms as Ru Tarn's shrill screech died off, all wondering what was going on.

"This is message," she said to the old man as Besmir himself appeared from a long corridor.

"What in the name of the Gods was that?" he demanded, glaring at everyone.

"The Corbondrasi has gone mad, your Majesty!" the old servant cried, trying to gather up the shattered glass with his fingers. "Insane!"

Besmir turned his attention to her, frowning.

"Ru Tarn?" he asked.

"Ru Tarn is having information," she said, "about P...P..." she struggled to say the word. "Porantillia," she finally managed.

Shame, guilt and nausea washed through Ru Tarn's feathered chest at having to speak the forbidden name but her duty to the royal family came first and she forced herself to quash her feelings.

Besmir glanced from her face to the book she hugged like a precious child, her feathered arms wrapped around it, before gesturing for her to follow him. He led her to an area of the house she had not been in before, a private living room filled with simple, functional furnishings and a few personal decorations.

Furnished exactly as Ru Tarn had come to expect from Besmir, each piece was simply built but well made. The king bought furniture to last, not to show off. His manner of dress was the same. Simple clothing without ostentation but well made and sewn to last, the one nod to decoration was the stag he had embroidered on his chest. Ru Tarn had heard that every stag the king had embroidered on *his* clothing had been put there by his wife.

Her eyes cut to the queen who sat in a padded chair at the far end of the room, her feet propped on a stool and covered in thick blankets despite the summer heat. She looked pale and worn, the loss of her son had aged her years in just a few days and Ru Tarn's heart went out to the young queen.

Zaynorth sat at a table by a window, his graying head balanced on one hand as he poured over some massive tome she could not see the title of. His brother, Herofic, stared out of the window, his broad back radiating hostility and rage. Neither brother paid her much attention as she entered but Ru Tarn knew it was not ignorance that made them dismiss her so easily.

"Your Majesties," Ru Tarn began, "all Corbondrasi suffer same loss. Ru Tarn also offer all resources of Boranash to help fin..." she trailed off as Besmir raised his hand.

"This isn't a state meeting, Ru Tarn," he said. "This is my home. Have a seat, have a drink, and tell us what you know."

The king hooked one of the chairs around the table with his foot, pulling it out for her to sit on. It made a goose-honk as the leg scraped across the flagstone but no one paid any attention. Ru Tarn stepped lightly across the room and folded herself into the offered seat as Besmir began pacing up and down the room like a caged animal. She gently put the book on the table in front of her noting Zaynorth's eyes flick to it before returning to his own book.

"This Ru Tarn family copy of holy writings given to Corbondrasi by Mwondi at dawn of time," she said, stroking her soft fingers over the worn cover. "Mwondi being God of hatchlings, of Corbondrasi babies." Ru Tarn looked at Besmir who was watching her closely. "It mention P...Porantillia. I sorry, name is forbidden to Corbondrasi. Is something no nice Corbondrasi to be saying," she explained.

"What's it say?" Besmir asked, uninterested in her explanation of her embarrassment.

Ru Tarn opened the ancient book, hand copied generations before by Corbondrasi scribes. The smell of leather and old parchment rose from the tome along with the subtle addition of dried blood. She stared lovingly at the elegant curls and loops of writing that had been committed to the parchment so long ago, turning each page until she saw the passage she sought.

"Ru Tarn try and translate," she said as Zaynorth and Herofic both turned their attention to her. "I, Mwondi, abhor the creature known as Porantillia. Be her name stricken from all history, from all...time," Ru Tarn read.

"Her?" Zaynorth asked in shock.

"She who is destroyer of worlds...destroyer of Gods," Ru Tarn carried on, reading the ancient Corbondrasi tongue was hard enough but translating it into Gazluthian was even more challenging. "Speak not her name or suffer the fate of Gratallach, the lover who spurned her attentions."

"This is all wonderful," Besmir said, "but is there anything in there that can actually help me get my son back?"

Ru Tarn looked up into his eyes, sympathy in her heart and shook her head slowly, her plumage hissing as it moved.

"Writings tell...Porantillia was lover to Gratallach. Gratallach leave her for other. Gratallach and new lover have children. Children are Gods Mwondi, Cathantor, Sharise. Porantillia...take revenge on Gratallach for leaving. Seal him for all time in middle of sun to burn forever." Ru Tarn felt her mouth dry out. "I sorry, this difficult for Ru Tarn. Corbondrasi taught from hatchlings never to be speaking this words."

"Why is that?" Zaynorth asked.

"Writings sacred to Corbondrasi, not meant for...outsiders. They teachings of God Mwondi, God of Corbondrasi hatchlings," Ru Tarn said apologetically.

"Well then, thank you for anything you can tell us," Besmir said.

"It is because Ru Tarn is friends with king that Ru Tarn do this," she said, "and because Ru Tarn is liking Joranas."

At the mention of his name Arteera sniffed, making a strangled, choking sound in her throat that drew both Besmir and Ru Tarn's attention. The king went to his wife in an attempt to comfort her but she rose, fleeing from the room through a door Ru Tarn had not noticed before.

The Corbondrasi ambassador looked away when she saw Besmir's expression of despair and the utter self-loathing in his face. Zaynorth caught her eye, his expression one of gratitude that she had not watched Besmir at his lowest point.

"So what can we do?" Besmir asked as he threw himself into a chair beside Ru Tarn, grabbing a goblet and filling it with wine. "How do I get into a plane of existence that, as far as I know, is only accessible to spirits?" Besmir gulped his wine and refilled the goblet almost immediately.

"Corbondrasi shaman," Ru Tarn said.

Besmir looked at her with a puzzled expression.

"Corbondrasi shaman know more about these writings than Ru Tarn," she said. "Ru Tarn go with you to Boranash. Ask King grant audience with master shaman. He tell you what to do."

"I can't just leave now," Besmir said, draining his third cup of wine in as many minutes. "What about Arteera? She needs me here."

Zaynorth slammed the book he had been reading shut with a bang that made Ru Tarn jump.

"We do not seem to have any other ideas regarding what is to be done," he said. "I have had scholars searching both day and night in the palace archives as well as the university library. There does not appear to be even mention of this

Porantillia anywhere in our literature, Besmir, this looks to be the only lead you might have."

"What about Gazluth?" Besmir asked.

"What about it?" Herofic demanded turning from the window. "What about Gazluth? Does it not owe you? After everything you have done since you ended your uncle, can the people not manage without you for a while?"

Ru Tarn saw his anger, fueled by his emotional pain, turning his lips almost white. His fists clenched at his sides and he shook with the feeling running through his body as he stared at Besmir. The king looked almost afraid, something Ru Tarn had never seen in him since she had arrived almost eight years before.

He rubbed his eyes as if to rid himself of the confusion she saw in them.

"You're right," he finally said, "of course you're right. I've got to go," he added, turning to Ru Tarn. "Please make any arrangements you feel necessary."

"Look, lad," Herofic said, sighing apologetically. "I do not wish to be hard on you but if someone needs to give you a kick in the right direction, I will be there with my heaviest boots on."

Besmir grunted a laugh, wiping his eyes. He stood, skirting round Ru Tarn to embrace the old man.

"I wouldn't have it any other way," he said. "Now all I have to do is break the news to my wife."

***

Joranas became aware of two things initially. First he heard a low whistle as wind blew over a hole somewhere. Second was the heat. Summer in Gazluth was warm and damp, perfect for sustaining the grasslands that fed the thousands of cattle the population owned but this felt uncomfortably hot. Panic gripped his chest at the thought he must be in an oven like the children in some of the stories his mother used to read. His mind thrashed, trying to wake his body but it would not respond.

Maybe I'm dead. Maybe I'm in Hell.

Eventually he calmed a little, if he were in an oven, or in Hell, surely this would be more painful? Joranas concentrated on what he could feel and hear. A gentle but hot breeze washed over his skin, bringing no relief from the searing heat. There was a gritty feel to the wind as it washed over him and the air he breathed was dry, dusty. Nothing came to his ears save the incessant whine of the wind, a low moan he tried to ignore.

Footsteps!

He could hear the crunch of footsteps on gravel or dusty stone and they were approaching. Finally he would be saved.

Unless...

Someone came close to him, he could feel their proximity, as if they were checking on him, making sure he was alive. A rustle and a sigh. Then breathing. Heavy breaths, long and slow.

Joranas' mind conjured images of nightmare creatures with horns and impossibly long teeth waiting to rip him to shreds.

That's stupid. Why would a monster wait to eat?

So it hurts more? So it scares you more?

Time passed and Joranas might have slept. It felt cooler now, so cold in fact he was shivering. Chills shot down his body as gooseflesh broke out. A ticking sound came to his ears and he realized it was his own teeth clattering against each other. Tiredness eventually took him again and he drifted off into a fitful sleep.

His eyes flicked open. Bright, painful light made the backs of them ache and he squinted, dulling the lancing agony. He found himself surrounded by sandy yellow-brown and orange, gritty floor and walls came together to form a cave around him and his mind fought to understand his surroundings as he looked.

His arms felt heavy, his legs ached as if the muscles had been beaten. Joranas recalled learning to ride a horse a few years back, something had spooked the gentle mare he had been on and she had thrown her inexperienced rider to the ground. His leg had slammed into a log with a sickening crunch, aching for days as it did now. His stomach rumbled, hunger gripping him as he tried to move. Joranas just managed to roll over, seeing for the first time his surroundings fully.

His empty stomach flipped as his eyes took in the vastness that stretched off into the distance. He could see for what looked like miles, leagues even. And everywhere he looked all he saw was barren, dry sand. The cave mouth opened onto a landscape unlike anything he had ever seen. Even the brief trip he had made with his parents to the coast had not had this amount of sand. Plus, that had been a light yellow color while now he was surrounded by rusty orange.

Slowly, awkwardly, and painfully, Joranas pulled himself into a seated position with his back to the cave wall. It was fairly shallow but deep enough to keep the baking sun from cooking him alive. He swallowed, the dry click of his throat a desperate sound and his face screwed up as tears threatened to come.

Stop that!

Oddly it had been his mother's voice that barked inside his head. Joranas would have expected such to come from his father but the Queen's voice had come to him.

Grow up.

His mother's voice cut into his mind, snapping him from his self pity and bringing him back to reality. He had to take stock. He had to survive.

Joranas looked around the interior of the cave. As his attention had been diverted outside before, he had failed to notice the small cache of items just opposite where he reclined. A few plant stems had been carefully laid beside a length of dried meat and there looked to be a nest of some kind, a pile of dry brush and twigs that had been flattened in the middle.

Joranas half crawled, half dragged himself over to the items, picking up one of the plant stems. As thick as his middle finger and dark green, it looked to have sections to it and felt cold to the touch. Joranas shook it, overjoyed when he heard the sound of liquid inside. He ripped a hole in the stem with his teeth and sucked, sweet water flooding his mouth and making the back of his jaws tingle. Thoughtlessly, did the same to three more stems before realizing he should conserve some and put the fourth back.

They're not yours either.

That thought shocked him. But of course, these things had been gathered by someone else. The heavy breather that had been here before. Joranas picked up the jerky, chewing the salty meat but not wanting to know what animal it came from.

Are they going to be angry?

Joranas found he did not care. If whoever had gathered these items had not wanted him to have them, they should have hidden them or taken them wherever they went. Joranas looked around to see if any clue as to the stranger's identity might lay within the cave but it was bare save for the few items he found.

Boosted by the small meal, Joranas moved over to the cave mouth, staring out into the vastness of the desert he was in. His eyes picked out nothing of any significance. All he could see were piles and piles of shivering sand. Orange waves with streams of sand lifted from their peaks by the wind. Hot sun beat onto his head like a club when he leaned out too far and Joranas ducked back inside the cave as fast as he could, curling up against the far wall and staring at the cracked ceiling.

I'm never leaving here. Not alive any way.

His eyes drooped, fatigue robbing him of the will to stay awake and he fell asleep almost instantly.

He jumped awake when something touched him. Joranas flicked his eyes open to see the outline of someone, someone big, trying to bury him. He screamed wordlessly, thrashing his arms and legs against the soft down he was under. The figure squatted and Joranas calmed a little, realizing he was not being buried but covered against the chill that had come with night again.

His keen eyesight allowed him to see the stranger in the near dark of the cave and Joranas studied the man from beneath his warm covering.

It was difficult to tell how tall he might be as he squatted, arms wrapped around knees, but his head almost reached the cave roof and Joranas had been able to stand upright earlier so he knew the man was tall. Bulky too. Joranas could see the thick cords of muscle on the stranger's arms and legs. His neck, too, was thick with muscle, leading up to a square jaw that had a dent in the chin. Emerald eyes sparkled in the darkness as the stranger examined Joranas in return and the young boy felt almost instantly at ease. They were kind eyes, filled with a friendly openness he recognized.

"Who are you?" Joranas asked in a cracked, dry voice.

"Who are you?" the stranger echoed, his voice a deep, baritone rumble.

"I'm Joranas."

The stranger tilted his head to one side like a dog listening to its master. Long, brown hair fell to his shoulders, shifting as he moved. The stranger frowned.

"Joranas," he said.

"Yes. I'm Joranas," the boy said. "Who are you?"

"I do not know," the stranger said, puzzled. "I met Joranas before, in the other place. He was not nice. Are you nice?"

Joranas nodded.

"Very nice," he said nervously. "Are you?"

"I do not know," the stranger said.

"Where are we?" Joranas asked.

"Here, in this place."

Joranas sighed. He was obviously impaired in some way, probably the intense sun had boiled his brains. Joranas looked and smiled, at least he had brought some more of the liquid filled stems.

"I'm sorry," he said carefully. "I used up the plants."

"Plants," the stranger echoed.

Joranas pointed at the stems, miming drinking from them. The stranger copied his mime, looking so comical Joranas laughed. The stranger did too.

"So you don't know your name at all?" Joranas asked

"No."

"What am I going to call you then?" Joranas asked.

"Joranas," the stranger said in a matter of fact tone.

"No that's my name, it would just get confusing," he looked up, thinking. "What about calling you Whint?"

"Whint," the stranger said. A broad smile crossed his face, revealing a set of straight, white teeth.

"Are you cold?" Joranas asked.

Whint tilted his head again, staring at Joranas. It was as if he understood the words Joranas said but not the meaning they conveyed, even though it was a simple enough question.

"Cold," Whint said.

"You covered me because I was shivering," Joranas said. "Aren't you cold too?"

"No," Whint replied.

"Is there anyone else near here?" Joranas asked.

"No."

"Any buildings or anything at all?"

"No."

"How did we get here?" Joranas asked.

"We arrived," Whint said.

"Well that explains it all, then," Joranas muttered.

He thought back to before he had woken here, trying to remember what had happened. His thoughts were hazy and indistinct, like when he had taken a bottle of wine and drunk some to be like his father. He recalled exploring the palace at night, unable to sleep. Could remember the strange statues in the Hall of Kings and then…the door had been open! The door his father had said had evil inside had been open and Joranas had gone in. He could remember the odd table, the strange feelings it gave him as he got closer to it and then…

"I touched it," he said.

"I touched it," Whint repeated.

Joranas looked at the man, trying to see if he was just copying him or he had touched the table as well.

How can he have known what you were thinking?

"I want to have a look outside," Joranas said a little nervously. "Can I get past?"

Whint stared at him for what seemed like far too long but eventually he shuffled over to where he had made his little nest of twigs and brush. Joranas watched as the large man crawled into it, curling up and getting comfortable. A wash of sadness rolled through Joranas when he watched Whint put his thumb in his mouth and begin to suck. Joranas ducked outside, the chill biting at him.

Chapter Six

"Of course I am going with you," Arteera said as she began to select a few items to take with her. "If you are traveling to Boranash to try and find my son, I shall be there too."

"And what about Gazluth?" he asked. "Who's going to look after the country if we both go?"

Arteera actually sneered at him, her lip curling as she stared at her husband.

"I really don't care," she said. "This is my *son* we're talking about here!" she shouted, more animated than he had seen her for days. "Not some trade agreement, not something that will bring money into the country or help make the people's lives better. My *son*!" she repeated, staring at him with a burning rage in her tear-filled eyes.

"Our son," Besmir said.

"Oh, you do remember that then?" Arteera asked sarcastically. "That he is your son as well?" she arched her eyebrows at Besmir who's confusion only grew. "Because it would seem you have so many more things that are more important than your wife or son," she snapped at him. "Did you know he thinks you have no love in your heart for him? Did you know he tries so hard for you to see him?"

"What do you mean see him? I see him every day," Besmir said, anger beginning to heat his chest.

"You do not see his achievements, you never praise him for anything he does and he does so much to try and get your attention."

Besmir shook his head, a bitter laugh crawling up his throat.

"So I'm a useless father and husband then?" he spat at Arteera. "Maybe you will both see the truth when I march into Hell to save my boy."

"I didn't say you were a useless father or husband," Arteera said in a gentler tone. "There is no need for the histrionics either," she said. "March into Hell!" she mimicked.

"Arteera," Besmir said in a patient voice, "you do realize this trip to Boranash is so I can do exactly that?" he asked. "I've got to find a way to *physically* enter the world my father's spirit lives in and then let this Porantillia, whoever she is, do whatever she likes to me?"

Arteera stared at Besmir, two red spots appearing on her cheeks as she considered his words.

"Why would she want you?" she asked, afraid of his answer. "How does she even know you exist?"

"Remember Tiernon?" Besmir asked sarcastically. "Remember all the demons he summoned?" Arteera nodded slowly. "At least one of them came from that blackness she is trapped in. I was there when something was born. Some evil, dark thing I burned the life from as soon as it emerged, but there were more, so many more."

Besmir trailed off, recalling his sojourn in the Hell dimension when creatures his father had called Ghoma had feasted on his eternal soul. He shivered at the recollection, shaking his head to clear the memories.

"That's how she knows about me. I killed Tiernon who she was either helping or controlling and now she wants revenge. So she's taken Joranas because she knows I'll do anything to save him." Besmir rubbed his chest hard.

"What's wrong?" Arteera asked, pointing at his chest.

"I've got this...pain, I suppose you could call it. But it's more like...a hollow...inside my chest," he turned his agonized face to her and her heart melted. "It won't go, Arteera," he added, sobbing. "No matter what I do I can't get rid of it."

The Queen of Gazluth walked over to her husband and took his hand gently. She lifted it, kissing his fingers before placing it between her breasts.

"Why did you not say?" she asked as tears rolled down her cheeks. "I have its twin within me."

"She's taken our son," Besmir said in a child like voice.

"I know," Arteera sobbed. "I miss him so."

"Me too," Besmir said. "I promise I'll do anything I can to get him back," Besmir declared. "Anything."

Arteera kissed him long and hard.

"But I could not bear to lose you either," she said, her voice rising to a squeak.

Besmir sniffed, looking down to where their hands met.

"Then I'd better find a way to get back to you, hadn't I?" he asked.

Arteera nodded hard, her hair bouncing.

"You better," she said, "or I will come and drag you from Hell myself."

***

Besmir, Zaynorth, Herofic, Ru Tarn and Arteera accompanied by Ru Tarn's assistant, Qi Noss, were escorted quietly from Morantine's north gate by a small group of White Blades led by Norvasil. Few people were abroad at this unholy hour and of those few that might have seen them, Zaynorth gave the illusion they were never there. Ru Tarn and Qi Noss had both raised concerns about not having enough protection but Besmir had pointed out that if there was anything on the way they could not handle or avoid, a few added soldiers would probably not be of any more use.

The land north of the capital rose steadily out of the valley the city had been built in, through farmland and some of the best vineyards in the country. They passed friendly farmers as they rode, exchanging pleasantries as they skirted fields.

"None of them will ever know they've just said good morning to the Queen," Besmir said, smiling at Arteera.

She smiled coyly back at Besmir, their little argument, followed by sharing of feelings, had strengthened them once more and she was truly grateful for it. She steered her horse alongside his and they rode together in friendly silence.

"I must say it has been a long time since I have traveled," Zaynorth announced. "Hopefully we can recall how it is done."

"You moan and complain about how sore your backside is," Herofic grunted, making them laugh.

"Now I remember," Zaynorth said playing along.

The party chatted amiably as they rode north-east through the rolling grasslands of Gazluth. Immense herds of cattle grazed lazily in the warm sun, eyeing the small party with uninterested stares as they chewed endlessly at the grass. Once, Besmir's keen eyes picked out a pair of people watching them from the top of a large rock that thrust from the ground like a giant thumb.

"Probably want to make sure we are not about to pilfer any of their cattle," Zaynorth said when he followed Besmir's eye line.

Besmir nodded and they rode on.

As the sun waned, heating their backs, Norvasil approached Besmir, steering his massive horse next to the king.

"Rogen says there is a hamlet up ahead, just a small place but there is an inn if you would like to stop for the night."

Besmir looked at his tired wife and the exhausted appearance Zaynorth was attempting to hide. He wanted nothing more but to gallop north, get to Boranash as fast as he could to save his son, killing horses if need be. Had he believed he would get away with it he would do so now. He also knew how insular the Corbondrasi could be and a lone horseman attempting to gain access to the royal family would most likely be filled with crossbow bolts. Gritting his teeth in frustration Besmir nodded.

Loran's End turned out to be quite a busy little place set at the intersection of two well traveled roads. The outskirts had been trampled into mud by the passage of thousands of hooves, horse and cattle had been driven round the outside of the town. The few buildings there were clean and well maintained, however, and the small party made for the center of town where a large building sat with a stable attached to the side.

Imposing and stone built, the Gorky Tavern had obviously grown over time as the different building styles and materials showed. The upper floors hung over the lower, using some building technique Besmir did not understand or fully trust. A pair of severe-looking men armed with clubs stood by the main door, one with an obviously broken nose and the other missing an eye. Besmir dropped from his horse and approached.

"Trouble?" he asked.

Broken nose grinned, revealing he had several teeth missing as well as his broken nose.

"Not with me and Jarks here," he grunted. "Ain't no one stupid enough to start nothing," he spoke with a slight buzzing hiss from his broken nose. "Stables round the side, give your horses over to young Besmir if you want to stay."

"Sorry, did you say Besmir?" Zaynorth asked with a smirk.

"Yep. What of it?"

"Oh nothing," Zaynorth said. "It is just not that common of a name."

"Quite a few folks round these parts called Besmir," he buzzed. "After the King, you know, and what he done for us."

Besmir glanced at Arteera who returned his look with a tiny, tired smile as they made their way round the building to where the stables were.

The pungent smell of horse manure rose from a large midden stirred by a young lad of around ten who dumped a barrow full of fresh dung on top. He turned and the ache in Besmir's chest doubled when he saw the similarities to Joranas. Of a similar height and build to his son he wore an almost identical, serious expression and Besmir turned to see if Arteera felt the same.

Her lower lip trembled as she looked at the boy but she did not allow her tears to flow in public. Besmir knew she would wait until they were alone to express her hollow sadness.

"Evening mister, mistress," the young Besmir said as he pushed his squeaking barrow back towards the stable door. "You staying?"

The King nodded, handing his reins to the lad who clucked his tongue and led his horse inside. He came back out a few seconds later and took Arteera's horse, leading that in too.

"Fine mounts you got here," he said, casting a professional eye over the horses. "Good bloodlines. Where you get them?"

"Morantine," Besmir said, his voice almost a whisper.

The young lad's eyes widened as he stared at them, taking Zaynorth's mount and leading it inside.

"You been to the capital?" he said in wonder. "You ever see the King there?" he asked. "My momma named me after King Besmir on account of how he saved the whole world from some bad man. You ever see him?"

The young Besmir squinted up at them, his head tilted to one side, waiting for a reply. Arteera turned her head, leaning against Besmir as waves of sadness threatened to drown her.

"No," the King said hoarsely. "No, I've never seen him."

Besmir reached into the purse hanging from his belt and pulled out a single gold coin. It glinted in the final rays of sunlight, catching the young boy's eye. He gaped at the coin as if unable to believe such wealth could exist. Besmir held it out.

"Do a good job and this is yours," he said, smiling when the young man snatched the coin from his fingers.

"Oh, I will, Sir," the stable hand said. "I shall look after these horses like they was my own."

Both Besmir and his wife smiled when the lad bowed to them. Arteera gripped his hand tightly as the youth disappeared inside to scrub, feed and water their horses. The couple stayed there for a while, both lost in their own memories as the rest of the party brought their horses in.

***

Ru Tarn had stayed in better places during her life. She had also stayed in far worse. The tavern was clean at least, the Corbondrasi noted as she changed from her traveling clothes into a dress that displayed her plumage more fully. She carefully applied the near priceless oils that kept her feathers in immaculate condition before arranging the soft down around her eyes to her utter satisfaction. Qi Noss knocked on the door.

"Shall I escort you down, my lady?" he asked through the wood.

"No, thank you, Qi Noss, I will make my way down...ah!"

Ru Tarn's words were cut short by a stabbing pain in the lower part of her abdomen. She bent forward, her breath caught as an agonizing wave of nauseating pain ripped through her.

"No, no, no," she whispered. "This cannot be happening now."

"Ru Tarn?" Qi Noss said in a worried voice from outside. "Are you well?"

"I am fine," she managed. "I will be down soon."

Ru Tarn waited as the agony slowly dissipated from her lower belly. This was not right. Her time was four months hence.

I should not be producing an egg now!

The tavern's main room was bustling with people when she walked down the stairs. A few heads turned as she entered, mainly locals or those who were not of her party. She saw the dark green feathers of Qi Noss who was having a conversation with the massive leader of the White Blades, Norvasil, but was not looking for his company. Her lavender eyes grazed over the crowd sitting at simple wooden tables as they ate and drank. At the farthest end, nestled in a corner she saw the table she had been searching for and started in their direction.

"May Ru Tarn join you?" she asked, approaching the table.

Zaynorth and Herofic both looked up in surprise, the Corbondrasi ambassador had never paid either of them much attention in the past.

"Of course, my lady," Herofic said as they both stood.

Herofic glanced at his brother in confusion as he helped seat the Corbondrasi but Zaynorth shrugged.

"Will you be dining this evening?" Zaynorth asked.

"Ru Tarn is hungry," she said. "What should she have?"

The Corbondrasi ambassador gave Herofic a coy smile, blinking her lavender eyes several times.

"Well, that depends on your tastes..." Zaynorth said at a loss. "Do you like meat?"

"Meat is acceptable to Ru Tarn," she said. "What is this meat?" she pointed to Herofic's plate.

"This is beef, ambassador," he said. "Would you like so..."

His words trailed off as she dipped her feathered fingers into his dinner and took a slice of the roasted leg. She tilted her head back and dropped the thing into her mouth whole, gravy dripping down her chin and from her fingers as she looked at them again.

"Tasty," she said. "Ru Tarn wants wine now," she added.

"Ambassador, are you feeling quite well?" Zaynorth asked as he passed a pewter goblet to her. The Corbondrasi lifted the wine that sat chilling on the table and lifted it to her mouth, drinking straight from the bottle.

"Ru Tarn fine," she said, wiping her mouth with the back of her hand and belching softly.

The Corbondrasi ambassador leaned back in her chair, studying the pair of older men as they spoke about Besmir in low tones.

"There will be a reckoning when we find this Porantillia," Herofic said darkly. "Taking Joranas has all but broken him," he added, nodding at the king.

Zaynorth nodded as he chewed thoughtfully at a chunk of meat in gravy.

"It's certainly a blow to him. Arteera as well," the illusion mage said. "I miss the lad, too." His voice went hoarse as he spoke.

Ru Tarn watched the interaction with interest. Both men came across as fiercely loyal to their king as well as one being a capable warrior while the other a mage of some esteem. Ru

Tarn drained the wine bottle, beginning to feel the first effects warming her insides. She casually dipped her fingers into Herofic's meal once more, taking a second slice of meat and virtually swallowing it whole.

Ru Tarn's rational mind was screaming at her to stop. To show some decorum and leave, go through the biological process of oviparity in private. Her biological imperative, however, had other ideas and Ru Tarn wanted nothing more than to mate. She had no idea why her annual egg was coming so early and had no time to prepare the solutions her people had discovered years ago to ease the symptoms and get through the experience.

"Herofic has big muscles," she said abruptly.

The brothers stared at her in surprise as her tone had been similar to that used by someone appraising livestock.

The Corbondrasi reached out and stroked her feathered hand down his shoulder and arm.

"Strong. Male," she purred, fluttering the delicate feathers that lined her eyelids.

Herofic swallowed, smiling at her awkwardly before shifting his chair a little and continuing his whispered conference with Zaynorth.

"I just wish there was something I could do for the lad," Herofic said as they watched Besmir lead Arteera from the room.

Zaynorth nodded.

"I know, Herofic, I know," he said. "I even considered attempting to persuade them," he admitted. "But it would not have helped us to get Joranas back." He turned to Ru Tarn. "What are we likely to face in Boranash?" he asked.

"Boranash beautiful but harsh. Hot sand blows in air and many people live around coastline. One river flows down from mountains, feeding land around capital city but rest of Boranash is desert," she said. "Is there more wine for Ru Tarn?"

Zaynorth ordered another flagon of wine and looked at the Corbondrasi who was almost casually stroking his brother with her plumage. Herofic looked distinctly awkward making Zaynorth grin at his discomfort.

"I rather meant what are these shamen like? Are we likely to face opposition in seeking their aid?"

Ru Tarn snorted rudely, her face twisting into a mask of derision.

"Secretive and exclusive," she grunted. "Shamen are thinking they better than other Corbondrasi, blessed by Mwondi so better. Ru Tarn is thinking this is only way Besmir can get Joranas back though," she added.

The Corbondrasi ambassador sighed and leaned heavily against Herofic, pushing her obviously feminine body against him as she wrapped herself around his arm, humming contentedly deep in her throat.

Zaynorth smirked as he rose, pushing his hands into the base of his spine and groaning at the ache.

"I might turn in for the night," he said. "This return to traveling has taken its toll and my old bones are in need of a comfortable bed."

"Will you not stay for another drink, brother?" Herofic asked with a worried glance at Ru Tarn.

Zaynorth feigned a yawn, stretching expansively as he grinned at Herofic, unseen by the Corbondrasi ambassador.

"No, brother, I really should get some sleep in preparation for our ride tomorrow. Good evening, Madam ambassador," he said to Ru Tarn, nodding his head in a bow.

"Ru Tarn bids you farewell," she said, scouring Herofic's body with her lavender eyes.

Herofic made a rude gesture at his brother as he left. Zaynorth made his way between the chairs and tables, chuckling to himself as he did so.

Herofic coughed nervously and shifted to extricate himself from her feathered embrace.

"I, uh, I should turn in as well," Herofic mumbled. "All this traveling has taken a toll on my old bones."

"Ru Tarn coming with Herofic," the Corbondrasi purred in a deep voice.

"I can see you to your room," Herofic said in a gentlemanly fashion, "then I'll bid you goodnight."

Ru Tarn grunted an almost hostile chirp and released Herofic's arm. She stood on unsteady feet and made her way through the tables and patrons, ignoring Herofic entirely.

Chapter Seven

Joranas could not understand how somewhere that was as hot as a flame during the day could be this cold at night. Pinpoints of light twinkled in the dark blue velvet sky as a dark shape flickered around, emitting a high-pitched squeal. Joranas watched the alien-looking thing as it swooped and dove, soon joined by another of its kind.

A low chill that was nothing to do with the temperature drained Joranas of courage as he stood there and he ducked back into the relative safety of the cave before either of the black, fluttering things could attack him.

Joranas hugged his knees and rocked slightly as he thought about his mother. Would she be worried about him? Was she looking for him even now?

I just want to go home.

A solitary tear rolled down Joranas' face before he lay back down, pulling the soft material over him. Almost instantly he felt his own warmth reflected back into him and thanked the Gods for Whint's having found this material. Drowsiness came with the warmth and he soon fell asleep once more.

Burning sun woke Joranas, somehow managing to penetrate the cave and slash at his eyes. He rolled but could not manage to get comfortable again. Sighing he rose and blinked several times, squinting against the brightness.

"We have to go," Whint said.

"What? Where?" Joranas asked in surprise.

"This way," Whint said vaguely, pointing towards the rising sun.

"We can't...I mean it's far too hot, the sun's going to cook us alive," Joranas said as panic gripped his guts.

"We have to go," Whint repeated before striding from the cave and out into the morning light.

Joranas was torn between fear of being left here alone and his fear of venturing out into the sun. He had not forgotten the midnight creatures that had been flickering around last night either, the last thing he wanted was to encounter one of them in the light. He stepped toward the cave mouth, staring after Whint who was purposefully striding across the cracked, broken earth.

Without water, supplies, we're doomed.

Joranas looked back at the little cave, grabbed the few plant stems that remained and set off after Whint.

***

His tongue felt too large. Joranas tried to move it inside his mouth but there was simply no way to make it fit. His limbs ached as if he had been beaten and something was trying to punch its way from inside his head. His eyes burned and felt as if they had filled with grit every time he blinked.

This is madness. I am going to die.

Joranas found he no longer cared. Vast, empty and barren, the landscape stretched off in all directions with nothing to be seen. Heat shimmers made it appear as if waves rolled in from some vast sea, spurring him on for a few seconds before his brain caught up with reality and misery came crashing down on him again.

Somehow Whint had found what looked to be an ancient road buried in the blowing sands. Joranas strayed off the edge frequently, stumbling and falling, his mouth filling with baked soil and sand. Not even knowing what drove him on anymore, Joranas crawled back up to the better footing and dragged himself up to his feet.

Noon sun beat down on his young head and shoulders like a physical blow, the heat becoming intolerable and in a state of delirium he collapsed to his knees before falling forward. Hot air caressed his back as he lay dying on the uncaring ground, the scouring kiss of desert air felt almost like the gentle touch of his mother stroking his back as she crooned some lullaby.

He became vaguely aware the world was bouncing around him. His arms and legs jerked loosely as he moved but there was no real understanding of why until he woke for a few seconds.

His eyes stared down at a pair of feet and legs that pounded along the dry roadway, tirelessly. The cracked ground he could see trailing off behind them took no footprints and gave no sign they had ever been there. Large muscles twitched and writhed beneath dark brown skin burned even darker by the kiss of the sun as Whint carried Joranas through the desert.

Eventually Joranas woke at a point where the world was still again and his eyes opened on a place that was so alien and so familiar at the same time he could barely believe it. Massive buildings stretched up into the sky around him. Impossibly tall towers that appeared to reach into the very sky were interspersed with smaller buildings that could have been shops or houses at one point. He was in a city, but a city like none he had seen before with incredibly huge architecture carved from gigantic blocks of stone his young mind refused to believe people could move.

It was also completely abandoned.

As Joranas looked around in surprised wonder at the place he realized there was no one else here. None of the sounds or smells he knew from home were present and his despair returned in a heartbeat. Furthermore he could see nothing made from wood or fabric. None of the buildings had doors attached but he could see where hinges had been attached to them.

How many years ago?

With no energy to move after his long day in the desert Joranas had to content himself with just looking around. He sat in the shadow of a tower but one that defied any of the building techniques he had seen from Morantine. The towers there were circular with wide bases that narrowed toward the top. Opposite him now was a square building that rose further than he could comprehend, its head lost to his vision. Dark circles punctuated its sides and Joranas realized they were windows, allowing light inside the construct. Even when he squinted he was unable to see the top of the thing and his mind shied away from what it might be like at the top as he wondered how the thing even remained standing.

A sound drew his attention and Joranas turned to see Whint rounding a corner, apparently unaffected by the heat. His dark brown skin gleamed in the late afternoon light, making it appear as if he glowed with some inner light. Joranas watched as the strange man laid an unfamiliar animal near him and proceeded to butcher it with a sharp piece of stone. Once he had cleaned and skinned it, he went into one of the buildings next to the one Joranas lay against and did not return for some time. When he did his hands were filled with cooked strips of meat that he held before Joranas' face. The enticing aroma of cooked meat filled the young boy's nostrils and saliva flooded his mouth. He reached out and took the meat, watching as Whint smiled his wide, easy smile.

"How did you know about this place, Whint?" Joranas asked as he wiped grease from his chin.

"I do not know," the big man said screwing his face up. "I get...things sometimes," he tried to explain, "in here." He tapped on his skull. "But I do not know where it comes from."

Joranas looked at the big man with sympathy. He had no idea where he was or how he had gotten there but not to know who he was or where he had come from must be horrible.

"Can't you remember anything?" he asked.

Whint stared at him for a long time, his eyes searching Joranas' face for answers.

"I remember being in a gray place," he said. "Empty. Then I met Joranas...the other Joranas...and broke his house. I went through the portal and arrived here," he beamed, his eyes twinkling with childish mirth. "You were in the cave and I knew I had to look after you. That is what I remember."

Joranas shook his head, recalling his previous thought that Whint had gone insane due to the heat of the sun. His father had told him a story once about a man who, kicked in the head by a horse, had forgotten who he was, his family, friends and whole life. Joranas wondered if that had happened to Whint too as he had not known his own name either.

Something screamed in the distance and Whint turned towards the sound, his face intent.

"Darkness is coming," he said. "We should go inside."

Without another word he lifted Joranas and carried him into the building he had used to cook the food in. Joranas' eyes picked out a deep trough filled with coals that glowed a dull red, remnants of the creature sizzled atop the metal mesh that sat over the flame and Joranas understood this was a cooking device of some kind. He also saw a raised block of stone with two stone benches down either side before Whint carried him through to another room. The large man laid him down on a stone platform he assumed to be a bed, covering him with more of the downy material he had found from somewhere. Whint turned to leave but Joranas stopped him.

"Whint?" the big man turned. "Thank you," he said.

Whint beamed his toothy smile again.

***

Besmir's company worked its way northwards through plains that became more arid and brown the farther they went. Rocky patches began to show through the dry soil and Besmir had difficulty believing it to be the same country. Temperatures rose during the day meaning they had to pause frequently to water their horses and by the time they reached the border town of Tinres they had all had enough of being in the saddle.

"Are we to remain anonymous here?" Zaynorth asked as he drew alongside Besmir when the gray walls hove into view.

Besmir looked at the garrison town, wondering what reception he might receive as king compared to that of a commoner. He could certainly make use of the facilities at the fortress and have a good meal, sleep in a bed and have a little luxury. He grinned.

"Something funny?" Arteera asked.

"Not really," Besmir said. "I was just thinking how nice it'd be to sleep in a bed. Ten years living as a king has made me weak and soft," he said. "Remember when all we had were a few tents and an ice cold river to bathe in?"

Arteera smiled recalling simpler times when she had first met Besmir and fallen for the eager young man who had promised to change the world for the better.

And he did. He did change it for the better, for a while at least.

"I do," she said. "But sleeping on the ground does not build the character of anyone," she added. "We should make this a royal visit."

"There's your answer, Zaynorth," Besmir said. "Norvasil, send word to the garrison commander. Tell him the king and queen have come for a visit," Besmir grinned, "then let the mayhem commence," he added.

Zaynorth chuckled.

***

"Ru Tarn must be speaking," the Corbondrasi ambassador stated as she guided her horse alongside Herofic's. She had been pointedly avoiding the stocky man ever since they had left the little hamlet of Loran's End but he had not been far from her thoughts.

"Madam ambassador," Herofic said awkwardly. "How are you?"

"Ru Tarn is...embarrassed," she admitted. "Ru Tarn was not telling Herofic everything," she trailed off, turning her head.

"You have no need for embarrassment," Herofic said, a little hurt. "I don't gossip..."

Ru Tarn laid a gentle hand on Herofic's arm and smiled at him warmly.

"Ru Tarn was not telling Herofic all the facts."

"All right," Herofic said, confused by this sudden conversation. "So what are all the facts?"

The Corbondrasi looked about, making sure they had strayed far enough from the rest of the party so as not to be overheard.

"Ru Tarn is having egg," she said, averting her eyes from his gaze.

Herofic stared at her for a while, utter confusion playing on his features as he considered her words.

"As did I," he said. "For breakfast this morning. We all did, did we not?"

"Herofic is not understand," Ru Tarn chirped in frustration. "Ru Tarn is having *egg*." The Corbondrasi stroked her feathered hand over her abdomen.

"Oh," Herofic said. "Oh!" he repeated, his eyes going wide. "You mean, you are having a baby?"

Ru Tarn looked around again, making sure no one had overheard his outburst. She glared at him, her lavender eyes burning into his own.

"Sorry," he said.

"What is Herofic knowing about Corbondrasi hatchlings?" she asked.

"Surprisingly it's not something I've made many inquiries about," he said with a chuckle.

"This is something Corbondrasi do not discuss," she said, "even to other Corbondrasi, but Ru Tarn is thinking Herofic should be knowing." The warrior nodded. "Corbondrasi females are having one egg every year," she said. "It is coming at same time every year so we are knowing when to be expecting it." Ru Tarn looked away, embarrassed at discussing her reproduction at all, let alone with a male from another species. "If Corbondrasi is not wanting to have hatchlings, she can rest and have special drink to make things easy while egg...goes away."

Herofic nodded silently. He could tell by her mannerisms and tone this was a difficult subject to discuss and had enough respect for the woman to let her explain it in her own time.

"Ru Tarn egg coming too soon," she said. "Ru Tarn not having place to be alone, not having drinks ready so Ru Tarn behaving oddly back at tavern for this reasons," she stopped, looking at him pointedly.

"Ah, I see," Herofic said.

"Ru Tarn is being sorry," she said. "If Corbondrasi not having special drink it making them...like madness. We not being able to control...urges...and looking for mate..."

"Mate?" Herofic asked in shock.

"Ru Tarn was thinking Herofic would be taking Ru Tarn's mind off problems back at tavern," she said.

"Did it work?" Herofic asked.

Ru Tarn looked away from his eyes, embarrassment and shame crawling through her as she recalled the random dalliance she had had after leaving the dining room in Loran's End. She shook her head but held her gaze from his.

"The one Ru Tarn..." She glanced at Herofic but his face was shadowed. "He is not being available for being father...he is having wife and hatchlings already..."

"Did you want me to deal with him?" Herofic asked in an almost savage voice.

"No!" Ru Tarn declared, her heartbeat doubling in shock. "Why would Herofic be doing this thing for Ru Tarn?"

"We are friends, you and I?" He asked.

Ru Tarn nodded, her plumage rustling in the darkness. A sense of wonder flowed through her. No matter how long she lived among these Gazluthians, no matter how much of their culture and mannerisms she experienced, they always seemed to surprise her.

"Well when someone uses a friend of mine badly," Herofic said. "I take offense. It's only natural for me to offer a little persuasion."

"That is being very kind and noble thing to offer but...it was being Ru Tarn that was doing the using," she said with a touch of embarrassment.

Herofic was silent for a few minutes before a chuckle bubbled up from his chest.

"What is being funny?" Ru Tarn demanded with an edge of anger.

"Oh Madam Ambassador you have made my day with this information," Herofic said. "I would urge you to share this with as many women as you can, they'll be able to explain it much better than I."

Herofic continued laughing, his chuckle infectious and Ru Tarn felt her own laugh rise in her chest.

"Might I ask if there's a stigma attached to your...particular situation?" Herofic gently asked a little later.

Ru Tarn sighed and nodded.

"Corbondrasi are being frowned upon for having hatchling without father but it is happening," she said.

"Anyone gives you trouble you send them to me," Herofic grunted. "This old ax of mine can change people's opinions quite fast," he said.

"Ru Tarn is thanking Herofic for his kindness," she said, looking into his eyes.

"Think nothing of it," Herofic said, "and if you need anything, even just to talk, you come see old Herofic. We'd better catch up with that lot," he added, pointing to the slowly dwindling column.

Chapter Eight

Besmir nodded as he walked along the rows of men and women who stood to attention for his inspection. Hastily arranged, the inspection had been yet another delay in his journey to Boranash and one he could do without. Yet Commander Traveel had virtually begged him, saying it would boost morale for her troops to see the king and gain his approval.

Besmir knew these soldiers had been polishing buttons and swords since the early hours of that morning and their efforts had paid off. Every man and woman there was impeccably turned out, their uniforms neat and weapons sharp. The citadel Traveel occupied was similarly spotless and neat, well kept and orderly.

Situated at the intersecting borders of Gazluth, Boranash and Waraval, Tinres was a surprisingly cosmopolitan place with people from all three countries mingling easily with one another alongside a few other races.

"Of course we do get our fair share of trouble here, your Majesty," Traveel had been telling Besmir at a meal the night before. "Just a few months back we put an end to a gang smuggling Corbondrasi spirits into Waraval."

"How well does it work here," Besmir had asked, "sharing the town with two other garrisons?"

Traveel had given a wry smile and held her hand up for another drink.

"We and the Corbondrasi get on extremely well, Majesty," the stocky commander had said, raising her goblet to Ru Tarn. "They take care of their issues and we do the same with ours. Problems only ever arise when Waravalians are involved, especially as they believe they own the world."

The group had laughed politely at that comment and the evening had passed uneventfully.

Besmir completed his inspection and gave a brief speech telling them all how proud he was to be there and what an excellent job they were all doing. He stepped down from the raised dais only to be greeted by Commander Traveel again.

"A tour of the fortress, perhaps?" she asked hopefully.

"Unfortunately, I've got pressing business in Boranash," Besmir said as kindly as he could. "We really must depart as soon as possible."

Chagrin flooded him as he realized he should have let Zaynorth maintain the illusion they were ordinary travelers. The stocky little commander wanted him to stay as long as possible.

"We can have all the necessary arrangements in place by tomorrow, Majesty," she said, nodding to one of her soldiers who dashed off on some errand.

"Commander," Besmir said with a sigh. "I appreciate the hospitality, especially as we arrived unannounced but I've got to leave. Now."

Besmir watched as the commander's face fell but she looked to accept his decision and turned to speak to another man who waited for instruction. Once he had trotted off she turned back to Besmir.

"I have arranged for your mounts to be readied, Sire," she told him. "You should be able to leave within the hour. Is there anything else you require?"

"No," Besmir said. "Thank you."

Something in her stance or attitude made Besmir want to explain his situation and once he began, the words fell from his mouth, unstoppable as a river. When he finished Commander Traveel stared at him with her mouth open.

"I will send word to the Corbondrasi at once, Majesty," she finally managed. "They can expedite your journey through Boranash to the capitol." Her honest face crumpled a little. "I was with you when we took the palace," she added. "I know what it cost us all and to have your son kidnapped as well...I cannot imagine what you and your wife are going through. I apologize for trying to keep you here," she added.

Besmir felt a warmth he had not experienced for a long time heat his chest and he held his hand out towards the shorter woman, smiling when she looked surprised at his offer. Her grip was strong when she shook his hand, her smile open and friendly.

An honor guard had formed around Besmir's party, mounted Gazluthian soldiers filing from the parade ground out into the streets before Besmir himself made an appearance. Crowds had formed to line the streets all hoping for a look at the king and queen that had appeared unannounced.

Besmir gritted his teeth at the slow pace he was forced to take while the front runners forced a path through people who had come out to gawk at him. His eyes picked out the dark blue and purple banners of the Corbondrasi flag and he sighed in relief, knowing he would soon be in Boranash when a man stepped out in front of his horse and grabbed the reins.

He wore a dark green uniform with black trousers and calf length boots polished to a mirror shine. Ribbons and medals adorned his chest and he looked up at Besmir with a self-important expression on his face.

"King Besmir," he said in a voice loud enough for all to hear. "I am General Kelloch and I extend the hospitality of the kingdom of Waraval to you and your party."

Commander Traveel drove her horse through the crowds, knocking people aside in her haste to get to him.

"This is not the time, Kelloch!" she hissed. "His Majesty is in a rush to visit Boranash."

"Yet Waraval is a much more pleasant land." Kelloch said. "I am sure His Majesty would rather visit our fair land before the wastes the bird-people live in."

"I'm going to Boranash," Besmir said sternly. "Let go of my horse."

Besmir's anger, despair and feelings of utter helplessness mingled in his chest, combining to create a painful pressure he could not bear.

"But Majesty," the Waravalian continued. "Waraval is such a pleasant land, temperate and beautiful. In comparison to Boranash...well there is no comparison," he finished with a wide smile.

"I've got pressing business in Boranash," Besmir said, raising his voice. "Now let go of my horse and stand aside!"

Kelloch's face fell slightly but he continued to hold the king's horse as he spoke again.

"Whatever business you have, I am sure we can make a better offer than our feathered cousins," he announced in his loudest voice. "Once you enter Waraval, I am sure you will see sense."

Besmir growled low in his throat, his anger towards this idiot boiling over and he jumped from his horse, thrusting his face at the general menacingly. Kelloch finally got the message when Besmir grabbed his collar with both hands, about to do some violence.

"Majesty?" Zaynorth called from behind him.

Besmir felt the old man's hand on his shoulder and looked to the side where his kind face appeared.

"Allow me to explain your situation to the good general," he said.

Besmir hesitated, torn between his desire to pummel the idiot into a bloody mess and his need to be on his way. He shrugged, releasing Kelloch and remounting his horse.

"As you wish, Zaynorth," he said. "Catch up when you're finished."

Zaynorth bowed his head slightly and watched Besmir ride off towards the waiting Corbondrasi, the queen and small party following.

"Wait!" Kelloch moaned, sensing his opportunity was slipping away.

He made a move towards Besmir as if to stop him.

"Wait!" Zaynorth snapped, forcing the inability to move into his mind. "You and I are to have a little talk," he added, a savage grin splitting his beard.

Kelloch's eyes rolled towards the old man as he strained uselessly against the illusion Zaynorth had planted in his head. Zaynorth leaned in and started to whisper in the general's ear.

***

The Corbondrasi in charge of their section of the town had already made preparations for the first leg of their journey into Boranash. Three mounted Corbondrasi, armed to the teeth with strange looking weapons met Besmir's White Blades led by Norvasil. The two small groups eyed each other warily until Norvasil grinned and held his hand out to one of the feathered men. The Corbondrasi smiled himself as he grabbed Norvasil's giant hand and the pair shook.

"Cal Trin, his brother Col Trin, and Mo Slir are to be escorting," Ru Tarn said, translating the Corbondrasi's words. "They are knowing best route and where is watering places," she added.

Besmir nodded and gave his thanks to the efficient Corbondrasi commander who bade them all good fortune and watched as the sad looking Gazluthian king rode through the north gate.

Zaynorth caught up just outside the town, as they were entering Boranash, his horse puffing hard after its brief gallop.

"What did you do?" Arteera asked.

"Made him believe he is a princess," Zaynorth said.

"What?" she asked as those who heard chuckled.

"I convinced the good general he is a princess of Waraval," the old mage repeated. "Small price to pay for being such an ass. I am sure he will be there now, demanding everyone call him your highness and looking for his pretty dresses."

"How long will it last?" Arteera asked.

"Not long," Zaynorth said in a sullen tone. "I didn't think I should make it permanent. A month, maybe."

"A month!" Arteera squeaked. "That man is going to think he is a princess for a month? What about his position?"

"I really don't care, Arteera," Zaynorth replied, using her name as they were not in a formal setting. "I think he got off lightly as it looked to me as if your husband was about to boil him inside his skin."

Besmir grunted noncommittally but Arteera saw the truth in his face.

"Your son is as dear to me as if he were my own," Zaynorth continued in a gruff voice. "Anyone standing in the way of getting him back is in for a world of trouble from me," he added, wiping a tear from his eye.

Arteera steered her horse over from beside Besmir and leaned over in her saddle, hugging the old man fiercely and awkwardly. Besmir watched as his wife and oldest friend comforted each other, Arteera sobbing as Zaynorth patted her back.

"Come now, Majesty," Zaynorth said. "Sit up straight or we are both likely to end up on the ground."

***

Besmir stood watching the group of soldiers as they chatted, worked at erecting tents or demonstrated different fighting tactics to the Corbondrasi. One of the women, in particular, stood out as she moved around the camp. His eyes followed her as she avoided speaking to anyone else, or joining in with any group. She was thin and lithe with shoulder length black hair, as many Gazluthians did. Hers, however, was too dark and lacked the natural shine of real hair. She was also having difficulty managing the sword that hung at her side and it fouled her steps twice as the king watched her.

He smelled the familiar perfume of his wife as she approached, spicy and sweet, so turned to take her into his arms.

"Who are you spying on?" she asked as she leaned her head on his shoulder.

Besmir nodded towards the woman who was now sitting with her back to one of the campfires.

"Oh?" Arteera asked, her eyebrow arching. "And why is she of so much interest to a married man?"

Besmir chuckled and kissed her.

"I noticed a couple of things," he said. "How she favors her left leg and her right foot sticks out way more than the left. She's tripped over that sword about eight times in half an hour and it looks as if someone's dyed her hair with boot polish and coal dust," he said, glancing back at the woman. "I've spent enough time with her to know Keluse anywhere, even with a disguise."

"Keluse!" Arteera cried. "What is she doing here and why is she pretending to be a guard?"

"Only one way to find out," Besmir said, leading Arteera over to where Keluse sat.

"What are you up to?" he demanded as soon as they were within earshot. "And who's looking after Ranyeen?"

Keluse looked up, her blue eyes giving her away instantly as a look of guilt crossed her face.

"Ranyeen's safe, Besmir," she said. "I left her with Ranyor's sister. I...I had to come," she said, "but I knew you wouldn't let me so I...kind of hid." Keluse played with her fingers nervously as she spoke.

Besmir shook his head but Arteera jumped at her friend and hugged her.

"I'm so glad you're here," the queen said, "but whatever did you do to your hair?"

"I've got a good mind to send you back," Besmir said grimly. "I wanted you in Morantine to make sure everything runs smoothly. What if something goes wrong while we're away?"

"Oh Besmir," Arteera moaned. "What is likely to happen?"

"Plus, as your apprentice, I should be with you," Keluse said.

"Apprentice!" Besmir grunted. "I think that finished about ten years ago!" he looked from his wife to his friend and back. "Oh, come on," he said. "It's farther back than forward now anyway. Just don't trip over that sword again," he added. "Send Norvasil to me," he told one of the White Blades as they passed him. "I need to see if he knew one of his soldiers was an impostor."

"Don't be too hard on him!" Keluse begged. "I didn't tell him and he's been a little preoccupied with planning and arranging this trip."

***

Ru Tarn felt hot. Her plumage itched and a throbbing need ached in her lower belly. Ignoring the problem had not helped and she had been out of sorts for days, snapping at people with virtually no provocation. She drew in the cool night air, happy to be back in her homeland but distracted by the massive needs her body was demanding of her.

Years ago, when she had reached the age a woman started producing an egg and her mother had explained it to her, they had brewed the drink that eased the symptoms and she had spent a week in an almost blissful daze as her egg had been taken back into her body. It had been the same ever since. Every year in early fall Ru Tarn would procure the plants and seeds needed to brew the medicinal draft all Corbondrasi women knew and spend a week indoors.

So why has it come early this year?

Cold fright gripped her as she wondered if there was something wrong. Some illnesses and diseases could be responsible for disrupting the egg cycle.

But they halt the egg not make it come early.

Ru Tarn had no idea what was going on and stuck in the middle of the Boranash out lands she had no one to ask. The Corbondrasi males would be of no use as oviparity was not a subject for discussion in Corbondrasi society and they would be clueless. She wandered aimlessly through the camp, lost in her own thoughts until she reached the edge and stared out at the landscape of Boranash.

Just two days ride into her homeland and the scenery had changed drastically. Gone were the lush grasslands and prairies of Gazluth, replaced by scrubby, hard plants that needed little water. Patches of dry earth had begun to show through as well, growing in size as they traveled. Increasingly rocky, the landscape had become barren and the temperature had risen significantly during the day. There was beauty here, Ru Tarn knew, and life but it was all a well kept secret, hidden from the eyes until uncovered by a hot wind or someone digging.

"You all right?" a deep voice asked from behind her.

A thrill ran up Ru Tarn's back and she shivered.

"Ru Tarn is being better," she said, squeezing her eyes closed and trying to fight the urge to throw herself at him.

Herofic moved alongside her, close enough for her to feel the heat his body gave off and smell his masculinity. Part of her knew this was all a side effect of her egg, changes inside her body making her want him so badly but that part was powerless to stop the urges she had to mate.

"Ru Tarn is needing something," she admitted turning to him in embarrassment. "Ru Tarn is having difficult time with egg and is needing..."

Herofic gripped her shoulders, turning her to face him and brought his face towards hers. Ru Tarn looked into his eyes and read what he was about to do, pulling back with an almost savage jerk.

"What is Herofic doing?" She demanded with wide eyes.

The Corbondrasi ambassador flapped her feathered hands before her face as if to blow away the kiss he had not even put there.

"Sorry," Herofic mumbled, backing off. "I-I thought that was what you meant..."

"No," Ru Tarn said, still flustered. "Herofic is being good friend but...but no. Ru Tarn was needing to talk, to be occupying mind of Ru Tarn so...urges are not being so..."

"Oh!" Herofic squealed his embarrassment obvious. "Maybe I should just go.."

"Please do not," Ru Tarn said in a small voice. "Ru Tarn is having difficult time and is needing Herofic like Herofic was saying. To talk to." The Corbondrasi made sure she spoke the last three words as slowly and clearly as she could.

Herofic smiled, still a little embarrassed and cast about for a comfortable spot to sit. He curled his legs beneath him and cleared his throat.

"Shall I tell you about how I met King Besmir?" He asked.

Ru Tarn sat a few feet from Herofic, facing him as she nodded then listened to his deep, somehow melodic voice as he regaled her of far off lands and sea voyages.

Hot wind blew in their faces carrying the smell of dry dust and empty lands as the small party trudged north through the increasingly desolate land. There was little opportunity for conversation as the wind snatched the words from their mouths and the sun threatened to desiccate them alive if they had their mouths open.

The Corbondrasi led them to a set of caves in the side of a hill where they all dismounted and started to shake the dust from inside their clothing.

"I will have to remember to empty this when I go home," Herofic said. "I have a great deal of Boranash in my navel."

The Corbondrasi laughed when Ru Tarn translated and one of them beckoned to Herofic who followed him to the back of the cave.

"You're my new best friend," he said clapping the feathered warrior on the shoulder. "Hey! There is a large pool back here, we can have a wash."

Herofic started to strip but the Corbondrasi stopped him, waving a canteen before his eyes.

"Ah, yes," he said a little sheepishly. "We should fill our drinking vessels before I get in."

With the horses fed and watered and all their canteens filled, Besmir, Arteera, Keluse, Herofic, and Zaynorth stripped, entering the cool water. Everyone in the pool fell silent, plagued by their own thoughts until Zaynorth chuckled.

"Remember when Joranas was about five and he asked that Ninsian woman if she was going to grow up one day?" he said. "I thought she was going to have a fit."

Besmir smiled and put one arm around Arteera who leaned into him.

"She was about the same height as him then," Besmir said. "It was a fair question."

"Yes, but she was almost a century old!" Zaynorth added and they all laughed.

"I remember when he and Ranyeen were going to run away together," Keluse said. "I forget why, but it was something I'd told her she couldn't do." Keluse smiled, looking down at her folded arms. "She went straight out, found Joranas and told him what an evil mother I was. He convinced her they should run away, do you remember?"

Besmir nodded and felt Arteera do the same.

"When we found them, they had two apples in a bag and were wandering up and down King's Avenue," Keluse carried on. "Said they were going to run away but they weren't allowed to go any further than the end of King's," she added in a sad voice.

Besmir felt something hot on his skin and looked down to see Arteera's tears running down his chest. He pulled her in close but she pulled away, turning to Keluse.

"We had better get this muck from your hair," she said sniffing. "I expect it has already stained."

"You don't have to do that," Keluse said as Arteera made her way round the pool towards her.

"I want to," the queen said. "I need to take my mind off the fact I'm never going to see Joranas again," she said in a matter of fact tone.

"Of course we're going to see him," Besmir reassured her in a gentle voice. "I promised, remember? I said I'll do anything to get him back safely."

"But what if you can't?" Arteera sobbed as she rubbed the strands of Keluse's hair in the water. "What if this shaman refuses to speak to us or cannot help?"

"Then I will find another way," Besmir said squeezing her shoulders gently. "I promise," he added, looking at Zaynorth with a pained expression.

"As will I, Arteera," the mage said.

"Me too," Herofic added in a sad voice.

Once they had all stripped the water from their bodies and dressed once more Besmir made his way farther back in the cave. Lines wandered up and down along the walls, reminding him of a stack of parchment that lay on his desk at home. Home. The word felt alien, foreign to his mind. Where was his home now? Gazluth? How could he ever return if they did not manage to get Joranas back? And if he did, would it ever feel like home again. Hate grew briefly in his chest, he hated Zaynorth forever seeking him out. If not for the old man,

Besmir could be living a life of freedom in the wild forests of Gravistard, the land he had grown up in.

The feeling disappeared as soon as it had come. If not for Zaynorth he would never have met Arteera, never had Joranas or met his own father, even if it had been in a Hell dimension. He would never have become king or helped save thousands of people.

Leaning his head against the wall Besmir let his eyes follow the lines that made up the layers of rock as they flowed back into the cave. His eye picked something out and he looked up to see something jutting from the rock. Walking towards it, his mind refused to believe what his eyes were telling him and he reached out for the object, almost afraid to touch it.

Its head was the same size as Besmir himself. A mass of teeth as long as his fingers lined its jaw and his fist could have fitted into its eye socket. Wonder and awe pulled at him as he examined the skeleton, thanking all the Gods the thing was dead.

"Sand Loper," Ru Tarn explained when he mentioned it. "There is being complete body at palace, Ru Tarn will showing it to you."

"Are there any living around here?" Besmir asked, afraid for them all.

"No," Ru Tarn shook her head with a hiss of feathers. "They are being all dead for long time now."

"It's incredible," Besmir said to his wife, "how anything that big could have lived."

"How long until we reach the capital?" the queen asked, uninterested in the immense beast.

"Ru Tarn is thinking we will be reaching Wit Vosad four day time," she said. "Wit Shull is being three day, but we can be taking boat up Shull river."

Arteera nodded and lay down on the cold floor, wrapping her blankets around herself and facing away from the group.

One of their Corbondrasi guides said something to Ru Tarn who translated.

"There are sometimes being bandits on road to Wit Vosad," she muttered quietly. "Army is killing some but they returning."

"I hope we run into some," Besmir said darkly. "I could take some anger out on them."

Chapter Nine

Almost a century of torment had twisted his already damaged mind into something that was unrecognizable as the man he had once been. He crouched naked at the base of the rocks, the only landmark for miles in any direction, and laughed until his ribs ached.

"Free!" he chanted. "I am finally free of you all."

Standing he stared out into the acid wind that scoured everything here bare, unblinking as the grit and dust blew into his eyes, uncaring that the very air ate at him. His mind did not register the searing agony that lanced up into his feet as he took his first steps here.

They gathered, always hungry, always ready to feed but he could hurt them now. After they had fed on his soul for nigh one hundred years, he was finally able to hurt them.

Flame exploded from his hands, ripping and burning the Ghoma who screamed and ran. His laughter echoed dully from the rock as he chased their fleeing backsides.

"Come back!" he screamed. "Come back, my friends. Do you want to play no more?"

A trail of devastated, burned and damaged bodies lay in his wake as he made his way through the gray landscape. Something tickled the back of his mind, some memory from another life but he could not remember what it was. Even had he recalled it with crystal clarity it would have made no difference whatsoever. The damage to his psyche had been so extensive that self preservation had long since been abandoned.

He trudged through the sharp ash, his feet cut to ribbons but instantly healing, wandering aimlessly. On the rare occasions he encountered something that lived he burned it to a crisp, laughing madly as it screamed and writhed.

Eventually he came to an end. The grayness just stopped being and blank, black nothing lay beyond. He approached the nothing, feeling its cold touch pulling at his fractured mind and recognition flooded him.

"Mother!" he wailed, smashing his face into the shards of ash at his feet.

A single word echoed from the blackness. A name he had not heard during his century in Hell.

"Tiernon."

***

Joranas felt stronger than he had in days. Whint had been gradually feeding him with cooked meat and cold water. Joranas had wondered where the strange creature had managed to get hold of cold water in this dead, arid city but found he did not really care. The strange man seemed harmless enough and was happy to look after Joranas while he recovered from their trek through the desert.

"I'm going to explore the city," Joranas said as Whint returned from one of his little trips.

"I'm going to explore the city." Whint echoed.

Joranas smiled, he had come to like the fact Whint repeated almost anything he said for some odd reason.

Joranas took a few shaky steps out of the house they used and started to stretch his aching muscles. He had been working on a plan for a little while now and was about to put it into practice. His feet crunched on the sandy cobblestones, the wind brought sand from the desert one day and scoured the streets clean the next. With a skin filled with the water Whint had found he crossed the street and entered the tall tower he had seen when he first arrived.

The bottom floor had several doors leading deeper into the building but Joranas dismissed these in favor of the steps that led upwards. It was dim inside the stairwell but his eyes picked out every detail clearly. A wonky step here, a cracked stone there, all easily avoided. His breath came in great gasps, his legs aching from lack of use as he pushed on, climbing up floor after floor until his legs finally gave way, dropping him on a flat floor.

There was no way he could climb any further even though the stairs continued so Joranas made his way into one of the rooms at the outer edge of the building. Within sat a similar set of items as in the house he and Whint had been using. A stone table with benches either side grew from the floor but as with the rest of the city, anything not made of stone had disintegrated long ago.

A large hole split the wall, rough edged and circular but Joranas could see it was not one of the windows. The edges appeared melted, the stone had run down to set again like ice. He reached a finger out and traced its smooth surface before his eyes were drawn outside.

The city stretched for miles!

He stood far higher than any other building and stared down at the dark maze below. Streets ran off in all directions, apparently at random, all lined with a multitude of buildings that must have been homes and shops at one time.

Why did everyone leave?

His hand rested on the cold stone but his mind wondered what could have made the hole.

Was it a war? Was that why they all left?

He squinted outside again and saw similar holes had been blasted in other buildings. Others had collapsed out into the street, a single wall the only sign a building had ever been there.

Joranas made his way through to the other side of the building. There was no hole here but the window allowed him to see a similar picture as the other side. The place had been vast. It must have been home to millions of people.

Where did they get food from in the middle of a desert?

Sadness overcame Joranas when he realized his plan to escape was a futile one. If he even managed to make it through the city without getting lost he would have the desert to contend with and with no idea where he was, which way would he even go?

He leaned his back against the wall and slid down it, the cold stone refreshing against his back. He sipped the last of his water and fought back the tears that threatened to come.

Crying is a waste of time.

His mind turned back to what could have melted the hole into solid stone a foot thick.

Magic. It had to have been magic.

The same kind of magic his father had been saying he could do. Maybe he could do it now.

But he's not here to show me. Plus he said it uses up your soul or life force or something.

Yet Joranas was young and realized he had years to live. Using up a little of his life could not hurt, could it? Especially as the time would come from the *other* end of his life when he was old and he was forced to eat soft foods because his teeth were gone.

But how?

Joranas concentrated, delving inside his own mind. It proved to be difficult as whenever he thought he might be getting somewhere an image would come into his mind. His mother's face or Ranyeen with her smile and head tilted to one side.

I wonder how she's doing?

No. He had to concentrate. Had to discover how to use the magic that flowed through his veins.

My veins. My veins.

In his mind Joranas pictured the fire he wanted to make flowing through his veins, trying to burst free. He held his hand out, seeing it in his own mind, the flame pouring from his hand.

A scream tore from his throat when his fingers caught light.

Joranas leaped up, shaking his hand to get rid of the flames. Once extinguished he looked at his hand in wonder. A little red, but not burned, a few singed hairs on his arm but there was no pain, no burned skin and his hand had been on *fire*.

Joranas smiled.

Let Crallan come for me now.

Joranas thought again, wondering if this was how he was meant to do it. If his father had had time to teach him, how would he do it? He had no idea but this was working. He could make fire come out of his hand!

Turning to face the window he pointed out into the open, concentrating on fire flowing through his veins again. He felt heat this time. A rush of intense heat that flowed through his body, down his outstretched arm and out. He opened his eyes to see a small flame shooting from his finger. About a foot long and bright yellow it was not particularly hot but pride swelled in his chest.

Not bad for my second try. Not bad at all.

***

The attack came on the second day after the caves. Besmir's small party had been headed for a well the Corbondrasi knew of. In awe of the vastness of Boranash, Besmir had almost forgotten the warning their guides had given.

"Cal Trin is thinking well is not too far," Ru Tarn announced.

Besmir noticed the Corbondrasi had adapted to live in this environment quite well. Their feathers protected them from the harsh sun whereas he and Arteera had started to go a dark red wherever the sun found a little patch of uncovered skin. They also had rows of feathers around their eyes that they could fluff up as protection from the flying dust when the hot winds whipped across them. Those from Gazluth had to make do with strips of cloth across their eyes and mouth, making it all the more difficult to breathe.

Pausing to let the harshest of the midday sun pass overhead the small party had relished the opportunity to rest and virtually collapsed into the shade of a hastily raised cloth. The thick canvas snapped in the wind but kept the worst of the sun off them and the horses as the Corbondrasi, who seemed unaffected by any of the heat, tended their mounts.

Arteera looked fit to drop as she lay with her head on a rock. Never the most robust of women she had remained thin even when food had become plentiful and the relentless sun and heat was beginning to take its toll on her.

"Try and drink something, love," Besmir said bringing a canteen to her lips.

She opened her eyes, peering out of the gauzy, white veil Ru Tarn had given her to keep the sun at bay. They fixed on Besmir, weakly and he could see how tired she was. He felt it himself but could not allow it to show.

His queen sipped at the warm water gratefully and she even managed a wan smile before closing her eyes again, her head slumping sideways.

"We will be reaching the river soon," Ru Tarn said, seeing Besmir's concern. "It will be being cooler and easier then."

Besmir nodded as he made himself comfortable and fell almost instantly asleep. Someone shook him a few seconds later and he opened his eyes to see the sun had crossed the sky into early afternoon. He frowned before it dawned on him he had been asleep for a couple of hours rather than seconds.

He stretched and groaned as muscles complained, watching as several other members of his party did the same.

Mounted and on the road again they carried on trudging through the hot, cracked earth when a shout roused Besmir from the stupor he had fallen into. The Corbondrasi Mo Slir had raised the alarm as people appeared from out of the ground on either side of the rough road they had been on.

For an instant only Besmir thought they were some kind of demons or monsters crawling from the dead earth to attack. It took a few moments for his brain to register they were just people who had dug holes to ambush travelers from.

They stopped, the Corbondrasi calling to the bandits who were making demands. Besmir looked around at the faces of his little group. They were in no mood for any of this, Keluse, Herofic, Zaynorth, Norvasil and even his wife looked angry, ready for a fight. A savage grin split Besmir's face as he saw Herofic heft his ax and he heeled his horse forwards to draw level with the Corbondrasi who were arguing with the leaders of the group.

"They are saying we must be giving them water and food," Ru Tarn explained to Besmir. "Gold is as well being demanded."

"Tell them I would not give them my urine if they were aflame," Besmir said, staring straight at the leader whose eyes locked onto his own.

He saw the moment the words hit the bandit as his dark purple eyes widened in shock. Besmir dragged the bright sword that hung at his side and started forwards advancing on the leader.

He leaped back and brought his hand to his feathered mouth, issuing a high-pitched scream that Besmir took as the order to attack.

Within a pair of heartbeats chaos had overtaken them all. The bandits that had been buried in the dry earth retreated as mounted bandits approached on beasts Besmir had only ever seen in books.

Panther like in appearance, each was about the size of a horse with immense teeth and clawed feet that also had wide pads to spread their weight on the dry soil and sand. There were a range of different fur colors from a sandy yellow to a mottled peach and brown.

As the mounted bandits approached their pedestrian counterparts they reached down, linking arms with one each and hauled them up on the back of their mounts.

The horses in Besmir's party started to show nerves as they caught scent of the large cats, pawing at the ground and tossing their heads as their riders fought to control them.

"We must be giving them things!" Ru Tarn cried. "If they are riding daasnu they can win!"

"You forget something," Besmir called back. "Why they call me the Hunter King."

His eyes appeared to go vacant as Besmir sent his mind hammering into the brain of the nearest daasnu. The large cat reared on its hind legs then fell to the ground, crushing both riders beneath its back. It rose and leaped at a second beast, hammering into the men riding it as they looked on in shock.

Arrows filled the air as the White Blades and Keluse fired. Besmir used the massive cat to slash and bite at the bandits, leaping from daasnu to daasnu as he forced them to throw their riders. When all their attackers were on foot and their mounts had run off into the desert, Besmir rode them down, slashing at them as they tried in vain to defend themselves. Herofic, the Corbondrasi and his White Blades joined the skirmish and before long the sand had been painted with blood.

A scream cut the air behind him and Besmir wheeled his horse to see a dark clad figure had dragged Arteera from her horse. He held her by the neck, a blade to her as he shouted something.

"Stop this or the queen dies!" he called in Gazluthian.

"Who are you?" Besmir demanded.

"Nobody you would know, *King* Besmir," the man spat. "Let my friends go or your queen dies," he added, jerking Arteera hard.

She screamed as the blade grazed her skin and Besmir held his hand up. Zaynorth looked at the man who held Arteera, steering his horse closer.

"Far enough old man," the bandit said.

"Of course," Zaynorth said politely. "However, you have forgotten one thing."

"Really?" the bandit asked "What?"

"You can no longer breathe," Zaynorth said.

The Gazluthian's eyes widened in terror and he released Arteera, dropping his blade as he clawed at his own throat. Besmir watched as Zaynorth stared at him, pouring the illusion into his mind that he could not breathe. So powerful was the old mage, so complete his illusion, that the bandit started to convulse as he collapsed to the sand still unable to take in breath. Not only Besmir's party but the few remaining bandits stopped to watch him slowly die. His lips turned blue as he pleaded with his eyes but Zaynorth continued to stare at him, his concentration diamond hard as he forced the man to suffocate himself to death.

"You should not have threatened my queen," Zaynorth said as he died.

Six of the remaining bandits threw their weapons away, kneeling in the dust when they saw what Zaynorth could do.

"What should we be doing with them?" Ru Tarn asked Besmir later.

"That's a Corbondrasi matter," he said. "Why don't you think of something?"

Besmir watched as she made her way to talk to her countrymen.

"Is she putting on weight?" he asked no one in particular.

Herofic stared at him with a squint.

"What?" he asked the old warrior.

Ru Tarn returned a few minutes later as the three other Corbondrasi dragged the bandits off to execute them in the desert.

"They would be using up water we are not having for them," she said in a disturbed voice. "It being kinder than letting Boranash kill them."

She turned and walked off, making her way over to Herofic and leaning into his embrace as the screams began.

"Wait!" Besmir said, concentrating.

As the final scream was cut off by a horrible gurgle, one of the daasnu appeared from behind a pile of dusty stones and dirt. It plodded across to where Besmir stood and halted for him to take the reins. The great beast stood just taller than the man himself and he looked at it with awe. Its feet were huge, two toed, padded things each toe the same size as Besmir's hand if he spread his fingers. Besmir ran his hand down the creature's flank, watching its fur spring back and muscles twitch beneath his touch. It turned its massive leonine head in curiosity, staring at Besmir as he examined it.

Besmir sent his thoughts out into the desert several more times, seeking out the other daasnu and bringing them back. In all, he brought four of the large cats back, each laden with the water and supplies its rider had owned.

The Corbondrasi who returned with grim expressions stared at the animals in surprise, twittering at each other in their own language as they stared at the daasnu.

"They are never seeing daasnu acting like this," Ru Tarn said in a subdued voice. "Daasnu are belonging to only one person normally."

"I've always had an affinity with animals," Besmir said.

He turned away from the gruesome scene as members of the White Blades checked each of the bandits, plunging blades into those who showed any signs of life. Ru Tarn started to retch as the stench of drying blood and feces reached them. Herofic followed the ambassador, rubbing her back gently as she leaned her hands on her knees.

Cal Trin had a nasty cut on his forearm that his brother was tending to. Besmir noticed Corbondrasi blood was a great deal darker than his own, something he had not noticed in the middle of battle. Col Trin plucked at the feathers lining the wound, muttering as his brother hissed. Once the edges of his cut had been plucked, Col Trin washed the injury before binding it tightly. Even through his layer of thick plumage Cal Trin looked pale.

"Maybe we should let him rest," Besmir suggested.

"It is being too exposed here," Ru Tarn said, trying to keep her gaze clear of the dead. "We are having to carry on."

Besmir nodded and turned his attention to the daasnu beside him. The large cat had planted its hind quarters on the hot sand and was busy licking one paw with its immense tongue.

"What do you think the chances are of me riding this thing?" he asked.

Ru Tarn chatted with the three Corbondrasi before turning back to Besmir, her lavender eyes piercing in the sun.

"Brothers are not ever seeing daasnu like this," she said. "Daasnu usually attacking anyone who is not owner," she shrugged. "King Besmir maybe having better luckiness."

The four Corbondrasi watched in fascination to see if the large creature would turn on Besmir, ripping him limb from limb. He could see the surprise in their oddly colored eyes when he jumped up into the saddle on its back without incident.

Besmir himself did not bother to enter the creature's mind again as he needed the animal to respond to him physically rather than mentally. Col Trin muttered something to his brother, the pair speaking in low tones as they watched the Gazluthian king.

"Is it being possible for them to ride a daasnu they are wondering?" Ru Tarn asked.

Besmir shrugged and the two Corbondrasi brothers approached an animal each, gingerly introducing themselves to the animal before leaping into the saddles. Each daasnu simply looked back at the man astride them with curiosity in their small eyes, shifting their weight slightly as they stood ready. Besmir could tell the brothers were impressed and happy with their new mounts and nodded to both men when they thanked him in awkward Gazluthian.

Chapter Ten

Confusion addled Besmir's mind when he woke beside a cool stream, its pristine water flowing over rocks and crystals that colored the water to make it look like a rainbow flowed across the land. He felt clean and warm but none of the oppressive heat that had been baking him in Boranash. His clothing was soft and fitted as if it had been tailored to his body, the ever present feeling of sand and grit in every crevice of his being was gone and even his skin felt baby-smooth when he moved.

His eyes roved over the immense, lush, green landscape, from the tree he had woken beneath to the rolling hills in the distance, the world teemed with life. Animals that ought to have been predator and prey moved past each other with what looked to be a primitive form of courtesy as Besmir looked on in amazement. A Crallcat that would normally pounce upon virtually anything that moved looked to give way to a deer that happily plodded towards its teeth and fangs. Both creatures carried on their way unharmed and innocent as Besmir gaped.

Overhead flocks of brightly-colored birds shared the skies and abundant trees with their brown and black cousins. Again Besmir watched as eagles and hawks ignored the smaller birds that might normally make an easy meal.

Besmir stood feeling the grass beneath his bare feet as soft as down, turning to stare at the man who approached him with a mixture of pain and joy in his heart.

He was simply dressed in tunic and loose trousers, still as tall and rangy as Besmir recalled. His black hair fell about his shoulders perfectly, shining blue in the warm sunlight. Deer and squirrel paused to nuzzle his hand as he walked towards Besmir with a serene expression on his face and the two men embraced, Besmir in shock that this man could be here after ten years in the grave.

"Ranyor," Besmir said in a hoarse voice. "What has happened to me?"

"Don't worry, my King," Ranyor said playfully, "you aren't dead. How is Keluse?"

Besmir detected the hint of sadness in Ranyor's voice. His beatific attitude slipping minutely as his features changed.

"She's well," Besmir said. "Still misses you, though," he added, "and Ranyeen is incredible..."

Besmir trailed off as he saw the expression of utter agony that crossed his friend's face. Ranyor had died before his daughter had entered the world and had never met the girl Besmir knew well.

"I'm sorry," Besmir said. "For everything."

Guilt hit the king hard as he was transported back to the night he had let Ranyor scout the city of Morantine alone and been killed by Tiernon or his demonic minions as a result.

"You are not to blame, Besmir," Ranyor said. "I chose my own fate that night...although I have regretted it since. Has Keluse...found another?" he asked in a halting voice.

"No," Besmir said. "She's completely devoted to raising Ranyeen. There will never be another in her eyes."

Ranyor nodded, still appearing pained and Besmir wondered if this afterlife was as perfect and heavenly as it appeared to be. Ranyor's head turned as if he could hear a voice Besmir could not and he nodded again.

"Come," he said abruptly, "there is someone you must meet."

Besmir struggled to keep up with his tall friend as the man strode through the paradise that seemed to stretch off infinitely. He watched as animals he had never laid eyes on wandered past him. Thick skinned creatures, red and dark blue, some with horns and some with wings, others with many more legs than Besmir had ever seen on an animal. Patterns and colors as diverse as fall leaves met his eyes changing his perception of himself to that of an ant trying to comprehend a building.

Besmir had considered himself to be a fairly important piece of the world. He had striven to change the lives of the people of Gazluth for the better. At first, by slaying Tiernon and accepting the position of king, then in his dealings as their king. Seeing the immensity, the diversity, of creatures that had lived before him was humbling, making Besmir see he was an almost infinitesimally small speck in an immense picture.

Ranyor led him through areas where people gathered to watch him pass, some raising their hands in a brief wave as others looked on with either disinterest or envy. A woman appeared from behind a tree, her black hair and pale skin proclaiming her Gazluthian heritage immediately, and approached Besmir. She looked him over critically as he stared back into eyes that he had seen in his own reflection almost every day, dark brown and large.

"M-mother?" Besmir asked uncertainly.

Rhianne grabbed her son in a tight hug, squeezing him for the first time in thirty five years.

"Oh, my boy," she sobbed in a hoarse voice. "My little Besmir."

The Hunter-King of Gazluth leaned into the mother he had never known in life and cried. Deep, wrenching sobs ripped from inside him as feelings he had buried deep inside him exploded.

"She's taken my son!" he bawled. "Porantillia's got my boy!"

"I know, love," Rhianne said gently, patting him on the back. "I know."

Besmir remained in the arms of his mother for as long as he could until Ranyor coughed politely and said they should continue.

"Why?" Besmir demanded. "Who's so important that I have to see them now?"

"You will see when we get there," Ranyor said cryptically.

"Go on, my love," Rhianne said gently. "We will be united one day."

"I met my father!" Besmir called as he allowed himself to be led from the spirit of his mother.

Her face screwed up into a mask of pain and tears and she turned, sprinting into the trees, away from his sight.

"What did I say?" Besmir asked.

"It's beautiful here," Ranyor said as he led Besmir through woods filled with people and animals, "and for many it is the perfect afterlife. I have freedom to do almost anything my heart desires," he added. "Unfortunately, what my heart desires is Keluse and that is impossible. I can't see her, speak to her, know anything about her. For your mother, it's the same. Yet I know one day Keluse will come to me...from what I recall, your father's spirit resides in Hell, Besmir. She has no hope of seeing him again. Ever."

Besmir wondered what it would do to someone to be surrounded by so much beauty but still be miserable.

Then maybe this is another kind of Hell.

Ranyor led him to the edge of a glade filled with a myriad of flowers. The scent of so many blooms perfumed the air sweetly and his friend bade him farewell as he pointed him in the direction he should go.

"Don't tell Keluse of me, please," he asked. "It would only cause her pain to be reminded of me, but know I wait for the day we are reunited and can spend eternity in each other's arms. Goodbye, Besmir," Ranyor said as he faded from sight.

Besmir swallowed and turned to look into the glade. Brightly lit and with a clear pond in the middle it was surrounded by a multitude of trees filled with birds and animals that peered at him as he entered. Taking his first steps into the glade felt strange to Besmir, as if he had entered yet another world. Quiet descended upon him, the sounds of nature fading from his ears as he walked.

"Hello?" he called. "I'm here."

Turning in a slow circle Besmir scanned the whole glade for someone, anyone who might be here but could see no one else. The sensation of being watched hit him, though, and he turned to be overwhelmed by a *presence*. Besmir's mind shied away from the entity that faded into view, exuding from the trees, grasses, flowers and animals that shared the glade until it stood before him.

Antlers graced a head that was part deer and part fox. Reptilian eyes peered at Besmir in curiosity at the same time as the figure's nose twitched like a rabbit. Clothed in living ferns and grasses it floated towards Besmir over the surface of the pond. When Besmir looked, however, the creature's feet appeared to be *part* of the pond. The crystal clear waters becoming the soles of the hooves it had for feet.

Odd though the being looked, it was his *presence* that affected Besmir most. An overwhelming aura that pressed against his conscious mind with unrelenting force. Although similar in physical size to Besmir himself the being radiated an immensity that was impossible to withstand. A timeless being older than the world, it seemed to Besmir and he fell to his knees before the God of Afterlife, sobbing at his *presence*.

"Hello, Besmir," Cathantor said in a conversational tone of voice.

His voice was that of multitudes, similar to Porantillia, but Cathantor's dripped with kindness and love whereas hers had sounded like a nation in torment. If Cathantor was a choir, Porantillia was its damned opposite.

Besmir looked up from where he groveled, seeing the smile that had crossed Cathantor's face. Each element that made up the God was separate, distinguishable as an individual animal, yet they all flowed into one perfect being that radiated love and acceptance.

"You can get up, you know," Cathantor said in an amused voice.

Shaking and weak, Besmir rose but could not look into the God's eyes so kept his gaze averted.

"Well, this is an odd turn of events isn't it?" Cathantor asked. "I don't expect you quite understand why I've brought you here, do you?"

"You talk like me," Besmir blurted the first thing that came into his head.

Cathantor laughed, the sound like a healing light in Besmir's soul and even he smiled.

"I'm everything to everyone, Besmir. Of course I talk like you."

Cathantor gestured with his oddly human hands and the pair started to walk. Besmir looked down to see the plants and flowers leaned towards Cathantor as he passed, birds and animals paid their respects to him with little touches and small noises that Besmir assumed he understood.

"I have a favor I need to ask," Cathantor stated in the voice of millions.

Besmir chilled with shocked awe as the God's words hit him.

Cathantor *wants a favor...from me?*

The God of Afterlife stopped and turned to Besmir, forcing the man to look into his timeless eyes. Besmir felt dizzy, buoyant and faint simultaneously but managed to concentrate as Cathantor reached out and grasped his shoulders.

"It's not going to be easy," he added, "but I need you to abandon your search for a way to get to Porantillia," he said.

Besmir saw that Cathantor had the forked tongue of a snake as he spoke.

"Joranas..." Besmir muttered, the force of Cathantor's will making him drowsy and compliant.

"He'll be fine," the God assured. "I'll take care of your son here."

Yes. That would be nice. Joranas would like it here.

Even as the thoughts flowed through Besmir's mind another part of him was screaming that this was wrong. Something was utterly, completely wrong with the whole situation but he could not understand what it was.

"Wait..." Besmir said, shaking his head.

Cathantor released him and turned toward the ocean they were abruptly at the edge of. Blue-green and topped with white crowns of foam, waves broke gently on the shore at Besmir's feet.

Something else started forward. Another *presence* that Besmir found pressing on his consciousness, unrelenting and vast. She came from the waves, was formed *of* the waves but was covered in scales, with fins and the smooth skin of a dolphin for a face. Tentacles flowed from her sides, beckoning Besmir toward her.

"I must also ask you abandon your quest, Besmir," Sharise said.

The siren song of her voice filled his soul with light and happiness to such a degree there was nothing Besmir would not do for her. If Sharise were to ask him to cut out his own eyes in that voice, he would do so.

Besmir smiled at the obviously feminine form of Sharise and nodded.

Of course. I'll return to Gazluth and continue to lead there. I'll forget all about my son...

Besmir's thoughts trailed off in confusion. What were they asking him to do? Abandon his son to die at the hands of Porantillia?

"Never!" he declared. "Leaving Joranas to his own fate is something I won't do."

The siren song of Sharise fell from his ears and he heard her true voice as she thundered her words at him, making him cower.

"Petty mortal, you are vain indeed. It is our will you shall not seek out Porantillia, for her freedom would signal the end of all things and this we forbid!"

Besmir cowered on the wet sand as Sharise blasted him with the immense power of her voice. Each word felt like a blow to his chest, the way he could feel the drumbeats of his soldiers on parade reverberating in his lungs.

"Leave this place," she continued. "Return to your throne and forget the name of Porantillia for all time."

Sharise pinned Besmir to the sand with her massive eyes, twin orbs the size of plates borrowed from some deep sea creature his mind shied from. After a few minutes she slowly slid back into the ocean, becoming one with the water and disappearing completely.

"Bit intense isn't she?" Cathantor asked. "But I had to get her to speak to you because I'm not so good at the intimidation side of things." The strange looking God of afterlife took a bright red shell from the surf and pressed in into Besmir's hand. "Sleep now," he said gently, "and know I love you."

Besmir felt his eyes closing as one of the waves washed over his body. Tiredness he could not battle drew him down into a dreamless sleep and paradise faded into darkness around him.

***

A deep growling gurgle brought him from the deepest sleep he had felt for ages. He sat up and rubbed his eyes, confused as to where he had woken. Sunlight burned the dark city without and the growl came again.

Joranas stood and walked across to the door, peering out with a squint at the three massive cat-like creatures that were advancing on Whint. Each one was about the size of a horse, thickly muscled beneath shining coats of dun colored fur and sported fangs as long as his index finger.

Joranas had seen a picture his father had of a Crallcat, a beautiful but vicious animal from Besmir's first homeland. These things were like massive versions of that and looked intent on feasting on Whint for breakfast.

Fear clamped bands of ice around Joranas' heart as he watched the lead cat crouch in readiness to pounce. Her muscles tensed and quivered as her narrow eyes focused on the dark skinned man who faced the three.

Whint himself seemed oblivious to any danger as he examined the massive creatures that were just about to kill him.

If they kill him, I'll be here on my own.

Joranas' fright grew at the thought of being stranded here alone and he tried to call a warning to the man who had been his only companion for weeks.

"Whint!" his squeaked whisper faded on the breeze. "Whint!" he managed a little louder this time.

Whint's attention was squarely focused on the animals that stalked him, however, and the young prince got no response at all. Joranas swallowed as he saw the lead beast feint at Whint, one huge, two toed paw lashing at his face. Whint made no move at all and Joranas watched the creature as confusion washed over its face, comical at any other time, frightening now. Indecision plagued the lead creature as it stared at Whint grumbling deep in its throat. Finally realizing there were three large creatures facing one small one the animal issued a bellowing roar and leaped at Whint.

Panic grabbed Joranas and before he knew what he was doing he had stepped outside and was running towards Whint who seemed perfectly happy to be in the jaws of a large cat. Joranas threw his arms out at the two large cats that turned towards him, teeth bared. Flames lanced from his hands, searing and burning the creatures and sending them running as their coats singed. Foul smelling smoke filled the little courtyard outside their home, the stench of burning hair and meat.

Joranas watched as the first creature mauled Whint, tossing him around with ease. He could not use his magic on the animal for fear of hitting Whint as well but if he could just get the creature's attention, he could draw it far enough away from his friend to burn it.

Joranas screamed wordlessly at the thing as it pinned Whint down with one paw, bringing the other up to strike. Helpless, Joranas could only watch as Whint grabbed at the powerful leg that held him.

Something changed then. One moment Whint was pinned beneath the large cat's paw, waiting for its death blow. The next he had twisted the leg, bringing a hissing scream from the cat as fur and muscle ripped. A river of hot blood sprung from the wound and Whint stood, apparently unharmed to face the, now limping, creature.

Nothing in its nature had prepared the cat for this eventuality and Joranas could see it had no intention of leaving. A fact that was proven when the thing attacked Whint again. This time the strange speaking man grabbed the cat's jaws as it bit at him. It flinched back, trying to shake him from its face but Whint held on grimly, his fingers digging into the cat's skin and even loosening one of its teeth.

Joranas watched in horrified awe as Whint forced the cat's jaws apart, levering them open further until the animal started to scream in pain. Even then Whint did not release the animal and with a sickening crunch Joranas watched the cat's lower jaw snap loose to hang at an odd angle.

Mewling in pain and fear the cat tried to run but Whint still held its face in his hands and hung on grimly as it shook him violently. When the animal paused to consider what to do, Whint vaulted onto its back, wrapping his arms about its throat and squeezing.

The cat dropped, rolling to try and dislodge the meal that was now about to kill it but Whint gripped it ever tighter with grim determination and Joranas saw more panic in the cat's eyes as it stood, collapsed and stood again. The second time it hit the ground it did not try and rise again, the light fading from its eyes as Whint cut it's air supply off. Eventually the massive cat gave a violent tremble as it died and Whint released his grip.

Joranas sprinted across, scared of the injuries Whint must have but needing to help if he could. His eyes roved over Whint's dark skin, the sunlight reflecting from it in blonde flashes as he moved.

Not a mark showed.

"Whint!" Joranas cried. "Are you hurt?"

"Are you hurt?" Whint asked as he stared at the immense carcass.

He looked at Joranas with almost sad eyes then gently lifted the boy's fingers, examining his hands.

"Fire," he said.

"I'm fine, Whint," Joranas assured him. "Are you?"

"I'm fine," Whint echoed.

It looked to Joranas as if he was unharmed. Somehow nothing the cat had done had harmed the odd man in any way but rather than being relieved Joranas felt nervous.

How can he not have any injuries? Not even a scratch?

"I wonder what they were?" Joranas asked as he looked at the mutilated carcass.

"Daasnu," Whint said after staring into the distance for a second.

Joranas had seen this before. It was as if Whint could get the information he needed. As if someone or some*thing* spoke inside his mind, telling him just enough to keep them both alive.

"I've never heard of that," Joranas said.

"I've never heard of that," Whint echoed.

Joranas looked at the dislocated jaw the daasnu had suffered. How much strength must it have taken to do that kind of damage? Joranas remembered a dog he and Ranyeen had befriended in Morantine. A mangy, rough street mutt they had both fallen in love with. Even when it was just playing, there was no way either he or Ranyeen had been able to pry its jaws open. Once it had a grip on a piece of old rope or cloth that had been it. This daasnu was the size of a horse with teeth the size of his fingers, it should have been able to bite Whint in half but somehow he had managed to dislocate the creature's jaw.

Joranas had known Whint was strange before but had put it down to desert heat or some kind of accident. Looking at the damage done to the massive cat and seeing as how Whint was unscathed in any way the young prince realized Whint was far more strange than he first thought.

He's not human!

Chapter Eleven

Collise was bigger than the other girls her age. At twelve she was taller, stockier and more mature than any of her peers. It was a confusing time for her as at one point she wanted to play with her dolls but in the next, her mind wandered to thoughts of Zanard, the blacksmith's apprentice. His hands. His lips.

Collise had not had an easy life. Her mother was a bitter woman, prone to savage attacks and fits of rage she inevitably took out on Collise. Her mother loved her, Collise knew, just not enough to stop hitting her. Poverty meant her mother had been forced to take handouts from the king and she hated that. A weekly allowance of grain, oats and honey along with some fruit was all they had sometimes.

"His horses eat better," her mother had spat bitterly on several occasions.

As she had always been a little different, Collise had also borne the brunt of some of the local bullies attention so spent much of her time alone, as today. She watched the play of sunlight on the river that flowed through the middle of Morantine on its way to wherever and wondered what life was like where the water ended up. Were there Goblins there? Dragons or princes that could take a young girl like her to places she had only ever heard of in stories?

So lost in her thoughts and fantasies as she squatted by the water, Collise did not hear the approaching footsteps until it was too late. The hands that shoved her were rough and strong and the chilly bite of the filthy water felt like knives to her skin as she hit the river.

Spluttering river water and other, more solid, items, Collise stood in the waist deep water, soaked through. Goosebumps broke out over her skin and she started to shiver at the same time as the stench of sewage hit her nose.

Tears of frustration and anger rolled down her face as she started to wade through the filthy water towards the laughing faces that had caused this. Three boys, just older than her, pointed and nudged each other as they laughed. Collise reached the bank where they confronted her as she tried to climb out.

"Get back in!" One of them cried, grinning. "Float out to sea with the rest of the filth."

Collise folded her arms and stared at them, all three were dressed in better clothing than she had ever had access to and must come from one of the merchant houses around here. The oldest had stopped laughing and was staring at her chest intently. Collise looked down to see the effect the chilly water had had on her body and that it had plastered her cheap dress to every curve and bump. She felt utterly naked.

"Well now, what have we here lads?" The oldest asked in a mocking voice. "You two should be kinder to a young lady." He held his hand out to Collise. "Come, let me help you," he said.

Collise looked at him, trying to determine if he was going to help or shove her back into the filthy river. He smiled and she reached her hand out, hoping he had come along after the other two had pushed her in. His fingers were warm and strong as he pulled her up onto the bank and guided her gently to the top.

"You boys need to learn the value of a lady," he said, glancing at their grinning faces. "Now, my lady, how are you going to pay for my help?" He asked.

"What?" Collise asked in confusion. "I don't have money. I can't pay you."

The older boy grinned a nasty grin as he looked her up and down.

"You have some way to pay me, right?" He asked in a dark voice.

Without warning the boy shoved Collise between two buildings and she fell backwards, hitting the ground hard. Leering down at her scared face he started to open his trews, displaying himself to her.

Disgust and fear roiled inside Collise but something else started to stir within her as well. A hot, tight feeling that threatened to burst her ribs and explode from inside her. A deep moan tore from her and he laughed.

"See lads? She can't wait for me to..."

His words ended in a scream as a gout of fire exploded from Collise's outstretched hand, engulfing him in flame. The youth windmilled his arms, still screaming as he tried to run from the fire that seared his flesh.

Collise stood up, her lips peeled back from her teeth as she casually set the other two boys alight, too. She looked at her untouched hand as all three threw themselves into the dirty river in an attempt to douse the flames.

"What's going on down here?" An old man demanded, staring at Collise.

His eyes lit on her feminine form as well and a sickness flooded her mouth with saliva. She turned and sprinted from the old man's leer as he called out to her fleeing back.

***

By the time night had fallen over the city, Collise had managed to clean herself up a little and dry out, but there were still brown stains on the front of her dress that stank of human waste. Reaching the single room she shared with her mother, she took a deep breath, sighing as she opened the crude door.

The low light revealed the poverty they lived in. Rotting blankets and moldy straw stolen from midden heaps formed a pair of crude beds they slept in. There was a small pile of wood, again stolen from the waste of others, beside a blackened patch in one corner. This was the fire that would heat the room, cook any food they might have and give off enough light for her to see her mother's bitter face as she slept.

"Where have you been?" her mother demanded as soon as Collise opened the door.

"Just out playing, mama," the girl said.

"Out playing." her mother echoed. "I wish I had the time to go out playi..." Her eyes widened as soon as she caught sight of her daughter. "What the...look at the state of you!" She screamed. "Covered in the Gods know what and that smell!" She wrinkled her nose.

Collise cowered as her mother approached, fists curled ready to punch.

"No, mama!" Collise cried, trying to cover herself with her arms as her mother slapped and punched her. "Please."

"I. Give. You. A. Good. Home," her mother punctuated each word with another slap or punch. Even a few kicks landed as the heat started to build in Collise's chest again.

""Stop it, mama, please," Collise begged. "I might burn you!"

Her mother stopped instantly, stepping back and staring at her daughter.

"What, girl?" She asked. "What did you just say to me?"

In a halting voice, punctuated by sobs and gasps, Collise revealed to her mother what had happened that day. Why she was filthy and what she had done to her potential attackers.

"You've lost your mind, child!" Her mother cried with yet another slap. "Making up stories and the like..."

Collise threw her hand at the far wall and unleashed a burst of flame.

"Praise the Gods!" Her mother cried when she had finished. "Your father got you on me by force but his legacy lives on in you!"

Cold fright dribbled through her then. What did her mother mean by that? Who had her father really been?

"Mama?" She asked, uncertainly.

"Can you do it again?" Her mother asked, eagerly.

Her face was lit up with an expression of eager expectancy as she stared at Collise.

"Go on," she urged. "Light up that fire for me, girl."

Collise concentrated, trying to bring the fire from her hands as she had done before. She felt warm but nowhere near the heat she had when she had burned the boys alive.

"Did you lie to me? Some kind of trick?" Her mother thundered, bringing her hand round across Collise's face.

The stinging slap made the heat explode from inside her chest, lancing along her arm almost painfully as she pointed at her mother.

The grim faced woman went white and dropped to the floor as soon as she felt the intense heat billowing towards her. Flames leaped over her back as she groveled on the floor, singing the hair on her head as Collise screamed her rage.

Looking at the corner of the room, she saw Collise had not only incinerated the small pile of wood but started to melt the stones in the wall as well.

"Yes!" She crowed in triumph. "Yes! Finally. After twelve long years of this poor life you have finally shown you are your father's daughter. A daughter of Tiernon!"

"What?" Collise asked in utter fright.

"King Tiernon took many of us from our homes. Kept us in cages for his own amusement and did to us what that boy wanted to do to you today, Collise. He put you in my belly back then but I never knew why. Now..."

"Why, mama?" Collise asked in a dim voice.

Her mother turned to her as if she was subhuman, staring at her with the same hate-filled eyes she had for years as a sneer curled her lip.

"Can you not see what this means?" She asked. "Are you that simple it remains unclear?" Her mother grunted a laugh. "It means, simple Collise, that you have royal blood in your veins. It means with good old King Besmir out of the way, you can be queen!"

Collise watched as her mother cavorted about their little room, muttering to herself and rubbing her hands together. She frowned, thinking as her mother plotted and schemed.

How can I be the queen when Besmir is already the King? It makes no sense.

Collise watched as her mother grinned and danced, her face alight with malice the like she had never seen. One thing Collise did know was that if she was going to somehow be queen, it would be her mother that was in charge.

*****

"It was the strangest dream I've ever had," Besmir said when he woke beside Arteera. "I can't believe how vivid it was."

"Hmm?" His wife hummed sleepily. "What happened?"

"I was in the Afterlife with Cathantor," he said folding her in his arms, "and Sharise the Goddess of the Sea. They said they wanted me to stop looking for a way to get to Porantillia and forget all about Joranas."

Arteera jumped, staring into his eyes.

"What did you say?" She demanded.

"I said yes at first," Besmir admitted, "because Sharise...her voice was...impossible to resist." Besmir frowned as he thought. "When I said I had to find him, get him back, her voice changed...it was terrible and frightening...what?" He asked.

Arteera was smiling at him in a way he had not seen for months. She wriggled closer, pressing herself against him tightly beneath their blankets and wrapping herself around him.

"Even if it was only a dream," she muttered into his ear, "you defied the Gods for our son. I lov...ouch!" Arteera cried. "What is this?"

Chill fingers raked through Besmir's chest when he saw the bright red shell she held in her hand.

"Besmir?" She asked as he rolled from their blankets. "Besmir, what is going on?"

"We need to talk to Zaynorth," he said, shaking. "That was no dream."

***

"So you believe the God of Afterlife and Goddess of the Sea told you *not* to seek Porantillia? To give up and return home?" Zaynorth asked as he turned the strange shell over in his hands. "And you said no?"

Besmir nodded, looking from face to face as he did so.

"Cathantor put that in my hand just before he sent me back," Besmir said. "I met people there, Zaynorth! I met my mother and..." he trailed off, glancing at Keluse. "Others," he added.

"I believe you," Zaynorth said. "However, why would the Gods seek to persuade you not to do this? Why not just make it so?" He asked, passing the shell back to Besmir. "Surely the Gods could erase all knowledge of this from us all?"

"I don't know," Besmir said, "but Sharise said releasing Porantillia would mean the end of everything, so what does that mean?"

"This is all pointless speculation," Herofic grunted rudely. "We need to get to see this shaman, sort out Porantillia and get your lad back. Then we can go home and think about Gods."

Besmir stared at the old warrior as he squatted on a rock. The sun was already hot, the dry wind full of gritty sand that got into every crevice and annoyed the skin but Herofic seemed to fare the worst. He was burned a deep, golden brown apart from the tops of his ears and tip of his nose, both of which were bright red. His hair had lightened by degrees in the sun, changing from its normal black to a lighter brown as the intense light bleached the color from it. He was more irritable and grouchy than normal and Besmir had to laugh.

"Oh that's all is it?" He asked, chuckling. "Just 'sort out' Porantillia and go home?"

"I will admit there might be a little more to it than that," Herofic said, "but sitting here discussing it while I slowly cook is getting us nowhere. We carry on or go home. Which is it?"

"Carry on," Besmir and Arteera said at the same time.

The pair looked tenderly at each other when they reached the same conclusion at the same time.

"There you are then," Herofic grunted, groaning as he stood. "Discussion over for now."

Wearily he lifted his leg up to the stirrup and bounced a few times to give him the lift to get on his horse again. It was not until his body crashed to the ground on the other side of his mount that anyone realized he was in trouble.

"Herofic?" Zaynorth called.

Besmir, Arteera and Ru Tarn shouted as well, each hoping the older man would get up and curse his own stupidity for falling. He did not. His horse stepped gingerly around his body as the whole group dashed across to his body.

"Sun is being too hot," Ru Tarn explained. "Must be getting him to shade quick."

Besmir and Zaynorth grabbed the hefty man by the arms and lifted him between them, half-carrying his body towards a shadowed area the Corbondrasi were attaching a canvas roof to. They laid Herofic on a few blankets and Ru Tarn squatted beside him, laying a feathered hand on his burned forehead, frowning. She paused then ran her fingertips down his skin, rubbing them together and sniffing the pads. Turning to Besmir with a shake of her head, the Corbondrasi ambassador told them,

"Herofic not using the cream Ru Tarn has been giving you."

Anger and concern filled Besmir in equal measure as he stared down at his friend. He glanced at the concerned faces of Zaynorth and Arteera.

"Stubborn old fool," the king grunted. "Why wouldn't he use it? How long do you think before he wakes up?"

"Not being as simple as that," Ru Tarn said with concern. "Sun can be killing if Herofic not doing what he should," she muttered something to her countrymen in Corbondrasi and the feathered men danced off into the rocks. "Must be making stretcher to carry him," she explained. "And hope he is being strong enough to live."

Besmir slumped to a hot rock, grinding his teeth in frustration at the added hold up. His eyes fell to Herofic's hand, clasped tightly in Ru Tarn's own before looking at her concerned face.

If he doesn't die I'm going to kill him!

Chapter Twelve

"Madam, you cannot just barge into the king's residence!" Besmir's housecarl, Branisi cried.

"Can and will!" Collise's mother muttered as she tried to shove her way into Besmir's house. "My daughter is a child of Tiernon and has as much right to be here as the king."

Branisi sighed, signaling for the guards to throw this harridan out but urging them not to hurt her or the child that looked on with doe-like eyes. Not for the first time, Branisi wished Besmir had left another in charge of his affairs. True, there were a number of staff to tackle the day to day running of the country, but he had instructed Branisi to take care of his personal affairs.

This is certainly a personal affair.

"Collise!" The woman cried. "Burn them!"

Branisi's eyes fell to the girl, widening in surprise as she raised her arm towards the household guard. Her chest tightened as she waited for the child to do something but relaxed after a few seconds when nothing happened.

"But mama..." The girl mewled.

"Collise!"

The girl stared in confusion as her mother was shoved rudely towards the doorway.

"Leave Mama alone!" Collise called weakly.

The guards reached where she stood, shoving her mother towards the door and back out into the street, pushing the girl as well. Branisi watched in satisfaction as the pair were steered out of the royal residence. It was not until one of the guards cried out that Branisi realized the child was dangerous.

"I don't want to hurt no one!" Collise cried. "But I can't always make it stop!"

Horror crawled through Branisi as she watched her friend's clothing catch light when he dropped to the floor, rolling frantically while his comrades tried to extinguish the flames. His screams split the air as Collise's mother watched with a sneer on her face.

"Collise, stop, please!" Branisi called, locking eyes with the girl.

She could see the fright and confusion in her face and felt a little sorry for her. It was obvious she was scared of her mother, even though it was Collise that wielded power. Collise's eyes flicked from Branisi to her mother and back uncertainly but the flames died down, leaving the man to groan on the floor.

"He needs a medic," Branisi said gently. "Can I send for one?"

"Let him die," the wizened hag spat.

Branisi ignored her, concentrating her attention on the child, realizing she would have to befriend her.

"Your Highness?" she asked Collise.

A little smile crossed her young face as Collise nodded and Branisi issued orders to get the fallen guard to a medic.

"Thank you for that, Highness," Branisi said. "I am called Branisi and am here to help you in any way I can."

"Then get us food," Collise's mother demanded. "And a bath. Clean clothes and soft furniture."

Branisi ignored the woman again, addressing her daughter directly.

"What would you like, your highness?" She asked.

If I can separate these two I might be able to make friends with the girl.

"I am a bit hungry," Collise said.

"Then let us get you something to eat," Branisi said, guiding the girl through to the kitchen. Collise's mother watched her with narrowed eyes, fully aware of what she was trying to do.

"Come on, mama," Collise said as she trotted through the house.

Her eyes darted from one wonder to the next as Branisi led her along a corridor, it was obvious she had lived poorly as she trailed her fingers along the walls, touching everything her eyes landed on and smiling.

"Cook will get you anything you want," Branisi said as they wandered into the kitchen.

Nashal looked inquiringly at Branisi as she stared at the pair of filthy people that had just appeared in her kitchen.

Branisi widened her eyes and nodded slightly at the cook who shrugged and waited.

"What would you like, highness?" Nashal's eyes widened at Branisi's address.

"Bread and cheese?" Collise asked. "Can I have that?"

"Of cours…"

"Stupid girl!" Her mother spat. "You can have anything you want and you ask for bread and cheese?" She sneered at her daughter before turning to Nashal. "Honey," she demanded. "Some good meat and pastries, you must have some pastries here. Come on!" She added as Nashal stood there, hands on hips.

"Bread and cheese, your Highness?" Nashal asked. "Do you want something to drink as well?"

"Milk?" Collise asked, uncertain.

"Good choice." Nashal smiled as she started slicing bread and cheese.

Collise's mother eyed Nashal and Branisi as they charmed her simple daughter. Neither woman would meet her eyes and she knew what they were up to, trying to befriend her daughter, drive a wedge between them and control Collise.

"Yes, love," she said. "A good choice. You always liked a little milk, remember?"

Collise nodded, smiling at her mother with a white mustache.

***

Besmir stared in surprise at the verdant valley below him. Trees and shrubs in a range of greens provided shade for buildings and people as they went about their business. Vast fields, pregnant with crops, were tended and irrigated by the brightly colored Corbondrasi. In contrast to the rest of Boranash they had arrived in a paradise.

The small party had been slowed by Herofic's need to be stretchered but one of the Corbondrasi had gone ahead to get a message through to the king and queen that they had been delayed. Now a party of Corbondrasi in military uniforms greeted Besmir at the edge of the greenery, saluting them all.

"Your Majesties," the leader greeted them in Gazluthian. "Let us be caring for your wounded." He gestured and a pair of Corbondrasi with leather satchels darted across to Herofic, assessing his well being. "Please to be resting here." He gestured to a large, covered wagon. "Will be to river soon," he added before saluting and issuing commands in the whistling tongue of the Corbondrasi.

Besmir led Arteera up into the back of the wagon watching as she lowered herself gratefully onto a soft cushion. Jugs of liquid sat surrounded by goblets and Besmir poured them all a cup of chilled water lightly flavored with fruit. Besmir drained his gratefully and filled it again before slumping down beside his wife. None in the wagon spoke, exhaustion and heat having sapped their will. Almost as soon as Besmir had sunk into the soft furnishings inside the wagon, his eyes drooped and he fell into a deep sleep.

When he awoke, confused and disorientated, Besmir discovered he had been moved while he slept and heard the telltale creaks and groans of a ship. The gentle sway of the floor beneath him and swishing of waves as they broke over the bow told him everything. A sense of relief washed through him then as he knew they were on their way upriver to the Corbondrasi capital.

Besmir stretched and looked around the cabin which was well appointed and clean. Clothing had been laid out for him and he sensed the hand of his wife when he saw the choices included anything she favored him in. A gentle smile crossed his face as he dressed in a simple, white shirt and leather trews. The skin over his face felt tight and he reached up to feel where someone had treated his sunburn.

Herofic.

Besmir stepped from the room he was in straight out onto the dark deck of the ship. A froth of stars overhead glittered in the velvet sky and a lone gull cried to any who might listen as it soared high above them.

"How is he?" Besmir asked as he approached his group of friends.

Arteera leaned into him slipping an arm around his back and sighing. A cool wind whipped her hair around Besmir's face and he breathed her scent in deeply.

"Not good," Zaynorth said, his careworn face looking older than usual. "He was not covering his head against the sun and has heat stroke and the burns are quite severe."

"I should have noticed," Besmir said, shaking his head. "Made him cover up."

"You have had other things to concern yourself with," Zaynorth said, "and he is a grown man, we should be able to trust him to care for himself." The old man's irritability was tempered with obvious concern for his brother.

"How long until we get to the palace?" Besmir asked.

"Captain is thinking tomorrow afternoon," Ru Tarn said, wincing and doubling over.

"Are you all right?" Arteera asked.

"Yes...I am being...fine," Ru Tarn chirped.

The ambassador turned and limped off towards a door set into one of the cabins aboard. Besmir watched her go, a twinge of concern for her well being tugging at his mind.

"Any more Gods come to visit you in your dreams?" Arteera asked as Besmir led her away from the others and towards the prow.

Besmir shook his head.

"Not today," he said.

The ship was making good time in the wind, her sails bellied out and pulling them northwards. They passed a small settlement with piers jutting out into the river. Boats and nets had been carefully stowed and the warm glow of fires lit the simple homes and Besmir sighed.

"What?" His wife asked.

"I just wondered when it got so complicated," Besmir told her, leaning on the rail.

"A decade ago, when you went and declared yourself King," Arteera said.

"Yes," Besmir grunted a laugh. "Should have been content to stay in those tents."

The couple fell silent as Arteera drew abstract shapes on the back of his hand.

"I wonder what Joranas is doing right now?" the Queen said.

"Getting dirty and ripping his clothes I'd imagine," Besmir said with a chuckle.

Arteera smiled sadly, a gentle sob issuing from her chest.

"I will get him back," Besmir said with determination as he stared upriver.

***

A shiver of awe and overwhelming sense of his own insignificance hit Besmir when the sun rose the following morning. He had kissed Arteera and left her in the cabin they had been assigned to see the sunrise over Boranash. In the distance, his eyes picked out a darker patch on the horizon and he squinted to get a better view.

Wit Shull, the Corbondrasi capital city was immense. Besmir had believed Morantine to be a great, cosmopolitan city but the size and grandeur of Wit Shull made it look like a country fair. As the royal yacht slid gracefully upriver, Besmir's wonder grew. The almost endless fields that had stretched away on both sides of the wide river gave way to small dwellings interspersed with large warehouses he assumed were filled with the produce from the fields.

Arteera gasped as she joined him a little later, her eyes gleaming at the brightly colored buildings and even more brightly colored citizens. Main construction was of sandstone, easily harvested from the surrounding desert but each building had some kind of decorative feature, even if it was as simple as a lone band running round it.

Spires and towers exploded into the air like fireworks, riots of color with jade and sapphire, rose and peach greeting Besmir's eye at every turn. At first glance these colors appeared random but Besmir soon picked out associations between color and building type.

"It is being way of telling people what building is being used for," Ru Tarn explained when he asked about it. "Green is being guard building, red is tavern or inn, blue is places of learning or advice."

The Corbondrasi ambassador did not seem bothered by the pains she had been the previous evening although she sounded tired and her plumage appeared faded.

Now they were surrounded by buildings on both sides of the narrowing river the wind all but faded to nothing and crew members appeared from below decks to take up long poles. Each would dip their pole into the water at the bow, finding an anchor point, before walking the length of the boat to propel it forward. Working silently and in pairs, the Corbondrasi worked tirelessly to power the boat against the current.

"Does not look to have changed much," Zaynorth said as he approached them.

"When were you here?" Besmir asked.

"I came with your father, thirty years past," the old mage said. "Your grandfather arranged the visit but was not well enough to make the voyage so Joranas went in his place." Zaynorth stared into the city as if seeing the past. "Here, look at the palace," he added, pointing.

Besmir gawped at the sprawling buildings, each looked to be covered in gold and he shivered at the expense, frowning at such waste.

A different culture, different people, keep your opinions to yourself.

Banners and flags danced lazily in the hot breeze making Besmir wonder if the configuration meant something, some signal the royal family was in residence. His keen eyes picked out numerous figures high among the rooftops, camouflaged but not from his gaze. Each was heavily armed with a longbow and sword, their own gazes raking the river and buildings for any potential threat.

"How big is this place?" Besmir asked as the palace slid by them on both sides. Every so often a bridge soared overhead, connecting the two sides of the palace and Corbondrasi peered over the edge as the royal vessel swum by beneath them.

"This is being difficult to answer," Ru Tarn said. "Palace and city becoming one many years ago so is being difficult to tell where palace ends and city begins," she shrugged. "We are being here soon," she added, pointing.

Besmir followed her gaze and saw a large dock protruding into the river. Like everything else here it was large and colorful, the whole trees that had been driven into the riverbed had been painted in a pattern and shade was provided by lengths of colorful cloth making it look as if they were docking inside a rainbow.

Besmir took Arteera's arm as the hollow thump issued through the ship, telling him they had moored successfully. Crew darted about in a carefully practiced dance to lower a large walkway down from the deck to the dock, kneeling as they finished their assigned tasks.

Besmir had been dreading the pomp and ceremony of a royal visit, his only goal in being here the recovery of Joranas. Anything else was a distraction or hold up stopping him from getting his boy back. The hunter king of Gazluth prepared himself for the fanfares and flowery speeches as he helped Arteera down from the ship.

Silence greeted them. He stared out at the dock, leading inside the buildings, to see a few armed guards lining the walls and a pair of Corbondrasi who must have been sent to meet them.

The male was powerfully built, muscular and strong with dark red and green plumage easily visible beneath the thin clothing he wore. As Besmir approached he found himself staring into a pair of mint green eyes the like of which he had never come across before. The piercing stare felt as if it burrowed deep inside Besmir's very soul, able to pick out his deepest fears and secrets.

The female was slightly shorter than her male counterpart, round and matronly with sky blue and azure plumage. With wide hips and small breasts she had pale gray eyes that also did not miss a thing.

Ru Tarn followed Besmir and Arteera down to the dock falling to her knees before the pair and staring at the floor.

"King Besmir, Queen Arteera, may I be presenting to you Vi Rhane, Light of Heaven and King of all Boranash?"

Besmir felt a shill shock through him.

This is the king?

He had been expecting a demonstration of power and wealth, marching bands and parades but one of the most powerful leaders in the world stood simply before him wearing an unadorned, thin shirt and light trousers.

Vi Rhane stepped forwards and thrust his hand out at Besmir who looked at it as if unsure as to its purpose. The Corbondrasi king let his arm fall slowly.

"My apologies," he said in a deeper voice than Besmir had ever heard from a Corbondrasi. "I was under the impression Gazluthians shook hands upon greeting."

Besmir shook his head as if waking from a dream, his eyes focused on the Corbondrasi king and he bowed low.

"No, your majesty, it is I who should apologize," he said. "You surprised me...I wasn't expecting you to be so..."

A wry smile twisted Vi Rhane's face then and he offered his hand again. This time Besmir took it, feeling the softness of the feathers covering his hand.

"Normal?" Vi Rhane asked. "This is my queen, Su Rhane."

Besmir bowed to the queen who offered him a curtsy before turning to Arteera. The Corbondrasi queen stared at Besmir's slender wife with a look of sadness in her face. Her gray eyes expressing the sorrow and loss Arteera felt.

"Oh, love," Su Rhane said as she enveloped Arteera in a feathery hug.

Arteera clung to the queen, sobbing while the Corbondrasi tried to comfort the woman she had just met.

Chapter Thirteen

"Considering the circumstances, I did not think it prudent to have a massive greeting ceremony," Vi Rhane said quietly as he and Besmir strolled through the palace.

Besmir had met many Corbondrasi since becoming king of Gazluth and understood their languages were so vastly different it was incredibly difficult for any Corbondrasi to speak his tongue. Vi Rhane, however, spoke as if he was almost a native of Gazluth with an extensive vocabulary and virtually no accent whatsoever.

"I'm grateful, your majesty," Besmir said. "It might seem rude but all I want is to find my son."

"Completely understandable," Vi Rhane said. "And please, call me Vi Rhane."

"And I am just Besmir. I have to say your Gazluthian is amazing."

"Thank you," Vi Rhane said. "I have an excellent teacher, one you may have heard of?" Besmir raised his eyebrows in question. "Founsalla Pira, your ambassador here?"

"Ah, yes," Besmir said nodding. "I've never actually met him in person but I've read his reports, he comes across as a capable man."

The Corbondrasi king hummed and scratched his head.

"Capable? Yes I suppose he is but very...unusual. You know his mother was Corbondrasi and his father from Gazluth?"

"I didn't think that was possible," Besmir said in surprise.

"It is an incredibly rare happening," Vi Rhane said as they passed a group of female Corbondrasi practicing a dance in a courtyard. "Probably as there are few couplings of our two peoples."

Vi Rhane led them to a group of buildings that were slightly separate from the rest. Less showy and more practical than the rest of the palace buildings, Besmir assumed these were to be his quarters for the time being.

"The Gazluthian embassy," Vi Rhane said. "Please feel free to refresh yourselves and change before we meet later. If there is anything you need just ask Founsalla and it will be arranged."

"I was hoping to be able to speak to you regarding the master shaman," Besmir said hopefully.

Vi Rhane nodded.

"Of course, I'll have him come straight over."

***

"He is utterly insane," Founsalla Pira said. "Lives in his own filth and squalor. Spends much of his time yanking his own feathers out." The Corbondrasi-Gazluthian hybrid shuddered at the thought.

Besmir was still surprised at Founsalla's appearance. Tall and thin to the point of emaciation he had obvious Gazluthian features. Dark brown hair covered his head but his face had a down of feathers that spread down his arms but ended at his wrists. He had none of the bright colors other Corbondrasi sported and all his plumage appeared to be small, downy feathers rather than the large, spouting ones other Corbondrasi had. He wore his heavy ambassadorial robes despite the intense heat and did not appear to suffer for it.

"Honestly, your majesty, even if they do locate the madman I cannot see what use he might be. He is a broken minded, gibbering wreck."

"I need to know if he knows anything about Porantillia," Besmir said.

At the mention of her name, Founsalla stepped back from Besmir and made a protective sign.

"Please, majesty, do not use that word here," he begged. "It is not one to be used in polite Corbondrasi society."

"She came to me in a dream, said she had my boy and I had to go to see her, physically, to get him back," Besmir stated flatly. "Oh and she is trapped in some kind of nothingness the other side of hell," he added.

Founsalla stroked his chin and nodded slowly.

"I can see how that might be a problem," he said. "Yet I still cannot see how that cavorting lunatic Lor Tas can be of any help."

"It's the only hope we've got," Besmir said sadly.

"Then I hope they can locate him, majesty," Founsalla said without much conviction.

***

"What ails you, little sister?" Queen Su Rhane asked Ru Tarn as the Corbondrasi ambassador presented herself.

"It is nothing, majesty," Ru Tarn lied. "There is no need to worry yourself with my problems."

Su Rhane chirped a snort and held out a small, wooden cup filled with honey. Minute birds flashed over to where she held the sweet goodness out, perching on the edge of the bowl and the queen's hand to dip tiny beaks into the sugar.

"As queen it is my sworn duty to worry about the problems my people have," Su Rhane said, running a gentle finger over the head of one of the birds. "As your aunt, my duty is doubled. So tell me, Ru Tarn, what ails you?"

Ru Tarn crossed to the window, sitting beside her aunt and leaned her head against the stonework, watching the birds feasting on the honey the queen held.

"My egg came early," she said. "Months too early."

The queen's head snapped round, startling the birds and causing them to scatter in all directions.

"As I was not expecting it, I did not have the proper preparations in place," she added. "No *pytarrah* juice, plus we were traveling."

"Dear niece that must have been an awful situation. Might I ask what actual measures you took?"

Ru Tarn looked down, embarrassed as she admitted to her dalliance with a married Corbandrasi..

"I have not expelled yet," Ru Tarn said bitterly.

The Corbondrasi queen looked shocked.

"Not to be brutal but there are measures one can take if wished," she said.

Tears rolled down Ru Tarn's face then, soaking her peach-pink feathers and making them dark.

"I don't know what to do," she wailed. "If I rid myself of the egg now it might cause so much damage I can't have another in future. If I have the hatchling I lose my position and the respect that comes with it as well as hurting you."

"My feelings are secondary in this, but can I ask who the father actually is?"

"My assistant, Qi Noss," Ru Tarn said with a look of embarrassment.

"And does he know any of this?"

"No, I've been speaking to a friend of mine though," Ru Tarn said.

"Good, what did she suggest?"

"He, aunt, it's one of King Besmir's friends, a man named Herofic."

"A male!" Su Rhane squawked in shock. "No, don't panic I was surprised, that's all. Maybe I should meet this Gazluthian," Su Rhane said.

"He is currently in the infirmary being treated for heatstroke and sunburn," Ru Tarn told her.

"A stubborn Gazluthian," the queen mused as she offered the honey out to the birds once more. "An interesting choice, my niece."

Ru Tarn stared at her queen and aunt as if she had not even considered the possibility. Now the words had been spoke aloud the realization hit her that she did have more than feelings of friendship towards Herofic.

***

Besmir recoiled from the stench that rose from the thing that had dragged itself before the Gazluthian embassy. A mixture of unwashed body and excrement wafted from Lor Tas with every movement and it was all Besmir could do to stop himself from ordering someone to douse the creature in water.

His dirty skin bore the marks and bruises where he had, apparently, pulled his own feathers out and Besmir could see a few of the larger holes had small blood trails running from them. A featherless Corbondrasi was a strange thing to behold as his skull was a completely different shape once stripped back to skin. Wearing nothing but a filthy rag around his waist the head shaman of Boranash squatted with his arms around his knees as he squinted up at Besmir with blood red eyes.

"The hunter king of Gazluth is seeking Lor Tas," the shaman said.

His voice was the high-pitched squeak of a Corbondrasi but his words were Gazluthian and easily understandable.

"I do," Besmir said, covering his nose with one hand.

Lor Tas giggled a hissing sound, slapping the floor with both hands.

"Smelly Lor Tas is upsetting the king?" He asked sarcastically.

"Actually yes," Besmir said. "You stink."

Lor Tas laughed again, rolling in a circle on his back and kicking his dirty feet in glee.

"Oh Lor Tas is liking the truth. So many others are lying to Lor Tas so Lor Tas will tell them what they are wanting to know. King Besmir is not being a liar but Lor Tas is not being able to help."

"You don't even know what I want," Besmir said as Founsalla Pira joined them.

"Mwondi came to Lor Tas," the shaman said. "Mwondi is telling Lor Tas Lor Tas cannot be helping Besmir king."

"Porantillia took my son," Besmir said.

Lor Tas recoiled as if he had been doused in acid. He folded himself into a ball and rolled backwards away from Besmir at the mere mention of her name. He drew symbols on the ground and mewled strange noises. Founsalla Pira shook his head.

"I am sorry, majesty," he said. "It is as I feared. His madness is obvious and complete, I doubt there are any answers here."

Besmir heard the steady drum of marching feet and an honor guard appeared escorting the Corbondrasi king and queen. They approached Lor Tas carefully, keeping a gap of several feet as if the shaman was some poisonous creature about to strike.

"More kings and queens for Lor Tas," the filthy shaman chirped. "Kings and queens everywhere," he chanted, rocking on his heels. "Enough for Lor Tas to make a living chess set."

"Has he told you anything?" Vi Rhane asked expectantly.

Besmir shook his head.

"Nothing," he said sadly, his heart sinking. "I think this has been a complete waste of time."

Besmir looked down at the prone form of the shaman as he prostrated himself before some unseen being, hate and despair mixing in his chest.

"I really am sorry," the Corbondrasi king said genuinely. "If there is anything I can do, I offer the resources of my kingdom and people to achieve it."

"Well, thank yo..."

Besmir trailed off as Lor Tas moaned and threw himself backwards. His entire frame trembled as if freezing, limbs shaking like leaves in a breeze. It was the fact he began to float that made everyone stop and stare at him. Easily a foot above the ground the shaman's jerking feet cast cavorting shadows on the ground. His head lolled, rolling forward so his chin was to his chest and his arms hung limply at his sides.

Besmir watched in awe as something appeared *around* Lor Tas' body, as if he wore the shadowy thing like a coat. Muscular arms rippled forth, overlaying the Corbondrasi shaman's own but twice the size and ending in claws. His head became engulfed within another, massive, head its glowing eyes staring at them all dispassionately.

Besmir watched as the Corbondrasi king and queen fell to their knees, leaning their heads to the ground, any other Corbondrasi following suit and bowing to the shaman. Besmir frowned as the enveloped shaman pointed at him.

"Mortal," his voice echoed around the palace like granite exploding. "Thou hast been advised by my brethren to turn from thy present course lest you bring about the cessation of all life."

"My lord Mwondi..." Vi Rhane began but the God ignored him in favor of Besmir.

"Why dost thou seek that which cannot be found?" Mwondi asked.

"Porantillia?" Besmir asked even though fear clutched his heart. "She's taken my son."

Mwondi raised his vast head, the beginnings of horns rising from his forehead, and fixed Besmir with a steel eyed glare.

"Thee mortals breed endlessly," the God rumbled. "Have thy mate bear another child."

Besmir heard Arteera sob behind him and rage burned his fear away. No one, not even a God should speak to her in that way. He strode towards the flickering form surrounding Lor Tas. Mwondi's large face showed surprise as he watched the small human walk towards him.

"That's not an option," Besmir spat. "I want my son back!"

"Impudent human!" Mwondi thundered. "Porantillia reclines in Hell, if it is Hell thee seeks, then Hell I shall cast thee into. Meet with her and suffer thy fate!"

The form of Mwondi lashed forward, his clawed hands wrapping around and *through* Besmir who screamed in agony.

Arteera watched as her husband defied a living God before her eyes, pride and love vying with utter terror as the massive thing grabbed Besmir before they both disappeared.

***

Collise stared out of the window and sighed. Her mother seemed happy to be living in the royal household but to Collise it felt like a prison. True she was dressed in the finest clothes Gazluth had to offer, her skin and hair glowed with cleanliness and they had somehow even managed to get the stink of poverty off her. Young women had been sent to curl and braid her hair, adding oils and perfumes to each strand as they brushed it yet none of them seemed to want to know *her*. It felt as if she was a job, something they must do, a task they had to complete as quickly and efficiently as possible before they could leave.

Collise caught the glances they gave each other as they worked in silence. Derisory stares and little sneers she was not supposed to see painted their faces. Collise hated them.

I will never be anything more than an illegitimate child of Tiernon.

"What are you sitting there for child?" Collise's mother, Deremona, demanded as she hobbled across the room towards her daughter.

Collise turned to see her mother had bought another dress. This one was the color of red wine, trimmed with silver and gold embroidery and came with a heavy gold chain that pulled at her sagging neck. Her hair had been pulled back into a severe bun and she had another new piece of jewelry draped over her skull like a fishing net. This net, however, had been crafted from gold and had gemstones dripping from it like tears.

"Everyone hates me," Collise told her mother sadly.

"Nonsense," she snapped. "They *fear* you just as they did your father. Do you think Tiernon sat moping at the window, bothered about what people thought of him?"

Collise shook her head slowly.

"Of course not. He was too busy taking what he wanted, gathering power and wealth, just as you should be doing."

"But...King Besmir killed Tiernon," Collise said with an air of confusion. "Would he not just come and kill me too?"

A nasty, scheming smile wriggled across Deremona's face then and she clasped her hands before her in glee.

"Not when you have his friends as hostages," she said.

Both women turned when the gentle knock came and Branisi entered the room, offering a small bow. Collise beamed, her whole face lighting up as she trotted over to the housecarl, embracing her in a tight hug.

"Good morning, your highness," Branisi said to Collise. "And to your highness," she added with a nod to Collise's mother.

"What do you want?" Deremona snapped.

Branisi moved over to a table and deposited a number of sheets of parchment, arranging them in some order Collise could not begin to fathom.

"There are a few details that need your highness's attention," Branisi said calmly. "Both the Ninsian and Waravalian ambassadors are requesting an audience as is the chairman of the Board of Commerce. I believe they wish to discuss trade agreements and such, shall I show them in?"

Collise's face fell at the thought of having to discuss anything with a man. What did she know about trade agreements? They would probably try and bully her and a sick lump grew in her throat at the thought. She looked at her mother who saw her distress and shook her head in disappointment.

"I thought you were supposed to deal with all that," Deremona said, giving Branisi an arch look.

"My duties are such only when the monarch is unavailable," the housecarl said. "Now your daughter has asserted her claim to the throne my duties are to assist your highness's by organizing your schedule."

Collise watched her mother's face as she stared at Branisi. She could see the hate and anger boiling just below the surface but did not really understand why she was so angry.

"Very well, Branisi," Deremona said in a falsely pleasant voice, "then I have the pleasure of delivering some excellent news to you. Collise and I were discussing things just before you arrived and she decided *you* should take care of all these little meetings."

Collise was about to speak when Deremona stared at her with wide eyes, silencing her daughter. Collise turned back to the window and stared out over Morantine as her mother carried on.

"Collise and I have full confidence in your abilities and we are both sure you can secure the most profitable deal for us." Deremona gave Branisi a nasty smile. "After all, we would hate to have to find another housecarl. That is all," she added dismissively.

Branisi smiled sweetly and bowed once more before leaving the room. Collise stroked the side of her own face as she stared out of the window, curling a lock of hair around her finger and pulling it hard.

"Stop that!" Deremona snapped. "I have only just managed to get those servant girls to make your hair look normal and I will not have you ruining your look by pulling your hair out."

"Why are you so angry, mama?" Collise asked, letting her hand fall.

"Don't mistake determination for anger, Collise," Deremona said. "Everything I do is for your benefit, remember that."

"I don't see how spending money on dresses and jewels benefits me," Collise murmured.

Her head snapped sideways with the slap her mother delivered, making her cheek sting and eyes water.

"Ungrateful little..." Deremona growled. "Do you think people will take me seriously if I was dressed in rags?"

"No mama!" Collise begged as her mother slapped her head and face.

The young woman brought her hands up in a vain attempt to ward off the blows her mother was raining down on her but several of them still landed.

"Want me poor and starving do you?" Deremona screeched. "After all I have done for you..."

"Stop, mama! Please. I am sorry," Collise begged.

Eventually, spent and panting, Deremona stepped back from her daughter.

"Never question me again," she growled. "Never, you hear?"

Collise nodded mutely, wiping tears from her cheeks as her mother turned and left her alone in the room. She sniffed and thought about her mother, how she managed to alienate everyone and turn them against Collise.

She makes them hate me. She is the problem.

***

Branisi strode along the corridor that ran the length of the royal household. Guards snapped to attention as soon as they saw the look of thunder on her face, the clenched jaw and balled fists. Servants dodged out of her path as she made her way down the rear staircase to enter the kitchens.

Aromatic steam wafted out the door as soon as she opened it and Branisi felt her chest loosen a little when she entered the familiar surrounds. The scent of warm bread made her mouth water and the pig that was slowly roasting on a spit over the apple-wood fire looked as if it was just about ready. Sprigs of herbs and other ingredients hung from racks and sat on shelves while a cook toiled to make some pastries on the massive table that dominated the room.

Branisi grabbed a stool and leaned an elbow on the table, watching the woman fold and mix, roll out the pastry and add a little filling to the delicate shapes she cut from it. After a few minutes she stared at Branisi, wiping her hands on a cloth.

"Something wrong?" Nashal asked

Branisi gaped at Nashal as if she had lost her mind.

"Is there something wrong?" Branisi asked sarcastically. "Yes, I think I can categorically say there is something wrong," she ran her hands through her hair. "Have you ever poisoned anyone?" Branisi asked.

Nashal's eyebrows shot up and she leaned one fist on her hip.

"Are you saying my cooking is not up to standard?" She asked.

"No," Branisi said with a chuckle. "I meant on purpose. I wouldn't be too upset if Deremona accidentally died horribly."

"Well I nurture and feed, not poison and kill so you will just have to look elsewhere for someone to off her," Nashal said as she slid the trays of pastries into a brick oven and slapped the door shut. "She cannot be all that bad, can she?"

"The woman is a harridan," Branisi said, "and spending money as if there is an infinite supply," She sighed. "It's not that I don't sympathize with her situation. I saw Tiernon's breeding pits when King Besmir discovered them and she hasn't had much of a life since we got them all out but..." Branisi trailed off.

"What?"

"It's not our fault," she said. "King Besmir has done his utmost to care for those women Tiernon used. He housed them, fed them and provided clothing, yet where is the gratitude? Where are the thanks? There are none. Rather she seeks to usurp the throne from Besmir and take as much as she can in the process." Branisi shook her head.

Nashal reached out and took one of her hands, kneading her flesh gently.

"Surely it's Collise that would take the throne?"

"She is the heir," Branisi said, "yet her mother controls her. Collise fears Deremona and will do anything to avoid her anger, but she's the one who can wield magic," the housecarl sighed again. "It's a shame, without her mother Collise is a pleasant young woman, if a little naive."

"I'm sure King Besmir will sort everything when he comes back," Nashal said confidently.

"If he has anything to come back to," Branisi muttered. "So, no poison then?" She asked again.

"No. No poison."

Chapter Fourteen

Hell was little different Besmir discovered. The scouring, acid wind that blew almost constantly was still there. The gray ash that covered the ground like a million tiny knives ready to pierce anything that touched it was still there.

It was Besmir who was different.

When he had been here before, his body had remained in Gazluth and it had been his immortal spirit that had been sent here. Creatures called Ghoma had feasted upon him while the acid had burned his lungs from inside his chest. Yet his spirit had repaired itself despite the agony he felt.

Now, however, Besmir's *body* was here as well and the effects of this world were leaving a more permanent mark on him. His hands and face were raw, scoured down by the incessant wind even though he had tried to cover them with cloth cut from his clothes. The back of his throat was sore from breathing the toxic atmosphere and he started to cough up blood as he tramped across the almost endless plain.

That had been another difference he noticed. The spirit of his father had been sent here to guard the portal to the world of the living and had taught him how he could use his will to fly from one area to another. In his physical body, Besmir was unable to do the same. Directionless and lost he carried on, hoping he was not walking in a circle and waiting for something to appear in the bleak landscape.

"Father!" He called, the wind stealing his voice.

Besmir recalled some of the creatures that existed here and decided against calling again. Concentrating on putting one foot in front of the other he constructed a picture of his son in his mind. A symbol of why he was here and Besmir lost himself in the image as he plodded through Hell.

It took awhile for him to realize something was different, yet when he looked up the wind had died down and a lone figure stood before him. Horns rose from its head and his heart leaped.

"Father?"

"In a manner of speaking I suppose I am," Cathantor said.

Now closer Besmir was able to see the varying forms that the God chose to display himself. Numerous animals blended together to produce the thing that stood before him, clothed in living fur and various skins.

"Are you here to stop me?" Besmir asked in a cracked voice.

"Here's the thing," Cathantor said. "Even I have rules I must follow. When we created man we gave you all free will so you could choose your own destinies, shape your own fates. That also means I can't force you to do anything or not to do something. You see?"

Besmir stared at the God of the Afterlife, his cracked, dry lips starting to bleed as he fought to form the words that wanted to escape.

"Don't get me wrong," Cathantor continued. "I can make things difficult for you. Put obstacles in your path and try to steer you wrong. I just can't understand what Mwondi was thinking when he brought you here, this is the last place I would ever want you to be."

"He thinks I'm going to die," Besmir croaked. "He thinks Porantillia's going to kill me."

"Oh, she'll kill us all," Cathantor said in an almost conversational tone. "We barely managed to contain her last time and we lost one of our own in the process. No, I'm afraid if you let her out of her eternal prison we're all done for."

Besmir's jaw dropped at that news.

A God died when they went against her?

Cathantor nodded, reading Besmir's thoughts as if he had spoken them aloud.

"So you see if you do let her out, Joranas is dead any way. As are you along with anyone you care for and myself of course."

"But why?" Besmir asked like a child asking a parent something. "Why does she want us all dead?"

"We remind her of the great betrayal," Cathantor said. "She hates me as I represent the offspring that should have been hers and she hates you because you are our creations."

Besmir shook his head.

"I don't understand," he said.

"At the dawn of time there was Porantillia and her lover Gratallach. They cavorted among the stars playing like children, finding joy in discovery and in each other," Cathantor said. "Eventually, however, Gratallach created another, a third being, Coranstansia. Her beauty was so great it transcended all else and Gratallach was smitten. He followed Coranstansia through the heavens and across vast worlds spurning Porantillia utterly."

Besmir realized as the God spoke that, if this were all true, Cathantor was speaking about his parents. Besmir swallowed, his dry mouth working as he listened to the story Cathantor laid out before him.

"Twisted by hate, rejection and loneliness Porantillia plotted her revenge. She came against Coranstansia again and again but each time Gratallach aided his new love and together they thwarted Porantillia's plans. You'll be surprised to find she wasn't the happiest when Sharise, Mwondi and I were born along with Deurine."

"Deurine?" Besmir asked, shivering as a sudden chill hit him.

Cathantor nodded, his antlers swaying dangerously.

"My sister was...lost when we bound Porantillia in the absence," he said sadly. "When Porantillia discovered our birth, she left and we believed she had exiled herself. Childish really," the God added with a self deprecating smirk. "Instead she was changing. Becoming a malevolent force with such infinite patience she waited until we had all but forgotten about her. Then she attacked." Cathantor fixed Besmir with a pain filled look. "You mortals might fear death, might balk against it but it is part of your existence, something you must finally accept. We are supposed to be eternal, so our own death is inconceivable and not an easy thing to bring about but Porantillia managed it."

Besmir looked at Cathantor, a living God that he had been taught to revere, and saw he was as flawed as any human. He, Sharise and Mwondi might be powerful and immortal but they were just as fallible as people, Besmir realized. His lip peeled back in a sneer and a rush of anger flooded his chest.

"You're like children!" Besmir accused. "Powerful yes, but like children all the same..." his eyes widened as realization hit him. "And we're your toys!" He gasped. "We have lives and loves, suffer losses and pain...all for your *entertainment?*"

"Speak not to me in such a fashion, mortal!" Cathantor bellowed in a completely different voice.

Flames dripped from his mouth as if he were chewing lit tar and Besmir fell back, grazing and cutting his hands as soon as they touched the ashen surface of Hell. He cowered, hiding his face from the rage Cathantor had just exploded into, yet when the God spoke again his tone was pleasant and conversational once more.

"Porantillia came against Gratallach, hammering at him with dark powers that stunned him enough for her to seal him in the heart of a sun to burn forever." Cathantor swallowed hard, his deer like neck working. "We cannot free my father," he said. "His screams haunt my days and nights endlessly. With Gratallach sealed in a star, Porantillia turned her attention to Coranstansia who had never been her match."

Besmir saw a single tear glimmer in Cathantor's animal eye, rolling down his furry cheek as the memories of his mother came back.

"The battle was immense," Cathantor said quietly. "My siblings and I could only watch, as if we were to have added our own powers the universe would have died. Coranstansia...mother tried in vain to fend her off but Porantillia's wrath was so incredible, so immense she didn't stand a chance. Eventually Porantillia drove mother into the heart of a planet, the energy she used so great the world exploded and Coranstansia was no more," Cathantor trailed off, staring at the blank horizon as if he could see his mother there.

Besmir got slowly to his feet, tired and aching, wearied by a thousand cuts and sighed. Something nagged at his mind, some deeply buried idea that would not leave him alone. Yet the more he concentrated, the more elusive it became.

"The rest of us went into hiding," Cathantor continued, "but Porantillia attacked our creations. Any world we had seeded with life she murdered, taking no prisoners. It was Mwondi who came up with the idea of the absence," Cathantor explained. "A prison fashioned from the very grief she had caused."

A bitter smile split Cathantor's deer head at the recollection and he spread his arms wide.

"We followed her to the last place any of our creations lived. Your world, Besmir. In the middle of a rain of fire we confronted her, binding her in the absence created from our pain and sorrow. Mwondi ripped his chest open first, followed by Sharise and then me. Deurine was the youngest," Cathantor said fondly. "She felt the loss so much more, so deeply that when she tore the despair from her chest there was nothing left of her to carry on and she faded from existence." Cathantor laid a gentle hand on Besmir's shoulder, his touch reassuring and kind. "So you see I do understand what it's like to lose one you love," the God continued, "but I can't let you get to her. I'm sorry," he said.

Besmir frowned. Why would a God be sorry? The idea that had been nagging at him surfaced then, alarm bells screaming inside his head.

"Why are you telling me all this?" He demanded.

Cathantor's face twisted into a horrible parody of itself and he shook his head, antlers waving almost sadly.

"Do you remember how time passes faster here than on your world?"

Besmir recalled his time here, years ago, when he and his father had spent what felt like a century together yet only a few weeks had passed in Gazluth. He nodded, his neck aching.

"I truly am sorry," Cathantor said again. "You can be with your mother in the afterlife," he added in a quiet voice.

Besmir looked down at his hands as they had begun to ache. His skin sagged from his bones as if he had aged a hundred years in a few minutes and horrified fright grabbed his chest. A fluttering sensation in his chest signaled his heart was about to fail and Besmir drew in a deep breath, cursing Cathantor with his dwindling breath.

He was keeping me here. All the time, keeping me from getting to Porantillia so I'd die of old age in Hell.

Besmir watched as Cathantor faded from sight, his form becoming indistinct before vanishing utterly. The wind returned to rasp across his now ancient skin with Cathantor's departure and pain ripped at every joint and tendon as he grew older by the minute. Besmir fell painfully to his hands and knees, the diamond sharp ash shredding his hands even more.

Desperately Besmir reached his weak arm out in a silent plea to anyone to help him. With his energy spent, however, he could not even keep his arm raised and it fell to the ash once more.

***

Joranas had given Whint a wide berth since he had come to the realization the man was not human. Whint did not seem to mind. Or even notice, Joranas thought. The young prince's skin had turned a golden brown in the almost endless sun, his body gradually changing and adapting to this harsh environment.

He had also started to look after himself a little more. Initially dependent on Whint for all his food and water, Joranas had followed the dark-skinned man as he foraged and hunted learning the best places to find food and water. Whatever race had built this city had included large stone tanks that filled during the rare downpours and stored the water in shaded places where it remained cool. Whint had an almost innate ability to find these cisterns and get fresh water for them.

The same people who had designed the water systems had also included an irrigation system that dripped water to fruit trees in a few gardens in the city. Now overgrown and wild with self seeded offspring the gardens were unruly places but could provide a morsel or two of fruit for the odd pair. Whint had shown Joranas the trees one afternoon, pointing to the apples that grew high in the branches.

"Food," he had said.

"Yes they look like really juicy apples," Joranas had said.

"Juicy apples," Whint repeated. "Climb up," he had pointed.

Joranas had been surprised, that had been the first time the dark-skinned man had asked anything of him, Previously he had been content to carry out any and all tasks relating to feeding and watering them both from hunting and getting water to cooking and finding firewood. That had marked a change in their relationship, as if Whint understood Joranas had some kind of power inside him and was not quite as fragile as he had first believed.

Joranas had scaled the trees easily, finding hand and foot holds among the tangled branches, then picked the fruit and tossed it to a waiting Whint who stalked off as soon as he had caught the last apple.

"Hey!" Joranas had called. "Wait for me!"

"Wait for me!" Whint had called back as he carried on walking.

Joranas had tried on a few occasions to ask Whint why they were in the city, who had brought them there and if they were ever likely to leave. His answers had been the same frustrating echoing of Joranas' words that he had been giving since they had met leaving Joranas with little option but to grin and bear it.

"I want to go home," he said once he had climbed for the apples.

"Where is home?" Whint asked in a surprising turn of events.

"Gazluth," Joranas said. "A city called Morantine."

"Morantine," Whint repeated.

"So can we go?" Joranas asked hopefully.

Whint stared at him with a blank expression for a long time before turning away and shaking his head.

"Can we go?" The dark-skinned man echoed.

Rage and despair flooded Joranas then. Whint was the problem. Whint was keeping him here against his will. It was Whint, Joranas wanted to hurt. The hot pressure in his chest flowed down his arms, filling his fingers with a tingling weight her had come to recognize.

Fire.

Tears rolled down his cheeks as he fought to contain the heat that threatened to explode from him. Part of him didn't really want to hurt Whint while another part didn't believe he *could* hurt him.

"Water," Whint said as he pointed at the tears flooding Joranas's cheeks.

"They're called tears, Whint," Joranas explained. "I get them when I'm sad or hurt."

"Are you hurt?" Whint asked, his kind eyes glued to Joranas.

"In here," Joranas said, pointing to his chest.

"In here," Whint repeated his words and action, sadly. "Why?"

"I miss my family," Joranas sobbed.

"I miss my family," Whint echoed.

"You don't have one!" Joranas shouted.. "Not one you remember any way. So how can you miss them?"

"How can you miss them?" Whint said.

"Stop copying everything I say!" Joranas yelled, his face reddening with the force of his screams.

Whint looked about to say something but clamped his mouth shut and stared at the horizon.

"I'm leaving," Joranas said. "Don't try and stop me or I'll burn you."

"You cannot leave," Whint said. "I have to keep you safe here."

"Why?" Joranas demanded. "Who told you to?"

"I don't know," Whint said. "But you aren't allowed to leave."

"You're going to have to kill me then," Joranas declared.

Whint's face fell and he looked as if he were about to cry himself but he stood and approached Joranas.

"It hurts in here?" he pointed to his chest.

Joranas nodded, more tears flowing down his face. Whint reached out a gentle finger and caught one, bringing it up to his face for inspection.

"Tears," he said. "You should go home," he eventually added after watching Joranas' tear evaporate.

"Really?" Joranas asked expectantly.

"Really?" Whint echoed before falling to the floor and convulsing.

Collise was sure everyone hated her now. Even Branisi avoided her as much as she could and it was all because of her mother. Deremona had alienated and belittled any and everyone she could since they had come here and Collise had had enough of her. It had been bad enough when they had been living in the poor house but at least Collise had been able to get away, to run and hide and play without her mother. In fact, Deremona had seemed more than happy her daughter was gone, until it turned out she had some power.

Now Deremona wouldn't let Collise out of her sight. She spoke for her, chose her outfits and kept her virtually isolated from the rest of the world like she was some kind of pet.

I might be simple but I am not *stupid. She only keeps me here because I can burn things.*

Collise sat in a chair in the only room she ever saw apart from her bedchamber and while it was comfortable, it still felt like a prison. She had books and embroidery, games and all manner of things to pass the time but all Collise wanted was a friend.

The door opened and Deremona walked in, wrinkling her nose as soon as she entered.

"Order a bath, Collise," she said. "There is an air about the room."

This was yet another change Collise had noticed in her mother. In addition to keeping Collise separate from just about everyone else, she had begun to speak differently as well. Gone was the common language she had used for as long as Collise could recall, to be replaced with terms, phrases and manners of speech she thought sounded more royal. Collise thought they made her mother sound ridiculous.

"Can I go out if I have a bath?" Collise asked. "King Besmir and Queen Arteera used to go out and see their people so why can I not?"

Her mother moaned, rolling her eyes and throwing her arms out.

"We have been through this, my dear," she said as if speaking to a toddler. "The populace will see you as a usurper, someone come to take the throne from their precious Besmir. Nobody will want you to go out in the streets. Why they might even throw things at you and you wouldn't want that, would you?"

"No, mama," Collise said. "But I'm so lonely in here on my own, all I want is to have a friend."

"And we've been through that as well," Deremona said, losing patience with her daughter. "Anyone who comes in here is going to try and use you to get what they want. They will not want to be your friend but try and get as much gold out of you as they can. That's why you sit in here alone," she added. "Besides which, you have me," she said lightly. "So how alone can you be?"

Collise folded her arms, sitting back in her chair and pouting her bottom lip.

"Branisi could come and keep me company," Collise said in a childish voice. "She wouldn't try and get things from me."

"Branisi could come and keep me company," her mother echoed in a mocking voice. "Branisi this and Branisi that." Her expression changed, lips peeling back from her teeth in a snarl of anger. "Branisi is the worst of them all!" Deremona yelled throwing her hands up. "She wants rid of *me* so she can control you."

Collise frowned, wondering if what her mother said was true. Branisi had never shown any malice towards either of them. In fact, the housecarl had been like a friend to Collise until her mother appeared and shooed her away. The more Collise thought about things, the more she realized it was Deremona who was the problem and she was not going to stand for it any longer.

"I don't think that's right, mama," Collise said in a trembling voice. "Branisi is nice, she would never try and get between us."

Deremona stared at Collise with an expression that showed she could not believe it was her daughter speaking.

"I beg your pardon?" Deremona said in a deceptively calm voice.

"Branisi is nice," Collise repeated. "It's you who keeps everyone away from me. You who wants gold and riches from me." Collise wanted to stop saying things but could not. "I have heard them speaking in whispers about you," she said. "About how you think Tiernon chose you, how you were special but that's a lie. He forced himself on you and you hated me because I was born." Collise had both fists balled at her sides and her chin thrust out at her mother like a battering ram.

"Idiot girl!" Deremona screamed, launching herself at Collise. "You know nothing of the ways of the world. That's why you need me to tell you what to do. What to think."

Her mother punctuated every sentence with slaps and punches as Collise cowered, covering her head and face to ward off the blows. Tears rolled down her bright red cheeks and the pain of humiliation tugged at her chest as she cringed in the corner.

No!

The flash of rage pulsed along her arms, exploding from her hands and engulfing her mother in a ball of flame. Her piercing screech split the air, grating over Collise's ears which, for some reason, angered Collise further. She stood, pointing her hands at her mother, flames belching forth to wrap around Deremona's writhing body as she thrashed and yowled in agony.

"You leave me alone!" Collise shouted as she burned her mother alive. "Stop hitting me! Stop calling me names!"

Collise burned her mother until she stopped moving and the mewling sounds ceased. Realization hit her then and her body started to shake, knees weakening as she looked at the charred husk of flesh that had been her mother. A wail of utter pain resounded around the room as soon as the impact of what she had done hit her.

"Mama!" She begged. "Mama, I'm sorry. Please be alive. Don't be dead. Please. Please."

Hands gripped her shoulders gently, lifting her from the pile of cooked and burned meat that had been her mother just a few short minutes before. The blurred face of Branisi hovered before her and Collise tried to speak, to tell her what had happened but she could not force words from her tight throat.

"Calm now," Branisi said. "Calm down and tell me what happened."

In broken and jerking sentences, Collise managed to convey the essence of what had happened to the housecarl who listened as the girl laid it all before her. Collise listened as Branisi gave orders for her mother's remains to be taken from the room along with the charred rug she had died on.

"I'm a murderer," Collise said absently.

"No," Branisi explained. "This was self defense." She gestured to the charred husk. "Your mother was hitting you as we all know she had done before and all you did was stop her."

The housecarl's voice was persuasive and Collise started to let herself believe Branisi's words. An ache still grew in her chest but it was the pain of loss rather than the tug of guilt.

"Yes," she said. "All I did was stop her."

Chapter Fifteen

White foam bubbled from the corners of Whint's mouth as his head thrummed and heels kicked against the ground. Joranas held his fingers to his mouth, eyes wide in shock and indecision as he watched the only other person for miles dying before him.

"Whint!" He cried. "Whint what can I do?"

Unable to reply Whint carried on convulsing on the ground, his skull making an awful, hollow sound as it cracked repeatedly on the floor. Joranas' body unlocked itself and he dropped to the floor, cradling the dark-skinned man's head on his knees.

"I'm here," he said. "I'm not going anywhere."

As soon as the words left his lips Whint's fit began to subside and a horrible suspicion crawled through Joranas.

Whoever is controlling him will kill him if I try and go.

Whint's breathing slowed and the tremors that ravaged his body ceased completely as Joranas watched, leaving the odd man in a calm state of sleep. After only a few minutes Whint opened his eyes, squinting against the sun to look up at Joranas, a wide smile crossing his face.

"Still here," he said, sitting up.

"Still here," Joranas repeated.

Both laughed when Joranas repeated the phrase as it was normally Whint that echoed anything he heard.

Joranas stood, wondering why he was so concerned about Whint's fate. He barely knew the man and although Whint had been nothing but kind to him, he did not feel he owed Whint anything. So why had he been so terrified when Whint lay dying at his feet? Joranas was at a loss to understand any of the strange feelings that coursed through him, at one point he felt about to cry at the loneliness and loss he felt. The next a burning anger might overtake him making him want to lash out and destroy things.

He's your friend.

Joranas looked at the departing back of the man who had almost just died and realized his thought had been right. Whatever force was controlling Whint, whatever odd thing he might be, he was Joranas' friend. The only one he had at the moment.

"Whint, wait!" Joranas called as he trotted after the strange man.

"Wait!" Whint repeated, his voice carried off by the wind.

Joranas smiled, wondering what life would be like if Whint was no longer there to repeat his words.

***

A thousand knives cut into Besmir's chest and belly. The searing pain brought his consciousness back from the brink of death and he looked up to where something was dragging him through the sharp ash of Hell. A moan escaped his lips and the thing paused for a second before continuing to pull him through the gray ash.

Besmir looked to where the thing that dragged him had hold of his arm. Its fingers dug into his flesh but there was no pain even though it looked as if the thing had snapped the bones in his wrist. From there, his gaze moved up, following the line of its arm, until he saw a shoulder, neck, and head. Wisps of fine hair sprouted from its translucent scalp and Besmir could make out a few strips of substance that might have been cloth or flesh wrapped about the thing's form.

His consciousness fled for a time, delving into the depths of blackness in which he could still feel the pain of being dragged across the gray ash. Eventually the quality of the pain changed and he understood he had stopped moving. With a monumental effort of will, Besmir forced his eyes open.

The gray ash of Hell still cradled his form but, just before him, the surface curved and disappeared into a cold blackness that he had only encountered once before. Whatever had been dragging him had brought him to the edge of the absence, right to Porantillia's doorstep.

Wearily Besmir turned his ancient head, the muscles barely able to support his head as he sought to discover who or what had brought him here. A shock of complete horror jerked through him when he saw the insanely grinning face that lay beside him.

Tiernon's spirit had been ravaged beyond anything Besmir could have believed. Even so it was obviously his uncle that lay there. Besmir's mind whirled when he realized he had doomed Tiernon to this plane a decade before. With the increased passage of time here, Tiernon must have spent centuries being tortured by the things that inhabited this world. Besmir shuddered. No wonder Tiernon looked as if he was a broken shell of his former self. His heart hardened when he recalled the atrocities Tiernon had carried out, however, the women and children dead by his hand.

No, this is what he deserves.

"I'm here," Besmir said.

The cracked whisper that came from his throat was barely loud enough for him to hear and he swallowed, his ancient throat clicking dryly, before trying again.

"Porantillia," he whispered. "I'm here."

No reply came and Besmir felt his body continuing to die. His breaths came ever more slowly and his heartbeat was erratic, pounding one second and almost stopping the next.

Beside him Tiernon's spirit sat up, the fixed rictus of his grin a horrible sight to behold. It looked to Besmir as if Tiernon had enjoyed everything that had happened to him here. As if, rather than a punishment, his sojourn in Hell had been a holiday.

Slack jawed and vacant of expression, however, Tiernon reached out and pushed Besmir, tipping him into the midnight cold of the absence.

***

It consumed him utterly. The absence wormed its way into every part of his psyche and body, sapping his will and energy. Initially depression and despair consumed him pulling his mind down into a spiral of misery from which there was no hope of escape. Besmir's thoughts revolved around every mistake, real or perceived, he had ever made. Any offhand comment he had made to Arteera without thinking or any time he had put something before spending time with Joranas came to the forefront of his mind to be relived and analyzed. Hours, possibly days or years, passed in this state, with Besmir focused entirely on every negative aspect of his existence.

Eventually, drained and weak, Besmir could barely feel anything. There was no pain, no sadness, no joy. No *anything*. The absence had pulled everything from him, leaving him cold and empty.

"Dost thou like my prison?" Porantillia asked.

Her voice was the multitude he had heard in his dream but Besmir could not muster the will to care, let alone answer. A single thought echoed inside his head.

Let me die.

"Thou hast been here the time it takes for a bird's heart to beat and this is the result," Porantillia mocked. "It has been my home for thousands of years. Is it possible for thee to even comprehend the torture I have been forced to endure?"

Besmir drifted through the absolute cold created from the anguish of four Gods, unable to bring himself to care about anything. Joranas did not matter. Arteera did not matter. Nor did Gazluth and its people. Nothing mattered now that he was here.

Besmir floated, unable to muster the will to live and felt his mind slipping away. It did not matter. Once he had ceased to exist, once the absence had drained him completely there would be nothing left at all.

At the point his final thoughts began to fade, Besmir felt something tickle at the base of his skull. His will dribbled back bringing thoughts of his son and wife with it.

What was I thinking?

"Hello!" Besmir called, his words hollow and empty.

"Thou hast no need to shout," Porantillia said from every direction.

"Where's my son?" Besmir demanded.

"Safe," the voices said together.

"What do you want me for?" he asked.

A single pinpoint of light appeared in the distance, growing fast as it approached Besmir. Arms and legs sprouted from the central mass along with a head so, by the time Porantillia reached where Besmir hung in the absence, she was fully formed.

His gaze raked over her form, more beautiful and sensual than any human could possibly hope to be. Long hair draped her perfect skin, inviting his touch by its very existence. Besmir's hands ached as he fought for control, his palms almost needing to touch her body. Utterly naked, nothing was hidden from his gaze and Besmir's entire body responded to Porantillia's sensuality with animalistic desire.

Porantillia chuckled, a deep throaty sound that could drive men insane.

"In truth, I could have chosen anyone to free me," Porantillia said, grazing her naked buttocks over Besmir. "However, thou chose to thwart my deal with Tiernon and I became sore vexed with thee for that."

Besmir clamped his teeth together as Porantillia breathed down his neck, sending tingles shooting down his entire body, the warmth of her breath like a lifeline in this place.

"I have lent thee some of my will to live in this prison lest thou become lost ere we leave."

"I'm not going to set you free," Besmir declared hotly.

Porantillia drew back, clothing shimmering into existence to cover her nudity, and fixed Besmir with a stern look.

"Thou shalt aid in my release or thy son shall die horribly and thou shalt witness it."

"You can't be allowed out," Besmir said vehemently. "You'll kill everyone."

"My thoughts of vengeance have waned over the millennia," Porantillia assured him. "Cathantor and Mwondi may keep their little pets, I no longer seek their destruction, merely release from this prison."

"How is it someone so powerful needs me to escape?"

"When it was that the bastard offspring of Gratallach did seek to imprison me here they also destroyed my celestial host," Porantillia said.

Besmir frowned, not understanding.

"Cathantor along with his merry little brothers and sisters killed my body," she spat, the million voices that issued from her throat all sounding equally angry. "Tiernon was to become my host until thy sword ended him. When it was that I sensed the opportunity to kidnap thy son I realized my plans could come to fruition."

"And you think I'm just going to let you have my body to do as you please?" Besmir asked in a mocking tone. "You don't know me at all."

"I need not know thee, Besmir," Porantillia said triumphantly. "As thy form is mine for the taking!"

Porantillia darted towards Besmir, diving for his chest almost as if she were aiming for a pool of water. Hands clasped prayer-like before her, she shot towards him like an arrow. Besmir struggled in vain to avoid her, but nothing he tried made any difference to the position of his body. Helplessly, he watched as Porantillia dove into his chest, filling his body with her light.

***

It felt to Besmir as if he were a passenger in his own body. He could see and hear, feel the world around him but had absolutely no control whatsoever. Worse, he could recall her memories, thousands of centuries of memories that cut into him. He could feel the hollow hate when Gratallach took another.

Why am I not good enough? What does she have I do not?

He had flown into a jealous rage when they had borne offspring.

Mine. They should have been mine!

Besmir thrilled in the satisfaction as he slammed into Gratallach, smashing at him with raw, hate-fueled power. Gratallach bellowed in raw agony as Besmir carried on his attack, shoving his immense body towards a star. Gratallach screamed as the heat seared his immortal body, burning and irradiating him at the same time as the intense pressure ground at him.

Besmir floated in the star's corona, listening to his former lover screaming his agony. He knew these were Porantillia's memories but was living them as if they were his own. With Gratallach imprisoned in a flaming Hell, Besmir turned his attention to Coranstansia.

Gratallach's lover cowered on a planet she had brought to life. Blue and red trees filled the valley she was in but Besmir located her with ease. He dropped into the atmosphere, barely feeling the burn as he flew down to the surface of the planet. He saw the army she had gathered, pathetic and weak creatures Besmir smashed into pulp with a thought. Coranstansia lit the sky with burning power aimed at Besmir but he sneered as he batted it aside. This would be no battle of powers, he would rip her to shreds with his hands.

He drew near, ignorant of the screams coming from the simple creatures Coranstansia had surrounded herself with and grabbed her body, launching them both out into space.

"What hast thou done with Gratallach?" Coranstansia begged. "Does he live still?"

"He lives," Besmir said darkly. "If thee were any more than a child thee would be aware I cannot end Gratallach. Thee, however...thee is a different matter."

Besmir swept around one of the planet's moons, shoving Coranstansia before him and using the moon's gravity to speed up. He aimed at the planet he had drawn Coranstansia from and streaked towards it at incredible speed.

"I shall end thy children," Besmir told the other Goddess as he released her.

He watched as Coranstansia slipped into the atmosphere, her immense form punching through the gases and burning incandescently. He had achieved such a velocity that

Coranstansia smashed through the crust and deep into the molten core. Unable to remain together the planet cracked like an egg, magma exploding over the surface as it exploded. Coranstansia, along with the lives she had created, perished in a shower of burning rock. What remained of her body mingled with the cooling parts of the planet as it slowly drifted into a new orbit around the nearby star.

Thousands of other memories flooded Besmir as he fought to control his own body, the deaths of entire worlds at his hands simply because the beings that resided there had been created by Sharise or Mwondi.

His mind shied away from trying to recall when they had trapped him in the absence, that hated eternal prison of despair where he had spent millennia, his will slowly being drained.

He watched as Mwondi led his brothers and sisters to attack her body, shredding the very fibers of her being and scattering it across the universe to be lost forever.

"Thou hast been cast into the absence to serve out thy days where thou cannot destroy us or our creations," Mwondi had said.

Besmir recalled screaming then, screaming for thousands of years before plotting his escape, plotting his revenge.

All these memories came to him as soon as Porantillia took him over and Besmir had to assume she was able to recall his life too, wondering if she was as affected by the loss of Joranas as he had felt when it had happened.

Besmir watched as he approached a lighter area and realized this was the entrance to Hell, the border where the absence began. The pathetic remains of Tiernon's soul, shredded and battered, still lay before the entrance and a flash of hate flicked through him when he saw it.

Porantillia raised Besmir's right hand and grabbed Tiernon's soul, flinging it into the absence as they passed. Both felt satisfaction as he disappeared into the blackness to be drained of what little energy he had left.

Besmir watched as Porantillia walked his body through Hell. Her incredible life force maintained his form easily despite the acidic winds and needle sharp ashes that threatened to shred his skin. Like a passenger in his own body Besmir could only watch as Porantillia crossed the apparently endless gray landscape of Hell towards a destination only she knew.

When he began to recognize a few of the features his eyes picked up Besmir started to thrash inside his mind. The alternating stripes of gray, the pond fed by a stream that began in midair and the tree he saw were all features his father had crafted through the power of his will.

No! Porantillia leave him alone.

Porantillia gave no sign she even heard Besmir's shout, however, and approached the house as if she belonged there.

"Besmir?" Joranas senior demanded in shock. "By the Gods, son, what are you doing here?"

Besmir's father had changed even further since he had seen him last. The horns that swept back from his skull had grown longer and begun to twist, spiraling away from his head like a parody of hair. The heavy scales that covered his body had thickened to the point it looked as if he was having difficulty in moving, his limbs limited in their range of motion until he was forced to shuffle along.

"Don't worry, father," Besmir heard himself say. "I got trapped here but now I need to get back. My son needs me."

The real Besmir felt a flash of hate for Porantillia when he heard her use the son she had kidnapped and put at risk as an excuse.

"Wait," Joranas senior said. "How did you get trapped *here*?"

"It's a long story, father, I really have to get back to Gazluth."

"There's something you need to know first," Joranas senior said. "Some*thing* came through here not long ago. I think *she* sent it. It knew about the portal and it was...tough." His father's voice was muffled by the heavy scaling around his mouth. "I tried to fight it but it was far too strong," he added. "I thought you ought to know."

"Thank you father," Porantillia said with Besmir's voice. "I should not worry about him. I really do need to return now."

Joranas senior raised his head in acknowledgment but made no move to assist his son.

"Father?" Besmir heard Porantillia ask with his voice.

The real Besmir smiled inside his own mind at the knowledge his father knew something was amiss.

"It has been a long time since you rested here with me," Joranas senior stated calmly. "Can you not stay for even a brief conversation?"

"No, father," Porantillia said with an edge of exasperation. "I have to get back to try and find my son."

"Of course," Joranas said. "It is a shame we cannot catch up. Still, I wish you the best on your return." The large, demonic spirit spread his scaled hands to the empty garden he had fashioned with his thoughts.

"What are we doing out here?" Porantillia asked.

"Waiting," Joranas said calmly.

"For what?"

"For you to tell me who you really are and where my son is."

Porantillia laughed through Besmir's throat before cocking his hip in a feminine way and tilting his head.

"The portal," she demanded. "Now!"

Joranas senior lashed out at Besmir, his taloned hand a blur of speed as he aimed for his son's eyes. Porantillia, however, anticipated the attack and Besmir watched as his father's hand exploded from a barrier she conjured. Joranas stumbled back, clutching his hand as it healed instantly.

"Open the portal," Porantillia said as she used Besmir's hand to grip Joranas' throat.

Besmir watched helplessly as his fingers clamped around his father's throat, digging in hard. While it was true his father's spirit could not be choked, the pain and panic he felt was just as real.

Besmir thrashed and screamed inside his own mind, completely unable to affect Porantillia in any way. Her triumph rang in his mind as she squeezed Joranas' throat, shaking him as a dog would with a rope. His father rained fruitless blows against him but Porantillia's barrier reflected his attacks, both physical and magical. Lightning flowed from Joranas' hands dripping from the shield Porantillia had erected in the same way his fire had.

Unable to stop her from torturing his father Besmir searched through her memories for something that might halt her. Looking back through her long history Besmir found the memory of a face, a being she had loved and a single word came to him.

Gratallach.

Besmir latched onto the image, strengthening it in his own mind and lashing it at the part of him that was now Porantillia. Hate filled sorrow flooded his mind then as she recalled what she had done to her former love. The searing heat that swallowed him when she sealed him inside a star had ripped at her too but it had been his screams of agony that hurt her more.

Porantillia jerked away from the memories, releasing Joranas reflexively and Besmir watched his father flinch back, falling to the ashen surface of Hell.

"No!" Porantillia shouted. "Stay thee from my thoughts!"

"Then give me back my body!" Besmir shouted inside his own mind.

From the floor, Besmir's father sent a wave of boiling heat flashing at them. Distracted by Besmir's use of her memories, Porantillia did not manage to protect herself from the initial blast and searing agony burned her face.

Besmir recoiled in agony as well, feeling the jet of flame cooking his skin.

Father, no!

Yet he knew his father was unaware he was trapped within his own body as he intensified the gout of flame that erupted from his clawed hands. Porantillia managed to construct a barrier, protecting Besmir's skin and allowing her to heal them both. Besmir felt blessed coolness wash over his face, a relief from the savage sting his father's burns had caused.

Porantillia lashed out with Besmir's arm. Strengthened by her incredible powers he could only watch as his own fist hammered through his father's soul. Joranas bellowed an inhuman sound that crashed against Besmir's ears and clutched at the arm that Porantillia was using to rummage around inside him with. She jerked Besmir's hand free of his father but dragged a length of something from inside him, vital parts that should never have seen the light of day.

Joranas fell back to his knees from where Porantillia had lifted him, some of his wound already beginning to heal, but she had further plans and Besmir screamed inside his own head when Porantillia wrenched his father's head sideways, twisting and pulling with incredible force. Porantilia ripped the head from Besmir's father's spirit with a sickening popping sound, ending his existence in Hell.

Still holding the horned head of Joranas senior in one hand, Porantillia casually approached the house he had built here and waited for it to fall back to the dust from which he had created it. Now she had destroyed his soul, Joranas senior's power no longer supported the house he had crafted to hide the portal back to Besmir's world.

Besmir felt nausea crawl up his very arm from the contact with his father's head. Porantillia had shown no mercy in dealing with his father and Besmir knew she had none within her. Sorrow gnawed painfully at his chest as he watched the lines and decorations his father had lovingly crafted failing, twisting and returning to the gray surface of the planet.

In just a few minutes, everything Joranas had fashioned was gone. Porantillia discarded the fading head and strode over to the almost black sphere that would take her and Besmir to his world.

He felt a spike of triumph leap from her when she let his body fall forwards and into the darkness between worlds.

Chapter Sixteen

Herofic became aware of a few things at the same time. To begin with he was laying in some kind of bed. Deep nagging aches ran the length of his body combined with a soreness on his skin that felt as if he had been dragged through fire. Without opening his eyes he reached up to feel the skin on his face. His fingers found crusty scabs that had been covered in some buttery substance and he frowned, sniffing at it for identification.

Something soft tickled over his face, gently moving his hand away and Herofic opened his eyes, blinking at the brightness that made the backs of his eyes ache. The room he was in was light and airy, with a cool breeze to take the heat out. Dark green plants had been brought in here and he could smell their foliage. Herofic himself was naked, covered only by a thin sheet, his muscular chest open to the air. To his left a long, thin table sat along one wall with a number of items that Herofic could not identify in pots and jars. His eyes lit on the most readily identifiable item there, however, a jug of water. He reached for it but his weakened body refused to move and he lay back, turning his head a little.

Ru Tarn sat beside his bed, offering a concerned expression as she leaned over to pass him the water. Herofic sucked greedily at the liquid, almost choking in his desperation to drink. The Corbondrasi ambassador took the cup from him for a second.

"Being slowly," she said.

Herofic sipped the cool water as he studied the Corbondrasi woman. She appeared subtly different to when he had last seen her but he could not pinpoint the exact cause. Her plumage and feathers were the same shade of coral pink and peach they had been but somehow it was as if they were more vibrant, a deeper hue and she shone with the oils her body secreted to keep her feathers healthy. The Ru Tarn Herofic had known had been fairly direct and business like, always ready to deal with whatever life threw her way. Now, however, Herofic thought she was distracted by something, her feathered hands were in constant motion, fixing her dress and absently preening her feathers. Her lavender eyes darted about the room, not remaining on one point for long before darting to another place and off again. She could barely bring herself to look at Herofic at all.

"Are you all right?" Herofic managed to whisper hoarsely.

"Ru Tarn should be asking Herofic that," she muttered. "Herofic is being almost killed by sun and heat."

Herofic caught her fleeting expression, her feathered face caught somewhere between disapproval and complete fear, her reaction making him wonder what was really happening.

"Little bit of sun never hurt anyone," Herofic said stubbornly.

Ru Tarn's eyes widened and she fixed Herofic with a stare more intense than he had seen since he had opened his eyes.

"This is being Boranash!" She said in a tone of disapproval. "Sun and heat is being so great it killing even Corbondrasi sometimes," she looked away from his eyes. "Herofic is being lucky he is not dying. Why is Herofic not using creams Ru Tarn giving him?"

Herofic felt a flash of embarrassment then, his face feeling hot as he stumbled for an explanation.

"I...ah, did not use the cream as...well the thing is." Herofic muttered, sipping the water again. "It smelled...like something a woman would wear."

Ru Tarn stared at Herofic, her lavender eyes blinking a few times in complete disbelief. Eventually a small chirp erupted from her chest, a Corbondrasi giggle. Unable to stop herself, Ru Tarn began to laugh uncontrollably. She folded at the waist, her chirps and squeaks turning to silent shakes of her body as her lungs emptied. Herofic chuckled as well, although not quite sure what had been so amusing.

"Oh Herofic is being funny," Ru Tarn eventually managed. "To be thinking Herofic nearly died so he is not smelling like a woman!"

Abruptly her expression changed and Herofic watched as the calm, pleasant Corbondrasi turned into an angry and savage being.

"Herofic is being stupid Gazluth!" She said, her command of the language slipping as her anger grew. "Why is it mattering what Herofic is smelling like? King Besmir was smelling same! Herofic's brother was smelling same! All men from Gazluth be smelling same so why is it mattering what Herofic is smelling like?"

Her outraged stare demanded an answer from him but just as Herofic was about to try and explain himself her expression changed again and the Corbondrasi dissolved into a flood of tears, her shoulders shaking as she sobbed.

"Ru Tarn cannot be doing this," she said in a thick voice. "Ru Tarn cannot be..."

Herofic reached out and gently wiped the tears from her face.

"What is wrong?" He asked gently.

"Ru Tarn is sorry," she finally managed to blurt. "Ru Tarn has something to be telling Herofic," she added. Herofic waited for her to continue. She looked down at her belly and stroked a hand over her abdomen. Herofic understood the gesture immediately and a happiness spread through his chest at her news.

"So you are pregnant?" He asked. "With a baby?"

"Hatchling," Ru Tarn corrected him gently.

"How long until he arrives?" Herofic asked.

"He?" Ru Tarn giggled. "Ru Tarn will be laying egg soon, then Ru Tarn must be caring for egg for around five months then hatching happening."

"Five months!" Herofic cried.

"Gazluthian women are being pregnant for nine months," Ru Tarn said defensively.

"I know," Herofic said, "it just seems such a long time," he added. "So why the tears?"

"I am having problem," she explained. "Laying of egg is being difficult for Corbondrasi and Corbondrasi needing male to help with caring for egg after laying but..."

"But you haven't got anyone to do that for you," Herofic muttered, understanding coming to him. "What about friends or servants?"

Ru Tarn drew back from him aghast, her expression as horrified as if he had asked to eat her impending young with a salad.

"This thing is not done!" She cried, pacing beside his bed. "There are being rules. If Ru Tarn is having this hatchling, Ru Tarn will have to be hiding and still not having male to help caring for egg."

"I'll do it," Herofic said.

The Corbondrasi stared at him as if he had lost his mind. She blinked slowly and then blinked again before smiling at him kindly.

"Sun is being too hot," she said, patting his hand. "Gazluth man is not being able to look after egg."

"An egg?" Herofic asked with a chuffed laugh. "How much trouble can one egg be?"

"Is not being trouble," she said in a halting voice. "Is just not being done..."

"So we'd be the first," Herofic said. "Nothing wrong with that is there?"

"Not being wrong," Ru Tarn said thoughtfully. "Being different so Corbondrasi not liking it."

"Tough," Herofic grunted. "Are we doing this or not?" He watched the Corbondrasi ambassador sit beside his bed and look at the floor as she considered his words. Her smile told him her answer before she even spoke.

"Herofic is being kind man to offer this," she said. "But Ru Tarn is thinking Herofic not knowing what he is getting himself into. Herofic does not need to be doing this."

"I never had children," Herofic said. "There never seemed to be time with all the wars and fighting, slipping from on crisis to the next. I just thought I could be part of a child's life." His tone was somber, surprising even him and Ru Tarn looked at him with sympathetic eyes.

"Ru Tarn not knowing Herofic is feeling like this," she said. "So if this is something Herofic is wanting to do, not feeling he is having to do, then yes."

Herofic felt the smile cross his face, scabs cracking as his skin stretched.

***

Previously, when Besmir had been in Hell, he had been there in spirit so upon his return his immortal being found his mortal body and he was restored. As he had been in Hell physically this time, his body returned to where it had left from and he found himself staring at the Gazluthian embassy in the heart of the Corbondrasi capital.

Porantillia panned Besmir's eyes over the building, marrying what she saw with his memories as she studied the colorful patterns and designs around them. Hardy, arid, desert loving plants had been artfully placed, their thick succulent leaves adding a structural element to the floral display. Dusk had fallen over Wit Shull bringing the chill of the desert night and the Gazluthian guards posted outside stomped their feet, blowing warm air through their fingers, steam rising into the air. One paused, his eyes going wide as he caught sight of his king and within a few heartbeats the alarm had been raised.

"Majesty," another guard breathed, her eyes wide as she approached. "Are you well?"

Porantillia nodded shortly, shoving past her towards the embassy buildings as Besmir struggled, fruitlessly fighting to control his own body.

He watched as Arteera appeared, her face pale in the dim light, lines of worry carved into her forehead and a deep ache throbbed in his chest to see her in such a state.

How long was I gone this time?

Besmir felt the warmth of her body as she threw herself at him, wrapping herself unashamedly around him despite the many eyes that posed unasked questions. Porantillia patted her back awkwardly and Arteera pulled back, staring into Besmir's eyes questioningly.

That's my Arteera. You know something's not right.

Even with her access to his memories, Porantillia was a completely different person to the man the gathered people knew and her behaviors and answers to their questions would reveal her almost immediately, Besmir knew.

"Did you find Joranas?" His wife asked as soon as she had pulled back.

"No," Porantillia said, "there was no sign of him." She did manage to make it sound as if Besmir was breaking inside when she spoke.

The real Besmir could only watch from inside his own body as Arteera folded herself into a chair, curling up and hugging her knees as if it would stop the pain.

"What news of Porantillia?" Zaynorth asked.

"Her," Besmir heard himself say. "She tricked me into releasing her from the absence before she managed to escape."

"Were you able to discover any of her plans?" Zaynorth asked.

"None." Besmir's voice sounded filled with disappointment and his rage grew.

What are you up to, Porantillia? You said I could have my son back!

My plans are incomplete. Thy son remains safe for the nonce,

I won't let you get away with this!

Thou art powerless to halt me.

"What do we do next?" Zaynorth asked, his face a mask of despair. "How do we get Joranas back?"

"I don't know," Besmir's voice said.

From inside his body Besmir watched as his old friend frowned, glancing at Arteera and Norvasil. He tried to keep his knowledge from Porantillia, guarding his thoughts as much as possible.

"Wine," Besmir demanded.

"It's right there." Arteera pointed to a table with goblets and decanter atop.

"Then serve me, woman!" Porantillia snapped in Besmir's voice. "I've just crawled through Hell and refuse to pour my own wine."

"Of course, my lord," Arteera said, her face pale.

She looked at Zaynorth as she approached, picking up the large decanter and pouring wine into a goblet before passing it to Porantillia. She drained the wine noisily and held the goblet out again, shaking it impatiently. Besmir heard the sound as his wife filled the goblet once more but Porantillia pointedly ignored his friends and family, staring at the blank wall as she drank.

Her oversight and self confidence proved to be misplaced when Besmir felt a savage impact across the back of his skull.

The blow was accompanied by a deep 'thwok' sound that echoed through his head as darkness took them both down.

***

How is it thy comrades knew something was amiss? Porantilia demanded.

Leave my body and give me my son back! Besmir said.

Never. She promised.

They won't let you go. Besmir told her. *Zaynorth and Arteera will keep you prisoner until you leave my body!*

Fool! I am eternal, think thou that I cannot merely wait for this vessel to die?

***

The voice was immensely persuasive, worming its gentle way into Porantillia's mind as she woke from the blow that had rendered both her and Besmir unconscious.

"You cannot see," it said, "yet there is no need for concern. You are completely in control and safely hidden."

Porantillia felt assured the voice was correct, especially as it was not the voice of her host. In all her planning and scheming she had not anticipated he would be as strong a presence as he had been. Besmir should have been a silent passenger within his own mind at worst, utterly destroyed and driven insane by her memories at best. Yet it seemed he was able to see into her past, uncover the secrets she had buried and locked away from herself and Porantillia hated Besmir all the more for that ability.

She had been forced to relive the utter humiliation of Gratallach's betrayal time and again as Besmir rifled through her thoughts. Every feeling she had spent centuries burying he had raked up, putting her through the pain and frustration again.

Yet, even as she had access to his pathetic memories, his companions had realized something was amiss and bludgeoned them both over the back of the head.

"All that you need to do to secure release is to speak your name," the voice told her.

Of course, it is as simple as saying my name.

"Porantillia," she said in a deep male voice.

Porantillia heard gasps and cries of alarm as she opened her eyes. Besmir's friend sat before her, stroking his beard as he studied the face before him.

"You have forgotten how to use your power," Zaynorth said calmly.

Porantillia felt the warm wash of certainty roll through her with his words.

That is correct, I have forgotten how to use my powers.

"It would benefit you immensely to remember where Joranas is," Zaynorth said.

Another warm feeling raked over Porantillia and she smiled, looking around at the people in the room. Zaynorth sat before her and there was an immense warrior with a red, braided beard but his name would not come to her. Behind Zaynorth stood a thin woman with light hair. She was pinching her lips in horror, her skin a waxy, pale color as her blue eyes pierced into Porantillia.

"Joranas is in Ludavar," Porantillia found herself saying. "Tended by a demon."

Further gasps issued around her and Porantillia frowned as something tugged at her mind.

This is all wrong.

"You are beginning to feel weary," Zaynorth said.

A flush of exhaustion rolled through Porantillia but she fought it.

No! He is an illusion mage!

"Thy tricks will no longer work on me, mage," Porantillia spat in Besmir's voice. "Release me immediately!"

"Yet, you cannot move," Zaynorth said in the same calm voice he had been using all along.

Porantillia felt her borrowed limbs lock up, her entire body halting as Zaynorth's persuasion invaded her mind.

How is it possible?

Yet no matter how hard she struggled, fought to move, she was unable.

These are merely mortals! How can one be so powerful?

Porantillia considered the issue as she carried on trying to move. Perhaps it was the effect of being inside Besmir's body that allowed this Zaynorth power over her. Certainly there would have been no possibility of one such as he being able to stop her doing anything in her original form. Almost limitless power to create or destroy had been hers to wield, yet at present she was at the mercy of a mortal illusion mage.

Anger rolled through Porantillia then, fueled by the chemicals pulsing through Besmir's blood.

How do males manage to function?

"I am losing her," she heard Zaynorth say as her arm moved. "Her power exceeds mine by an immeasurable amount."

"Correct, mage," Porantillia said. "It would be wise in the extreme to facilitate my freedom."

Porantillia watched as Zaynorth shook his head, his long, iron gray hair waving.

"Yet you do not wish to leave," he said. "Your only need is to restore Besmir."

Zaynorth leaned in close to Porantillia, staring into her borrowed eyes.

No. Resist hi...

There really did not seem to be any reason to go anywhere else and she was so incredibly tired, probably from her time in the absence, that she could sleep while Besmir took control of the body again. It was his after all and once she woke she could just shove him aside and resume control again.

"I do not wish to leave," Porantillia said. "I am feeling sleepy."

"A nice long sleep would refresh you," Zaynorth assured her.

"Hmm..." Porantillia hummed as Besmir's eyes started to close.

As she felt herself slipping into unconsciousness, Porantillia heaved herself from within Besmir.

Chapter Seventeen

"Besmir?" Arteera said softly into his ear. "Is that you my love?"

Something throbbed at the back of his neck. A painful, tight lump that felt as if someone had...

"You hit me," he slurred. "Over the back of the head with a wine decanter."

Arteera sniffed a laugh.

"That hurt," Besmir added, opening his groggy eyes and lifting his head to look at his wife.

His limbs would not move correctly, something rough and tight held his wrists and it took a few seconds to realize he was tied to a chair.

"Safety precautions," he muttered, straining against the ropes. "Wise choice."

"What happened?" Zaynorth asked.

"I had a nice long chat in Hell with our old friend Cathantor," Besmir said. "Apparently the Gods can't actually force us to do anything we don't want. He did try to keep me in Hell long enough to die though. Strangely it was Tiernon and Porantillia that actually saved me."

Zaynorth sat back and tugged at his beard again.

"Tiernon! I do not believe this mad creature is truly Besmir," he said. "Maybe this Porantillia is attempting to deceive us once more."

"No," Arteera said. "That is my husband. The way he speaks, his tones and inflections are completely different to when he first arrived."

"She's gone," Besmir said in a miserable tone.

Nowhere within his mind could Besmir feel or sense any sign of Porantillia's presence. Somehow she had left him, taking her thoughts and memories with her.

"What?" Arteera asked, untying his wrists.

"Porantillia needed a body to leave the absence, the Gods destroyed hers when they sealed her inside," Besmir explained. "She stole mine thinking I would die or go mad but for some reason I didn't. But now I can't feel her at all, can't go through her memories like I could. She's gone."

"Good," Arteera said.

"Not good, love," Besmir said, rubbing his wrists and stretching. "I could hear her thoughts while we shared a body."He looked at each face in turn solemnly. "Despite anything she told me, her sole purpose is vengeance," he added. "Against the Gods and anything they created."

"That would be us," Zaynorth observed.

Besmir nodded and Arteera slumped into a chair.

"I just want Joranas back," she said in a small voice, "and now we know where he is." She looked at Zaynorth gratefully. "Ludavar, wherever that might be."

"I beg your Majesties pardon," the half Corbondrasi ambassador, Founsalla Pira said, "but I believe I have heard of such a place. It is the stuff of legend, folklore and hearsay," he said grimly.

Besmir stared at the strange looking hybrid and held one hand up in question.

"Far to the north of Boranash is an uninhabited land of ruins and desolation, abandoned centuries ago for a reason long forgotten. That is where Ludavar supposedly lies."

"Looks as if we have a trip then," Besmir said.

"The land is cursed, sire," Founsalla said. "Nothing lives there any longer."

"If that's where my son is being kept, that's where I'm headed," Besmir said grimly.

"I shall be going too," Arteera said.

"And I," Zaynorth added.

Besmir watched Founsalla's face change from disbelief to respect as one by one Besmir's companions added their support. It was not until all others had spoken that Besmir searched the large room for Keluse. She did not appear to be anywhere he could see so he asked.

"Has anyone seen Keluse? Where did she go?"

The White Blades made a brief search of the embassy but could not locate Besmir's former apprentice and friend. The king frowned knowing it was unlike her to just disappear without telling anyone where she was going and a nasty suspicion grew in his mind.

"Porantillia," he said grimly. "What if she's taken Keluse over? We need help from King Vi Rhane."

"How do you know?" His wife asked. "Could you tell that was what she was planning before I knocked you out?"

"No, love," Besmir said. "But I can't feel any trace of her inside me anymore and now Keluse has disappeared without a word to anyone. Founsalla, can you get me an audience with the king?"

"Of course, majesty," the Gazluthian ambassador said before leaving.

"I need to clean up a little," Besmir said. "Hell is a dirty place."

***

Besmir stared at his hands as he waited in an antechamber for the Corbondrasi king. It played over and over in his mind, the texture of his father's horns as Porantillia had wrenched his head from his body. The sickening lurch as his spirit had given way, separating into two sections. Worse was the feeling he had of her carrying his father's head, as if she had instantly forgotten it was in her hand, as if his life, his spirit, meant nothing.

"Tell me," Arteera murmured gently as she rubbed his back with a soft hand.

Haltingly, in a pained voice, Besmir told her of Porantillia and what she had done, how he had been powerless to halt her and how he had been able to feel and see everything.

"I don't even know if his spirit could survive such trauma," Besmir said as he stared out over the palace buildings. "When I journeyed there before, my spirit could feel pain but not be harmed..."

"By the Gods!" Arteera said.

Anger pulled a grimace across Besmir face and his hands tightened their grip on the stonework he leaned against.

"The Gods," he spat disdainfully. "This is their doing in the first place. Cathantor made the deal with my father that kept him in Hell, then he tried to hinder my progress so I died of old age there. Do you know what he told me?" Besmir asked, his eyes wide.

Arteera shook her head, a worried expression on her face.

"Cathantor, the *God*, said he hasn't got any power over any of us. None. The Gods can't force us to do anything, they can only guide, suggest or hinder." Besmir's voice took on a mocking tone. "I'm done with them," he carried on. "If we're ever to get Joranas back we're going to have to do it ourselves."

"I think..." Arteera began but the door opened and a Corbondrasi guard ushered them into the throne room.

Besmir led his wife through a room filled with opulence and wealth. Part of him was awed at the gilded metalwork and marble columns supporting the ceiling while another part railed at the waste such luxury must have cost. He knew that somewhere in this kingdom someone could benefit from the gold used as decoration. His eyes wandered over paintings depicting various Corbondrasi he assumed were former members of the royal family, each dressed in swathes of silk embroidered in silver and gold thread. A cream carpet ran the length of the room, leading straight to where the king and queen sat on gilded thrones so intricately carved Besmir could have spent several hours looking at the various scenes depicted there. Royal guards lined the hall on both sides lending an official air to the proceedings and Besmir knew this was not an informal meeting as they had had before.

"Your majesty," Besmir said, bowing to Vi Rhane before turning and offering a bow to his queen.

The Corbondrasi royal couple were dressed in similar silken attire to that which had been depicted in the paintings Besmir had passed. Light material flowed over their colorful plumage, allowing what little air circulating to cool them. A simple crown of beaten gold adorned Vi Rhane's head while his queen sported a diamond encrusted silver tiara.

"Friends," Vi Rhane said. "We have arranged refreshments to be served outside."

The Corbondrasi king offered his arm to his queen and she laid her feathered hand on it, allowing him to lead her onto a raised platform that gave them an almost complete view of the city.

"Your ambassador has advised us as to your plans," Vi Rhane said as servants appeared with trays of sliced fruit and honey. "Ludavar is in an abandoned land, barren and hostile. It was she whose name is forbidden that made it that way centuries ago."

"So when can we leave?" Besmir asked, impatience nagging at the back of his skull.

"It isn't going to be an easy path," Vi Rhane warned them. "The land of Aristulia is hostile and filled with savage creatures. You will only be able to take a small party as water will be difficult to find."

"If you're suggesting we abandon my son to Porantillia..."

Besmir halted as the Corbondrasi king held one hand up, his face showing distress at the use of the forbidden name.

"I am simply warning you of the dangers and hardships you are likely to face," he mumbled. "If our daughter had been taken, I would do anything I could to see her returned. We will provide as much help as we can within Boranash, however once you have crossed into Aristulia we cannot offer much assistance."

Besmir nodded gratefully.

"We are having an ancient map copied," Su Rhane said. "The only known image of the land you wish to enter. As it will take our scribes some time to complete and the day is waning I suggest you take the opportunity to rest today. We will arrange supplies and mounts for you to leave at first light." The queen lowered her eyes for a second before addressing Arteera. "I cannot begin to know what you are feeling at present," she said in a softer voice. "If there's anything I can do, please let me know."

Besmir watched his wife embrace the older Corbondrasi queen, the two sharing a bond he could not and an irrational stab of jealousy lanced into him for a second but he shoved it aside, ashamed.

"I want to give you both my heartfelt thanks," Besmir said, "for everything you've done for us. Under different circumstances..." he trailed off, his throat closing.

"When you recover your son," Su Rhane said, "bring him here, we would love to meet him."

Besmir's heart swelled at her words. Even if she believed they were doomed to failure, the Corbondrasi queen spoke as if they had already recovered Joranas.

***

Collise heard the shouting before the explosive thump and dashed across to see what was happening. She opened the door leading to the hallway and stared out at the scene before her.

Two guards lay sprawled on the carpet, weapons scattered and eyes devoid of all life. Branisi held her arms out in surrender as someone Collise could not see made their way inside her house.

Anger rose in her chest, heating her ribs and threatening to burst out, burning whoever the invader was.

"Who is it? Who is there?" Collise demanded as she approached Branisi.

Peering round her housecarl, Collise laid eyes on a boy of around her own age. His hair had been sheared close to his skull, he had dirty brown skin and his clothing had seen better days, ill fitting with rips and stains. Collise saw the expression on his face, his jaw set and eyes locked onto her as he examined her from head to foot. A ripple of pleasure made her smile and the newcomer smirked back.

"Who are you?" Collise asked.

"Merin," he said in a voice that wavered between boyish soprano and manly baritone. "*King* Merin," he added. "Tiernon was my father. Who are you?"

"Collise. Queen of Gazluth," she said. "Tiernon was my father, too."

Branisi looked from Collise to Merin and back as she lowered her hands and shook her head.

"How many more are going to appear?" She whispered as Collise walked down the stairs.

"You can't be queen," Merin said, "as I am king." He folded his arms and stuck his chin out like a child having a tantrum.

"I'm already queen," Collise said, "so you will have to go away."

"You're the one who will be leaving." Merin said raising his hands.

Collise saw Branisi throw herself aside at the same time as something massive and unseen slammed into her chest. She flew backwards, hitting the wall hard enough to make her ears ring and slumped at the base, groggy and weak. The outline of something was coming slowly towards her and something burned inside her chest, leaping from her hand and hitting it.

Merin shrieked as flames coursed over his body and he dropped, rolling madly to try and put them out. Disorientated as she was Collise could not keep her focus enough to carry on burning him and Merin managed to put the flames out, rolling to his knees and facing her.

Collise struggled up, head pounding and looked for Merin, ready to burn him as she had done her mother but he ducked down a side corridor to get away. Collise stumbled after him, her eyes unfocused as Branisi shouted behind her.

"Collise, wait!"

Yet anger drove the girl now.

Who is he to come in here and attack me? I will make him pay.

Collise chased Merin along the corridor, throwing fire at him but missing and setting flame to tapestries and the walls themselves with her power. Merin turned and loosed a barrage of force at her, knocking both her and her flame aside. Collise rejoiced when she heard him cry out and heard the hair singe on the side of his head, burning it even shorter than it had been. The stench of burning hair and cooking flesh reached her nostrils and a grin spread over her face.

The blast that slammed into her chest a second later smashed all the breath from her. She felt something snap painfully in her chest and squealed as she was thrown back through the air to land in a heap, back scraping painfully along the carpeted floor. She dragged a ragged breath in, her ribs clicking and sending agony lancing through her chest. Tears blurred her vision as she struggled up into a sitting position to see the dark outline of her attacker slowly approaching her.

Collise lashed out with her fire but the agony in her ribs as the pressure built fouled her power meaning nothing but a little spark of flame fell from her palm. Merin smiled nastily, the side of his face she had burned not working as well as the side that remained intact. Raw, pink flesh covered in angry looking scabs and blisters that had burst covered his cheek and the side of his head. Collise also noticed he walked with a slight limp now and a savage satisfaction rolled through her.

Merin closed, approaching where she lay against the base of the wall. He looked as worn and tired as she felt under his injuries and she wondered if he was about to attack her again or leave her here. Merin slowly squatted beside her, fixing his pained eyes on her with grim satisfaction.

"Mother said you would be easy to beat," he said, "just like the others were." His voice warbled but with pain this time. "Now it's time for you to sleep the long sleep."

His grin widened a little and Collise knew he was about to slam her with his power again. Hot pressure grew in her chest and she felt her ribs grinding against each other again, wrenching a grunt from her throat. She leaned over as if she was about to whisper something to him and he actually leaned in to hear her.

Collise slapped her hand against his face and unleashed the burning pressure inside her. Merin's eyes went wide as soon as the heat flowed into his skull, cooking his brain alive. A scream tore from his throat as he keeled over sideways trying to escape the searing pain she was inflicting on him. Collise managed to hang on, broiling his head with the savage power she could barely control.

Merin's eyes rolled back into his head and his limbs started to shake, hands and feet tapping on the carpet in a tattoo of agony. The smell of waste filled the air as he lost control of his bladder and bowels gave way. Foam appeared on his lips and a puff of air escaped his lungs, a low moan of agony as he died.

Collise collapsed back against the wall, staring at the young man she had just killed.

That is the second person dead because of me!

"Branisi!" She called. "I think my ribs are broken."

The housecarl appeared, pale and shaken at the sight that greeted her eyes.

"By the Gods what happened?" She asked, staring at the dead boy before her.

"He attacked me," Collise said defensively. "You saw him. Broke my ribs, too," she added.

Collise let herself drift as Branisi shouted orders to the royal staff, telling them to clear the bodies and extinguish the flames that still crackled here and there.

Collise let them help her up, her chest aching as they moved her, and get her back to her bedchamber. Collise lowered herself into the soft bed Besmir had shared with his queen and waited for someone to come and tend her injuries.

Her thoughts drifted back to what Branisi had said earlier.

How many more half brothers and sisters do I have?

Was this going to be her life from now on? Was she going to have to defend her place here every week? Collise made a mental note to speak to Branisi about it when she came back.

Chapter Eighteen

The morning sun crept over the Corbondrasi capital, chasing the shadows away as Besmir and his small company made their way through the city. The king was accompanied by his wife, Zaynorth, Norvasil and the odd hybrid ambassador Founsalla Pira. They were being escorted through the city by a squadron of Corbondrasi royal guards who made sure they were given a wide berth by the citizens already abroad at this early hour.

Besmir had stepped out of his embassy that morning to be greeted by the two Corbondrasi brothers, Col and Cal Trin. Both were smiling as he trotted over and hugged them. The immense daasnu he had tamed in the desert was also there and the large creature almost leaped at him, nudging him with its massive head and licking his face while growling her happiness at seeing him again.

Arteera approached her own mount, the great beast not quite as enthusiastic as Besmir's but still greeting her energetically. Besmir glanced at his wife seeing the smile on her face and feeling his chest ease at the sight of it. He smiled himself as the daasnu tried to run her rough tongue up his face again. The Corbondrasi brothers tweeted laughter at the antics of the large cat as it danced at the sight of the Gazluthian king.

Just as he was about to clamber on the back of the big cat, Besmir noticed a small group of people approaching. His heart leaped to see Herofic trailing along behind the Corbondrasi king and queen who was followed by Ru Tarn. Although overjoyed to see him, Besmir could see he was troubled by something and his heart felt almost heavy again.

"Good day to you," Vi Rhane said to them all.

The Corbondrasi brothers knelt as their king approached, bowing their feathered heads to him and his queen. Besmir nodded his own head and ran his hand down the large cat's side.

"A fine beast," Vi Rhane said, nodding at the daasnu.

"She is," Besmir agreed.

Although he was speaking to the Corbondrasi king, Besmir was trying to make eye contact with Herofic who was almost hiding behind the Corbondrasi and staring down at the ground.

"My guards will escort you from the city and halfway to the border," the Corbondrasi king said. "Supplies and provisions will meet you there."

Besmir approached the Corbondrasi king, his hand out ready to shake. Vi Rhane had other ideas, however, and grabbed Besmir in a massive hug, clapping his back with his feathered hand.

"Thank you," Besmir said. "For everything."

"You are most welcome, brother," Vi Rhane muttered in his ear. "For the care you have shown to my wife's niece if for nothing else," he said, releasing Besmir.

Besmir glanced at Ru Tarn who stood behind the queen, hands clasped demurely before her as she watched the two kings together. She looked almost embarrassed to be there, Besmir thought, as if she were out of place and he frowned at her, glancing at Herofic who still would not meet his eyes.

"What's going on?" he asked.

Herofic looked up then, the skin on his forehead red and peeling, scabs and fresh, pink skin on his cheeks. His eyes were wet, as if on the verge of crying and a sudden fear chilled Besmir's core when he considered what might be wrong.

"Herofic?" He asked. "Really, what's wrong?"

"I will not be able to come, lad," Herofic mumbled in a subdued voice. "I want to but..."

"Herofic's injuries are being too severe for traveling," Ru Tarn said.

"You'll get better though?" Besmir asked. "There's nothing...permanent?"

"No," Herofic said. "I mean yes, I will recover fully. I just feel I'm letting you down by not being able to go with you."

"This is the best place for you to be," Besmir said. "Get rested, get well and get ready to see Joranas when we bring him back here."

"I will, lad," Herofic said gruffly. "I will."

Herofic made his way slowly over to Zaynorth and grabbed him in a big hug, whispering something to the old man that made him smile and look shocked at the same time. Desperate to be on his way Besmir didn't pry for whatever the information might be, knowing he would probably find out later on.

"We should ride," he had said and the party had set off.

Now they had reached the outskirts of the city, the midday sun burning hotly down on their heads as they rode. Besmir adjusted the white headscarf he wore, longing to tear the boiling thing off but remembering what had happened to Herofic.

Oh, to feel the wind in my hair.

Once free of the confines of the city, the royal guard picked up the pace, leading the small party north along the bank of the river. They passed a few wagons and caravans traveling in the opposite direction, drivers and teamsters giving way to the approaching guards happily, raising hands in greeting as they passed.

They camped the first night by the side of the road in a field of grasses and wildflowers that had spread from the waters brought by the river. Besmir let his daasnu loose to hunt and she darted off into the dusk, nose to the ground for any sign of quarry. The damper air near the river held more heat allowing them to camp without tents and Besmir felt grateful for the respite from the heat.

"What makes you believe the creature will return, sire?" Pira asked as they sat eating a small meal of honey cakes and fruit.

"Didn't you see her reaction when I came out of the embassy?" Besmir asked. "She's as loyal as a dog, she'll be back as soon as she's fed."

Pira shrugged his thin shoulders as if it made no difference to him and fell silent for a few moments.

"May I ask what it's like where Mwondi took you?" he asked.

Zaynorth and Arteera leaned in as Besmir sighed and began to speak.

"My father told me it's another world," he started, "but it's nothing like this." He swept his arm around the landscape. "It's barren. Bare and gray. The ground's covered in this sand that's like walking over broken glass and the wind's like a constant acid that's blowing in your face no matter which direction you're facing." Besmir paused thinking. "Overhead, the sky's constantly dark, no stars and no daylight. The things that live there, the things Porantillia birthed to try and come here, try and strip the life from anything that sets foot anywhere near them. It's a hostile and truly horrific place."

"Worse than Waraval?" Pira asked with a completely straight face.

"Even worse than that," Besmir grunted with a laugh.

After a brief meal Besmir lay beneath his bedroll listening to the sounds of Boranash around him. Insects chatted and chirped at each other while birds flew in giant patterns overhead all twisting and turning at the same time. From a distant upthrust of rock a cloud of dark, winged creatures emerged, screeching and moaning as they began their nightly hunt for food. Grateful for the ring of Corbondrasi soldiers around him Besmir let his eyes drift closed.

Movement beside him brought him back from the edge of sleep and his eyes snapped open to find Arteera arranging her blankets beside his. She pulled herself close, wrapping an arm across his chest. Besmir rolled to face her, studying her features in the firelight.

Still as beautiful as she was when I met her.

His eyes traced the lines of her face, her delicate nose and defined cheekbones, the full lips and long, dark eyelashes. Arteera smiled almost shyly under his scrutiny and leaned in to kiss him.

"Thank you my husband," she whispered.

Besmir frowned.

"What for?"

"For everything you've done to try and get our son back," she whispered. "For all you're still doing to find my baby." Her voice turned hoarse and she sniffed in a deep breath. "There's nothing I can do to help..."

"You help by supporting me," Besmir said cutting her off. "After everything we've been through, you're still here, at my side. You don't question anything I do, trusting me to get him back and that means more than anything you might think you should be doing." Besmir took her chin in his fingers, forcing her to meet his gaze when she looked away. "There would be no point to anything if I didn't have you."

He watched as she blushed in the dim light from the fire, her face coloring in a way that made his chest ache warmly.

"You have friends and Gazluth," she murmured.

"Worthless without you," Besmir said pulling her against him.

"Riches beyond that of most," she added.

"You're my most valuable treasure," Besmir said with a grin.

His wife smiled back before tucking her head beneath his chin and sighing. Besmir let the warmth from her body lull him to sleep.

***

No matter how hard he tried, Joranas found he could not recall his mother's face. He remembered the spicy perfume that always hovered around her, the sound of her voice when she was gently chiding him for ripping his clothes, but his mind refused to recall what her face looked like.

Tears blurred the bright world around him, the dark lines of the buildings around him wavering as the tightness in his chest grew.

"More water," Whint said as he appeared from behind a building.

Joranas sniffed, wiping his eyes and swallowing the lump in his throat. He watched as the dark skinned man casually butchered some poor creature they were going to feast on. He watched the play of light on the muscles that twitched and bulged beneath his skin as he worked, wondering again where he had come from.

"I can't remember what my mother looks like," Joranas mumbled as Whint spilled the creature's intestines to the ground.

The big man paused, his dark eyes searching the cobblestones for inspiration.

"Is she pretty?" He asked.

Joranas nodded.

"What color is her hair?"

"Black like mine," Joranas answered. "It catches the light, shining with blue and red patches," he said absently. "And it's long, almost halfway down her back."

"What are her eyes like?" Whint asked as he stripped the skin from the animal's carcass.

"They look like deer's eyes," Joranas said, his heart beating a little faster. "Big and brown and full of love when she looks at me."

"What about her mouth?"

Joranas frowned, thinking hard.

"It's small," he said in a halting voice. "But when she smiles it makes me feel happy and you can see her teeth."

Joranas felt a smile cross his own face as the image of his mother's smile came to him.

Whint paused, his hands coated in drying blood, and looked at Joranas.

"I think you can remember her," he said almost sadly.

Joranas sniffed again as he realized he could remember her. His father, too, and Zaynorth, Keluse, and Ranyeen. Anyone who was special or important to him leaped almost instantly into his mind and he jumped up, running over to hug Whint.

"Thank you," he sobbed.

"Thank you," Whint repeated. "What for?"

Joranas looked up, realizing Whint had no idea what he had done and also coming to understand he was not hugging him in return, just standing beneath the hot sun with the remains of a dead creature in his right hand.

"You helped me remember my family," he said. "Can you remember any of yours?"

"I do not think I have a family," Whint said.

"You must have a mother and father," Joranas insisted. "Try and remember anything you can."

He had no idea why it was so important to him that Whint remember where he was from or who his loved ones were but it seemed vital.

To make him human.

Whint stared up into the sun, screwing his face up in thought while Joranas stepped back. The dark skinned man stayed like that for minutes before relaxing his face and looking back at Joranas.

"I cannot remember anyone," he said in a sad voice. "And I can no longer hear the voice," he added.

Joranas frowned.

"W-what voice?" He asked nervously.

"The one that told me things," Whint said cryptically.

Joranas realized from the way he spoke that Whint believed he had a similar voice guiding him as well.

"I don't understand," Joranas told him.

"If there was something I needed to know, the voice told me. If there was something I did not understand, the voice explained it to me," Whint said. "But now it has gone," he added.

Joranas looked at his distraught face and felt the need to help him well up.

"I'll help you," he said. "I can explain things and show you how to do things."

Whint beamed, his white teeth gleaming as he turned his face towards Joranas.

"I'll help you," he repeated.

***

Besmir woke to find the side of his face was damp and hot. He opened his eyes to discover a group of people, including

Zaynorth and his wife, staring down at him with ridiculous grins plastered across their faces.

"It must be love," Zaynorth said, turning to Arteera.

His wife chuffed a laugh, her eyes full of mirth as she looked at him.

"Looks that way," she said, biting her lip to keep the laughter in.

Besmir heard as well as felt something hot puff against the side of his face and turned to see the large, blunt face of the large daasnu asleep beside him. The massive cat had laid beside him and fallen asleep with her face next to his, breathing wetly against him. He looked back at the group, now joined by Cal Trin who was also smirking and made a rude gesture.

Founsalla Pira joined the line of onlookers, his face a carefully crafted expressionless mask.

"Good morning, sire," he said. "Did you both sleep well?"

Besmir sat up, ignoring the laughter the comment got and wiped the side of his face where the great cat had soaked him.

"I'm the king, you know," he said in a grumpy voice. "You shouldn't be laughing at me."

Besmir smiled as Arteera started laughing harder, the sight a rare blessing these days.

"It's so sweet the way she is with you," Arteera muttered, stroking the great cat's head and ears. "After you rescued her from that nasty man."

Besmir rolled his eyes as she spoke in a childish voice to the daasnu.

"You should name her something," she added.

"What do you suggest?" Besmir asked.

"Pusskins?" Pira spouted dryly and immediately. "Your majesty," he added with a mocking little bow.

Besmir squinted at the odd Corbondrasi-Gazluthian hybrid with a growing sense of kinship. He had read numerous reports and missives from Pira since becoming king but none of them had given any sign of this wry sense of humor. Founsalla Pira didn't seem interested in Besmir's status in the least and the king liked his style.

Besmir stood, watching as the daasnu rolled to her feet beside him and laughed at the silly name Pira had come up with.

"Remember when Norvasil called his ox Zaynorth?" Besmir said with a chuckle.

Even the old mage laughed.

"Simpler times," Zaynorth said.

"What shall I call you then?" Besmir asked the great cat as it nuzzled his stomach wanting to be stroked. "When I was a boy, the Duke that found me had a horse called Teghime, an old Gravistardian word for faithful. That sounds about right to me," he said. "Teghime."

The leader of the royal guards approached them and spoke in his native language.

"The good captain believes it's time we continue our journey," Pira translated.

Besmir and the others packed the few belongings they had and clambered aboard their massive mounts, the remainder mounting the fresh horses Vi Rhane had supplied.

They followed the path of the river northwards until mid afternoon, the waters running ever clearer the further they rode. The skittish horses were not particularly happy with the daasnu behind them so Besmir, Arteera and Cal Trin rode at the head of the column, flanked by guards.

As this was one of the main routes through Boranash they passed large caravans heading for the capital laden with goods and wares, animals and foodstuffs. One wagon was filled with spices, the aroma greeting them on the wind before they were in earshot of the driver.

"Why are there so many guards?" Arteera asked, counting the grim looking, armed Corbondrasi around the wagon.

"Many of the spices are more expensive than gold, majesty," Pira explained. "Certain ones take a lifetime to grow and harvest."

Besmir's eyes picked out a line of hills to the northwest, gentle mounds to begin with but growing into fractured, jagged squat mountains in the distance. He sighed when the captain indicated they should turn away from the river and start for the hills.

As he rode, Besmir considered where Porantillia could be, how she had escaped with Keluse, if indeed she had, and what she had planned for his friend. Also playing in his thoughts was the mention Porantillia had made to Zaynorth that his son was in the care of a demon. He had experienced some of Porantillia's creations personally and knew none of them were capable of caring for a child. Besmir pursed his lips and rode on.

Chapter Nineteen

Porantillia felt confusion shiver through her mind.

What is wrong with me?

Since making the leap into the woman, Porantillia had been experiencing strange thoughts and feelings that were not her own. She understood they must be coming from the body's original owner but not how. She had leaped from Besmir when the illusion mage had somehow managed to make her reveal some of her plans.

Escaping the palace had been simple. Porantillia had made her way to the river that ran through the middle of the city, picking through the woman's memories to help her. Once there, she had dived into the water, swimming against the current with the woman's lithe, strong body a much better host for Porantillia.

She shivered when she recalled the feeling of being inside Besmir. She could not begin to understand how male creatures managed to exist with the thoughts of violence and lust barely far from their mind. If Porantillia had not found another host she thought she might have been trapped inside Besmir, a slave to his base feelings and thoughts of violence.

Porantillia had crawled from the river, suffusing the woman's body with power to revitalize it, and made her way to the top of the bank where she found herself on a road surrounded by buildings. Approaching one she had heard laughter, singing and smelled the pungent odor of fermented drinks. Knowing she needed a mount to travel more quickly, Porantillia rounded the building to where a small stabling area had been set up, the smell of manure heavy in the air as she approached.

Untying one of the horses, Porantillia felt something odd in her chest. Something heavy and unpleasant she did not like.

Guilt. It is the woman's guilt, nothing more.

"Stop! Thief!" A Corbondrasi had shouted at her.

The commotion his shout caused brought more people flooding from the tavern and Porantillia had found herself facing eight or nine armed men.

"I am in need of this animal," she told them.

"Well you can't have it, it's mine!" One of the men called.

"Let go of the reins and clear off before we call the watch," another demanded.

Porantillia had planned to begin her extermination of life once she had recovered the body she had created but if these few were about to give her trouble she could make an exception.

"Come take it from me," she had said, glancing at the horse.

The Corbondrasi had looked at one another for a few seconds, unsure as to what to do when she had challenged them. No one seemed particularly keen to attack a woman but finally the horse's owner had stepped forward and reached for the reins. Porantillia had sneered as she almost casually lashed at him with her power. Once powerful enough to destroy a Goddess like Coranstansia, Porantillia was now limited and weakened by the woman's body but she still wielded enough force to smash a hole through the Corbondrasi.

Blood and entrails along with pieces of his spine had exploded from the man's back as he folded in half and flew against the wall of the tavern. Her grin had been wide as she watched the other Corbondrasi fall back in fear and shock. Flame had lanced from her hands then, igniting the tavern and many of the people inside, their screams echoing through this part of the city.

She had bounced into the saddle, turning the horse northwards and disregarding the ache in her chest. There was no way she was about to give in to the feelings of the woman whose body she had stolen. Porantillia knew she was strong willed, but it did not matter. She was eternal, immortal and no creation of those pathetic Gods would control her. Grimly she rode north through the city, into the night, trying to push Keluse aside.

It had never occurred to Porantillia, in all her years of imprisonment, that she would have any limitations once freed from the absence. Now clear of the hated thing, she was disappointed to find there were a number of things she could not do. Her celestial form had been capable of traveling at the speed of thought and she had been able to soar through the cosmos between worlds virtually at will. These human forms were so fragile that such ideas would bring instant destruction to them meaning Porantillia had to employ traditional modes of transport.

She found herself grinding Keluse's teeth as she rode, her backside already aching from the unfamiliar saddle.

***

Keluse had screamed silently when the icy waters hit her body. She struggled to move her hands, to blink her eyes, to do anything that meant the *thing* that had stolen her body was not in full control but nothing she did worked. When she felt herself dragged from the water she was weak and aching but something pleasant and warm, refreshing, washed through her, revitalizing and bringing her body back to life.

She could hear what Porantillia was planning. She wanted to steal a horse and ride north towards something...something that was waiting for her yet Keluse could not see what it might be.

Vainly, she tried to stop Porantillia from taking the horse. It belonged to someone, it might be their livelihood, the only thing they had left and she was about to casually take it to serve her own selfish needs.

Keluse watched her own hands untie the reins, her foot step into the stirrup and felt the cold as she sat in the saddle.

Evil!

She hurled the word at the other consciousness inside her, getting nothing but mocking laughter in return. Sadness washed through her then as her thoughts turned to Ranyeen and what the future might hold for the girl. Keluse knew that if anything happened to her Besmir and Arteera would ensure she was cared for but the thought of never seeing her daughter again caused physical pain.

She never met her father and now she might never see me again.

Keluse raged and cried within the prison of her mind, cursing herself for coming here. True she had always had a bond with Besmir, following his lead ever since he had chosen her as his apprentice years before. He had saved her from the dire fate she had faced at the hands of her own father and offered her a quality of life she could never have hoped for in Gravistard. His words and deeds through the years had bound them together as more than master and apprentice, more than friends. Besmir had become her family. The brother she had never had and like the father hers should have been despite their being almost the same age.

Yet, Ranyeen was her flesh and blood. She had carried her alone, given birth to her, alone and cared for her alone. That was where she belonged, where she should be, not stuck in some burning foreign country possessed by the malevolent spirit of an insane God.

The hollow that grew in her chest was so deep and intense Porantillia could feel it. Keluse knew it affected her when she heard the other being's thoughts.

Thy grief is pointless, woman. Thy offspring will need to function as an orphan.

What manner of woman was this Porantillia? What had happened to make her so utterly twisted and evil.

Keluse's mind flashed into the past, rifling through Porantillia's memories as if they were her own. She saw the face of Gratallach, filling her with love and gentle thoughts. They flowed through the heavens together shaping worlds and bringing life to dead rock, sharing themselves freely and intimately until they became almost one.

Not until Gratallach created the third of their kind, turning his face from Porantillia, had she felt the dark seed of jealousy germinate within her, growing into a vast, all encompassing rage that burned inside Porantillia. Jealousy had turned to hate and that hate grew to immense proportions, blurring all reason until Porantillia had managed to do the unthinkable. Upon seeing their happiness at bearing children, Porantillia had managed to force her former love into the heart of a star.

Keluse tried to pull her mind from the soul wrenching screams Gratallach had bellowed as she watched. The tiniest trace of guilt Porantillia had felt washed away by the glee she had that he would feel the same pain she had endured when he turned from her to Coranstansia.

Thy curiosity will be satisfied, woman.

Porantillia spat the thought at her as she fought to wrench her mind from the horrific images and memories Porantillia had. The Goddess had murdered and destroyed on an unimaginable scale after sealing Gratallach in the sun. Whole galaxies she had brought life to with him had been crushed by her vengeance and cruelty. Keluse felt the intense pain, sorrow and loss Porantillia had felt after Gratallach had spurned her affections and knew she wanted nothing that lived because of him to exist any longer. She would destroy anything that had the power of Gratallach within it, even if that meant the devastation of worlds she had helped to create.

Now thee has thy answer.

Porantillia's thought came to Keluse as she finally managed to pull her mind from the awful memories the Goddess recalled.

It's not fair, Keluse sent out. *To punish innocent beings for something Gratallach did.*

Thou art foolish and naive. The seed of his treachery lies in the heart of all he has created. Porantillia spat within her mind. *Thou hast seen it firsthand, thy father sold thee to another who sought to use thy body for his own pleasure. Soon these flaws shall be wiped from history, allowing mine own impressions to become the template for life.*

Keluse realized Porantillia was not against *life.* Her sole purpose was to destroy the negative feelings Gratallach had created within her. By extinguishing the flame of life wherever she could she sought to rid the universe of greed, hate, jealousy, rage and her own suspicions she had not been good enough for Gratallach.

It won't make any difference. Keluse thought. *Even if you manage to kill every living thing those feelings will still haunt you. Deep within your heart they will fester, eating at you and fouling anything you create.*

Keluse waited for a response, some thought from Porantillia that she understood or at least considered her words but nothing echoed from inside her but silence. Her body rode on into the evening, guided by Porantillia and her hate.

So be it. The thought came eventually.

***

Besmir crested a rise atop his newly named daasnu, Teghime, and scanned the horizon for anything unusual. His hope had been to spot Keluse and Porantillia, running her down and stopping her.

How?

That question had been plaguing him for some time now and it was one he still had no answer for. How was he, a mortal human, albeit a powerful one, supposed to stop an eternal Goddess in the body of his best friend? Especially when other immortal beings had failed to contain her.

His eyes found nothing but further hills, virtually barren and lifeless. As nothing had passed this way for centuries apart from a few lone travelers seeking to plunder or learn from the old cities, they were having to make their own path through the wilderness. Teghime led the small group with Cal Trin ranging ahead on his daasnu. Much of the ground was hard packed earth, dry and cracked, littered with stones and debris. Occasionally Besmir saw the evidence of flash floods where savage waters had cut through the dirt, carving a path through the bedrock, wearing it smooth and making the going a little easier.

Scrubby grass and hardy plants made their home here, clinging to life where there seemed to be no hope and Besmir wondered how his son could possibly exist in a land this harsh, especially as he had a demonic companion.

Hope and reason fought inside him as he waited for the rest of his party to catch up, the horses nowhere near as sure footed as the daasnu in this land. Part of him considered that Porantillia would keep Joranas alive, keeping him safe as a bargaining tool or shield.

She doesn't think like you, or need him now she has Keluse.

That thought brought his mood crashing back down. Of course she had no need to keep his son alive. Porantillia had only done so in order to force him to present himself at the absence.

Joranas is as good as dead already.

Besmir gritted his teeth and clamped down on that morbid thought. To begin thinking like that was to doom the whole trip and he vowed never to let his son down in that manner. Until he had Joranas back in his arms he would forge ahead.

"We must rest a while," Zaynorth said as he drew alongside Besmir. "These horses are worn out."

Besmir looked at the mount the old man sat on. Sweat coated her flanks and her head was bowed, sniffing at the brown grass for any kind of moisture. While he knew Zaynorth was right, knew they were finished without the horses, he raged inside at the hold up.

He had toyed with the idea of leaving them, of spurring Teghime north through the barren countryside to try and find Joranas. It had taken all his willpower to stop him, reasoning he would need all their eyes and ears to find a single boy in a whole country.

Gently he reached his mind out towards the horse, feeling the weary animal's willingness to carry on but also the tiredness and thirst she felt. He nodded to the old man, leading them down into the shade of some rocks in the channel left by storm water.

There was a cooling breeze here, the wind channeled by the rocks and the floodwaters had piled up a small quantity of driftwood and brush when it had washed through. Col Trin tied his horse to the root of a bleached tree that lay against the rock wall. Besmir watched as he took a small spade from his saddle bags and knelt at the base of one of the walls, scraping at the dry sand.

"What's that all about?" Besmir asked Pira as the wiry ambassador secured his own mount.

Pira chirruped something in Corbondrasi, the digging man replying before he turned back to Besmir.

"He is attempting to find water, sire," Pira said. "Apparently moisture can be found, for the horses at least, if one knows where to look."

Besmir wandered across to where the Corbondrasi labored, scraping at what was now sand until he had dug down around a foot. Besmir watched as the sand changed color at that point, darkening with the water that was there. Col Trin carried on digging, even the sounds coming from the sand were wet now and before long the king saw there was a small pool of water forming in the bottom. It was a dark red color and had foamy scum on top but it was water nonetheless.

"Incredible," he muttered, unable to believe there was any water here.

"Yes," Col Trin said, looking up. "Wet."

Besmir was shocked when the Corbondrasi dipped his spade into the water and flung it out of the hole, wasting it but understood when he watched the hole fill back up with almost clear water.

Col Trin led the horses, one by one to the watering hole he had dug, letting them drink their fill before returning them to the makeshift corral they had set up. Besmir sat with his wife, Zaynorth and Pira who looked to be suffering as much as any of the Gazluthians.

"I'm a city man, sire," he said when Besmir commented. "More used to social functions and gala events than arid canyons and desert sands."

"Why did you agree to come then?" Besmir asked as he chewed on a piece of dried meat that had come as part of their provisions.

"You're my king and needed someone to translate any instructions to the Trin brothers," Pira said as if Besmir ought to have known. "With Ru Tarn indisposed, the task falls to me."

"Indisposed?" Arteera asked weakly.

Pira glanced at them both, his hawk-like eyes piercing as he assessed their expressions.

"You are unaware, I see," he commented.

"My brother and the good lady ambassador are expecting a child," Zaynorth said gruffly.

Besmir felt his mouth fall open and turned to look at Arteera who wore an expression not to much different to his own.

"How...I mean when...and how?" Besmir stumbled over his own words in his surprise.

"In the normal manner, I would suppose, sire," Pira said dryly. "As to when I could not even offer a guess without a great deal more information. King Vi Rhane informed me Ru Tarn would not be able to accompany you as she was expecting and as your subject, as well as a dual speaker, he advised it was my duty to assist you."

"What do you know about this?" Besmir demanded of Zaynorth.

The old mage turned his bearded face towards Besmir, confused and a little hurt.

"Nothing," he said in a quiet voice. "He only told me outside the embassy before we were due to leave." The old man looked away. "I knew they had been...close, but not to the extent that she is pregnant. He has never kept anything of importance from me before," Zaynorth added sadly.

"Maybe he didn't know," Besmir said. "After all, when he did say anything it was to you. And he'd been laid up for days. Maybe she didn't tell him."

Zaynorth looked hopeful but his tone did not change when he muttered.

"Maybe."

They fell silent for a few moments, the warm breeze moaning as it blew across an opening in the rock.

"Isn't it really rare for a Gazluthian and Corbondrasi to have children?" Besmir asked eventually.

"Yes, sire," Pira said, "and I have no idea how it works with a Corbondrasi mother. I was born in Gazluth to a Gazluthian woman, my father was Corbondrasi and I was born in the normal way but..." Pira trailed off as if he had said too much.

"Go on, what?" Besmir urged.

"Not something we discuss in Corbondrasi society," Pira said. "However, were you aware Corbondrasi females lay eggs?"

"Eggs!" Besmir cried, casting a guilty glance at Col Trin. "No, I hadn't a clue, I assumed it was all the same as with us."

Pira shook his head.

"It's an incredibly private and personal thing, certainly not discussed with strangers."

Indeed Besmir thought he could see some color coming to the ambassador's cheeks as he spoke.

Besmir was just about to say something more when the sound of galloping feet came to his ears and he looked up to see the form of Cal Trin approaching. His blue plumage looked windswept and unkempt, filled with dust and dirt collected from riding so hard and the daasnu he rode was breathing hard, his sides swelling and shrinking fast as it stood there.

"He has seen a lone rider!" Pira translated as the Corbondrasi tweeted shrilly.

Chapter Twenty

It was not particularly fun being queen Collise decided as she took several deep breaths to try and keep her lungs clear. No one wanted to be friends with her in case she burned them or cooked them inside their clothes.

But I wouldn't do that unless they came at me first.

Even Branisi was making fewer visits to see her and she had been one of the kinder ones, even when her mother had been alive. Collise sighed, wincing at the pain in her chest, and gingerly stood to cross to the window and stare out at the familiar scene below.

Her house, or rather King Besmir's house, overlooked the main avenue that had led up to what had been the palace. Hoards of people passed by her window each day, all of them destined for somewhere else, not one wanted to see her and all she wanted was a visitor. It hadn't been her idea to come here and take over from King Besmir while he was off doing whatever kings did. That idea had come from her mother and now she was dead so could Collise not just leave?

How will you survive then, idiot?

That was her mother's voice, reminding her she was stupid, reminding her she couldn't take care of herself. If she left here now she would have no money and nowhere to live. No, she was stuck here until either King Besmir came back and killed her like he had done her father or another one of her half siblings arrived at the front door to challenge her.

Collise had begun to wonder the same question Branisi had muttered as she had been battling the boy that had come to challenge her. How many more children had Tiernon fathered and how may could use the power they had? She watched enviously as a group of children ran past, weaving and ducking through the crowds, laughing as they played some game or other.

That's all I really want.

Then make them do what you want.

Her mother's voice echoed unpleasantly through her head. Yet Deremona was right. Collise had the magic in her, Collise was the queen and people had to do as she said or else.

"Branisi!" she cried, wincing again as she forgot her ribs. "Branisi, I want to go out."

The door opened to admit the housecarl who looked pale and tired.

"Sorry?" She asked abruptly. "What?"

"I want to go out. Into the city to meet the people," Collise said. "Arrange it."

Branisi frowned and took a step forwards.

"Forgive me for reminding you, highness, but did you not say everyone hated you? I thought you had decided it would be better if you remained inside."

"I've changed my mind," Collise said with her nose in the air. "I want to go and meet the people. I'm the queen and they have to do what I say," she added in a petulant voice.

Branisi shook her head but said she would arrange a trip and turned to leave.

"Branisi?" Collise said as the housecarl reached for the door handle.

"Highness?"

"You can stay here," Collise told her in a satisfied voice.

"As you wish, highness," Branisi said as she left the room.

Collise felt disappointed. She had thought telling Branisi to stay here as she went out would have upset the woman but if anything she had appeared relieved.

Good. I don't want her with me anyway.

A little later, after Collise had changed into suitable attire to meet her people, a long dress trimmed with ermine and deep cerise in color, Branisi opened the door and introduced her escort for the royal visit. Three young men and a woman of similar age stood to attention in the hallway outside, all armed and armored as well as being in full dress uniform. Collise noticed each sported the white stag of Besmir over their heart, signaling they were his troops and loyal to the king.

"About time," Collise said. "We will leave now."

Branisi stood aside as Collise walked past her, the four guards falling in behind her. Another servant opened the main door and Collise stepped outside, savoring the warm air that greeted her, full of the scents of her city. Branisi stood at the door watching her leave as groups of people gathered to watch the odd procession. Collise heard them whispering questions and rumors as she passed but ignored them for now, heading down the avenue towards the large market she knew would be on.

The heavenly scents of cooking meats and baking bread mixed in the air with the less attractive smells of unwashed bodies and sweating animals when Collise reached the market. She had been here a few times as a child to gawk at the numerous wares from all across the land and even some from foreign countries, none of which she could have afforded at the time. Now, however, she had the treasury at her command and would spend it as she pleased.

People gave way as soon as they saw the royal guards, all hoping for a glance at whoever had come among them. Besmir was a man of the people and trusted them with the life of his son as well as his wife. The king could often be found walking among the populace, greeting people and chatting with them amiably. Collise had seen it herself in years past, when she had collected the small amount of honey and grain the king had allowed her and her mother, he had been there giving his blessings and the occasional coin.

Now it was Collise's turn to be worshiped, for people to fawn at her sleeves and beg for a morsel of her time.

Except...

Except no one appeared to be doing that. People stared, pointed at the strange girl dressed in royal clothing with royal guards but none seemed to want to approach her, to know her.

To be her friend.

Collise approached one of the stalls, a dark cloth laid over a table with jewelry laid out over its surface. Her eyes roved over the glittering pieces, coveting each but seeking the perfect piece she would have. It came in the form of a golden chain with a white opal surrounded by thoranite gemstones at its center. The fine chain shone in the afternoon light and it looked as if the opal glowed with inner light.

Beautiful.

"That," Collise said pointing at the chain.

"An excellent choice, young miss," the vendor said as he unhooked the chain. "This is six hundred gold."

Collise swallowed. That kind of money had been more than she had ever seen in her life and this man wanted it for a single necklace?

Of course he does, you're not poor anymore.

"Claim it from the treasury," Collise said, holding her hand out for the piece.

The jeweler looked nervous, his expression apologetic as he folded the chain into one hand.

"Many apologies, miss, yet I don't know who you are to claim the treasury will reimburse me. Have you any form of currency?"

Collise felt her cheeks heat up and a tightness grow in her chest. What did this man think that she was some impostor?

"I am Collise Fringor," she shouted, drawing the attention of passers by who stopped to gawk at her. "Heir to the throne and your queen!"

Collise felt her cheeks burn hotter when some of the people around her began to laugh behind their hands.

"Since when has Besmir had a daughter?" Someone called.

"You're no queen!" Another shouted.

"Who are you really, and why did you get your friends to dress up as royal guards?" Another voice demanded.

Collise spun, turning from face to face, her confusion, fear and anger growing. This was not how it was meant to be. They were supposed to love her like they did King Besmir not call her names and shout at her in the street.

"Tiernon was my father!" Collise shouted, silencing some of the voices. "King Tiernon Fringor and I am his daughter."

"Pah!" An old lady spat before her feet. "Old Tiernon was insane. Only reason he had any children was to use them as slaves. You is no more queen or princess than I am," she added in an unkind voice. "Go back and crawl under whatever rock it is you was living under."

Numerous cheers and catcalls followed the old woman's remarks and Collise felt the burn of embarrassment in her chest and face as she turned to leave. Not until the first piece of fruit hit her did it occur to Collise she was in any danger.

Although soft and almost over ripe, the *guala* fruit still made her cheek sting when it burst spraying red juice all over her face and staining the ermine trim of her dress.

Laughter followed her attack and Collise turned to the guards behind her.

"Do something!" She shouted at them.

"What would you have us do, highness?" One of the men asked in a sarcastic voice. "Attack the people?"

Even her own guards were mocking her, snide little smirks on their faces.

Burn them!

Her mother's voice screamed inside her head and Collise lashed her hand out at the old woman without even pausing to consider. She shrieked as her clothing and hair lit as easily as if drenched in oil and ran off through the crowd, people dancing out of her way, only to fall and roll madly on the ground in a futile attempt to quench the searing heat that consumed her.

After that the screaming began in earnest. Those who had experienced Tiernon's savagery years before were joined in voice by those who watched Collise burn an old woman to death, all scattering and yelling madly, leaving her in the middle of an empty market. Collise hung her head, even the guards had taken the opportunity to leave her and the only other person anywhere near her lay a blackened and charred husk on the ground.

Collise sighed, her ribs aching and stooped to collect the golden chain the jeweler had dropped in his mad flight from her wrath. Sadly she looped it over her head, the piece cold against her skin and started back for her house.

If this is how they want it to be.

***

Teghime sensed the urgency from Besmir and galloped madly over the terrain, her large, two-toed paws digging up little puffs of dry earth as she streaked across the ground.

Besmir grinned savagely, grit and dust gathering on his teeth as the hot air flowed across his face, through his hair. From the corner of his eye he could see the hindquarters of Cal Trin's daasnu bunching and flexing as he led Besmir towards where he had seen the other rider. The Corbondrasi slowed his massive cat at the crest of a ridge overlooking a vast plain. Besmir halted, staring down at the grassland below crisscrossed by animal tracks. Dark green and brown vegetation stretched as far as his eye could see, merging with the azure sky in the distance. A few scrubby trees had sprung up here and there providing cover and shade for the herd of buffalo that must number in the thousand.

He scrutinized the land before him, searching for any sign of the rider Cal Trin had reported but saw nothing. The Corbondrasi shielded his eyes with one feathered hand, pointing with the other and chirping in his strange language.

Besmir squinted his eyes tearing up with the brightness but he just made out an ant sized speck in the far distance.

"Is it her?" Arteera asked as she reigned her own daasnu in. "Is it Keluse?"

"No idea," Besmir said absently as he struggled to focus on, let alone identify, the figure. "But who else is likely to be out here alone?"

The hunter freed his mind, his consciousness flashing through the intervening distance until he slammed into the brain of the rider's horse.

The mare was tired and confused, thirsty and hungry as Besmir slowed her to a stop. The rider on her back was unfamiliar to her and had not been kind. Besmir felt the rider dig their heels into the mare's flanks.

"Onward!" He heard Keluse's voice.

As soon as he realized it was her, Besmir threw the horse into a mad bucking. Kicking and jumping with the last of the animal's strength to try and dislodge her. Eventually he made the mare drop to the ground, rolling onto her back and knocking his friend free. He turned the horse to see her roll free, coming to a standing position in one fluid movement and casting a hand towards him.

Pain exploded up the horse's legs and chest, transferring to Besmir, as the Goddess did something to the mare's heart. Within the animal, Besmir could do nothing but endure the torture as the mare suffered a massive heart attack. Throwing himself free of the dying horse Besmir flowed across to one of the buffalo that was contentedly munching grass. He turned the massive creature towards Porantillia and started forwards.

You'll kill Keluse!

Reluctantly he slowed the headlong charge the buffalo was now in, turning the great beast as it panted and blew, before pulling his mind from it. Flashing back to his own body he panted, clutching his chest where he could still feel a ghost of the pain the mare had felt.

"Besmir!" Arteera was screaming. "Besmir, what's happening? Are you all right?"

"Yes," he managed through the dissipating pain. "It was her...them...Porantillia in Keluse's body," he gasped in a deep breath. "She killed her horse," he frowned, thinking. "Killed it because she knew it was me controlling it!"

"How could Porantillia know it was you?"

"Not Porantillia. Keluse!" Besmir cried. "When Porantillia took over my body, I knew her thoughts, her memories and she knew mine. It was as if we were the same for a while, melded together as one being. That makes things even more difficult."

"Why?" Arteera asked with a frown.

"In order to stop her, I've got to out think Keluse, not just Porantillia," he explained.

"Wait, why are we chasing her now?" Arteera asked. "I thought we were going to get Joranas back."

"We are, love," Besmir said gently. "But Keluse is my oldest friend, I can't just abandon her to whatever Porantillia might do," he said, "and she still wants to destroy everybody in this world. I have to stop her or getting to Joranas will be for nothing."

Besmir watched as his wife's face fell, the expression of hopefulness that had been there replaced by a blank stare that he had seen more often recently. Arteera was gradually drawing into herself, shutting herself off from him as well as the rest of the world in an attempt to ignore the pain inside. Each time another blow came, each time another piece of bad news or bad luck hit them her face returned to this new expression and Besmir hated it.

Arteera clucked her tongue, turning her daasnu away from the edge of the cliff. Besmir watched her straight back sway as she left, cursing himself for not knowing what to do to help her.

***

Porantillia sent a wave of power at the horse, speeding up its heart until it could go no faster and the delicate vessels covering the great muscle began to rupture. The mare screamed, her front legs buckling as Porantillia destroyed the nerves running to and from the heart, interrupting the electrical signals that regulated the thing. Eventually the horse's heart could take no further interference and ceased functioning entirely. It had been a slow and painful death, one

Porantillia would not have chosen for the beast had she not read the woman's thoughts that the mare's odd behavior was because of Besmir.

Porantillia had not bothered to plunder his thoughts or memories when she had wrested control of Besmir's body, considering them to be far too base and simple to be of any use to her. The woman she was now in control of had extensive recollections of Besmir, however, and Porantillia began to study them as she turned to walk north. She discovered he was able to control animals, using them however he saw fit and made a mental note to watch for any creature that was behaving oddly.

The loss of the mare did not bother the Goddess, she would either find another creature to use or it would take longer for her to walk. Either eventuality would mean she reached her goal and the body she had fashioned.

What body?

Silence, woman!

She snapped the thought across at the other consciousness inside her body as she continued to look through the memories Keluse had of Besmir.

Thee had a child?

Yes, Ranyeen.

Warm love suffused the thought but Porantillia slapped it aside, ignoring the happiness Keluse felt.

At what point did I begin to use thy name? The Goddess wondered. *Thy child will likely never see thee again, Keluse. Thou hast forsaken her for the needs of another. A male.*

He's nothing like Gratallach... Keluse began

Think not his name! Porantillia thundered inside her own mind. *Think nothing of the great betrayer. His time is past.*

Then why do you still love him?

Thou art pathetic in the extreme to believe such. If thy plan is to attempt to persuade me to believe I still have feelings for that one, thou art sorely mistaken.

You're lying to yourself. Keluse said quietly. *But I can see everything. Even the things you hide from yourself and I know you're still hurt because you still love hi...*

Silence!

Porantillia bellowed the word as hard as she could, silencing the woman efficiently. To think that she felt anything but hate for Gratallach was infantile. But then was not hate still a feeling she had for him? To be truly free of any attachment to him would she not have to be indifferent towards him?

Not wanting to do so but unable to stop herself Porantillia considered Keluse's words as she stepped through the ankle high grass.

Chapter Twenty One

"Where are the guards that escorted me to the market?" Collise demanded as she entered the house she had been using.

Branisi stared at the unkempt girl, taking in her red eyes and the angry set of her mouth. Something had happened and she had not heard about it yet but the housecarl thought she was about to.

"If they aren't with you, highness..." Branisi said, watching Collise's hands for any sign she might be about to throw fire around.

Since exterminating her mother by accident Collise had started to become angry, unmanageable and a little violent.

"Well they're obviously not with me, are they Branisi?" The girl demanded with eyes wide. "They haven't been with me since they abandoned me with everyone else back at the market."

"Might I ask what happened?" Branisi said cautiously.

Initially she had believed she could befriend the girl, splitting her from her tyrant of a mother and winning her over. As soon as Deremona had been take care of, however, Collise had begun to make demands that meant Branisi had less time to spend with her. Eventually the housecarl had only seen her for a few minutes each day, leaving her alone for hours on end, to think and probably come to the wrong conclusions.

"I burned an old lady," Collise said with no particular empathy.

"Why?" Branisi demanded as a cold jolt of shock slapped her chest.

"She was nasty," Collise said, "and they were throwing fruit."

She pointed to where her dress had been stained, some of the juice still visible on her face and Branisi sighed.

"Why did they throw fruit at you?" She asked gently.

"They all hate me because Tiernon was my father," Collise said, breaking down in tears.

Branisi put her arm around the girl's shoulders and guided her towards the rooms she had been using.

"Come on," she said. "Tell me everything that happened and I'll see if I can help."

Collise let herself be led, content to be guided for the time being. Branisi considered their plight and wondered when the king might return to deal with this situation. She hoped it would be soon but hadn't received word from him for some time.

"I haven't really ever been good at making friends," Collise said as she and Branisi sat down on a sofa. "I know I'm not the cleverest person in the city but why should that make a difference?"

"It should not," Branisi said.

Despite the girl's actions she sounded so sad that the housecarl felt a pang of sadness for her. It was obvious she was lonely, her harridan of a mother had more than likely kept her in a virtual prison her whole life and now she was free Collise probably thought she should be able to have all the things she wanted.

"When I told the people in the market that Tiernon was my father they shouted at me, told me to go away. Why?"

Her eyes searched Branisi's face earnestly looking for an answer and the housecarl realized no one had bothered to tell her what her father had been like.

"Have you ever heard about your father?" She asked. "What he was like?"

Collise shook her head.

"Ah, well there is no nice way to put this but he was a very bad person," Branisi nearly choked on her own understatement. "He killed many of his own people and did despicable things to others. You realize he forced himself on your mother to get you?"

"I knew that," Collise said in a small voice, "but not the other things." Her face screwed up in thought. "So people hate me because Tiernon was evil?"

"That's part of it," Branisi said, cursing her words as soon as she uttered them.

"What else is there?" Collise demanded with a furrowed brow. "Why do they love King Besmir and not me?"

"The thing is..." Branisi started. "The King is...he has done many things for Gazluth. Good things that have made people's lives better and helped the whole country grow. Understand?"

Collise nodded eagerly her face alight with childish glee.

"Yes, I understand," she said. "I understand we should throw a big party, invite everyone in the city for food, drink and dancing." Collise stood and twirled. "And I'll pay for it all!"

***

Besmir could no more begin to understand the workings of northern Boranash than he could attempt to decipher the female mind. Until now the weather had been almost unbearably hot, sapping the strength and will of even the Corbondrasi brothers who lived here. The last day had brought cold winds and torrents of rain that caused flash flooding over massive areas. He looked on in dismay as an inch of water deepened until a completely new lake had formed before them. Rivers that had not been there a few hours previously, feeding into the proto-lake and swelling it.

Even then he had tried to push them on, tried to continue his hunt for Porantillia but the very land around them conspired to stop their progress. Again he was shown how well the daasnu had adapted to life in this land as their large feet spread their weight out making it possible for them to traverse the boggy ground. The horses, on the other hand, began to get stuck in deepening mud as the rain continued to fall. They were forced to stop and dig hooves from the sucking earth as icy rain beat down on them.

"I can't do this," Arteera said as she shivered uncontrollably atop her daasnu. "If I freeze to death what good am I to Joranas?"

Besmir swore beneath his breath.

"Ask if the Trin brothers can find us shelter!" He called to Founsalla Pira who had wrapped himself in a deeply hooded cloak.

Besmir carried on laboring to pull one of their recalcitrant horses free as Pira whistled and tweeted back and forth with the Corbondrasi.

Half an hour later they were all huddled in a small cave, horses and daasnu included. The ceiling was low and conditions were cramped but they were dry and free of the sucking mud that plagued every step. Besmir's only solace lie in the fact that if they were having a hard time, Porantillia would be even worse off on foot.

What little dry items they could pile between them was set alight and everyone there held their hands out to the small blaze in an attempt to absorb some heat. Besmir smiled at the odd selection of palms, some with feathers, others without as he shivered beside his wife.

"Cal Trin seems to think this will be over by the morning and suggests we take as much rest as we can until then," Pira translated. "I was aware the weather could be fickle up here but not to such an extent."

Besmir nodded and pulled some fresh clothing from his pack, stripping his wet attire off and changing into the welcoming warmth. Arteera lay staring into the glowing embers of the fire, mesmerized, so he left her with her thoughts and moved to the mouth of the cave, staring out at the rain swept plains before him.

Showers of raindrops swept over the surface of the standing water as he watched, creating patterns almost as hypnotizing as those his wife studied. His eyes followed the path of a floating bush as it drifted across the floodplain, twisting and turning in the current and wind before disappearing from his sight.

"I hate this land," he said as Zaynorth approached from behind.

"There is beauty here," the old man grunted, "yet it comes at a high price," he added holding his hand out to the rain swept landscape. "I have some concerns," he said after a few moments silence.

Besmir turned, fixing his old friend with a look of half amusement.

"*You* have concerns?" he said in a tone of disbelief. "I have more than a few myself. Go on then, let me have them."

Zaynorth scowled at Besmir for a moment, not appreciating his tone but made nothing of it as he spoke.

"I have no idea what we are actually doing out here," he started. "Are we trying to rescue Joranas or after Porantillia?"

"Both," Besmir said. "Next?"

"What are you planning to do to Porantillia if you actually catch up with her?"

"I really don't know," Besmir said. "If I come up with something I'll be sure to let you in on it."

"None of this is my fault you realize?" Zaynorth snapped. "So moderate your tone, boy."

Besmir felt the sting of his words before he smiled and allowed a little laugh.

"I'm sorry old friend," he said. "These things have been plaguing me for a while now and I still don't have the answers. I desperately want Joranas back but I also know Porantillia must be stopped. Yet to stop her must I end Keluse? Is Keluse already doomed? Gone? And what does Porantillia want that's all the way out here any way?"

Zaynorth shrugged, his face becoming passive again.

"I doubt you're likely to approve of this but what about attempting to seek the Gods for advice?"

Besmir felt bleakness creep into his soul. What would the point of that be? The Gods were ineffectual, powerless against Porantillia. He shook his head.

"No. If anything is to be done I think it's down to us," he murmured.

The pair fell silent until Besmir turned to his old friend.

"Do you think people speak to Vi Rhane the way you just spoke to me?"

Zaynorth grinned and turned his back on his king.

True to his prediction the rain ceased overnight and by the time the silver, pre-dawn, light had spread over the land, the surface water had drained away. It was still a few hours until the knee deep mud was dry enough to walk over and by that time the air had grown hot and humid.

Besmir stared out of the cave in wonder, however, when his eyes took in the sight that greeted him. Where there had been a foot of standing water the day before, the desert was now a riot of color with billions of small flowers all vying for the kiss of an insect to pollinate them.

"Come look at this, love," he called to Arteera, his voice a quiet whisper.

She joined him and he heard a little gasp escape her throat as she took in the sight.

Every color imaginable was represented by the little flowers, patches of them flowing into other patches of color with blue and red mingling and purple flowers sprouting between. An orange and yellow section was so vividly bright it looked as if the sun was rising again just before them. Flies and even butterflies drifted from flower to flower doing their job of pollinating them as they filled up on the sweet nectar the flowers offered.

"It is beautiful," Arteera breathed, her hand creeping into his.

Besmir said nothing, turning to study her face as she stared out at the floral display nature had created. His heart still beat a little faster when he looked at her and he felt enormously grateful for that fact.

"We should be off," he said, squeezing her fingers gently.

Besmir was surprised to discover the ground was virtually as hard as it had been before all the rain and they made good time, heading northeast towards the base of a mountain range, the largest of which spouted smoke and ash into the air.

"Mount Ashod," Pira said. "Lies on the border with Aristulia."

The sight of the grumbling volcano spurred Besmir on, knowing they were within sight of the strange country where his son was supposedly being held. By midday it looked barely any closer to his eyes and he slumped in his saddle, an air of defeat draping itself around his shoulders.

The following day brought them close to the base of the mountain. Gray soil saturated with sulphurous waters rendered the ground completely devoid of any life while geysers and hot springs jetted either warm or boiling water dozens of feet into the air. Besmir felt the sting of hot water on his face as the wind brought some of the hot spray to him and wondered how hot it must be coming from the ground to still scald him now. Some of the earth was jagged with rock while just a few feet away lie soggy bogs that had to be skirted for fear of losing a horse. All the while they were being gradually coated with a fine layer of ash and grit from the rumbling monster beside them.

Besmir saw the danger just before it hit them.

***

Porantillia strode on through the deluge. The rain didn't bother her in the least, a simple flex of her power and Keluse's body would be restored. Plus, the woman was waterproof so what did it matter if her clothing was wet? Still, the hot water at the base of the mountain felt pleasant against her skin and brought memories flooding to the surface of Keluse's mind.

Porantillia watched as a younger Keluse lowered herself into a hot tub, relaxing in the water until someone else, a man, joined her. She examined the feelings of apprehension and desire Keluse had had at the time, unable to understand them.

Speak of this.

No. It's private.

Porantillia laughed.

Nothing remains private between thee and I any longer. Why did thee fear this man and want him simultaneously?

If we haven't got any secrets you should know. Keluse thought stubbornly.

Porantillia felt one of her eyebrows rise. This was truly galling. Before her incarceration within the absence she had borne virtually limitless power. To manipulate the mind of such a simple creature as this would have been the work of a thought. Now forced to share the body of that simple creature she found herself powerless to affect it in any way and that limitation brought anger.

She flashed through Keluse's memories, searching for anything that she might be able to use as a lever to force her to explain. Eventually the Goddess settled on an intimate memory, playing the scene over and over in an attempt to embarrass Keluse.

Sadness rose in her chest, making Porantillia's throat close as she walked between the hot springs and she reached up to hook a tear down from her eye.

Why?

I loved him more than life. Keluse thought.

Porantillia rifled through Keluse's memories of Ranyor and saw the moment when Besmir had explained he had perished at the hands of Tiernon. Porantillia frowned as the feelings of despair, grief, loneliness, loss and misery pulled at her afresh. Keluse's feelings affected Porantillia this time and she didn't like them at all.

Besmir again. Porantillia thought. *Thy mate perished as a result of Besmir.*

Porantillia watched as Keluse looked through *her* memories then, seeing into her plans to control Tiernon in order to bring him to the absence and inhabit his body as she had done to Besmir.

Tiernon murdered my husband. Keluse spat the thought at Porantillia. *But you drove him mad with your demons and that damned altar! You killed Ranyor. No one else.*

Porantillia felt blazing hatred explode through her from Keluse. A raging torrent of negativity all aimed at her. Her face fell as she realized she had caused this to be and a minute part of her began to consider how many others she had hurt in her vengeful quest.

Her pondering brought her to the far side of the volcano and the rough transition between Boranash and Aristulia. There was nothing to mark the border between the countries, no marker stone or signpost yet the feelings that sprung up within the Goddess signaled everything she needed to know.

Warmth spread through her and not from Keluse. Satisfaction swelled within her when she saw the land she had started to cleanse so long ago. A shiver of trepidation followed this as the recollection of the four children of Gratallach had appeared to seal her in the ice cold nothing of the absence.

"Not this time," she said aloud. "Thee hast nothing to bind me with on this occasion."

***

"Run!" Besmir screamed as the creatures charged for the small party.

He wheeled Teghime, drawing the blade that hung at his side as he was far too close for his bow, and slashed at the fist beast that neared.

"Oskapi!" he heard Zaynorth bellow. "How can there be?"

Yet the semi-human creatures were there and in number. Blunt faces with flattened noses and inch long, yellow tusks that jutted from their lower jaws. He heard his wife scream when she saw them lumbering towards her, the shrill sound whipped away by the wind. The shock of impact jarred his upper arm when his sword bit into the shoulder of the lead creature.

Besmir stared directly into the creature's eyes when his blow landed, clashing deeply into the muscle. Pain exploded across the thing's brutish face and it bellowed an oddly human scream. Besmir recalled the story Herofic had told them about how these animals had once been men and how they had murdered the only woman Zaynorth had ever loved. He cast a quick glance at his old friend as he dodged between the beasts. The illusion mage wore an expression of disgust and anger at the appearance of the Oskapi, but a sword had appeared in his hand and he was making sure Arteera was protected.

Oskapi flowed at them, at least twenty in number, some female. Each carried some kind of crude club or even the large bone of something they had killed or found. Their grunts and excited squeals rang in his ears as they chased him down. He thrust the blade of his sword at a second creature, lancing it in the throat and sending it tumbling down in front of the others. A few stumbled over their dying comrade but soon rejoined the chase.

In a desperate bid to try and turn the tide, Besmir threw his mind at one of the Oskapi. It was filled with a savage joy. Driven by the need to kill and smash, the thing was capable of rational thought and Besmir shied away from the thing as soon as the image of Keluse came to him.

Porantillia! I should have known.

As he re-entered his body something slammed into his shoulder knocking him from the back of Teghime to land painfully on the ground. Breath refused to enter his lungs as he rolled on the floor and all he could see was legs. One of the Oskapi kicked him in the ribs as it ran past but another paused, half a tree raised in both hands ready to smash the life from him. A light brown blur shot over the top of him, the deep bellow of a growl exploding from its throat as it smashed into the Oskapi. Teghime sank her teeth into the thing's thick neck, ripping through skin, muscle and cartilage, blood spraying as she bore it to the ground.

Struggling to his feet the King of Gazluth turned to see Col and Cal Trin, along with Founsalla Pira, charging towards the Oskapi. His heart swelled to see them coming to his aid but he also knew they did not stand a chance against the ravening monsters, especially driven by whatever madness Porantillia had installed in them.

Fire leaped from his hands flowing over the nearest Oskapi and making them scream horribly. Both dropped to the ground in an attempt to douse the flames searing their skin but Besmir would not allow it and they died in horrible agony. Lightning flashed into another three, felling them as Besmir turned his attention to them. The trio fell writhing to the ground shaking and fitting with the electricity flowing through them. Some of the following Oskapi paused, staring at their fallen comrades with dismay when they saw them twitching on the floor.

The Trin brothers and Pira slammed into the stationary creatures, stabbing and slashing at them as they stood there apparently confused. Besmir realized his attack and murder of their comrades had shocked them out of whatever spell Porantillia had put on them.

"Hold!" He cried when he realized the fight had gone out of them.

At the same time as his order rang across the earth one of the Oskapi lashed out with her club. A half hearted blow it nonetheless caught Col Trin on the temple hard enough to knock him from his horse to land hard on the ground. Besmir stared at the Corbondrasi as he lay there not moving, a pool of blood spreading rapidly across the earth.

Cal Trin screamed when he saw his brother fall. He threw himself from his daasnu, hurling his sword at the Oskapi that had attacked his brother. It bounced off the creature harmlessly and stuck in the soil. The Oskapi glanced at it absently before stooping to grab at one of her fallen comrades.

Besmir watched the creatures as they cleared their dead, astounded by the fact they did it. He realized they were far more man than animal and must have feelings for their dead. One passed by close to where he stood, ignoring him completely in order to scoop up the charred remains of one of his tribe. Besmir watched the play of muscles beneath the thing's skin as he moved. With their dead supported between them the strange humanoids shuffled back the way they had come.

Besmir turned his attention to the fallen Corbondrasi, pounding over to where his brother knelt beside the feathered man.

"How is he?" Besmir asked the rake thin Pira.

"Not good, majesty, I doubt he will recover from this."

Besmir swore.

"Tell his brother we need to get him into the shade," he said.

Besmir took hold of the fallen Corbondrasi at the same time as Pira translated his words. Col Trin nodded and helped Besmir lift his brother. The Corbondrasi's head lolled horribly and Founsalla leaped to support it as the two men bore his body across to where Zaynorth and Arteera were preparing a pallet for him.

"Are you hurt?" Arteera asked in a high voice.

"Not as badly as he is," Besmir said as he laid Col Trin on the sandy ground his wife and friend had scraped flat.

Besmir hugged his wife briefly, making sure she was fine before busying himself gathering sticks and logs for a fire. Arteera hacked some bandages from a spare piece of cloth, wadding more to absorb the blood leaking from the Corbondrasi's head.

Cal Trin knelt beside his brother, holding his hand and stroking the plumage on his head as he whispered gentle whistles and warbled softly to him.

Besmir's heart ached to see the love Cal Trin had for his brother, especially as he was laid low because of Besmir himself.

Arteera made her way across to where he stood, slipping an arm around his waist.

"This isn't your fault," she said gently.

"Stay out of my head, woman," he joked. "You know me too well."

"It's true, though," she said. "It's not your fault."

"Still it makes me feel bad people have to die in order to save Joranas."

"I know," she said, rubbing her hand over his chest.

Col Trin's labored breathing whistled from his throat, slowing as time passed, until he took his final breath four hours after he had been slammed from his horse.

Cal Trin wailed, throwing his head back while Besmir and the others turned their faces from his grief. Once he had fallen silent Besmir turned back to see him cutting the plumage from his brother's body with a knife. The Corbondrasi gently removed several of the feathers that sprouted from his forehead, clutching them to his chest. After a long moment of silence that Besmir thought he might be using to pray, Cal Trin rose and approached them, his eyes bloodshot and wet with tears.

"Take this as sign you were friend to my brother," Founsalla Pira translated the Corbondrasi's words.

Cal Trin passed a single feather to each of them before carefully wrapping the rest and packing them in his saddlebags.

"Porantillia sent them," Besmir said quietly.

"What?" Zaynorth demanded.

"The Oskapi," Besmir said grimly. "One had the image of Keluse in his mind when I tried to control it. It had to have been her."

Zaynorth shook his head, an expression of disbelief on his face.

"Don't underestimate their savagery," the old man said. "They are capable of despicable acts and wanton destruction."

Besmir knew Zaynorth held a grudge against the creatures known as Oskapi but had to make a point of what he had noticed.

"Yet they were virtually ignorant of us once a few had been killed and the compulsion had been removed from their minds."

Zaynorth grunted noncommittally as Besmir turned to see Cal Trin readying his daasnu for travel.

"Should we not bury him?" He asked Pira.

"It's not the Corbondrasi way, majesty," the thin ambassador said. "Customs dictate the dead are laid to rest in the open to return their bodies to the cycle of life. Cal Trin will likely leave his brother here for the wildlife to consume."

Besmir felt a shock run through him until he considered the Gazluthian method of leaving the dead in holes dug in the ground was little different. Their bodies would be returned to the earth, just via a different method. He nodded and clicked his tongue, summoning Teghime to him. Within the space of a few minutes they were trotting silently northwest once more.

Chapter Twenty Two

Buildings stretched off before her eyes as Porantillia strode down towards the abandoned city of Herintula. Centuries had passed since she had been here but the place remained largely untouched. Construction techniques honed over generations meant the dark stone blocks that had been fitted together had remained in place for the most part. Even where Porantillia had attacked the city, slamming her power through the walls and melting holes straight through the stone, the buildings had stood the test of time. While nothing remained of any of the organic materials apart from a few stains and any metalwork had long since turned to rust, the buildings were almost all intact.

Porantillia felt a strange affinity with the place even though she had been trying to destroy everyone that lived here the last time she had stood within its boundaries. Almost like a homecoming she recalled the screams and fear as people scattered from her.

How impressive. Keluse sent, her thought laced with sarcasm. *Murdering the innocent with power they couldn't stand against.*

Silence, woman! Porantillia snapped back.

No. Keluse thought. *My daughter was the victim of a bigger child who threatened and beat her friend Joranas. That child was a bully and you are exactly the same.*

Thy thinking is flawed. Porantillia sent back. *My purpose was not to intimidate but to exterminate. All life created by Gratallach or his offspring is flawed and needs removal.*

The Goddess had been suffering from pains in the legs of her hijacked body for some time, none of which could be assuaged by use of her powers. At the center of Herintula sat what had been the mayoral home, larger building that had been decorated with carved animals and plants from the surrounding area. Porantillia made for it, her gait slow and pain great.

What ails thy body? She asked.

Exhaustion. It looks as if even you have to rest sometimes. Keluse said. *Walking me for miles and miles for days without any sleep will do that to a person, you know?*

I find it difficult to believe such weak creatures managed to thrive as successfully as thy species did. Porantillia thought, her words laced with malice.

The Goddess strode into the mayor's house, looking about. Dust and plant debris had gathered in the corners, carried there by the desert winds, casting a dusty, brown hue over the dark stones. She sat, resting her back against the stone wall and let her eyes flutter closed.

Is this what thee had in mind? She asked Keluse.

No answer came from Keluse as she had already fallen into unconsciousness. Porantillia grunted, still unable to believe such weak creatures could ever have been able to survive.

Pre-dawn light greeted the Goddess when she finally woke, Keluse's body stretching almost automatically.

What? She wondered. *What was that?*

It's called sleep. Keluse explained. *Don't Gods and Goddesses sleep?*

I cannot believe mortals have to enter a state of unconsciousness to feel refreshed. Porantillia thought. *The phenomenon is most disconcerting. Could one not be easily attacked?*

That's why we have doors and buildings to keep people out. Keluse told her. *Until someone comes along and starts melting through the walls.*

Porantillia ignored the comment, concentrating on the lack of pain coming from Keluse's legs. How was it possible that a long rest did more to revitalize the body than her power could? It made no sense to the Goddess but she put it aside and stood, feeling only a few minor aches.

So what now? Keluse thought as Porantillia guided her body outside the house.

Now we send a welcome party for your best friend. Porantillia replied in a nasty tone.

Keluse saw the large forms at the same time Porantillia did, fright clawing at her as she looked at them.

So not all the residents deserted this city. Porantillia thought.

What are they? Keluse asked in disgust.

Former residents of this land. Porantillia explained as she approached the group. *Mutated and changed by...my power.* Porantillia thought with a sense of wonder.

The Oskapi turned as they started to notice her approaching, baring their teeth and howling warnings at her. Porantillia sent a wave of energy at them, whipping each member up into a frenzy of hate and fear all aimed at Besmir.

Keluse screamed within her mind as she sent the slavering quasi-animals against her friends but Porantillia ignored her, laughing as they loped off abandoning their crude homes and meager possessions.

Porantillia looked at their homes as she strode past. Several buildings had been used for what looked like a number of generations. A midden pile of bones and damp waste matter built up at the back of each home. She saw they lived in family groups, each occupying a separate dwelling, the families filing out of their homes as each got the impression they were under attack.

Incredible. Porantillia thought. *Even after I killed almost every citizen here, some returned.*

Her sense of wonder sent waves of anger through Keluse who shot her own thoughts at Porantillia.

This was their home! Of course they came back. What kind of thing are you to not understand that? You created life in other places but you've got no idea of what it is to live. If this is what you were always like, I'm not surprised Gratallach took another to love.

Keluse spat the thought before she realized she was about to do so, instantly regretting letting it slip in her rant against the Goddess. Porantillia closed herself off, silencing her mind but Keluse could feel the swirling hate and despair combined with self loathing the being felt. That Gratallach had hurt her beyond belief was not at question but to consider it had been her fault, even in part, had never occurred to Porantillia in all her long years.

When Keluse eventually started getting images and thoughts from Porantillia again they were filled with violent, vengeful ideas to cause harm to Keluse herself. The Goddess even considered hacking off Keluse's hand while she still remained inside her as a punishment.

Porantillia stood, statue still, in the middle of the Oskapi settlement and considered numerous forms of torture and disfigurement. From tearing out her blonde hair to slashing her face with sharp rocks, Porantillia considered each. Only a tiny portion of her remained rational as she thought of the horrific things she would do to Keluse's body.

Eventually Porantillia managed to calm her mind enough to rationalize the fact she would have to endure the pain of whatever she did to Keluse as well. While this did not seem to bother Porantillia in the slightest she also needed Keluse's body to be fit and well.

Thee has not had an easy escape. Porantillia warned Keluse as she continued through the dead city. *Soon we shall reach my goal and as soon as I have reclaimed the treasure there I will do things to thee that will make Gratallach's imprisonment seem pleasant.*

Keluse remained silent, retreating as far from the malevolent thing that had stolen her body as was possible. She curled her consciousness into a ball, locking herself away as she turned over the horrors she had seen Porantillia planning for her.

Help me Besmir. She thought quietly. *Please.*

***

Besmir trotted along astride Teghime, the atmosphere understandably subdued now they had suffered the loss of one of their party. His eyes scanned the horizon as they rode, their course following that of the Oskapi as they had retreated. Eventually they came to an ancient city, the walls half buried in sand, into which the Oskapi tracks led. Besmir reigned in, dropping to the ground and looking out the map the Corbondrasi king had had made for him. Sealed in an oiled, leather case the rolled up vellum was fresh and new with clear markings in Gazluthian.

"I think it would be best to skirt this city," he said as the remainder of his party gathered round. "The Oskapi are in there somewhere as well as any number of other things we don't want to encounter."

The king squinted off into the distance, rolling hills of scrub grass and stunted bushes that had baked virtually dead in the sun reaching as far as his vision could penetrate.

"Where is he?" Arteera asked, her dry throat making her sound like an ancient hag. "Where is Joranas?"

Cal Trin silently handed her a canteen as Besmir pointed to where Ludavar lay on the map. Arteera laid a hand on his arm in thanks as she took the water from the grieving Corbondrasi and sipped it carefully.

"This is where Porantillia said he is," Besmir stated.

Arteera stared at the spot on the newly copied map as if she could see her son rendered on the surface. As if she could reach out and stroke his face, push the hair back from his forehead as she had done almost every day of his life. A lump grew in Besmir's throat to see her looking so lost and he vowed to himself again he would do anything it took to get his son back.

"We'll rest here for half an hour then continue," he said in a gruff voice.

The King of Gazluth wondered where the original builders of the city had managed to get all the stone to build it. Although not massive in comparison even to his capital of

Morantine, the city must have taken generations to build and nowhere in the landscape around him had he seen any of the dark rocks the buildings had been built from. He steered closer to the outer wall, examining the stones that had been shaped and fitted with such incredible precision it did not appear as if he could get a finger between them, even now.

The rock was a dark gray, almost slate color, with a crystalline structure inside that shone when it caught the sunlight. Like nothing he had seen before, the stones must have been brought from somewhere else and his mind shuddered at the cost of such an undertaking. Who had the Aristulians been before Porantillia had come to begin her cleansing of the world?

Once past the city he didn't even know the name of, Besmir turned northwest once more, finding an easier path in the cracked earth. Almost as if a road had been built, or worn, here centuries before it led in the same direction they were headed and although partially buried by the dry soil and sand the going was easier for the horses at least on the road. Besmir knew they would make better time on this and hoped it would take them all the way to the city they sought.

Dusk came, bringing the chill down across his shoulders and Besmir shivered. Looking up he saw the day fading into night as the sun fell and for a few minutes the light blue sky was peppered with stars as day and night mingled.

"What is that?" Pira asked, pointing to a dark shape in the distance.

Besmir squinted in the growing dark spotting the darker outline of something regularly shaped on the side of the road they traveled.

"Might be a building," he said. "Somewhere to escape this cold at least," he added as he nudged Teghime into a trot.

On approach to it, Besmir saw it was a single storey building set off to one side of the road. Built from the same gray stone as the city they had skirted Besmir assumed it to be some kind of way station as it did not appear to be military in style. Walls and roof were all intact, the same attention to detail and exquisite craftsmanship used here as in the city meaning the building had stood up to the sun and weather for centuries. Two things demonstrated the age of the building. First, there was a pile of sand and earth thrown up against the side of it like a snowdrift and second, as with the city, every trace of organic material had perished, every scrap of metal long since turned to orange rust.

Besmir held his hand up as he sent his mind inside the building to make sure there would be no nasty surprises. He wanted no more encounters with any Oskapi or other inhabitants of Aristulia.

"It's clear," he said as soon as he returned to his body.

They filed in through the surprisingly wide doorway, taking the animals inside with them. Besmir noticed it was significantly warmer inside the building and laid his hand on the stone. His eyebrows shot up as he felt the stone was not only warm but as smooth as glass to his hand. He felt around, not even able to feel where the stones joined and wondered again at the people that had built such things.

There were a number of rooms that Besmir was eager to explore, but the animals demanded attention first. He loosed Teghime and Arteera's daasnu so they could hunt, Cal Trin's mount joining them a few seconds later. He, Zaynorth and Founsalla Pira started to unload the horses, brushing them down and pouring water from their dwindling supply into a bucket.

Besmir fed them oats and turned to see Cal Trin had already folded himself in his blankets, his face turned towards the dark wall. Besmir sighed, wondering what it must be like to be among virtual strangers, only one of whom spoke your language, and to be grieving for the brother you had just lost.

"We'll have to keep an eye on him," Zaynorth muttered when he caught Besmir's stare.

The king nodded his agreement, squinting in the now almost complete darkness. Breaking one of his self enforced rules, Besmir lit a fire with his magic, the tiny cost to his life force a negligible thing. Pira had collected armloads of dry shrubs from outside and soon they had a fire to see by.

"I thought you said you were no good out here," Besmir said as Pira returned with another load of combustible material.

"Ah, but I'm a fast learner, majesty," the ambassador replied.

"You might as well drop all that majesty stuff," Besmir said. "There's no need out here."

Pira executed a little bow.

"As you wish, my king," he said with a grin.

Besmir shook his head, smiling at the half Corbondrasi's humor as he rifled through packs for something to eat.

"I meant to ask about that," Besmir said as he unwrapped a package of dried meat and sniffed it. "How come you work for me and not Vi Rhane?"

"I was born in Gazluth," Pira said shortly, looking at Besmir with a shrug. "Remember I told you my mother was Gazluthian?"

Besmir nodded as Arteera sat beside him.

"So father was working in Gazluth, they met and I came along some time later. I only really escaped to Boranash when things went awry with Tiernon," he added bluntly. "I was lucky enough to be able to take refuge in Boranash where I gained some notoriety being half Gazluthian. King Vi Rhane summoned me and after hearing my tale offered me dual citizenship." He looked at Besmir with an expression of gratitude. "When you ended Tiernon and freed the country I returned to try and help rebuild some of what had been lost. Father was a merchant bringing spices and dry goods in and exporting beef from Gazluth so we were well off financially,"

Pira trailed off as if embarrassed by revealing so much about his life. "Eventually King Vi Rhane asked me to return and teach him Gazluthian. It was his idea I work as ambassador to the Corbondrasi so he contacted you to make the suggestion and I have been there ever since. I am honored to be considered a Corbondrasi citizen but my heart lies in the greensward of Gazluth and you are my king," Pira finished with a lowering of his odd head, his hair falling forward to cover the feathers that grew there.

"I'm glad to have finally met you in person," Besmir said quietly, "and want to thank you for coming on this journey. I won't forget it."

"And none of us who saw what Tiernon did will ever forget what you did for them," Pira said hotly. "My mother and I were lucky enough to be able to live in Boranash but many others were not. We all lost friends and family to Tiernon, but his tyranny stopped because of your actions."

"I wasn't alone," Besmir said pointing to Arteera and Zaynorth. "There were hundreds of us there in the end. Plus the real enemy, the one who was coercing Tiernon was Porantillia."

Besmir felt a pang of guilt slap through him when he realized that Tiernon had been nothing more than Porantillia's puppet. Zaynorth looked over, reading his thoughts and rumbled.

"He was always unkind, even before she got her claws into him. Jealous of your father and envious of his position as first born and heir to the throne. Don't waste any time believing he was different."

Besmir let the old man's words sink in but still wondered if he had been justified in his killing of Tiernon.

He stood and stretched, lighting a torch from the fire.

"I'm going to have a look in the other rooms," he told them. "Keep an eye on the food."

With that the king stepped lightly through from the main room into a smaller one at the rear. Devoid of anything apart from three raised blocks that were about large enough for him to lay on, Besmir wandered through into another room.

This had a large block in the middle, with smaller blocks around the outside.

Obviously a table surrounded by benches.

Besmir realized whoever had built this place had used stone to build furnishings as well, meaning the blocks in the first room he had passed through might have been beds. His eye was drawn to a large carving on one wall and he approached, holding the torch high to get a better look.

It looked to be a map. Similar to the one he had been supplied with but far more detailed. Representations had been made of several different cities, each carved in detail on the wall and joined by almost straight roads. Other roads led to places that were not cities but areas Besmir could not determine.

Possibly mines or quarries for stone.

Besmir dashed back to where the others were slowly cooking and rifled through the packs until he found the rolled up map.

"What have you discovered?" Zaynorth asked when he saw Besmir's urgency.

"There's a map in there that looks to be far more detailed than this," he said. "I want to compare them and possibly update this one."

The old man followed Besmir back through to the room where Besmir spread his map on the table and studied them both. There were numerous similarities indicating the map Vi Rhane had provided was fairly accurate but the map carved into the wall had far more towns and cities on it, all linked by a network of roads. It continued much farther north as well, Besmir noticed. Where his map ended with Ludavar at the northern edge of the map, on the carved map, Ludavar city lay almost at the heart of the country of Aristulia making Besmir wonder if it was the capital.

Zaynorth approached the wall, running his fingers over the details there in wonder.

"Incredible," he breathed, pulling his beard. "All these details yet the surface is as smooth as glass."

Besmir felt for himself, astounded as his fingertips drifted over what looked like a carving of a city but felt nothing.

"Whoever they were," Besmir said respectfully, "they built a massive kingdom."

Zaynorth hummed his agreement, turning to peer through another door Besmir had not explored yet. His gasp and wide eyes told Besmir he needed to see what the old man had found and he trotted across to the doorway, torch in hand to see what Zaynorth had discovered.

Points of light reflected his torch as Besmir looked into the gloom. His meager flame was barely able to penetrate the vast cavern inside but his eyes picked out enough to be able to understand the civilization had been far more advanced and strange than he had first thought.

Carefully he stepped inside, gravel crunching underfoot, making sure there was somewhere *to* put his foot. Just before him stood a railing, the metalwork protected by the building so it remained in place but rusted nevertheless, at the edge of an immense pit. It was impossible to see the far side or bottom of the chasm they had opened in the earth but Besmir could tell it was vast. Nothing echoed back when he called, not a whisper of his voice to bounce off the walls or roof and come back to his ears. Besmir shied away from the edge, not wanting to get too close to what was probably a perilous drop into nothing.

"By the Gods!" Zaynorth whispered, making Besmir jump. "How did they make this?"

"I've got no idea," Besmir replied. "But now we know where they got all the stone for the city back there."

"Dug it out of here, you mean?" Zaynorth gasped.

"That would be my guess," Besmir said. "We should leave, I don't feel safe in here."

He and Zaynorth filed back into the map room where Besmir took another look at the image. If he was right and the building they were in was next to a quarry for the stone, there were seven other similar locations marked on it. He wondered how much rock they had pulled from each quarry and how many buildings it had made.

"We should get back," Besmir said. "Dinner must be almost rea..."

The dire howl that echoed through the building cut his words off.

Chapter Twenty Three

Ru Tarn screamed as another wave of agony rolled through her abdomen and down her legs. It felt as if she were being ripped apart from within and there was no way she could take any more.

"I cannot do this!" She screamed as Su Rhane rubbed her back.

Her body had been trying to lay her egg for six hours. Six long, painful, endless hours.

"Where is he?" Ru Tarn had demanded, her red rimmed eyes locking onto her aunt.

"I sent him away, dear," Su Rhane said calmly. "This is no place for a man, let alone a *Gazluthian* man."

"But I want him here!" Ru Tarn had cried.

Now her aunt stood before Ru Tarn, taking her hands and making her waddle around the room.

"Come, this will help move things along," she said.

Behind her Ru Tarn felt someone massaging her lower back, the relief like bliss.

"Harder," she told the servant.

The Corbondrasi woman obliged and Ru Tarn moaned as the relief from the woman's hands turned into another wave of agony ripping her in two.

"If you know what is good for you you *will* let me in!"

The shout came from outside the door and in a voice Ru Tarn recognized.

"Herofic!" She called.

What followed was a number of shouts, the sound of metal on metal as if weapons had been used against armor and the terrified chirruping of Corbondrasi royal guards.

"He has gone mad!" One cried.

"Call for reinforcements!" Someone else shouted.

After a few moments in which Ru Tarn let herself be led around the room, the door opened and Herofic stepped in. Relief suffused Ru Tarn as soon as she saw him. He looked calm but grim as he stared at Su Rhane.

"I said I wanted to be here," Herofic grumbled rudely to the queen.

"Corbondrasi women have been doing this for centuries," the queen said. "Without the need for male intervention."

"Well we do things a little differently in Gazluth," Herofic muttered. Ru Tarn was simultaneously shocked and awed by Herofic's words. No one ever spoke to the queen this way but the fact was he was doing it for her and her hatchling was doubly impressive.. She smiled at him weakly before turning away when the pain started once more.

"Then it's lucky we are not in your country but Boranash," Su Rhane said. "And this is not a birth but the laying of her egg so you may as well leave."

"I will not," Herofic said.

Ru Tarn watched as her aunt's eyes narrowed and she knew the older woman was considering having him removed by force, calling guards in to drag him away.

"Your majesty," she said in Corbondrasi. "Please allow him to stay."

"Oh, very well," Su Rhane said after a moment's thought. "What damage can one Gazluthian do?" Switching to his language, she added. "If you are to stay you must do as I instruct."

Herofic nodded, taking one of Ru Tarn's hands as another wave of agony ripped through her. This time something felt as if it gave way deep inside her and she shrieked as the egg shifted in her belly. She squeezed Herofic's hand, sure she was hurting him, but he made no complaint, gently guiding her around the room with her aunt.

"It's coming!" She cried in Corbondrasi but even Herofic understood.

"You're doing an amazing job!" He said. "I'm here and not going anywhere."

The queen looked over at him, an odd expression on her face and Ru Tarn thought she could see her aunt reevaluating Herofic by the second.

Nature took hold of Ru Tarn then, making her knees weaken so the egg did not fall from a great height and become damaged. She crouched, hanging on to Herofic and her aunt for support and stared into his face as she bore down with all her strength.

Rather than fear or disgust, Ru Tarn could only see wonder in Herofic's face as she finally managed to lay her egg.

Panting, sweating and spent Ru Tarn let herself be led back to the bed where she would spend the next day or so sleeping and recovering, her egg by her side. The odd swimming sensation that took hold of her mind was not particularly unpleasant and Ru Tarn was more than happy to give in to it despite the worried shouts and voices calling her name. The floor came up to meet her and she lay there for a few seconds as grayness crept in at the edges of her vision.

***

She could hear his voice but it sounded distant and muffled, as if heard through water or from another room. Other voices joined his but Ru Tarn could make no sense of anything any of them said. Something tugged at the edges of her thoughts, something of great importance but she had no idea what it might be. The Corbondrasi knew something had happened to her but the memory of it eluded her completely and so she drifted in the dark haven of unconsciousness.

Birdsong. The first real sense of anything solid was birdsong. Ru Tarn let her eyes flicker open to see the bright green and cream of her aunt's private quarters. The tiny birds her aunt doted on, feeding them honey every day, were lined up on the window ledge demanding her attention.

My egg!

Ru Tarn tried to call out but her voice was weak and issued from her throat as a weak trill. She tried to move but something deep inside her abdomen tugged hard, sending a wave of nauseating pain up through her. She lay back, panting through her pain as she struggled to recall what had happened. That she had laid her egg was clear but anything after that was hazy and indistinct.

"Quiet, my little ones," Su Rhane whispered to the birds as she entered the room with two small bowls in her hands. "You will wake the patient."

The queen's eyes flickered over to Ru Tarn and her expression changed from nervously worried to cautiously hopeful.

"Ru?" She asked, using the intimate form of her niece's name. "Ru Tarn are you awake?"

The Corbondrasi queen dumped the bowls of honey on the windowsill for the birds and rushed to Ru Tarn's bedside.

"My egg?" The ambassador asked weakly.

"Is perfectly safe with Herofic," Su Rhane said, gripping her hand.

Ru Tarn frowned. It was unheard of for a male to care for the egg. He may have some supporting role in its care but it always fell to the mother to care for her egg. Su Rhane laughed at her expression.

"He is certainly a wind for change that one," she muttered with a giggle. "Your Gazluthian friend flatly refused to let me or anyone else look after your egg. He wears a sash with it nestled against his skin, strutting about the palace proudly and talking to it!"

Su Rhane held her hand up when she saw her niece's expression of concern.

"No need to worry," she said. "He has cut a path through the ladies at court. They all think it's the greatest, sweetest thing anyone could do and have been berating their husbands for not being as forward as he is"

The queen helped Ru Tarn sit up a little and offered some sweetened fruit water to sip.

"What happened?" She asked her aunt when her throat was lubricated.

"You had some complications," Su Rhane said in a strained voice. "Whether it was because your egg came early we'll never know," the queen paused when Ru Tarn went to speak. "I have no doubts about Herofic," she said, frowning as she looked away. "In fact if he had not insisted on being there, you may not be here now."

"Just what did happen?" Ru Tarn asked, concerned now.

"You laid your egg," her aunt explained in a gentle voice, "and all seemed well for a few seconds but you fainted and as you fell...there was bleeding...clots almost the same size as your egg and I believed you were..."

Su Rhane's eyes teared up and she pulled Ru Tarn's hand up to kiss her fingers, stroking the side of her face.

"My dear girl," she said in a hoarse voice. "I thought that day I lost my sister was the most painful thing I could go through but seeing you laid low like that..." The queen took a deep breath and continued. "Herofic was incredible," she said. "Almost as if he had done it before he used pads and cloths to stop the bleeding and then carried you to the healer. He would not leave your side until we were sure you would live..."

"How long has it been?" Ru Tarn asked.

"Just over a week," the queen replied. "Let me send for Herofic," she added.

"Yes I'd like to see my egg but I must look a complete mess, not fit for visitors."

Su Rhane smiled and went to a chest of drawers, removing a delicate brush and bottle of expensive plumage oil.

"This is the good stuff," she said with a smirk. "Don't think you will be having it often."

Ru Tarn let the queen of Boranash oil and preen her feathers, making the coral and pink plumage shine in the morning sun.

When Herofic entered a little later she took in the sight of him, proud and happy to carry her egg.

The taut, thick muscle and sinew he had built up over a lifetime of wielding a heavy battleaxe were now the cradle for a light blue, oval egg with just a sprinkling of darker speckles.

Herofic's dark eyes met her lavender ones and something passed between them. An unspoken communication that spoke volumes, telling her everything she needed to know. She watched his smile of relief widen as her own face stretched into an expression of joy.

"You tried to die," Herofic said gruffly.

"Herofic was not letting me," she replied.

The warrior crossed to her bed, sitting gently on the side and reaching into the length of cloth he had slung from shoulder to waist and up his back. Nestled within was her perfectly formed egg and he brought it out to lay on her chest.

"Meet Orlane," he said.

Ru Tarn frowned not knowing what he was talking about and he laughed.

"My family has an odd tradition," he explained. "No one knows exactly why, but any unborn baby we call Orlane." Herofic looked at Ru Tarn and shrugged. "Does your family not have any strange traditions you can think of?"

"Not being as strange as Herofic's family," Ru Tarn replied with a smile.

She tried to lift her egg but felt so weak her arms could barely support themselves let alone that. Herofic reached gently and took hold of the precious thing, lifting it to her ear.

Among the rushes and squeaks, thrumming and low growls coming from within was the satisfying thump of a rapid heartbeat and Ru Tarn felt her face grinning again. "Good and strong," he muttered.

Ru Tarn reached slowly across and took his rough hand in her feathered one.

"Thanking you for saving Ru Tarn's life," she said. "And thanking you for not leaving Ru Tarn."

"Why would I leave you?" Herofic asked in genuine confusion.

"Ru Tarn was being nearly dead," she said in a strained voice. "Ru Tarn would not be blaming you for leaving."

"I said I'd help look after Orlane and I will," Herofic rumbled in a deep voice. "Leaving was never an option."

Ru Tarn listened to the sound of her hatchling inside the cocoon of its egg as a lump rose in her throat.

***

Collise couldn't understand what the people of Morantine wanted from her. She had arranged a street party for them with free food, wine, musicians and entertainers yet still they spurned her. They avoided her in the street, especially since word had spread of her burning of the old woman, and some still called her names but from the shadows where they could not be seen.

The young girl sighed as she walked down the steps from her house, alone as usual. People melted from her path as she turned to walk up the tree lined avenue towards the old palace complex.

The great buildings hadn't really held much interest to her before but recently she had wondered if there was anything in her father's palace that could help guide her. Give her some idea as to how to make people like her. Branisi had told her that King Besmir had the palace locked up tightly to stop anyone from getting inside but Collise wanted to go and see for herself.

Her bright green dress flowed around her ankles and her hair bounced as she walked, people staring at her as she passed but not making eye contact with her. The day was sunny and warm, mid-morning sun caressing her back as she walked boldly up to the door in the curtain wall and looked at it curiously.

Thick and strong looking the gate had been built from oak and iron, designed to withstand an attack if one ever came, she thought. Collise's first thought was to burn through the thing but realized it would take hours even if it did work. She had no idea how hot her fire could be but it was probably not hot enough to melt iron.

Tracing her fingers over the gate made something odd tug inside her chest and she leaned against the gate, resting her head on it. A feeling of detachment washed over Collise as she stood there, as if she was no longer inside her own body but had somehow become part of the gate. It was extraordinarily odd but when she finally returned and opened her eyes, the gate was open.

Collise took a breath and shoved the gate, opening it and stepping inside.

Something had set fire to the overgrown trees and plants inside. The ground had a thin layer of pale gray ash over it, as undisturbed as fresh fallen snow. Blackened, charred branches lay to both sides of the path she could see had been burned through the middle of this shrubbery. Her eyes followed the path all the way to the palace building itself and widened when she saw where her father had lived.

Apprehension gripped her chest as she walked towards the blank, dead eyes of the palace buildings, dark windows that had once contained glass now stood gaping in the morning sun.

Not eyes. More like mouths.

The thought made Collise shiver but she managed to force herself onward, reaching a door that would let her in.

Her hand shook as she reached for the handle but she kept telling herself this was just an empty building, her father was not here, over and over like a mantra. Ice cold iron greeted her hand and a deep click echoed from the door as she turned the handle. It slid open on silent hinges, revealing a dark world of dust and insects.

Collise took a brave step inside, the temperature dropping as she entered, and looked around. Details were hard to make out but she could see walls and floor were damp with moss growing in places. As her eyes adjusted to the dark interior she started to pick out a few more shapes, darker patches were doors or hallways while the walls came to her as lighter patches.

Heart pounding, Collise tiptoed through the entrance hall and into a large room. Unable to see the walls or ceiling she gingerly stepped across the dusty floor. Coming to a thick pillar she stopped, finding a large metal construct there. Filled with candles and candle stubs, she realized this would have been lit at one point bringing life to the room.

Without a thought Collise raised her hand, a gout of flame rushing forth and lighting several of the candles. A warm glow issued, chasing the shadows away and Collise walked around the throne room, igniting any candles or lamps she found.

Her eyes fell on the throne and she crossed to it, walking up the few steps to the raised dais and laying a tentative finger on the dusty, gilded seat. A pile of rotting cloth lay in a bundled heap behind it, giving off a damp, mushroom like smell that she actually found quite pleasant. Collise sat in her father's throne.

My throne.

Feeling the hardness cut into her. She would have to get some cushions if she was going to use it. She sat there for a little while, pretending she was surrounded by gaily dressed courtiers all vying for her attention. Eventually bored she jumped down from the dais and turned to the door at the back of the room.

She took a lantern from the wall, lit the wick with a touch of her finger and held it before her as she walked along the corridor she found herself in. Damp and musty it smelled of mildew and rot, making her nose wrinkle as she progressed.

The scream that tore from her throat was accompanied by a wave of fire that lanced from her hand when a figure crept out of the darkness. Flames curled around the person, incinerating his clothing and licking up his body as she sent wave after wave of fire at whoever this was.

Eventually, realizing there was no screaming or running, Collise extinguished her flame and looked at what was there. Dead, stone eyes stared out of a blackened, charred face as the last vestiges of his clothing burned away.

A mad laugh bubbled up inside Collise when she saw it was a statue. Lifelike and wearing old clothing but a statue nonetheless. She chuckled to herself as she carried on down the Hall Of Kings, coming across more statues as she went.

Piles of splintered wood lay at the far end of the hall and she looked around to see there had been a door blocking one of the rooms at one point. Stepping inside she held up the lamp to see a table, ornately carved and inlaid with silver in strange patterns. Collise wondered at the strange thing as it seemed so completely out of place in this dying, crumbling building. The wood looked clean, polished and bright, reflecting the light from her lamp as she ran her fingers across its surface.

An odd feeling pulsed through Collise then. A similar detachment to when she had opened the palace gate. This time, however, rather than leaving her body, it felt as if something came *in*.

Collise took her hand from the table and walked from the room.

Who are you? The voice came from inside Collise but had not been her.

I am Collise. Who are you?

The girl felt a presence within her, as if she were not alone inside her own head and her heartbeat hammered in her chest when the thought came back to her.

Tiernon. I am Tiernon.

Chapter Twenty Four

"What in the name of the Gods was that?" Zaynorth demanded as the grunting howl droned on.

"I've got no idea," Besmir said, "but we need to get back to the others and find out."

Grabbing the map he rolled it up roughly and sprinted across the room, skirted the room that had the raised platforms in it and dashed back into the room where his companions were.

Arteera was on her feet, staring around in fright. Founsalla Pira stood with his back to the wall at one side of the door, peering out and even Cal Trin had risen at the sound of whatever this was.

The horses whinnied and shuffled nervously as the sound drew to a close, leaving an eerie silence in its wake.

"No one said anything about massive beasts in this land," Besmir whispered as he grabbed his bow and slung a quiver of arrows over one shoulder.

"No one comes here to see if there are any," Pira said, still looking out into the darkness. "Expeditions stopped coming here when they failed to return," he looked round. "As I said it is a cursed land."

Arteera whimpered when the deep, grunting howl came again. Nothing with any trace of humanity left in it could have voiced the sound and Besmir went to her, wrapping one arm over her shoulder and feeling her body tremble.

"What is it?" She asked in a querulous voice.

"Let me see if I can find out," Besmir said.

He loosed his mind, floating free of his body and soaring up through the roof to look down on the landscape below. Lighting up the world like stars in the heavens were the traces of life around him. Bats chased insects off to one side, mice foraged for seeds in the scrub grass below at the same time as being hunted by wild cats. All this life, however, was overshadowed by the deformed thing that he could see.

He flashed over to it, trying to leap into its mind and take control of the thing so he could turn it from them. Once inside the creature Besmir discovered it had once been human and although it was a base and simple thing now, he could not control it in any way. He did manage to glean the fact it could smell them and the horses, both of which it thought of as an easy meal.

The Gazluthian king pulled back, hovering before the thing and wondering what power could have changed this thing so much. He flashed back to his body, feeling the warmth of life surrounding him again.

"It's some kind of mutation," he said grimly. "Similar to the Oskapi but much bigger and it can smell the horses."

Besmir avoided telling them it could smell them too, knowing the information would simply frighten them even more.

"Do you think it will just go away?" Arteera asked hopefully.

Besmir shook his head.

"It's hungry," he said. "But we might be able to hide from it. Take the horses through there and into some of the other rooms."

"By the Gods!" Pira shouted. "If we are to hide we had better be going soon, the thing is immense."

Besmir gently shoved Arteera towards the door leading to the room with the platforms inside as he stooped to grab their packs. Founsalla Pira was busy telling Cal Trin what was happening in the Corbondrasi tongue as they began leading the horses towards the door with Zaynorth.

Besmir watched as they rounded the corner, the horses needing virtually no encouragement to get away from the beast that was approaching, then turned to see it coming through the doorway.

It had worked itself up into a frenzy, not used to entering buildings to get food, and Besmir watched its chest heave as it growled and snarled its way inside. The firelight picked out a few features as it approached, sniffing the air. Thick, sinewy muscle flexed beneath a dark hide that featured shaggy fur in patches. It stood around eight feet in height and had to stoop to enter the room. Vaguely humanoid in shape, it had four limbs and a head but there the similarities ended. Besmir saw its arms were far longer than any human, hands almost grazing the floor as it shuffled across the room. Those hands were bunched into loose fists at the moment but each fist was easily the size of his head.

Besmir drew an arrow silently and put it to his bowstring, flexing the weapon a little. The creature's head came round as soon as his bow creaked and its violent eyes fixed on him. It let out a soul chilling scream, a challenge to Besmir as soon as it recognized he was a threat.

The hunter king drew his bow to full power and loosed the arrow. It shot across the room with a satisfying whoosh followed by the deep thump and grunt of pain as it hammered into the creature's chest.

Besmir's heart sank when he saw the arrow had barely penetrated the thing's tough hide and knew they were in trouble. He stepped back into the room his companions had escaped through, relieved to see they had already gone into the map room. He sprinted after them as the sound of massive feet pounded behind him.

Besmir turned to see the creature slam itself through the doorway, snapping pieces from the wall as it stumble through. He lanced fire towards it, singing and burning the hair from it and making the thing recoil from the heat.

By the time he had made it into the map room, Besmir was panting, adrenaline and fear making his body work hard.

Zaynorth was trying to steer his horse through into the cavernous room but the animal appeared to be fighting him for some reason. Besmir leaped across the stone table and lunged at the animal's hindquarters, slapping the muscle there hard. The horse leaped forward, hooves slipping and skidding on the stone floor, dragging the old man through the door with it.

Inside Besmir found Cal Trin and Pira had lit a number of torches, leaning them against walls and even just laying them on the floor as they prepared weapons to fight the monster.

Besmir saw they were on a platform that overlooked the immense pit but was still unable to see the bottom of it from where they were. Zaynorth had narrowly avoided being dragged over the side to fall into the pit by the horse Besmir had slapped and looked at his king with an angry glare as he led the animal over to the other horses.

Arteera's scream split the air as she saw the creature enter the room they were in. Fully revealed by the torchlight now, Besmir could see it was a blunt faced thing, almost like a bear with a flattened nose but with no fur to cover its ugliness. Its beady little eyes shone in the torchlight, swinging to focus on the horses as drool flowed from its mouth and down its chest.

Turning its attention to Besmir again the thing screamed, lumbering forward to lash at him with its long arms. He saw it had sharp, black claws at the end of its fingers when they passed within inches of his face, the breeze from the blow cold on his skin.

With its attention on Besmir, Cal Trin lashed forward, his blade stabbing at the thing's armpit, sinking in a little way. It turned with deceptive speed, hammering one hand into the Corbondrasi who crumpled under the blow, flying a few feet before landing hard against one wall.

Founsalla Pira stabbed at the thing as it turned back to Besmir, lancing his blade in behind its knee joint. It screamed as the metal bit into its leg, smashing one hand down against Pira's sword and wrenching it from his hand. Besmir saw the thin man fall back, clutching his shoulder with an expression of agony on his face.

Besmir loosed a barrage of lightning at the thing, making it writhe and twitch as its muscles contracted and a deep bellow issued from its mouth. Despite being ravaged by his power, the creature managed to reach for Besmir and he had to throw himself to one side, his lightning fading.

The king rolled to a stop, turning to see where the thing was going next. His heart almost stopped when he saw Zaynorth stepping across to confront the creature. The old man was muttering something as he walked confidently across to the beast.

"Zay!" Besmir cried. "Stop!"

The old mage ignored him and walked straight up to the creature, still muttering, his beard moving. The creature looked about, its gaze glossing over Besmir and the horses as he watched. It sniffed the air and grunted something before staring out into the darkness of the chasm. A snarl bared its teeth as it looked at something in the darkness and without warning the eight foot beast sprinted for the chasm.

Besmir rolled over as it passed him, following its passage as it raced towards the rusted remains of the railing. Centuries of decay had turned the rails into little more than piles of rust and the creature exploded over the edge, screaming as it fell to be swallowed by the blackness.

Cautiously Besmir approached the edge as the creature fell, still screaming, the sound becoming ever more faint until abruptly it ceased.

How deep is *it?*

He turned to where Cal Trin and Arteera were trying to help Founsalla Pira to his feet. It was obvious to Besmir the ambassador's shoulder had been dislocated by the savage blow the creature had delivered. Cal Trin himself looked to have labored breathing and was favoring his right leg and arm as he moved.

"What happened?" Besmir asked Zaynorth as the pair strode across to their companions.

"I made it believe the horses were running away and put the image of a floor in the chasm," Zaynorth replied. "The thing gave chase and fell into the pit."

Besmir could not believe the easy, almost casual way the old man explained what he had done.

"How did you know it would work?" He asked.

"I didn't," Zaynorth said. "Yet you said it was similar to the Oskapi and they were once human so..." The old mage spread his hands.

"And if it hadn't worked?" Besmir demanded.

"I expect it would have killed us all," Zaynorth said in a similarly blasé manner.

Founsalla Pira looked paler and sicker than he normally did when they crossed to where he had been propped against the wall. Arteera was busy piling the torches to form a makeshift campfire to keep them all warm.

"I must apologize, majesty," Pira said in a breathless, shaking voice. "I've been so remiss as to suffer a dislocated shoulder."

Besmir smiled, even in the midst of such pain the wiry ambassador kept his sense of humor.

"And I must apologize," Besmir said grimly. "As it's really going to hurt to pop that back in."

"I can help with that," Zaynorth said.

Besmir nodded and turned to Cal Trin who had lowered himself to the ground not far from Pira.

"How are you?" He asked, waiting for Pira to translate.

"I'm well enough," the ambassador spoke the other Corbondrasi's words for him. "Scrapes and bruises is all. I have springy bones that don't break easily."

Besmir nodded and turned back to Pira.

"I'm going to need you to lay on your back," he said.

The wiry half Corbondrasi shifted, grunting as he moved, but managed to lay down. Zaynorth knelt beside him and started mumbling words in his ear.

"The sun is warm on your face. You can smell the grasslands of Gazluth with every breath and a summer breeze brings the scent of apples to you."

Besmir saw Founsalla smile as the illusion took shape in his mind. Zaynorth nodded to him and carried on muttering as Besmir reached down and took hold of the man's wrist. He slowly drew the hand up, pushing down lightly on Pira's thin chest with his other hand until the joint jumped back in with a light thump.

The slightest moan came from his throat as the shoulder relocated but nothing like the screaming Besmir had heard from others. Besmir looked at Zaynorth who was still washing the man's brain with calming, peaceful images and wondered what his life would have been like if the creature had killed the old man. Growing up without a father had deprived Besmir of many of the qualities a good father imparted to his son but he had come to depend on the old man, seeing him as a substitute for his father in some strange way.

"Can you make a sling please, love?" He asked Arteera who was already cutting a large triangle from a piece of cloth.

"Far ahead of you," she said with a scared smile.

Besmir wrapped his arms around her, feeling the trembling in her body.

"It's dead," he assured her. "It's gone."

"*That* one is," she said. "What if there are more?"

Besmir watched the others glance nervously at each other until Zaynorth stood from Pira's side.

"Then we shall deal with them," he said confidently.

"I don't want you putting yourself in danger again," Besmir said to him.

"I am old," Zaynorth said in a weary voice. "If my life has to end in order to recover Joranas, I consider it to be a worthy trade."

"Well I don't!" Besmir growled. "You know how that boy feels about you. What do you think it would do if he knew you died to save him?" Besmir felt a pang of loss and pain stab straight up beneath his sternum. "There will be no more deaths to get Joranas back," he declared. "Apart from Porantillia," the king added with a savage grin.

"I agree," Arteera said in a quiet voice. "I want nothing more than to have my boy in my arms again but not at such cost."

The queen stepped over to Zaynorth and hugged the old man who looked mildly surprised at her actions.

"Come on now, lass," he said in a hoarse voice.

Besmir watched his wife and oldest friend hug, warmth spreading through his chest when the sound of footsteps came to them all.

Arteera's eyes went wide in fright.

"Not again!" She pleaded as something entered the firelight.

***

Collise screamed as she felt the teeth ripping at her. Every memory her father had was the same. He was in a gray place being eaten alive by savage monsters that looked as if they had sprung from a nightmare. She tried to pull her mind away from the hideous thoughts but they would not leave her.

I must be insane. This is what it's like to lose your mind!

Calm yourself, child!

Collise had no idea if that voice really did belong to her father or something inside her that called itself Tiernon. Either way she felt much calmer when it spoke, even though there was an edge of hostility and threat of violence to it.

Who are you?

I told you before! He snapped. *I am Tiernon, King of Gazluth.* There was a pause as he looked through Collise's short history. *Ah, it's too perfect.* Tiernon whispered in her mind. *You're my daughter.*

What's happening? Collise asked in panic.

Tiernon's thoughts took on a mocking, apologetic tone as he sent his thoughts at her.

I'm sorry but your time as queen must come to an end. I find myself in need of a body and yours presented itself so fortuitously. Feel free to spend the remainder of your time reveling in my memories. I have some business to attend to.

Collise felt herself pushed aside, inside her own body. Her hands came up and she looked at them, feeling his sense of wonder.

"So young," he purred in her voice. "So *innocent*," She heard her own nasty chuckle. "I'll soon change that," Tiernon said as he turned back down the Hall of Kings.

Once outside, he turned her face to the sun, soaking up the feeling of warmth and letting it wash away the chill of hell.

"So Besmir wouldn't use my palace," Tiernon said aloud.

Collise felt a coldness well up in her when Tiernon thought about Besmir. Fear and hate mingled with rage and the need for vengeance, the heady mix of negativity washing through Collise and overwhelming her senses.

Tiernon strode her body back through the overgrown and burned gardens towards the gate in the curtain wall. He paused outside in consideration of the people there, all wandering about without a care in the world, happy and free while he had been exiled in hell. Collise felt her teeth snap together and grind in anger.

We shall see who suffers now. Tiernon thought.

Collise watched as her body shoved through the crowds, making for the house she had been using. Tiernon cared nothing for the people he rudely bashed into and a number of them turned disapproving glares at her as she passed.

"Look where you're going!" One man finally shouted, pushing Collise's shoulder hard enough to make her stumble.

Tiernon didn't even hesitate. Collise watched in horror as her hand shot out, the hair on her forearm standing straight up as lightning lanced from her fingers and into his chest. The stranger jerked, his whole body going into spasm as electricity hammered through it. A small fire started on his chest where the power smashed into his body, setting light to his clothes.

Tiernon halted the power and watched in satisfaction as the man's body fell to the ground, dead. A second later the screaming began.

People scattered, shrieking in their fear as Tiernon moved off towards the house Besmir used.

"You can't do this!" Someone screamed.

"What?" Tiernon demanded, turning to face the woman.

She was slightly taller than Collise, in her late twenties or early thirties and dressed in a royal guards livery. Without weapons, Collise assumed she was on her way from her home to wherever she worked and had stumbled across this scene. Collise stared at her through the eyes she could not control and screamed warnings the woman could not hear as Tiernon chuckled inside her mind.

"I said you can't just murder people at will!" The guard said.

Collise saw she was pretty, with long hair and porcelain skin, large brown eyes and pink, bow shaped lips. Collise imagined what she would look like burned and smoldering on the ground.

"I believe I can," Tiernon said, raising Collise's hand.

Pain lanced up the arm as soon as he had pointed it at the woman and Collise laughed inside her mind as the guard twisted and pulled Tiernon off balance to slap into the ground.

Her mirth was short lived, however, as Tiernon glowed incandescently with rage. Flames exploded from the hand the guard had pinned at her back, scorching Collise's back as well as burning the guard. She cried out, letting go of the hand that had suddenly erupted in fire, and falling back as Tiernon rolled over.

"How dare you touch me!" He cried. "I am King Tiernon Fringor and now you die!"

Something caught Collise a glancing blow on the side of the temple, knocking her head around and making her vision blur. Tiernon struggled to make sense of the world around him as several dark shapes approached.

"Stop this, Collise!" Branisi cried.

Her words fell on deaf ears as Tiernon swung to throw flame at them all, missing as they scattered and his aim was fouled by the blow to Collise's head. Branisi chopped her arm downwards in an arc and several members of the royal guards rose up, firing solid little projectiles at Collise.

Tiernon had not possessed a body for some time and as he was not used to using Collise's, did not manage to erect any kind of barrier that would have easily stopped them before. He screamed in her high voice as the lead balls smashed into him, each impact stinging and burning as it hit. Distracted by the pain neither Tiernon or Collise saw the pellet that felled them. One of the guards, an expert in the use of these slingshots, managed to hit Collise directly at the base of her skull. Darkness crowded her vision as the blow rendered even Tiernon unconscious.

Chapter Twenty Five

"Teghime!" Besmir cried as soon as her furred paw stepped inside.

Relief hit him like a punch to the stomach and he noticed similar expressions on the faces of his friends as he grabbed the huge cat's ears and rubbed them hard. Teghime rumbled low in her throat, following the scent of the creature across to where it had plunged to death in the pit.

"It's gone, girl," Besmir said sending his thoughts into the daasnu to calm her.

With a final snuffle and grunt the creature trotted over and nudged Besmir until he started scratching her ears again.

"I'm guessing we'll have to stay here at least a couple of days," Besmir stated, trying to keep the disappointment from his voice.

"Don't worry," Pira said, "we Corbondrasi heal fast. I will ride in the morning."

Besmir glanced at him and Cal Trin before turning back to his wife.

"The least we can do is feed them," he said.

***

The following morning, light filtered into the building through some means Besmir could not begin to understand. He walked to the edge of the chasm and looked down into the darkness as the sun rose outside. His head swam as he stared down into the hole, unable to bring himself to believe people had dug to such a depth. There was no way he could see the bottom even now there was light flooding into the room and what he could see of the walls was sheets of jagged, broken rock that had been hewed from the depths.

Besmir stepped back, his head reeling with the immensity of the quarry.

Who were these people to have dug this, built these cities and then just left?

They packed, Pira slowed by his arm being bound, then led their animals back through the strange building and out into the already hot sun. Besmir helped the half Corbondrasi to mount his horse, making sure he was steady before leaping onto Teghime's back.

The creams and ointments Ru Tarn and the Corbondrasi King had provided them with had helped Besmir's skin turn from its usual pale color to a light nut brown. He found he could strip virtually naked and not feel the savage effects of the sun, enjoying the feeling of wind kissing his skin.

Water was still difficult to come by but with Cal Trin's expertise and experience in desert life they were able to get enough to survive. Days wore on as they trekked northeast, following roads that had long since sunk into the desert. Occasionally they saw other cities or individual buildings, all stacked from the same dark stone but avoided them entirely, not knowing what manner of things might inhabit the ruins.

Their food supplies began to run low and Besmir began to send his mind out, following Teghime as she loped across the hard ground in search of prey. Initially he sought out animals they could eat and laboriously walked them back to wherever they were camping, exhausting himself with the effort of ranging so far from his body. One evening, after a particularly hard day's riding, he fell into an exhausted sleep before her had ventured far at all. His consciousness drifted, loosed from his body, following paths at random.

He flowed upwards, carried by unseen forces, sailing north over hills and cresting the tops of a sea of trees. The forest had died years ago, the wood now bleached white with wisps of wood curling out here and there. It was vast, running for miles in any direction and at the western edge he saw a dark smudge almost the same size as the forest had been.

Knowledge flowed into him as he looked at it.

Ludavar. That's where Joranas lies.

Besmir knew the voice that had spoken those words in his mind and distaste flooded his mind. Cathantor chuckled at his hate and Besmir felt his mind sucked along by the God's power. They soared far above the world, out and up every detail growing smaller by the second until Besmir could see the edge of Boranash, where it met the sea on the far side of the immense Aziraz desert. Still farther Cathantor took him, up through clouds until he was able to see the world was like a ball. A green and blue ball floating in the night sky.

Fear gripped Besmir as he looked down at the world where his body lay thousands of miles away.

Where are we going? Am I dead now?

Cathantor didn't answer and Besmir wondered if the God had abandoned him here, leaving his consciousness floating in the night sky for eternity. Panic gripped him when he found he could not move. Normally he could consider a direction and his mind floated that way but here the rules seemed different and he began to scream, fright and panic overwhelming him.

The globe before him started to fade and he welcomed the darkness, calming and soothing as he fell into a deep slumber.

When he woke abruptly Besmir knew exactly where he was. He had been here before, met his mother Rhianne and been guided by Ranyor. The afterlife was as much a paradise as it had been on his previous visit. Vast green plains swayed lazily in the gentle breeze as herds of cows, buffalo and numerous other creatures wandered through them. A great forest, alive with a thousand different types of tree, stretched off into the distance and Besmir breathed deep lungfuls of the purest air he had ever smelled.

He could not begin to understand how he had a body here when his body lay in Aristulia but he stretched his arms out, seeing the familiar hands at the end of them. As before he saw someone approaching him and hoped it would be Ranyor again. He set off towards his old friend but soon realized his walk was different, the way his shoulders swayed was not how Ranyor moved and caution grabbed at him.

The man had a friendly smile as he came across to where Besmir stood staring out over the verdant grasslands. Just taller than Besmir he was obviously Gazluthian with the pale skin and dark hair Besmir's race nearly all shared. He had broad shoulders and the muscled torso of a swordsman. There was a certain familiarity to his features but Besmir could not recall ever having met this man before and turned to him.

"Hello," he said carefully but politely. "I'm Besmir."

"I know," the man said in a deep, mellow voice. "We've met before."

His knowing smile began to irritate Besmir as did the wrinkles of mirth around his eyes, both making Besmir feel as if he were being mocked.

"Then you have me at a disadvantage," Besmir snapped, "because I don't remember you at all."

"Although I did look somewhat different when we met," the man said. "I would have thought a boy would know his father."

"Joranas!" Besmir shouted, grabbing his father in a tight hug. "What happened? How? I watched Porantillia rip off your head!"

"And that was an agony I wish never to repeat," his father said with a wry twist of his lips. "When I woke up I was here, whole, and reunited with your mother."

Joranas' eyes misted at the thought of his wife but a smile crossed his face. Besmir saw he had a small scar leading up from the right side of his lips.

"I'm not sure why I am here, but I believe it's Cathantor's way of rewarding me for centuries of service in Hell."

"I'm so happy for you, father," Besmir said, "but shouldn't there be someone there to guard the portal?"

"Not since somebody released Porantillia," Joranas said, pursing his lips. "What were you thinking son?"

"She has my son!" Besmir cried. "And I will do anything to see his safe return."

"Anything?" Cathantor asked, appearing behind them.

Joranas dropped to one knee, bowing his head to the God but Besmir turned, staring directly into Cathantor's deer eyes, his own laced with malice.

"Yes. Anything," he said hotly.

"That's good," Cathantor said mildly. "Because my brother, sister and I have something we have to tell you. Come," He ordered.

Besmir ground his teeth and looked at his father who had gone pale and wore an expression of utter shock.

"Besmir!" He gasped. "You must show respect. That's Cathantor."

"I know who he is," Besmir grunted, "and what he's capable of. Or not. I refuse to be cowed by someone who sees us as playthings."

Besmir felt his father's stare as he trudged off across paradise behind the strange animal amalgam that made the body of the God. Besmir frowned as he walked, although he had been a hunter and tracker, reading signs in the ground and environment, he could not detect any sign of Cathantor's passing. He knew the God was there as he could see his brown, furred back, tail dragging in the grass, but there was nothing before Besmir to show he had walked this way. Not a hoof print, not a broken stem of grass or any other sign he had been there. The hunter king frowned and Cathantor turned, walking backwards and laughing.

"I'm not here," he said. "This place is for the spirits of those who've passed and I'm very much alive."

Cathantor paused and held an arm out to Besmir. It ended in two hard hooves rather than a hand and Besmir grabbed it awkwardly. He felt a jerk as if the universe had shifted around him and found himself at the edge of the sea where they had been before.

"Going to get your sister to shout at me again?" He asked.

Joranas gasped at the comment and Besmir turned, surprised to see him there as he had not touched Cathantor at all. The God himself responded with laughter as Sharise began to grow from the water before them.

Besmir watched as a section of the calm water grew upwards, reaching several feet in height before gaining any kind of recognizable shape. Legs, arms, body and head became distinct as the thing flowed towards them, still merged with the sea. Besmir had seen some of the Ninsians on a state visit who had a pastime that involved riding atop waves on a carved, wooden board. Sharise's approach was much the same, apart from the fact her feet merged with the water's surface and she had no need of a board.

Features appeared as she neared them. Kelp-like hair sprouted to fall down her face and chest, covering her breasts. Her face developed and Besmir was surprised to see she was quite ugly to his eyes. She had a large chin and sagging cheeks, a thin lipped mouth and dirty green eyes that regarded him with disinterest. Her belly was flat but had no navel and ran down to wide hips that were covered in shimmering fish scales, that glowed with a rainbow of color as she moved. Her legs and bottom were cloaked in the same scales and she stepped from the water to the sand at exactly the same point her appearance was complete.

Besmir turned as he sensed movement from beside him and saw his father was down on one knee again. The hunter king shook his head and turned back to the Gods.

"So what now?" He asked rudely.

Sharise turned to regard him with a baleful stare, utter displeasure on her face.

"Now, mortal, we await the arrival of our eldest," she thundered in a voice that could shake mountains.

Besmir saw she had barnacles attached to her arms and coral grew on her back as some kind of odd crustacean crawled through the kelp of her hair.

"Will he be long?" Besmir asked. "Because I've got something quite important to do at the moment."

Cathantor turned a warning glance on him but Sharise's expression flicked into rage and she grew before them, arms stretching out into tentacles with fleshy hooks along their surfaces. Her head flowed downwards, sucking the kelp into it as her shoulders melted and a sickening mouth grew in the middle of her chest. A ring of wrinkled muscles twitched constantly, sucking at the double row of almost human looking teeth there. Sharise snapped her teeth together, grabbing Besmir with her tentacles and lifting him towards her maw.

Although fright grabbed at Besmir, making his entrails squirm coldly, he knew Sharise could not do anything but threaten him. His father shrieked on the sand at his back but Besmir fought not to let his panic overwhelm him and remained as still as he had on the sand.

Sharise paused as soon as she realized he was not afraid and set him back on the sand, unscathed.

Joranas grabbed Besmir in a hug, his whole body shaking.

"Don't do this," he begged into Besmir's ear. "The Gods are all powerful and can destroy you with a thought."

Besmir knew his father was wrong but a lifetime of belief could not be changed in a few heartbeats and so Besmir clamped his mouth shut against the tide of words that wanted to flow from him.

"Maybe you should go and see mother," he managed.

"You will remain," Cathantor ordered.

Joranas gulped and bowed as something huge flapped its wings above them.

The bird had at least twenty feet of wingspan, each feather lovingly created in the mind of Mwondi as he glided in on unseen currents. The immense bird had yellow skinned feet with black talons easily capable of lifting an ox. His beak was around four feet, an orange blaze as it reflected the sunlight and his eyes were the piercing orbs of an eagle. Besmir had seen those eyes before but in a different form, outside the embassy in Wit Shull, the Corbondrasi capital.

The bird landed, his flapping wings driving a spray of cold sea in their faces as it skimmed the surface of the water. Mwondi flickered into his normal form before he had touched the ground, his feet landing lightly on the sand a few feet from them.

He looked almost normal, Besmir thought as he crossed the final few yards to where they stood. His arms ended in hands with fingers and he had a human form but he was feathered almost like a Corbondrasi but with none of the colorful plumage they displayed. Mwondi wore a coat of dark brown feathers, a few black, with lighter patches over his eyes.

The three Gods stood in silence, looking at each other as Besmir waited, his anxiousness growing by the second. Eventually he coughed loudly, slapping his chest to make even more noise.

"It is thy belief this is the one?" Mwondi asked Cathantor as he pointed at Besmir.

"I believe so, brother," Cathantor replied in a completely different voice to the one he spoke to Besmir in.

"Mortal," Mwondi said. "Thou hast been chosen to end Porantillia whom thee freed against our wishes."

Besmir looked at each God in turn, his face a mask of disbelief.

"Oh, right," he said. "That's it is it? Just end Porantillia?" He snorted a derisory laugh. "You three couldn't," he said. "Actually wasn't it four?"

Mwondi's face fell as he stared at Cathantor with utter sadness and pain carved into his feathered features.

"Thou hast been informed well," Mwondi said in a voice that brought despair to Besmir's heart.

His pain at the loss of his youngest sister was so great and eternal it would be too much for any mortal to bear. The Gods were supposed to live forever so the grief he, all of them, felt was a never ending torture they would bear until the universe died. While humans might eventually learn to cope with the death of a loved one, for the Gods it was impossible. Besmir heard all he needed to in Mwondi's voice as the God carried on.

"Deurine was the youngest and gave of herself to create the absence so much she faded to naught. Yet where we have failed, thee might succeed as Porantillia has bound herself to a living host and may yet be slain."

Horror overtook Besmir as he realized what they meant him to do.

"I-I can't," he begged. "I won't do it. There's no way I can kill Keluse!"

Chapter Twenty Six

Keluse's mind could not conceive of how large the city that lay before her was. Porantillia had brought them to the edge of a plain and a vast, dead forest, that had a city so large it out sized the Corbondrasi capital. Keluse took in the endless rows of buildings and myriad streets, all laid out in a grid like pattern. As far as she could tell the buildings might stretch on forever and every single one was devoid of any life.

It is barely changed. Porantillia thought. *I can imagine the people who lived here going about their mindless tasks like ants in a nest.*

Until you came here? Keluse thought.

Thy guess is correct, woman. The first people, who lived here, were favored by Gratallach so it was my initial target. I find amusement in stashing my new body here, along with the other prize.

Keluse was unable to understand what the Goddess was thinking about, her own mind still wrestling with the size of the city she was facing. Porantillia turned, seeking a way down into the valley, soon finding an easier path that would lead to the city.

They called it Ludavar. Porantillia thought as she strode down the scree filled path, skidding and sliding. *The great capital of Aristulia.* Her thoughts took on a mocking tone. *That came here, you know? Those half breeds that refer to themselves as Gods. Came here to mingle with their creations and be fawned over, worshiped. That is why I chose to begin here.*

But they stopped you, didn't they? Keluse asked.

They managed to bind me for a time. Porantillia replied. *Until thy friend Besmir released me.*

You tricked him and kidnapped his son!

And it was an easy thing to do. Porantillia gloated. *As simple as he is himself.*

You'll underestimate him. Keluse said. *He'll never let you get away with hurting his son.*

Mocking laughter echoed inside Keluse's head.

Idiot child! I have no need of the boy any longer. They have already failed. Their attempts to bind me have failed and once more I am to end the life of anything containing the life force of Gratallach.

Keluse tried to shroud her thoughts as she saw a curl of smoke rising far to the west side of the city, hoping it was only one person.

He is here! Porantillia thought.

Strange feelings flowed through Porantillia at the sight of the smoke. Part of her disregarded it completely while another feared it was Besmir and what Keluse believed he was capable of. Another feeling of loneliness struck her as she thought about why he was here. To save his son and friend. While not a being in the universe would lift a finger to come to her aid if she needed it.

It is good I do not need help from anyone in that case. Porantillia thought to herself.

Even you would like a friend of some kind. Keluse murmured, reading her thoughts.

I had one. Porantillia thought sadly. *He chose another.*

The Goddess slammed a door shut, clamping down on the feelings that plagued her as she marched towards the massive city of Ludavar and whatever she had secreted there.

***

"You have blinded me," Tiernon said when he finally came round.

Collise could feel the tight pain from the swelling at the base of her skull and the incessant banging thud that pounded through her head. True she could not see but there was no pain in her eyes, simply the feeling of cloth around them and she knew Branisi had blindfolded her.

Branisi! I am here. Help me! Collise screamed but the words would not come.

She heard her father chuckle in her voice and hated him for it. All the stories had been true! Tiernon was evil, selfish, violent and power hungry.

That may be true, daughter of mine, yet you burned your own mother to death.

It was an accident! Collise cried.

The first ones always are. Tiernon growled *Still now we are bound and blind there will be little chance of fun.*

Collise felt sick. Her father's idea of fun was burning people alive! Listening to them shriek and scream as the fire licked at them. Any notion she had had that he had received an unfair end at Besmir's sword were washed away as she flowed through his thoughts, seeing the disgusting things he had done.

That thing *made me this way.* Tiernon thought defensively. *Porantillia and her demonic beasts whispering in my ears day and night. I couldn't bear it. It was she who drove me to madness.*

You should have ended yourself. Collise thought spitefully.

So true, my child.

Collise felt a grin spread across her face and hated the way it must look.

Yet if I had, you would not exist.

Good! Collise snapped. *I wish I had never been born!*

And be denied the chance to meet your father? Tiernon asked with sarcasm lacing his thoughts.

Collise did not reply as she heard footsteps approaching, a door being opened.

"Who's there?" Tiernon called in her voice. He wanted to sound scared, as if it was she who asked rather than him.

"Branisi," her voice filled Collise with calm.

If anyone could help her it was Branisi. But how was she supposed to tell her Tiernon was in control of her when Tiernon *was* in control of her.

"Help me, I don't understand," Tiernon chirped in her high voice. "Why am I in the dark."

"We've bound you," Branisi said. "To stop you killing anyone else. When King Besmir returns he can deal with you."

"Besmir!" Tiernon spat, his stolen voice cracking. "He is the one who put me here!"

Collise could hear the confusion in Branisi's voice as she spoke.

"What are you saying? You never met the King."

"Idiot woman!" Tiernon raged. "I *am* the king! And you will release me if you value your life."

Collise heard Branisi sigh.

"It's true, then," she said, almost as if she were talking to herself. "They said you had gone mad but I had to hear it for myself."

"What are you wittering on about, woman?" Tiernon demanded. "Release me immediately."

Trapped inside her own body, unable to speak or move, Collise began to laugh.

What is so funny? Her father demanded.

You! She said with a giggle. *You don't sound anything like me. I talk completely different so all you are doing is making sure they keep you here.*

Collise laughed, the sensation odd as she could not feel her belly moving. For some reason she found that even funnier and guffaws of uncontrollable laughter rang from her mind, spreading through to Tiernon's consciousness.

He in turn started to laugh but as he was in Collise's body, sounded odd to his own ears and he began to laugh hard as well. Collise could hear his thoughts as he tried to stop laughing but they were all in vain. She could feel the ache from her belly now as her father laughed in her body.

"Oh, Collise," Branisi said sadly. "I'm so sorry."

For some reason her pity and sadness made them both laugh harder and Tiernon rocked in the chair he was tied to, trying to escape as Branisi left.

"May the Gods have pity on you," Branisi said as she closed the door, leaving a young girl tied and blindfolded in a stone cell.

"None have so far!" Tiernon cried to the empty room.

Why did you force yourself on my mother? Collise asked abruptly.

T'noch convinced me to breed as it would give me an army one day. The thought came to Collise laced with sadness and she reached out to look through his memories. Collise flinched back when she came across T'noch. A hideous, multi-jointed thing that should never have existed, even his memory of it frightened her.

How do you think I felt? Her father asked. *It whispered to me day and night until I didn't know whether its voice was in my head or not.*

A wave of repulsion washed over Collise as Tiernon thought back to some of the things he had done at T'noch's suggestion and she could tell he had some measure of guilt inside him.

Gods, what did I do?

Images came at Collise as she tried to hide. Vile memories he had of throwing fire at children in tents and burning down people's homes. She saw people, so many people, fade to nothing on the table she had touched in the palace, their dead husks discarded like trash.

She watched as a young girl, barely older than Collise, approached Tiernon in his throne room. She had been pretty, young and innocent and Tiernon had driven her insane, ripping her mind apart until she became little more than his pet.

He recalled sealing someone behind a thick wall of wood, leaving him to scream and beg as he left him there so starve alone in the darkness. Later the same man had been gradually sinking into a wall overlooking the horrible altar. Collise saw the man, *Shorava*, beginning to fuse with the wall, becoming part of it as he hung by the hands.

Stuck within the prison of her own body Collise screamed as the awful images, thoughts and memories flooded her mind.

Horror, fear and sadness mingled with nausea as hundreds lost their lives at the hands of her father.

Then there were the women. So many women he had used in the vilest of ways, Collise's mother included. Collise had come to understand what he had done to Deremona but to recall it in detail was more than she could bear.

With no outlet for her emotions, as she could not scream or cry, Collise felt her mind stretching as if it was about to give way or snap and she welcomed the break if it would let her be free of the horrible images he recalled.

***

Joranas looked over and smiled at Whint who was apparently always happy. Now he was helping the strange man around their little home, tasks got done in half the time and they spent many afternoons talking and lounging in the shade.

"Remember anything yet?" Joranas asked with a smirk.

"Actually, yes," Whint replied.

Joranas sat up, staring at the other man as he reclined at the base of a wall.

"Really?" He asked in surprise.

"Yes," Whint said again, moving into a cross-legged position and fixing the boy with a stern gaze. "I remember you are annoying," he finished with a grin.

Joranas stared at the odd man he had come to like with a smile spreading across his own face. He jumped up and darted across to where Whint started to laugh, launching himself at the dark skinned man and trying to wrestle him.

"Annoying, am I?" Joranas asked as Whint rolled backwards, digging his fingers into Joranas' ribs as he dragged the boy down.

Whint rolled, pinning Joranas to the ground and holding him there with one hand holding both wrists and his leg across Joranas' thighs. Joranas struggled, his muscles straining against the prison Whint had him in. It was pointless, Whint held him as securely as if he was bound and he gave up trying to lay there panting as the man looked at him.

"Oh dear," Whint said. "It looks as if you are stuck." Whint poked Joranas in the belly making him squirm. "What will you do?"

Joranas' eyes widened as he tried not to laugh but the feeling of Whint jabbing his finger into various soft places from belly to armpit grew too much and he yelled a laugh. He clamped his mouth shut against the sound but Whint continued tickling him until he could not stand it any longer and laughed until his stomach and ribs ached.

"Oh stop!" He begged, still laughing. "Please, Whint. Please."

"Will you admit you are annoying?" Whint asked with a smile.

"Never!" Joranas declared.

He screamed more laughter as Whint tickled him mercilessly and the lad tried again to get free but Whint held him fast.

"All right!" Joranas cried. "I submit!"

"And you are annoying?" Whint asked again, tilting his head to one side.

"Yes, I'm annoying," Joranas cried. "Now let me go."

Whint released him and Joranas rolled to one side, getting to his knees and then his feet to look down at Whint who squinted back up at him.

"Not as annoying as you are," Joranas said with a laugh as he sprinted off.

Behind him he heard Whint shout and jump up to give chase. Joranas' feet pounded over the dark cobbles as he ducked down streets and rounded corners to try and escape Whint. Excitement bubbled up in his chest as he sprinted between former homes and blacksmiths, the stonemasons and carpenters that had all long gone.

He had long since given up trying to decide what each building had been used for, some of them seemed to sprawl out inside, rooms upon rooms creating a labyrinth as confusing as the city itself. His wariness of the city and the strange things that might also live there, or visit, had also slowly dwindled since he knew Whint could handle anything that came at them and he could summon fire at will.

He dashed through a large, open square, the tall buildings set back, probably to allow for a market or public gathering. Eerie sounds echoed back from the buildings as his breathing came back to his ears but he heard nothing of Whint's feet. Joranas slowed as he approached an incredibly ornate building, the face of it covered in carvings of people and animals he could not identify. The people looked vaguely similar to people he had seen but many of the animals were completely unknown to him. He saw a large, two-legged creature with sharp teeth and a line of scales down its back chasing people and attacking them. Another was being hunted, arrows and spears jutting from its hide as it fell to the ground.

Joranas' mind seemed to flow into the carving, the world spiraling and whirling around him as he stood there, transfixed. Around him the city came to life, the strange people from the fresco before him appearing like wraiths to walk and laugh and talk. Unusual aromas came to him as more of the past appeared, spices and hot metal from the forges mixed with the heady aroma of roasting meat and bread baking. Joranas stared in wonder at the people, all of whom were taller than anyone he had seen before, far taller than Whint even was. They moved with a kind of fluid grace similar to some of the dancers he had seen with his parents, their long limbs almost floating in the hot air.

A group of children darted between the adults, laughing as they played some chasing game, Joranas thought about

Ranyeen back at home and wondered what she was doing at that very moment. One of the children caught the arm of a burly man, knocking the basket he carried to the ground. He turned his stern face to the child who looked a little afraid as he cradled his knee. Abruptly the man grinned and squatted beside the child, pointing to his knee and offering a piece of cloth he drew from his clothing. The lad nodded, relaxing into a smile of his own as the man patted his graze gently and helped him back up.

Joranas jumped when he turned to see three of the children staring at him. Each had paused just a few feet from where he stood and examined him with large, green eyes. One was a girl and Joranas felt something heavy in his belly as he looked at her. She had long, light brown hair that shone in the sunlight framing a face that he found intensely beautiful. Her small nose turned up at the tip and the dusting of freckles that garnished it migrated over her cheeks delicately. She was tall and thin but his eyes were drawn to the obvious signs of her gender and he felt his cheeks burn as he stared openly at her. One of her companions, a boy who might have been of a similar age to Joranas, pointed, muttering something to the other two. Joranas frowned as his finger was not pointed at himself but at something behind him. Turning, Joranas saw to his wonder, the building he had been looking at was alive with color. The carvings he had seen had been faithfully and meticulously painted to resemble real life. He ran his eyes over the frescoes, seeing far more now than he had when they were monochrome.

Joranas pulled his attention back to the girl who wore a little smile as she studied the scene. She looked so real, as if he could reach out and touch her bare shoulder, feeling the softness of her perfect skin...

He reached out but, just before his fingers were to touch her, they all turned their heads. Joranas looked to see everyone was staring in the same direction, some pointing but all with expressions of either fear or concern on their faces.

Something bright flashed in the distance and he saw some people open their mouths, screams he, thankfully, could not hear echoing from the stonework. Further flashes came from the same direction they all faced, followed by a glowing orb that smashed into one of the buildings, melting through the stone with sickening ease. More of the glowing orbs appeared, as if it was raining them, to melt through the stonework and set fire to the inhabitants and their possessions.

They ran then, fear carved on their faces as their feet pounded past him. Joranas could only watch as the girl he had been about to touch fell to the ground before him, hair and clothing alight as her friends tried in vain to put the flames out. Her back arched, limbs thrashing in agony as she burned alive, her skin turning black as he watched. She died seconds later, adults and children alike running past them as more people emerged from buildings on fire, thrashing and screaming in a mad attempt to stop their hair burning.

Pain and fear welled up in Joranas' chest as he watched the city burn before him. The square he faced was filled with corpses, all burned horribly. Flames licked from the buildings as anything flammable caught light and still the rain of glowing, purple orbs came.

Though blurred by his tears he saw another figure walking slowly through the square. Joranas rubbed the water from his eyes to see a woman, beautiful and terrible, making her way almost casually through the carnage. Joranas could see she was nothing like the people who had lived here as she was at least twice the size of any of them and looked completely different.

Her body was a voluptuous ode to femininity, strong and supple with taut muscles and long, amber hair. Large, round eyes as blue-green as the ocean gleamed with savage delight as she advanced making strange feelings erupt inside Joranas at the same time as revulsion washed through him. Her skin was a mottled red-pink color, darker in some places than others but what struck Joranas more than anything was that she was utterly naked. Nothing was covered with even the tiniest scrap of clothing and when the wind shifted, curling smoke and flame around, her hair blew back, revealing her heavy chest as well. She looked as if her only reason for existing was to breed.

She was also the one responsible for massacring the city.

Round arms raised and fingers cupped she brought forth wave upon wave of the purple orbs, launching them in all directions as she floated several feet from the ground. The expression on her face was one of vile satisfaction as she casually slaughtered hundreds of thousands of people.

Joranas did not want to see any more but he could not turn away, unable to close his eyes even though his tears blurred the scene. Eventually the woman, whatever she had been, passed through the square, naked buttocks on display.

Wherever he looked, men, women and children lay dead, their clothing and hair burned horribly and their faces beyond all recognition. Joranas slumped to his knees, falling sideways as the city burned around him. Thick, cloying smoke seared the back of his nose and throat as flames licked from the tall buildings around him.

Finally able to close his eyes, Joranas sat on the cobbled ground and wept for the loss of this graceful, loving and happy people. Something rocked his body and called his name. He looked up to see the concerned face of Whint staring back at him.

"Joranas?" The dark skinned man shouted. "Wake up!"

Whint shook him again, his grip tight and painful on Joranas' shoulders and making Joranas' head roll limply.

He came back slowly, as if waking from a stupor, the sights and sounds of the city being destroyed fading as he focused on Whint. The tall man knelt and looked into his eyes.

"What happened?" He asked in concern.

"I-I can't," Joranas said, his voice breaking. "It was horrible."

Whint frowned but gathered Joranas in his strong arms and carried him back to their makeshift home.

Chapter Twenty Seven

Besmir opened his eyes to the silver light of pre-dawn. Arteera slept beside him with Cal Trin and Founsalla Pira a little way off. A low fire smoldered at the center of their small camp with Zaynorth feeding a few thin branches into it as he brewed some tea. Sitting up gently to not wake his wife, Besmir rolled from his blankets and went to the fire, holding his hands out to it to ward off the night's cold.

Zaynorth looked up, his lined face filled with surprised concern.

"It's about time you woke," he said.

"Why? It's early morning," Besmir replied with a frown.

"You've been asleep for three days, lad," Zaynorth told him. "Arteera has been out of her mind with worry."

Besmir tried to think, to recall what had happened. He had been hunting, sending his thoughts out with the daasnu and...

"What's wrong?" Zaynorth demanded.

Besmir couldn't get his breath and he felt the blood drain from his face as his journey and meeting with the Gods came to him.

I can't tell them what they expect me to do.

"I just feel a bit sick," Besmir lied. "Got any of that tea to spare?"

"Of course," the old mage said. "Do you recall what you usually call this, though?"

Besmir smiled despite the memories flowing around his head.

"I call it horse urine," he said, "and I stand by the name, but you swear it makes you immortal so it might cure my sickness."

"I never said it makes me immortal," Zaynorth grumbled defensively. "I merely stated I am never unwell due to its healing properties."

Zaynorth poured a generous amount of the tea into a metal cup and passed it to his king. Besmir blew on it, sipping the bitter liquid and wincing.

"Yes, definitely something a horse would pass," he murmured with a smile.

"There is only one way you could actually know that, you realize?" Zaynorth asked with one eyebrow raised.

Besmir laughed, sipping more of the dire brew. Something grabbed him from behind sending half his cup hissing into the fire.

"What...?" He cried.

Arteera wrapped her arms around him, squeezing as hard as she could as Zaynorth chuckled.

"Besmir!" She warbled. "What happened? Why have you been asleep for days?"

"I don't know," he said, a pang of guilt at lying to her spiking through him. "I suppose I must have been exhausted from all the riding and then hunting each evening. It was quite tiring sending my thoughts out that far."

"Well don't do it again!" His wife ordered, squeezing in beside him.

"We have to eat, love," Besmir said.

Arteera's face changed to one of wonder as she exchanged a brief look with Zaynorth who smirked and sipped his tea.

"We have been," she said. "Teghime has been bringing us meat."

Besmir felt his eyebrows shoot up as he looked at his wife to see if she were mocking him. Arteera laughed at his expression.

"Really," she said. "She must have known you were unwell as she began dropping animals at your feet the first night."

Besmir looked at the large cat, curled in a bundle with the other daasnu, head on the rump of another cat and lightly snoring. He made a silent promise to himself to take her back to Gazluth with him when this was over. Maybe start a breeding program so others could benefit from the faithful creatures. Teghime opened her eyes, staring at him as if she knew he was thinking about her. She raised her head, yawned and tucked it back down behind the other cat's back. Besmir laughed.

"If only I felt that carefree," he said.

"Will you be able to ride?" Zaynorth asked as Founsalla Pira rose, nodding to Besmir without a word.

"Yes, I'm fine," Besmir said.

My body is anyway.

They broke camp after a brief breakfast, each member well rested after a three day break. Besmir's mind rolled over his strange journey as they rode for Ludavar. He could not understand why he had been kept asleep for three days when his trip had been so brief, no more than a few hours. Was this the Gods' way of hindering him again as Cathantor had tried to do in Hell. If so, why?

He felt Teghime slow beneath him and came out of his thoughts to stare down into the valley he had seen when Cathantor took him. The massive, dead forest was the same bleached wood stretching off for miles and the city, Ludavar, stood beside it, immense and labyrinthine.

Joranas is in there.

That was what Cathantor had told him before flying up into the night sky and on to the endless fields of the afterlife.

"By the Gods, it's immense!" Pira said as he reigned his horse in with his good arm.

The four people stared down at the sprawling mass of buildings and streets, each realizing what an immense task still faced them inside that city until Besmir spotted something.

"Look!" He yelled, pointing.

In the distance, barely visible through the boiling heat haze, a lone figure walked towards the gate leading into the city. It was impossible to tell who it was at this distance but Besmir guessed it to only be Porantillia in her stolen Keluse body.

If I hadn't been asleep for three days...

The thought came to Besmir as he watched Porantillia enter the city, heading for his son. He knew why Cathantor and the other Gods had kept him asleep, so she could enter the city first.

But that just puts Joranas in more danger.

Besmir's fist clenched on the reins and he gritted his teeth as he realized the Gods had been interfering *again*. His companions mistook his rage for anger at Porantillia but he did not bother to correct them as he turned Teghime and rode her down into the valley, galloping towards Ludavar in pursuit.

The walls loomed, taller than any he had seen as he approached, slowing the gigantic cat to fully appreciate the scale of the city. Towers, taller than he had ever seen, grew into the sky like dark fingers, dark holes he assumed to be windows dotting the sides.

"How did they even build these so tall?" Pira asked in wonder as he drew alongside on his puffing, heaving horse.

"I have no idea," Besmir said.

Arteera was paler than usual when he looked, her eyes, roving over the large buildings, wider than usual and he knew she was scared. Besmir steered Teghime over beside her daasnu.

"He's in there," he said. "Our little Joranas."

Arteera nodded.

"So is *she,*" she spat.

Besmir realize he had read his wife wrong. She was not frightened at all, this was rage and hate aimed at Porantillia he could see. His heart swelled with pride and love for the gentle seamstress he had married. He remembered, years ago before they were married, when he had been in need of an army to overthrow Tiernon, he had said that no force on earth was as determined and outright threatening as a mother whose young are threatened. The expression on Arteera's face was a perfect example of that. Given half a chance he thought she would rip Porantillia apart with teeth and nails if she could.

"What are you smiling at?" She demanded.

"You look ready to punch your way to the middle of this place," he said.

Arteera grinned at him and he grinned back, turning Teghime to enter Ludavar.

***

Tiernon's mind whirled like a draining pool. Unable to focus on any one thought he rolled over and over, endlessly reliving the horrors he had visited upon others.

Collise had no choice but to do so too. She watched as he tortured, maimed and killed people time and time again, both of them screaming in the madness. Of all the overriding thoughts that came to her, one stood out over all others.

It was T'noch! He made me do it!

The more she heard this thought cast out by her father, the more she wanted to find out the truth. With a huge effort of her young will, Collise managed to force her mind back through his thoughts and memories, traveling back to some of his earliest recollections.

He was with his brother, Joranas, and another boy called Zaynorth. His brother and Zaynorth were fast friends, not including Tiernon in much of what they got up to around the palace and Tiernon was left on his own for much of the time. Today, he felt good as they were letting him tag along. Being the younger brother to the crown prince was not always the easiest of lives but Tiernon loved Joranas and so he accepted his lot in life.

They took Tiernon to a part of the palace forbidden to them, an area where the women of the palace bathed, and climbed high onto the roof, cajoling and berating Tiernon until he joined them. Once there, Joranas made sure he was quiet as they peered through a crack in the wall at the women far below. When Tiernon came to take his turn he felt a wave of fatigue and heard Zaynorth muttering to him, his words unclear. When he was roughly woken by a guard later, he was hauled down a ladder and brought before his father who lectured him on not spying on women as they bathed. He could tell his father was disappointed, if not disgusted by the actions of a prince but something inside him stopped him from speaking out against Joranas.

Collise rummaged through the vaults of her father's mind, finding a few more occurrences of her uncle and his friend putting her father into awkward and embarrassing situations for their own amusement. More often they just abandoned him for other entertainments, not wishing him to tag along and the young Tiernon spent much of his time reading or studying.

Older, his brother had met Rhianne and fallen madly for her, germinating a seed of jealousy and hate in Tiernon's heart for them both.

Why should they be happy when I am not?

His brother took her as wife and they had a child.

That is King Besmir! Collise thought in amazement.

An unpleasant plan had started in Tiernon's mind, Collise saw the first tendrils of his idea to take the throne from his brother at their wedding. He would threaten the woman and the child as he could not best Joranas, especially with Zaynorth at his side.

Collise saw his plan succeed and he was crowned King of Gazluth when their father died, his brother in exile to afar land. Yet even though he was gone, Tiernon could not put thoughts of his brother and nephew from his mind. If they were to return he might lose the throne, so he ordered assassins to find and kill them all.

Collise drew back, unwilling to see any more. Her father *had* been evil in the beginning, letting hate and jealousy overtake him until he had his brother killed.

But King Besmir lived, he came back.

And he killed me. Tiernon's voice echoed in her thoughts, more rational and sane than she had heard it before.

Collise gasped inside her mind at his words but listened as her father continued.

You're correct, I should not have let some childish pranks affect me as they did but look to your own childhood of exile and exclusion and tell me you're not similar.

Collise felt a wash of shame at his words, she had burned an innocent woman for saying a few mean words while her father had endured it for years from his own brother.

***

Keluse could feel the anticipation as Porantillia strode through the deserted streets of the dark city. They were heading for something important to the Goddess, the body she kept thinking about, but Keluse was plagued by a sense of foreboding. Something was about to happen and even though Porantillia thought she was going to leave Keluse's body for this new one, Keluse had no idea whether she would survive the process.

Porantillia marched past buildings that had partially collapsed, recalling the time, centuries before, when she had come here to destroy them. Keluse saw the Goddess launching orbs of pure, raw energy at the city burning women and children alike.

All because of your jealousy. Keluse spat.

We have been through this, thee and I. Porantillia thought, sighing. *I do this to correct a wrong. To erase the flawed life created by Gratallach's putrid offspring and begin again.*

You're lying to yourself. Admit it. This is pure revenge because he took another. Well it happens! Get over it now.

Once I have erased the mistakes, it will never happen again. Porantillia insisted. *None again will feel the agony of betrayal.*

You will. Keluse thought quietly. *Unless you kill yourself as well, you are going to lose in this plan as his betrayal will still haunt you forever.*

That gave Porantillia pause, Keluse realized. The Goddess actually listened to what she had to say, rather than ignoring her words.

They marched on, Porantillia ignorant of Keluse's weariness and pain, past buildings that had holes melted through the walls. Porantillia's orbs had gone *through* solid rock and

Keluse shuddered at the thought of the fear and pain it must have caused.

The memory flashed into Porantillia's mind as soon as Keluse thought of it and she watched as the Goddess had made her way through the city, floating over the dead and burning corpses with a sick sense of glee in her.

Why did you enjoy it so much? Keluse asked.

What?

If exterminating all life is a simple case of erasing a mistake, why did you enjoy killing all those people?

It was a simple case of completing a task. Porantillia thought.

Liar! Keluse spat, knowing the truth. *You wanted these people to suffer because they were created by Gratallach's children!*

Speak not his name!

I'll speak anything I want! Keluse screamed inside her mind. *This is* my *body and I'll do as I please. Yes what Gratallach did was horrible and wrong but killing people who have never heard of him or you is worse. You had your revenge on him and Coranstansia centuries ago but you are still trying to punish everyone for things they haven't done. You're like a child having a tantrum...*

Keluse's thought cut off as agony lanced through her nose. Porantillia had slammed her face into a nearby wall, breaking her nose. Keluse watched in horror as the Goddess brought her head back and smashed it against the corner of a jutting windowsill, splitting her lip and snapping one of her front teeth.

Reeling from the pain and the savagery, Keluse silenced her thoughts.

Better. Porantillia sent to her. *Thee would do well to remain silent for thy remaining time.*

Keluse knew the Goddess could feel the pain as well as she could. She also knew nothing she said or thought could dissuade Porantillia from her course. She was determined to destroy all life and kill the Gods and there was nothing Keluse could do about it.

Chapter Twenty Eight

Besmir's eyes traced over the dark gray buildings in awe of their height and size. Many of them were completely intact, with just a few cracks radiating from the odd holes that Porantillia had melted through the stone. A few had seen better days, portions of them spewing out into the street like drunken sailors pouring from a tavern but most remained as intact as when the Goddess had attacked the place centuries before.

He looked inside a few of the buildings to see what remained. Many of them had similar stone tables and benches to the one he had seen in the map room at the quarry. Others had constructions within he could not fathom as he rode past.

Teghime snorted, sniffing the air for a scent he could not detect and grew anxious as she approached an intersection. Besmir dropped from her back, handing the reins to Arteera and drawing his sword. He put his back to a building that soared into the sky, hiding in its shadow as he edged towards the crossroads. Risking a peek Besmir saw the cause of his mount's concern and stepped from the shadow, waving his friends forward.

A large carcass, stripped almost entirely of flesh, lay against a wall. Besmir walked over to it, covering his mouth against the smell as a cloud of flies launched from the exposed bones.

He could see it had been a daasnu but wondered what had killed it, as snapping the massive jaw like that must have taken incredible strength.

He turned and walked back to Teghime, soothing the great cat with words and touches as Arteera and Cal Trin did with their mounts.

"Let's go," he said quietly before clambering back into the saddle.

Hours passed as they wandered through the dead city, past columns with statues at the top and fountains long dried up. A massive amphitheater had been dug and built with hundreds of tiers of seats facing a circular stage that had a curved wall behind it to reflect the sound.

Not knowing their destination was worrying, especially when much of the city looked the same and Besmir found himself wondering if they had passed a certain building or statue before. The confusion and bewilderment on his companions faces told him they were feeling the same thing.

Yet he pushed on as the heat of the day rose, steering his mount from side to side as he guided her from one tiny sliver of shade to another. It grew so hot they were forced to take shelter within one of the buildings, using the last of their water to quench their thirst and keep their animals alive.

Arteera drew a knife from Besmir's side.

"What are you up to?" He asked.

"You need a shave," she said. "Your beard is a complete mess and I will not have you reunited with our son looking like a vagrant."

Besmir knew better than to argue and let his wife trim his beard, shaving him as close as she could without cutting his skin. He felt raw and sore after she had finished but had to admit he felt a lot cooler.

"Your turn, old man," she said to Zaynorth who had lain down in the coolest part of the building he could find.

"I will thank you to keep your distance from my face with Besmir's hunting knife," Zaynorth told her. "Should I desire to be skinned, even by a queen, I will request it."

"You're being childish," Arteera said. "Let me give you a little trim so you look your best."

"We're burned, tired and dirty," he said. "Trimming my beard is not about to make me look my best."

"It won't matter if it makes no difference, then," she said brightly.

Zaynorth grunted something about women and sophistry that Besmir did not catch. The king grinned at his old friend as his wife started cutting at his beard.

With Arteera satisfied they all looked good enough to meet her son and the hottest part of the day over, the little company continued their trotting through the dead city.

Eerie sounds made Besmir think they were not alone on a number of occasions and his hand kept straying to his sword until he understood it was the stones themselves making the sounds. Heat and wind seemed to cause the creaking and sometimes wailing sounds, the stones expanding and then moving against each other as they passed. Apart from that, nothing stirred, not a single speck of life seemed to exist in the whole city.

By mid afternoon Besmir's mood had worsened to the point he wanted to blast holes through the walls himself.

Is there no end to this place?

He looked across at his companions, seeing similar dour expressions on their faces. Only Cal Trin seemed unaffected, his expression the same grim, grief stricken one he had worn since his brother had died.

Besmir stretched and stared ahead, jerking in surprise when he saw the figure walking ahead of them.

"Porantillia!" he bellowed loudly. "I've come for you!"

***

Joranas heard the footsteps pounding towards him and instantly knew it was not Whint. He stood, putting aside the stick he had been trying to carve with a sharp, stone knife he had found in one of the houses and looked toward where the footfalls came from. It seemed as if they were coming for an age, echoing from the buildings endlessly until Joranas thought he was going insane and imagining them.

When she finally appeared Joranas felt an irrational jolt of fear and utter confusion wash through him. It looked like

Keluse but a Keluse changed and mutated from the one he knew.

Although she had always been slender, the woman storming towards them was emaciated, as if she had not eaten for weeks. Blood had poured from her nose and mouth where she had smashed her face and her blonde hair looked greasy and far darker than it should. The sun had burned the tops of her ears, forehead, cheeks and nose where he could see bright red skin. Although she was running towards him, her right leg was failing to support her fully and she had a pronounced limp.

"K-Keluse?" He asked unable to believe it was her.

"Well met, Prince Joranas," the woman said in a very un-Keluse like way. "We shall have a formal introduction once I have dealt with thy parents."

"W-What?" Joranas asked, his mind reeling.

The false Keluse grabbed him, her grip deceptively strong and fingers digging in as she dragged him towards the building where his friend was.

"Whint!" Joranas cried. "Whint, help me!"

Relief flooded his young chest as Whint appeared, squinting in the afternoon light as his large frame emerged from the building. His relief was short lived, however, as Keluse shoved him towards Whint.

"Hold this," she commanded.

"Whint?" Joranas asked in fear as the dark skinned man's arms clamped around him like iron.

"Silence," Whint grunted as he hauled Joranas up off his feet.

Keluse stood beside Whint and both turned to face the same street she had entered through.

"What's going on?" Joranas asked, his voice wavering. "Who are you really?"

Keluse's face turned towards him, dried blood and crusted salt from sweat marring her skin and grinned horribly. Joranas saw one of her front teeth had been snapped off, a tiny sliver of white all that was left in the gum. Her skin looked *loose* as if she had aged twenty years since he had seen her a few months ago, hanging from her neck in jowls. Joranas stared at the woman he had known his whole life and knew this was not his friend's mother.

Things fell into place as he struggled against the unmovable arms that held him.

The thing that was talking to Whint is the same thing that has taken control of Keluse!

"Let me go!" Joranas shouted. "If you were ever my friend, Whint, just let me go!"

The dark skinned man never twitched once.

***

Besmir kicked Teghime into a run, her twin toes clicking on the cobblestones as he charged towards the dark figure of his friend. He skidded to a halt not far from where Porantillia had turned Keluse to face him. On her right a large man stood, muscular and strong, holding an urchin across the chest and head. His mahogany skin glistened with sweat and he shook with some unknown palsy. His face was strong and fine boned with a square jaw and framed with loose, dark curls. His eyes were wide, almost bulging despite the bright sun and his white teeth shone from the grimace he wore. Whoever he was it looked as if he was having trouble with something.

Besmir's eyes fell to the younger man the other carried, his eyes widening in horror when he finally recognized his own son. Something felt like a horse kicking him in the sternum as he stared at his altered boy.

Joranas' hair had been bleached by the sun and had grown long enough to touch his shoulders. What was left of his clothing had not covered much of his skin and the sun had burned him a hazelnut-brown, adding a heavy dusting of freckles across his shoulders and the tops of his arms. His eyes looked wild as he tried to stare at the man who held him, then toward Besmir himself.

Besmir heard Arteera make a small noise of despair when she caught up with him and saw Joranas. Yet he had no time to comfort her as he was staring at Keluse's face and the obvious damage that had been done. Despite the blood and missing tooth Porantillia wore a deranged, triumphant grin that set fires of hate inside his chest.

"Thee shall leave now or I kill thy child!" Porantillia shouted.

Besmir stepped forward, ignoring her completely.

"I know you want to kill everyone anyway," he said. "So I think I'll stay right here."

"So be it," Porantillia called.

***

Keluse felt something shift inside her and her pain doubled. Little cuts and scrapes she had barely been aware of shot to the fore as Porantillia tried to leave. She could feel the Goddess pulling her consciousness out through her skull, returning control of her body to Keluse.

"Besmir!" She cried.

Hope flared in her chest when his expression changed to one of recognition.

Yes it's me, your friend.

***

Joranas' heartbeat doubled as soon as he saw his father.

He came! He actually came for me!

Joranas felt a lightness in his chest and a smile spread over his face.

Unbelievably his father was riding one of the massive cats similar to the one Whint had killed, its light brown fur shining in the sunlight. The cat growled low in its throat as another of its kind joined it, this time with a woman on its back.

Joranas had to stare at her, his brain refusing to believe what his eyes were telling him.

It can't be her. Mama?

Her transformation was even more pronounced than his father's. Her skin glowed a deep, golden brown and her hair had lightened in the sun until it was almost the same color as Keluse's. Normally she wore long, flowing dresses and items she had sewn herself but his eyes picked out a pair of cloth leggings clinging to her skin and a shirt that might have fitted his father. A hat covered her head, warding off the sun and casting shade over her face.

Joranas heard Keluse threaten his life and his father refuse to leave. Whint stiffened behind him, his muscles tensing until it felt like Joranas was pressed against stone. The big man trembled, his whole body shaking as if he fought something. His breath came in little gasps and Joranas swore he could hear his friend repeating the same word over and over.

"No! No! No!"

***

Keluse knew something had gone wrong with Porantillia's plan. She had created the man who was holding Joranas, pulled him from her very essence and pushed him from the prison she had been in before Besmir had freed her. Her plan had been to come here and take control of the body. With it being part of her life force, Keluse knew she would not have the limitations she had while using Keluse's own form. Yet for some reason she was still anchored in Keluse's mind.

She could barely feel the connection the Goddess still had to her but knew it was there, like a gentle finger resting on the side of her head. Confusion broke over her like a wave when she felt Porantillia snap back inside her.

Yet Keluse remained in control.

No! It cannot be. Porantillia's angry thought rolled through Keluse's mind and she knew what she had to do to free the universe of her.

***

Besmir knew as soon as he heard her voice say his name that Keluse was back. He had no idea where Porantillia had gone to but he knew she was no longer in control of his friend. He took a few steps towards her as she walked towards him.

"Keluse..." he began, his voice breaking as he looked at the dire state of her body.

Porantillia had used his friend's body hard, aging her and wearing her down in horrible ways. She was limping and in obvious pain as she reached for him, leaning against him for support.

"Don't," she told him when she saw his expression. "She's back in here." Keluse tapped the side of her head. "But she can't do anything...at the moment."

Keluse broke off as Arteera approached, her gaze flicking between his friend and their son, tears rolling down her cheeks.

"What is going on?" She asked. "Who *is* that?" She pointed at the dark skinned man holding Joranas.

Keluse turned to Besmir's wife, taking her hand and looking into her eyes.

"Please, please take care of Ranyeen for me," she said.

Cold fright screwed tight inside Besmir's chest when she said those words. He knew she was not expecting to survive this and wondered if the Gods had been meddling again.

"Of course, we'll look after you both," Arteera said, confused.

Keluse smiled at her sadly, shaking her hands and turning back to Besmir.

"You're going to have to kill her while she's trapped," Keluse said.

"I can't!" Besmir cried. "Keluse, I can't."

"What are you talking about?" Arteera demanded. "How can you kill her?"

Keluse rolled her eyes towards the queen.

"Porantillia is still inside of me. She's trapped at the moment but I can feel her fighting for control and when she wins, it'll be too late."

Besmir watched his wife as understanding dropped into her, tears forming in her eyes.

"There must be some other way," she said.

Keluse made a clicking sound in her throat as she almost doubled over, grunting.

"There isn't," Keluse said. "She's nearly broken through. Besmir, do it!"

"How can I?" Besmir begged as sorrow mixed with despair in his chest.

"Kill me," Keluse said in a quiet voice. "Send me to be with Ranyor and end this before she destroys the world. Kill me!" Keluse ended her sentence in a shout.

Chapter Twenty Nine

This is going to hurt. Tiernon thought to Collise as heat flared from her palms.

Searing agony rolled up her arms as her father burned through the bindings that held them to the chair. She screamed inside her mind as Tiernon maintained the fire, searing through the leather, grunting through the pain himself.

With a final jerk Tiernon freed their wrists and flapped the flames out with a shake of their arms. He took the blindfold off and Collise saw they were in a stone cell, dark and damp. Reaching down he undid the rope that held their legs and rubbed the circulation back into their cold feet. Pain lanced up her arms from the blistered skin but Tiernon ignored it as he strode to the door.

Collise felt an immense pressure grow inside her as her father did something she could not begin to understand. She watched as he gestured with her hand, the pressure lancing along her arm and out through her finger. The dungeon door folded outwards with an explosive thump, splintering against the wall opposite.

Shaken and pale a face appeared from the gloom and dust, pointing a spear at Collise as he trembled. He died in agony when Tiernon lanced lightning through his heart. She screamed inside her mind as her father advanced along the stone corridor, casually lobbing fire at anything that moved. At an intersection he turned and made for a set of stairs leading upwards.

At the top sat a thick, oaken door firmly bolted and locked.

"Halt or die!" A voice called through the tiny grate.

Tiernon laughed in Collise's high pitched voice and gathered the pressure in their chest again, ready to burst the door.

"If you open the door and leave I might allow you to live!" Tiernon called back.

Collise felt a wave of hatred and disgust roll through her when she realized he had no intention of giving them a chance to run. He gestured and the door burst outward, massive chunks and splinters shredding the air as well as the guards in the room beyond.

Her mind shied away from the sight as Tiernon walked into the room full of dead and dying people, casting another fireball towards the door when he caught sight of a fleeing figure.

Stop! Just stop this! Collise begged.

Why would I do that? Now I have a fine, young body I can rule again. Tiernon thought back.

He stepped from the prison and out into the waning daylight, grinning as the fresh air washed over their face. Tiernon took a deep breath and turned for Kings Avenue.

Joranas could not hear any of what his parents said to Keluse but he became instantly aware when Keluse turned and screamed at Whint.

"Kill him!"

She turned back almost immediately but the damage seemed to be done as Whint tightened his grip around Joranas, easily cutting his breathing off. Panic gripped Joranas and he thrashed weakly, kicking at Whint even though he knew there was no hope of defeating the strong man.

With each breath released Whint squeezed a little tighter, meaning the next breath was lessened. Joranas weakened as he started to run out of air, his lungs burning and numbness beginning in his fingertips. Darkness started at the edges of his vision and his mind started to play tricks on him as he thought he could hear his mother screaming his name. Joranas smiled knowing she would never do such a thing.

When the end came it felt more like he was being dropped. The hot ground, baked solid by centuries of sun burning against his back.

Joranas dragged in a deep breath as his eyes snapped open. Whint stood over him with the stone knife he had been whittling with gripped tightly in his fist. Joranas swallowed as he thought the strong man was about to butcher him like he had done to so many animals.

"I..." Whint tried but he could not speak.

Instead he took the stone knife in both his hands and rammed it into his own chest.

***

NO! Porantillia thundered when she felt the body she had crafted over centuries stab itself.

She thrashed helplessly but could not make Keluse's body obey her in any way at all. Without control of the woman she could not even use her powers. Porantillia fought and pushed and struggled to get the same minuscule amount of control she had stolen to order the boy's death.

"She's too strong!" Keluse said. "Do it now, Besmir!"

Porantillia grinned knowing the man could never kill his friend. He would see all life falter and wither at her hands and Porantillia vowed to herself he would be the last to die.

Something gave inside Keluse, some part of her psyche that had been resisting Porantillia snapped and the Goddess shot forward wresting control of her body.

***

Besmir watched as his friend's face fell, her expression showing utter desperation then agony. Keluse bent forwards, her back twitching for a second as she stood up once more.

The expression on her face told him everything he needed to know. Porantillia's grin was as evil and hate filled as it had been before.

"Joranas!" Arteera screamed.

Besmir watched in horror as she lanced forward, plunging his hunting knife into Keluse's abdomen and up behind her ribs. His wife peeled her lips back from her teeth as she swirled the blade around inside Keluse, cutting and mincing her vital organs. Keluse's eyes widened in pain and shock. Her hands flapped at Arteera weakly as her muscles began to spasm. She grabbed Besmir as her knees began to buckle and Arteera wrenched her knife clear spilling a gout of hot blood over him and the floor. Gasping and unable to speak, Keluse smiled at him and then Arteera.

"Aberhh...." her final breath came out as nonsense and Besmir laid her gently on the cobblestones.

***

Joranas sucked in deep breaths savoring the sweet scent of his mother's skin. Her hair was as soft as it had ever been and her whispering in his ear just as wonderful. He could have stayed there forever, relishing the feel of her soft skin against his, the way she held him tight to her chest.

Yet he knew something was happening behind him. His father had stabbed Keluse and he was sobbing. Joranas needed to know what was going on. Reluctantly he pulled away from his mother's comforting embrace and turned. She pulled him back but stared at his father too.

As he watched his father weeping over the body of his friend he saw the air shimmer. He wiped his eyes thinking it was tears that caused it but when he looked again he saw the shimmering was more intense and shadows had appeared within it. Three shapes formed as Joranas watched, one had antlers, one covered in feathers and the third a woman.

"Thee hast done well, my child," the feathered one said to his father.

Besmir raised his head, dust washed into strange patterns by his tears, to look at the trio. Joranas saw his face change to anger.

"Happy now?" he asked. "Now she's dead and my friend, too?"

Joranas jumped at the tone of his father's voice, pain and hate filled.

"Of course we are not happy," the woman snapped in a voice like thunder rolling through the hills.

Joranas dropped to his knees. Not just because the voice had been so loud but because he realized these were the *Gods*. He panted in frightened awe as he looked upon the images of Cathantor, Sharise and Mwondi, each appearing in full glory.

"Don't touch her!" he heard his father shout.

Before his eyes, the three Gods lifted Keluse's body between them. His father stood, brandishing his sword at them as a golden light suffused her body. Joranas realized they were healing her body, repairing all the damage the thing inside her had done and he struggled to get from his mother's clutches. She clung to him tightly, crying out for him not to go but

Joranas was stronger now and pulled out of her arms, running to where his father stood.

"Wait, father!" he shouted, putting himself before Besmir. "They are healing her!"

"I don't care," his father growled. "You don't know what they've done I don't want them touching her!"

"It's what Ranyeen would want, father," Joranas pleaded. "Let them fix her."

Joranas watched the fight go out of his father. The hunter king stared at him as if realizing who he was for the first time and dropped his sword to the cobbles with a clang to pull Joranas to him.

"Oh my boy. Oh my son!" His father moaned as he lifted him against his chest, hugging him more tightly than his mother had.

***

Besmir felt the small body of his son pressed tightly against him, the chasm that had been in his chest for months filling with a glowing love for the boy.

The three Gods laid Keluse on a stretcher they conjured somehow, intact and beautiful. Her blonde hair framed a face restored, her nose had been put back, her blood cleaned and skin tight once more. Besmir was sure her broken tooth was repaired along with any damage his sword had done.

Pain grew in his chest when he thought of what he had done. He had his son back but at what cost. Col Trin and

Keluse and those were just the ones he knew of. Then there was the dark man that had held Joranas.

Besmir turned to look at the man as the Gods faded.

Good. Never bother me again.

We may have need of thee yet, my child. Mwondi's voice echoed inside his head.

Besmir led his son over to the dark skinned man, hearing Joranas sniff. He looked to see the tears flooding his eyes and reached for his shoulder, feeling his burned skin crisp beneath his fingers.

"Whint?" Joranas asked in a small voice.

He knelt beside the man who had tried to kill him and Besmir was about to pull him back but Arteera stopped him. Zaynorth trotted over as Joranas shook the man's arm in a futile attempt to wake him.

"He was never meant for this world," Cathantor said, making them all jump.

Besmir rolled his eyes getting a warning glance from Arteera who bowed, elbowing her husband in the ribs. He ignored her and turned his attention to his son.

"Porantillia crafted him of herself in the absence. He was a part of her, an extension of her and as such should have obeyed her every word but..." Cathantor looked at Joranas. "You managed to show him a better way."

"How is this better?" Joranas sobbed. "He's dead."

"Really, he was never alive but what he did, what he gave, was to save you." The God glanced at Besmir. "There is no greater gift," he added with a quick look at Keluse.

"I never said goodbye," Joranas said in a devastated voice.

"Maybe there is still time," Cathantor said as he faded.

"You are still annoying," the thing his son called Whint said in a deep voice.

Joranas leaped at him, hugging his torso but staying far from the knife that jutted from him.

"Whint!" Joranas cried in joy. "You're alive!"

"You're alive!" Whint repeated, stroking his son's face gently.

His eyes opened, fixing on Joranas kindly. Whatever else this thing might be, whether Porantillia created it or not, Cathantor had been right. Whint had killed himself to save his son and Besmir would remember that sacrifice for the rest of his life.

"Whint!" Joranas said, his voice squeaking as the dark skinned man's eyes started to shut.

"Jor...anas..." Whint said as his final breath left his body.

***

Helpless to do anything but watch Collise sobbed inside her own mind as her father strode through the center of Morantine ravaging people with lightning and fire. A few of the buildings along Kings Avenue were ablaze, chains of people with buckets trying to put them out as Tiernon walked among them. Few saw Collise's body walk past them, fewer still knowing it was Tiernon who had passed by.

"Open the doors!" Tiernon called when he reached Besmir's house.

Collise heard marching footsteps and knew any sent against her father would likely die. She also knew he was prepared for the same manner of attack that had seen them incarcerated in the first place and felt the hair rise on her arms and across her back as he erected a barrier around them. She heard the doors open at the same time as a group of heavily armed guards marched from a courtyard to the side.

Collise felt her father grin at the futility of their efforts and struggled against him when he raised her hand towards them. The lightning that lanced from her fingers leaped from guard to guard, running across their armor and making them jerk and twitch in a horrible parody of a dance. When she felt the power stop flowing, eight men and women lay dead. Tiernon swung to face Branisi whose face was pale with shock and grief as she steadied herself against the doorway.

"No way to welcome your queen," he said with a savage grin. "I can do this all night, have you the guards?"

Branisi shook her head slowly, her eyes fixed on the dead as she stepped aside. Tiernon guided Collise's body up the steps and into Besmir's house, looking around with disdain at the simple décor and furnishings.

What's the point of ruling a nation if you can't indulge in the finer things in life? Tiernon thought.

He marched into the royal family's private rooms and stood, hands fisted on hips as he looked around the room. His eyes lit on a large painting on one wall, the only particularly expensive thing he could see. His eyes traced over the curves and outlines of Arteera's face as she stared from the canvas. Collise felt sickness wash though her at the thoughts that raced through her father's mind as he gawped at the painting.

"So this is Besmir's wife," he said to no one in particular.

"You know it is," Branisi muttered from behind.

Tiernon spun Collise round to confront the housecarl. Branisi looked ill, her arms had folded across her chest protectively and she looked at the floor with a distant expression.

"This child's memories do her no justice," Tiernon said. "I wonder how she'll take to being mine upon her return?"

"What are you talking about?" Branisi demanded.

Collise felt a horrible grin spread across her face as her father smiled.

"When my nephew returns I shall treat him to the same fate he gave me!" Tiernon grunted with an edge of anger. "Then this little beauty will become my plaything."

Collise watched as realization dawned on Branisi's face. Her eyes came up to meet Collise's own and her mouth dropped open with a gasp.

"You really are Tiernon back from the dead, aren't you?"

"At your service," Tiernon replied with a mocking bow. "And now we have a lot of business to get through."

"What have you done with Collise?" Branisi asked.

"Dead," Tiernon lied. "And gone."

Collise felt a warmth run through her when she saw Branisi's face fall.

Did she actually like me?

I doubt it. Tiernon thought back. *Let's face it, there's nothing much to like.* He chuckled.

Collise could see him rifling through her memories and wondered what he was after.

"The cook!" He said with a little surprise. "You and she are lovers." It was not a question and Branisi's face hardened into something Collise had not seen before.

"You harm her and..."

"And what?" Tiernon demanded in Collise's high voice. "What will you do?" A sneer crossed Colllise's face as Branisi's face fell. "Worry not, your little sapphist will be perfectly safe as long as you do as I say."

Tiernon walked over and sat by the window, the same place Collise herself used to sit, and watched the mayhem without as people rushed to put out the fires and clear the dead.

"Come here," Tiernon muttered, "and kneel."

Collise could not see her but she heard Branisi's slow footsteps approach and the click of her knees as she knelt.

"Good," Tiernon said, turning to allow Collise to see Branisi on the floor. "Arrange for builders to start repairing the palace," he ordered. "I'll have somewhere proper to rule from. Then get me the highest ranking officials Besmir used to have so we can have a little talk. Bring me the best wine this dump has to offer," Tiernon grinned. "And get your little wife to prepare me a feast, this girl is hungry!"

Collise watched as Branisi stood, her head down and hair hanging across her face. Her entire demeanor was one of defeat and she trudged back across the room towards the door.

"Try to help her escape and I'll eviscerate her while you watch," Tiernon said in a dead voice.

Chapter Thirty

Besmir smiled as he watched his son play with Teghime. The great cat had accepted his son at first sniff and she doted on Joranas as much as she did Besmir himself. Joranas's laugh split the morning air as Teghime rolled on her back, nudging his legs so he fell to the sandy earth.

Joranas had shown them where to get water. Massive stone tanks had been built into the city to trap what rain did fall, storing it below ground in the cool. He also took them to a garden within the city. Overgrown trees and shrubs clung to life here, providing a little fruit and some firewood but Joranas had suggested it might be a nice place to leave Keluse and his friend Whint.

That had been an odd story. Told in sections as Joranas was grieving over Keluse and his friend, Besmir came to learn of the odd man that had looked after his son when Porantillia had stolen him. It soon became obvious that Joranas had come to love Whint, depending on him for more than food and protection and Besmir was careful not to say anything against him.

It would take Joranas a long time to recover from what had happened, Besmir thought as he watched the daasnu licking Joranas's face while the lad squealed laughter. Each night Joranas slept between Besmir and Arteera, holding each of his parents tightly to make sure he was not separated from them in the night. He often went around the group, gently touching each member in turn to make sure they were real before sitting down to a meal or turning in for the night.

Besmir shared worried glances with his companions when they watched his son carry out his rituals but he chose not to say anything, hoping the passage of time would help heal the scars.

"Joranas!" Besmir called.

His son trotted over, Teghime a few steps behind, his face the somber mask Besmir sometimes saw.

"Shall we take a ride?" He asked his son.

Joranas' face changed to one of anticipation and he nodded eagerly. Besmir mounted the great daasnu, offering his hand to his son and hauling him up to sit before him. With virtually no encouragement the large cat was off, galloping across the desert sand with long strides.

Besmir felt the warm air hit his face and reveled in the feeling of just having his son there. He thought it odd the mere fact of having Joranas back could change so much in him, but it did. Now, when he looked at Aristulia, he saw beauty and life where there had only been a cursed wasteland before. The range of rocky hills to the southeast glowed as the morning sun climbed into the air, orange and red shimmering in the desert heat while the slumbering giant Mount Ashod belched smoke into the air.

"What's happened to that mountain?" Joranas asked as he stared in wonder at the immense tower of smoke.

"It's called a volcano," Besmir said, ruffling his son's hair. "Sometimes liquid fire explodes out of them,"

"Why?"

"I have no idea," Besmir said. "None at all."

Joranas fell silent as he stared at the landscape before him, Besmir could tell he was worried or concerned about something but was unable to tell what it was. He slipped from the saddle, waiting for Joranas to drop down then let Teghime free for a while. He picked his way through the rocks and sand until he reached a sheltered area with shade and soft sand. There Besmir sat, swilling water from his canteen as Joranas plopped down beside him.

They sat in companionable silence for a few minutes until Besmir spoke.

"You know you can tell me anything?" He asked.

Joranas turned, squinting at his father with one eye. Besmir chuckled at his face.

"I mean you don't have to tell me anything, but if there's anything you want to talk about..."

Joranas looked away again, staring off into the distance where the volcano grumbled.

"It's just..." Joranas began. "When you said about that...volcano spitting fire..." He looked at Besmir again. "I can make fire too."

Besmir nodded, recalling what he had been teaching Joranas just prior to him being kidnapped.

"It's something I can help you learn to control," he said, "and we could explore other powers you might have."

Joranas looked down at the sand at his feet.

"I don't know if I want to," he muttered. "I don't want to hurt anyone."

"No," Besmir said. "But what if you hurt someone accidentally, because you can't control it?"

"When me and Whint..." Joranas paused, swallowing. "Before. I burned some animals like Teghime when they were attacking him," Joranas explained. "I still dream about their screams sometimes," he added. "Why do we have these powers?"

Besmir took a long breath, preparing to disappoint his son with his lack of knowledge.

"I don't know *why* we have them," he admitted. "But they're just a tool, like a hammer or sword."

He grinned when Joranas looked at him with a frown of puzzlement.

"If a man has a sword but has no idea how to use it, chances are he's going to hurt himself or someone else," Besmir said. "Same with power, if you don't know how to control it you might hurt someone else even if you don't mean to."

"So if I learn how to use this fire I've got I could choose never to use it at all?"

"Yes," Besmir nodded. "That'd be completely up to you."

"I miss Whint," Joranas said abruptly.

Besmir wrapped an arm around his small shoulders and pulled him in for a hug.

"Yes," he said in a kind voice. "That might take a long time to get used to."

"It hurts," Joranas said in a soft voice, as tears welled in his eyes.

"I know," Besmir said. "But one day you'll be able to think about him and the pain will be less. Then it gets smaller and smaller until you can remember the good times you had without much pain at all."

Joranas leaned against Besmir and cried softly for a while. Besmir let a few tears of his own flow when Keluse's shocked, pain filled face came to mind as he butchered her in an abandoned city.

***

"Gentlemen!" Tiernon shouted as he entered the conference room.

He had dressed Collise in a bright green dress with her hair worn up in a matching ribbon, madly pleased with himself that his whole demeanor would confuse this room full of old men. Collise watched from inside her mind as he trotted around the room, many of the men there watching her with puzzled faces.

"Who are you?" One asked as she passed.

Tiernon paused dramatically, turning to face the old man slowly with a shocked expression on his face.

"You mean you don't know?" He purred in a ridiculous voice.

"Look this is madness, we have a country to run while King Besmir is away and you've called us in here to play games." The old man stood. "I'm leaving."

"Take one step and your whole family dies," Tiernon said in Collise's sweetest voice.

"Just who do you think you are?" He demanded angrily.

Tiernon reached down and took the old man's hand. Collise felt the hairs on her arm rise as her father unleashed his attack. He stiffened, his body breaking wind as every muscle tightened. His eyes opened wide and rolled around in their sockets. Wisps of hair on his head began to smoke, curls of flame breaking out as Tiernon pulsed lightning through his body. The smell of urine and cooking meat filled the room as the old man died in silent agony.

Tiernon stopped and let go of his hand as his body went limp and crashed to the floor, head thumping on the table as he fell. Tiernon looked at the shocked faces of the other men who were all staring back at him.

"Who do I think I am?" Tiernon asked in a deceptively calm voice. "I'm King Tiernon Fringor and I've been given a second chance with this child's body." He let the information sink in but could see the looks of skepticism in their eyes. "You'll all realize I speak the truth when you return home," Tiernon told them. "I have taken the liberty of having your families rounded up. Currently your wives, children and grandchildren are being herded into stables somewhere should any of you decide to become difficult. I am more than happy to return them piece by piece if you don't comply with everything I say."

Tiernon looked round the room, satisfied that many of the men looked unsure whether to believe him or not. The rest looked as if they believed the words of the girl before them, believing she had their families even if they didn't believe she was Tiernon.

"What would you have us do, sire?" Another man asked, unable to tear his eyes from the dead man beside him.

"That's the spirit!" Tiernon chirped happily. "I want you to spread the word among your lackeys and lickspittles, tell them all I have returned and anyone who even *thought* of opposing me ten years ago is about to die in horrible pain. I also want Besmir. Alive."

Tiernon flicked his gaze around the room to each man, holding their attention with a dire stare that was immediately older than Collise's ten years.

"Off you go then," Tiernon said in a sweet voice, flipping his hand. "And," he flapped a hand at the smoking ruin of a man on the floor, "take that with you."

***

Wit Shull, the Corbondrasi capital, was draped in banners as Besmir and his now enlarged party rode along the banks of the river Shull. People had decorated any and everything they could, including themselves, as a party seemed to be underway.

Besmir had seen a plume of dust rising in the distance two days previously, a large party riding towards them.

"Probably come to greet us," Zaynorth said.

Yet Besmir had picked up on the slightest hint of nerves from the old man and shared them. For all they knew this could be a group of bandits come to rob and kill them. Weakened as they were by lack of numbers, they could not fight off a larger force even with Besmir and Joranas using magic.

Besmir rode on tensely as the dust cloud grew larger, the wind carrying it for miles to the east. Eventually he led his small group to one side of the road they were traveling on to let the larger group pass if they wanted.

"They are dressed in royal uniforms," Founsalla said as he peered into the distance. "I would guess we have been spotted and his majesty Vi Rhane has arranged an honor guard."

Besmir relaxed a little but could not do so fully until he saw them for himself. Leading the group was a tall Corbondrasi with purple plumage who dismounted and bowed.

"Your royal majesty," Pira translated for the man. "We are sent to escort you and your party back to the palace. Not too much farther we have supplies, fresh horses and wagons should you wish to rest."

"Thank you," Besmir said simply.

Weariness and grief had taken their toll on the whole party and Besmir knew he would have to relive the whole story any number of times as ever more people demanded to know what had happened in the strange, deserted country. He let the Corbondrasi captain take the lead, forming his men up around them protectively and guiding them towards the city.

Now, rested and back in Teghime's saddle, Besmir stared at the bright colors around him. Every hue seemed to be represented in the streets, with Corbondrasi having colored their already bright plumage. Most of the women wore jewels in their feathers and many people danced in the streets to music played on stringed instruments.

The party didn't halt as they passed, merely gave way to the riders, flowing back into the space behind them like water.

Keluse would've loved this. She always wanted to see it.

Besmir remembered Ranyor telling her about the Corbondrasi celebration. Three days of dancing and celebration to the God Mwondi when even the royal family mingled with everyone else and all gave what they could afford towards the feasting.

Yet now, both Ranyor and Keluse were dead and neither one could ever sing, dance or even feast again.

"What's wrong, my love?" Arteera asked when she saw his expression.

"I killed her," Besmir said. "And Ranyor died serving me. I'm not good to be around."

Arteera guided her daasnu closer and leaned across, taking his hand as people cheered and clapped around them.

"Look around you," she said. "All these people, every single one, is alive because of you. You've saved the entire *world* and I, for one, would want to be nowhere but around you."

Besmir nodded and rode grimly on, heading for the palace and the embassy where he could get some peace from the endless display of happiness.

*****

"Your majesty," Joranas said as he bowed to Vi Rhane.

The Corbondrasi king chuckled and offered his hand to shake.

"There's no need for such ceremony, Joranas, I am pleased to finally meet you. Your father told me many things about you when he was here. Please enjoy your stay and I am glad you are safe now."

"Thank you," Joranas said.

Besmir watched as he walked back over to stand beside him and whispered.

"What did you tell him about me?"

"That you can't leave the house without staining or tearing your clothes," Besmir said with a chuckle.

He heard his son huff and laughed again as Herofic and Ru Tarn came into the throne room. It was all he could do not to gape at the man who he had known for more than a decade.

Herofic wore an open shirt in the Corbondrasi style. Silken and light blue in color it clung to his muscled torso like a second skin. Light gray trousers, again silken, ballooned slightly as they dropped into a pair of calf length, supple black boots. He had scrubbed his skin and his dark hair had been oiled until it shone.

"That's nothing short of a miracle," Besmir whispered to his wife. "Who is that?"

Arteera gave him a warning glance but also had a smirk on her face.

"Apparently, he's set a precedent for men to carry eggs," she said. "Su Rhane told me many of the Corbondrasi noblewomen have been swooning at his feet."

Besmir shook his head, trying to reconcile the gruff, blunt, battle axe wielding man he knew with the almost debonair gentleman striding along the carpeted aisle towards him. Slung over one shoulder, dropping to the opposite hip and running up his back, Herofic wore a gold and silver sash with the most intricate embroidery he had ever seen. Nestled in the folds the king could just see the top of a light blue speckled egg.

"Oh," Arteera gushed. "He's matched his shirt color to her egg."

Besmir stared at his wife as tears of happiness sprung to her eyes, noting a number of Corbondrasi women dabbing at their own as he looked around the room. Zaynorth rolled his eyes at Besmir who tried not to laugh as an incredible fanfare blasted through the room.

Su Rhane appeared to float through the throne room, her king moving to take her arm as she made her way along the central aisle towards the throne where they both sat. What followed was a number of speeches and congratulations for Joranas' safe return. Once dealt with the party retired to an adjoining room and so began a formal dance and ball. Besmir watched as any number of Corbondrasi women approached Herofic, asking him to dance.

Late in the evening Herofic approached the small group gathered around the Gazluthian king.

Zaynorth pointed at the egg slung at Herofic's chest.The warrior grinned and stroked the shell.

"Let me show you something incredible," he said.

Herofic rose and dragged a large candelabra across towards them. Carefully he dipped his hand beneath the egg and lifted it out. Besmir could see it was about the size of the warrior's head and the speckling cover the surface. Herofic held the egg before the candlelight and Besmir heard Arteera gasp as they could all see the child twitching within.

"Amazing," Besmir said.

"I know," Herofic replied.

"I mean you're so old. How has she let you look after such a precious thing?" He grinned as Arteera poked him in the ribs.

Herofic tucked the egg back in the sash he wore and fixed Besmir with an angry look.

"Old or not, king or not, I will still kick you into next week, boy!"

Besmir chuckled and stood as Ru Tarn approached them.

"Madam ambassador," he greeted her formally but smiled warmly.

"Your majesty," she replied, spreading her arms in a curtsy.

"Herofic was just telling us how he is in need of a warm drink and blankets to soothe his aches and pains," Besmir said.

Besmir laughed at his own joke as he turned to see if Keluse found it as funny.

"What is being the matter?" Ru Tarn asked in concern when she saw Besmir's face fall.

The king frowned and shook his head.

"Nothing, nothing. Don't worry, I'm fine."

He clapped Herofic on the back foundering with the knowledge he had just forgotten Keluse was dead. Thoughts and feelings whirled in his head as he sat there, guilt and loss the primary ones. He turned when he felt a hand on his shoulder, looking into Arteera's knowing eyes with a jolt.

"We need to get this one to a bed," she muttered, dipping her gaze to Joranas. "Then you can tell me what is wrong."

"The same thing that's always going to be wrong," Besmir said in a suddenly exhausted voice.

***

Collise woke with a start, unsure of her whereabouts. She was cold and laying on something hard in near total darkness. She frowned as a wave of nausea rolled through her, the world around her spinning. Liquid flooded her mouth and her stomach squeezed, spilling its contents to the floor.

After several minutes of heaving Collise knelt, wiping her mouth with her arm and tried to recall what had happened. It came to her in broken pieces, filled with gaps and hazy memories. Tiernon had thrown himself some kind of deranged party. He had plied her young body with drink and smoked something that made her cough and her throat sore. His entertainments had been based around humiliating people, mostly women. The women and children he had had kidnapped while their husbands were at the meeting had been forced to strip and dance as he drank and laughed.

Using my body!

Abruptly it hit her. He was no longer in control. She could move her limbs, turn her head and a squeal of joy erupted from inside her. It echoed around the room and she jumped at how loud she had been.

Sitting in a puddle of her own making Collise searched inside her mind for any trace of her father. It felt strange to direct a thought at a certain point inside her head but with a little concentration she found she could do it.

He was still there.

Like a vicious predator lying in wait she could still feel his presence there malevolent and evil but sleeping.

Or unconscious. She thought.

Carefully to avoid waking him Collise got to her feet. Her legs ached as if she had been beaten and she wondered what would possess someone to drink so much if this was what it felt like the following day. Moonlight streamed in through windows high in one wall lighting the old throne room in the palace.

He must have come here while he was drunk, forgetting it's a ruin.

The builders had made a start on renovating the room, Collise saw as she walked across to the old throne and leaned against it. Piles of stone and bits of masonry lay beside mounds of sand and other things she had no idea what they were.

Collise took a deep breath and sighed, wondering if this was to be her life now. Only able to exist if her father were in a drunken stupor and forced to witness the sick debauchery he enjoyed so much.

Tears started to roll down her face the more she thought about it and she realized she would rather be dead than have some kind of half existence trapped as a prisoner inside her own body.

Maybe that's what I have to do. She thought. *Kill myself and my father. At least that way he can't torture anyone any longer.*

But how should she do it? Climb to the top of the palace and leap? Find a sword and open a vein? The answer came to her in a flash of young inspiration and she stood on unsteady legs, making for the door leading to the Hall of Kings.

The statues of Tiernon's ancestors–*her* ancestors, she thought–seemed to watch her with kind eyes as if the spirits of her forebears approved of her actions. It was not until she reached the far end of the hall she saw what appeared to be an extra statue staring at her. This one, however, was filmy and indistinct as she stared at it and realized she could see through it.

"*Mama?*" Collise whispered.

The spirit of Deremona smiled a more benevolent smile than she ever had in life.

"Collise," she said.

Her voice sounded distant, as if she were calling from down a long corridor and it made Collise shiver to think she was talking to the ghost of her mother, the mother she killed.

"I-I'm sorry, mama. I didn't mean to..."

"Hush now, child," her mother said. "In case *he* wakes. I'm the one who needs to be sorry. I should have been a better mother to a sweet girl like you but I was too caught up in my own selfish misery to see what a blessing I had right before me."

Collise tried to swallow the lump that grew in her throat but could not stop more tears from flowing down her cheeks. Panic hit her when she felt a flash of consciousness from Tiernon.

"Mama!" She hissed.

"I know, child," her mother said. "Follow me and be as quiet and gentle as you can."

Deremona floated a little way along the corridor and turned into the room in which the altar lay. Collise followed, fear pulling her back the other way when she thought of being in the same room as that thing again.

That's what put him inside my head in the first place.

It was unchanged inside the room. The altar stood in the middle, its silver inlay glowing a sick, pale, throbbing light that illuminated the room eerily. Collise stepped gingerly inside and pressed her back against the cold stone to be as far as possible from the hateful thing.

"Come close, Collise," Deremona said gently.

Collise shook her head, crying harder but trying to be quiet so Tiernon did not wake.

The shade of her mother drifted close, her misty eyes staring directly into those of her daughter.

"Trust me, child," she said gently. "Lay your hand on the table, there are some spirits here who wish to speak with your father."

Collise became aware of a host of other people, spirits like her mother, all staring at her from the far side of the altar. They all had a similar expression painted on their face, eager expectation.

"Come now, Collise," Deremona said. "Let us take him from inside your mind."

Collise took a step forward, her hand rising towards the table. A second step brought her halfway to touching its cold surface. Two more and she was there, hand hovering above the glowing metalwork as she looked at her mother's ghostly face.

"Trust me, child," her mother said. "Trust me more than I ever deserved in life and know I love you."

Collise let her hand drop.

Tiernon snapped awake.

Collise screamed as molten barbs ripped into her brain. Tiernon clung to her with every ounce of will his addled, broken mind could muster but thousands of spirits pulled at him. Shadowy figures leaped from the table, gripping Tiernon's spirit from *inside* Collise and dragging him free.

She could hear his screams matching her own as he was slowly pulled down her neck, into her shoulder and through her arm into the altar. The agony cut into Collise and her screams echoed through the old building as her father tried in vain to stay inside her body. Eventually she felt the last searing agony leave her hand and wrenched it from the surface of the altar, falling back and panting as the pain left her.

Collise looked up to see the spirit of a middle aged man floating above the altar. He was balding and wrinkled with a cruel mouth and nasty eyes.

Tiernon. She thought.

He was confused and bewildered as he stared back at her but turned as someone else appeared at his side. Her mother floated next to Tiernon, looking angrier and more fierce than she ever had in life.

"I've waited for this," Deremona growled in a horrific voice.

Her spirit dived at Tiernon's own and he flinched as she smashed through him, ripping a piece of his spirit and taking it with her. Another woman appeared and slammed through Tiernon, tearing another section from him as he screamed an echoing scream.

After that it became a frenzy of people, each one ripping a piece from Tiernon's shade, systematically tearing him to pieces as he screamed and screamed, his eyes wide with fear and pain.

"A fitting end for him," Deremona said from beside her daughter. "And now, my love, I must leave."

"But I don't want to be alone!" Collise cried.

"And you won't be," her mother said gently as her spirit faded. "Trust in Besmir."

Epilogue

Soft, sweet smelling grass cushioned her body as she lay in the warmth of the sun. Without opening her eyes she lay there basking in the glow as she tried to identify as many of the animals around her as she could from their calls.

An Orm warbler trilled his song to announce her presence at the same time as a Day Singer whistled to the rising sun, her song complex and almost worshipful. She managed to recognize a few more as she lay there but there were many more she did not know the names of and more still she had never heard before.

Keluse opened her eyes, blinking as the sun-bright world came to her. The greenest of green foliage waved lazily above her head. An immense oak tree spreading gnarled and thick branches to shade her from the brightest of the sun's rays. Her keen eyes picked out a squirrel as it bounded up the trunk and out along one of the branches bent on some errand. Birds flew from branch to branch, their plumage ranging from dull browns to outrageous orange, red and blue.

She sat up and stared at the seemingly endless grassland she was at the edge of. Herds of cattle and deer roamed freely across the greensward, tearing at the grass and flowers as she scanned the horizon. The forest at her back looked to have patches of as many species of tree as there were, from pine and spruce to red leaved things she had never seen before.

Her memory jerked and she recalled the searing agony as Besmir had plunged his sword into her chest. Her hands automatically felt there but there was no injury and no pain. Keluse stood, her brain just about coming to the conclusion she was in the afterlife.

"I'm dead," she said aloud.

She stared about, realizing, apart from the wildlife, she was also alone.

Heart heavy Keluse started to walk. Not knowing where to go she trudged along the edge of the forest, her eyes flicking from one bright flower to the next. Scents came to her, the perfume from so many flowers, the mushroom-like scent of damp leaves from the forest floor and the musky scent of animals who were more than happy to approach her.

How many of these did I send here?

Her morose thought died as she looked up to see a lone figure trotting towards her. Her heart leaped in her chest at the thought of who it had to be and tears of joy rolled down her face as soon as it was confirmed.

He was as rangy as he had been in life. Tall and thin with his black hair and pale skin, Ranyor sprinted through the grass towards her.

Keluse started to run too, grass stems and leaves whipping at her calves as she pounded for her husband. They halted a few feet apart, wordlessly staring at each other for a few seconds before wrapping their arms around each other tightly. Her mouth found his and she thrilled at the feel of him as they kissed for the first time in a decade.

"Hello," Ranyor said, panting his hot breath over her face.

"Hello you," Keluse mumbled, not quite able to believe he was here.

"I don't think I will ever let you go," Ranyor said, pulling another kiss from her mouth.

"Fine by me," Keluse said.

***

Everyone who was not engaged in nefarious deeds lined the streets of Morantine to welcome the royal family home, with one exception. Collise wrung her hands as she paced the length of the sitting room, nervously awaiting the return of the man who might decide to slay her.

Every time she reached the window she peered out, hoping and not hoping to see him drawing nearer. Half of her wanted him to arrive and deal her fate while the other half wanted him to be called away again. The crowds were cheering and waving flags in anticipation of his return but Collise felt sick.

She tried to sit but her body would not remain still so she stood up and began pacing across the room again. From window to door and back again, waiting for King Besmir to come home.

Outside the cheering grew in volume and Collise knew he must be getting closer. She pressed her head against the window trying to get a glimpse of him as he rode slowly down Kings Avenue. Her brain refused to believe what she saw at first and Collise had to concentrate to be sure she was seeing what she was.

He was riding a massive cat!

The queen had one, too, and Prince Joranas rode with his mother as all three waved and smiled at the people who had come out to greet them. Collise watched as he slowly made his way home, to the house she had tried to steal, the *kingdom* she had tried to steal and nerves almost got the better of her as she ran for the door. Collise pulled it open, ready to flee but realized she still did not have anywhere to go and closed it again.

Eventually she could hear voices in the hallway beyond and closed her eyes as she heard Branisi's muffled voice talking quickly. A deeper voice replied and then she heard footsteps approaching.

Collise darted about, trying to find the best place to be when he opened the door. Should she sit in the chair, stand by the window or beside the fire? The choice was taken from her as she was halfway between window and hearth when the door opened.

Collise froze as she was confronted by a tall, bearded man. He wore brown trousers and jacket with a simple shirt, all of it unadorned save for the white stag that was his emblem. Calf length, brown boots graced his feet and he wore a sword at his hip.

Collise trembled at the thought of that cold blade sliding into her flesh.

Following him into the room, Queen Arteera peered curiously at Collise, her dark hair looking lighter than the young girl had thought. She wore a red velvet dress that came up to her neck and almost all the way to the floor, protecting her from the chill air. Her expression was one of guarded curiosity as she regarded Collise as if she was an animal prone to attacking.

Prince Joranas came in next, also looking at Collise but with much more interest than wariness. He had changed since Collise had seen him in the city, he was taller and the chubbiness of youth had faded, something had happened to his hair and skin while he had been away as they were both changed.

Collise stood for a heartbeat as she took all this in then fell to her knees before them.

"Please don't kill me, majesty!" She begged.

Tears rolled down her cheeks as she waited for whatever King Besmir was about to do. Her soft sobs echoed around the room as she knelt there. Collise had no idea what he was about to do to her but she was more than surprised when she felt strong hands lifting her to her feet. She opened her teary eyes to see the king standing before her.

"Hello, cousin," he said.

Made in the USA
Lexington, KY
15 October 2018